MEMORY'S LENS

LIAR
BOOK 1

WHITAKER WORDSWORTH

dedicated to my father

CONTENTS

懐剣 *kaiken (noun): an unadorned single- or double-bladed dagger often housed in a plain mount, formerly carried by men and women of the samurai class in feudal Japan, especially for self-defense indoors.*

The Kaiken's Inscription:

私は妄語。死と死者の証言を司る者
私の犠牲者にとって偽りは真実になる
囚われしは殺人鬼。そこに真実はない
記憶喪失を解き放ち偽りの記憶を植え付ける

ONE

IT JUST DID NOT add up. Hanna knew Theo could be lying. The doubt was already consuming her. She cherished their time together—happy memories. How could she forget? It was shameful and impossible.

"Don't you remember that day?" he asked again.

"Not really," she answered, her frayed memory offering nothing of their afternoon together.

Hanna looked down at the table between them. The surrounding activity of the café receded from her thoughts.

Glancing back up, Theo's inquisitive expression met her penitent eyes. He sat across from her, resting his elbows on their sticky wooden table, his interlaced fingers covering his tightly drawn lips. "We just stopped for coffee at my place that afternoon," he explained.

Pale afternoon light reached through the glass door of the café. Hanna and Theo watched two more groups of customers join the queue. She recognized them as fellow students from her university.

Theo merely monitored her. Then, pulling her attention back, he said, "Can you recall anything? Any details, like what we ate?"

She shrugged. "Kind of. I mean, that was three weeks ago. Can you remember exactly what you ate for lunch three Saturdays ago?"

He frowned. "Try. You ordered your coffee the same way then as you just did today. Isn't it like pairs of cards in a memory game?"

"That's an odd comparison, don't you think?"

"Oh, you don't remember that," he muttered, before urging her on. "What do you remember?"

The tattered images surfaced desperately from the murky pool of her memory. "It was a well-lit restaurant. I remember the candles and the white tablecloths. There was a line to get in and we talked about the story of Dr. Faustus. You walked me back to Penn Station. There were flurries."

"That was two weeks ago—not three."

"God, I'm such a mess."

As if deaf to her plight, he carried on, "How about Central Park? Or ice skating?" and she sprung to life, saying, "Oh yeah, those were fun! Ice skating last Saturday in the city and Central Park the Sunday before that. I thought it would be miserably cold, but it turned out to be a blast."

"Central Park was nice around Christmas too, wasn't it?"

"It was the best!" she chimed merrily, propelled by her crisp memories. Why was Theo's recollection always so much clearer than hers?

Hanna paused, and her jovial tone turned pensive. "But memory is mysterious. I read an article about it recently in a magazine at the library. Some memories can sit for ages, unnoticed. Then something reminds you and suddenly you rediscover this dormant memory just sitting there. Other memories are unwelcome, like embarrassing ones that come up by some association in your mind. Every time you have a nice memory, you can't help but remember that one incident too."

Theo reciprocated her pensive tone, adding, "Sometimes you don't remember the original memory. You just recall remembering it or the outcome. Sometimes, memories are incomplete, so we fill in the details with our imagination. Memories can mix in our subconscious. Other times, we only remember the feeling more than the actual events or precisely when they occurred."

Grave concern darkened her countenance. She leaned forward. "I don't want to end up like those abducted people in the news coming back unable to remember anything of it. I know I'm forgetful, but I feel like there's something more. I feel like sometimes it's hard to remember parts of our dates, like I have these little gaps in my memory. Mostly they're just details, but I've lost stuff at school too. Theo, why can't I remember?"

"I don't know," he said, dismissing her.

"Will you help me remember?"

"Of course, but how?"

Desire to somehow answer hastened her tongue to form the next word, but the approach of their drinks stole his attention. The server set each mug down, cheerfully oblivious to their exchange.

Elusive, Theo sat before her just out of reach of the truth's light. A direct attack would yield no result. Spooking him would only prompt his retreat. How would he ever reveal why she only forgot time spent with him? Who else would know but him? But there he was, pleasant and innocent, with no logical explanation for her fragmented memories. Better to test his temperament.

"You're in a good mood today," she said, twirling her hair.

"Why do you lie?" Theo stabbed back.

She jerked her mug back onto the table with a thud. "Jesus, Theo, it's called being nice. And it's a little lie, not a big one." His sunken eyes lingered on the caffeine invisible in his black drink.

"Okay, maybe it's a stretch, but you're chattier than usual," she pointed out.

Theo retorted, "You don't have to lie to start a conversation with me."

Rosy color rushed to her cheeks. "That's not what I meant! Sometimes we tell little white lies to be nice. People can tell them every now and then. That's not a bad thing. You could even consider it moral, wouldn't you?"

"People tell huge lies all the time but that's considered immoral. What's the distinction? Frequency? Magnitude?" She froze. Like a bird that had finally come to rest in her hand, his attention provided a chance to draw out his sincere, but often cross, curiosity. Instead of a garden sparrow, though, it was a raptor weighing on her arm—its sharp talons digging into her.

"I don't know," she said. "The morality of a lie is measured by both its outcome and the truth it obscures? Lying itself is only considered immoral because you just assume the truth and consequences involved are for a bad purpose."

Thought gripped him. His eyes darted from her to the table to his coffee and back to her. "I hadn't considered that," he said.

Giddy excitement roused her to flick her bangs out of her eyes. She took a hearty gulp of her sweet coffee and let fly, "Well, yeah, I mean some things are definitely sin, like murder, but a little lie may change someone's memory for the better. Unlike the other commandments, I think it's a little more nuanced. It may be justified to bear false witness against your neighbor if it saves his life. Sometimes we just know that not telling someone something would leave them better off. What do you think?"

"Do you lie to me?"

"I'd never lie to you," she rushed to say. "You're so, how do I say . . . blunt. I feel like I can be myself around you because you are nobody but yourself. You're like the only person I could ever admit this to about lying. My family would just say I'm being immature. Emma would laugh at me."

Theo's astute eyes narrowed. "I don't believe you."

"But I'm telling you the truth," she said, her smile fading. Drawing out his honesty was backfiring.

"What's the point?" he said dismissively. "Even if you remembered this, there's no way to tell if you're sincere or not."

Annoyance twisted her fair features. "No, don't be mean. I thought you said you'd help me remember."

"That was gratuitous."

"Do you mean it?"

He paused again, but Hanna spotted reflection in his features. "Yes, I do," he said deliberately. Her hand reached across the table. His hand met hers with a gentle caress. Sweetest icings of indulgent confections would struggle to match his saccharine yet demure smile breaking free.

She pushed her hair behind her ears and asked, "What do you want to do for Valentine's Day? It's only two weeks away." His calculating silence perturbed Hanna. She rushed to add, "I mean, it's not like it has to be a big deal or anything."

"I haven't made plans yet. I suppose we should come up with something memorable."

That last word cut into her. She promptly qualified, "I'll remember for sure this time. It doesn't have to be expensive. No pressure. I could take you out too. How could I forget my own plans, right?"

"We could go to a photobooth," he suggested casually.

Amused, she replied, "That's curious. You mean like one of those ones where you take your picture together and it's on a timer and it has filters?" Before he could respond, she perked up, adding, "And it prints them out at the end? And there are usually props or hats in the photobooth?" He waited a moment, anticipating her next interjection. "We learned about them in Japanese class. They are called *purikura* in Japanese. Mostly popular with kids but it's not unheard of for high school or college students to go to them. It's kind of for girls but great for dates. I'd have so much fun just figuring out all the Japanese instructions in a real one."

"That."

Her pupils widened. She leaned forward. "It's a date."

"Now I'll have to find one."

She sat back and took another sip of her sweet coffee. Theo watched her lilac earrings dangling from their short silver chains.

"I doubt we'll find one here," she surmised while looking at his still-full coffee mug. "We'd have a better chance finding one in the city."

"How do you pose for a picture?"

"What on earth do you mean?"

"In a purikura booth, for example. How would you pose for so many pictures? How would you not look tired?" She found the sincerity anchoring his question incredible from anyone but him.

"I guess, like this," she mused and tilted her head, bearing a forced smile.

"Take a selfie. That way it will be genuine."

"Why don't we take one together?"

"You'll pose differently with me in the photo. First just you on your phone, then both of us on mine." She found it odd that he was so specific, but he always was.

"Alright. Your phone has a way better camera, but okay," she said as she took out her flip phone. Repeating the same pose as before, she smiled into the phone's tiny camera lens and snapped the picture. Theo rose and moved behind her. She stood to better match his height. He still lowered his head to be in the frame with her. Curiosity tantalized Hanna as he held his much smarter phone out in front of them. She smiled into its ample lens and saw Theo's thumb waiting above the glass touchscreen to capture the moment. Their two expectant faces stared back at them on the screen.

"What are you waiting for?" she asked, turning toward the real Theo. He snapped the picture as he kissed her lips.

"Hey, wait!" she playfully called after him as he swiftly returned to his seat.

"Send me the picture you took," he said, and Hanna obliged. He showed her his screen and flicked between the two photos. One showed Hanna trying to smile, eyelids weighed by doubt. The other showed her parted lips forming a startled grin, eyes wide open, looking into Theo's eyes, gently shut. He politely concluded, "You answered my question. Thank you."

Dismissively, Hanna joked, "Just don't get too crazy trying to get reactions for poses." He chuckled. She glanced at his coffee. "Still too hot?"

He took his first sip. "Just right," he said, then added, "You wore the earrings I gave you."

"Of course! This is a date, silly."

Clouds had gathered, crowding out the weak January sunlight, quick to wane in the afternoon. A steady stream of patrons kept the café staff busy. Hanna was mostly unaware of them, fixated instead on Theo's calculating eyes. She wondered how they would appear if she excited him—or scared him. He silently drank his sugarless, creamless coffee. She patiently waited, savoring his tempered manner, which she found regal.

"Grab your jacket. I'll walk you back," he said, checking his watch.

Over her sweater went her puffy black jacket. Theo's wool sweater spilled out the top and bottom of his black peacoat, its pockets weighed with contents. She put on her fluffy earmuffs and slung her hiking backpack, laden with books, over her shoulders. She wrapped her scarf around her neck twice and led Theo out of the busy café. A staff member was already on the way to clear their table. She interrupted her scarf wrapping to shout, "Sorry for taking so long!"

Theo corrected, "We were here for only twenty-two minutes."

Aghast, she asked, "You were counting?"

The staff member cleared Hanna's empty mug and Theo's, still half-full.

Greenberm's quaint downtown had little activity left for the day. Two cars scowled at a red traffic light with no cross traffic. Many found the idea of a stroll unenjoyable in the merciless cold and remained inside. The few forced to venture out hurried with lowered heads. A barren sidewalk led Hanna and Theo away from the café. Closed storefronts carried their passing reflections before handing them on to the next.

Hanna energetically looked back at Theo, his head held high. "You're not cold? You're not wearing a hat!"

"It's not that cold."

"Well, you didn't take the bike, so it must not be too warm either."

"I could've," he lied through a shiver. Gusts of wind whipped around his twine-colored hair, usually short but longer now after the holidays. The unforgiving wind chilled her legs in their black stockings, keeping a brisk pace. His long gait casually followed behind her, an unhurried rhythm of denim. The town slowly slipped behind them as the sidewalk led them up the road back to her university.

Hanna cleared her throat and called to him, "I wanted to thank you for the coffee today. I'm ready to study now. I'm pretty sure we've been there before, haven't we?"

Theo put his hands in his coat pockets. "We have not."

Joy faded from her steps. "I'm starting to get worried about my forgetfulness. I'm starting to think I have amnesia or something."

"What do you mean?"

She took in the barren birches above. "I just can't seem to shake this forgetfulness. I feel like I'm doing my best in school and stuff, but I'm sure my parents wish I would do better. But since starting college . . ." She trailed off. Theo witnessed her anguish weighing upon her. "I don't know what to do. I keep forgetting the dates we've had."

"Just afternoon coffee in the city."

"No, you've asked me about our dates before and I wasn't able to remember." She grimaced. "I can remember forgetting but can't remember the actual memories. I'm sorry."

"You don't have to apologize."

"Ask me something."

He hesitated. She grabbed his shoulders and stopped, holding him with her eyes. "Anything. You said you'd help me remember."

"What's your favorite class?"

"Japanese," she shot back promptly.

Detecting dissatisfaction, he gave it another shot. "Where did you go to high school?"

"King's Prep in Wakefield, New Jersey."

"Who is your best friend?"

"Emma, since third grade."

"What's your sister's name?"

"Lily Popov."

"When did we first meet?"

"Junior year at King's."

"When did we start dating?"

"Last June, after prom."

"But I have promises to keep."

"And miles to go before I sleep."

She gasped. He gently repeated, "And miles to go before I sleep. You remember."

Hanna sighed and resumed walking. She looked at Theo walking beside her. "You know I hated that poem when we had to memorize it. I haven't thought about it since junior year."

"See, your memories are still there." He grew concerned. "But it seems like others are having real bouts of amnesia. Have you seen those abductions in the news?"

Intrigued by the subject change, her pace quickened. "Yeah. I don't want to end up like them. People all over New York City, apparently, and even out here have been disappearing and turning up unable to remember anything." Hanna paused. "But the shorter ones could just be people getting blackout drunk," she said, qualifying her statement, though no objection was posed. "The longest one was like two days. Maybe it's something in the water—or aliens."

Theo added, "It seems random. The police can't find an explanation. It's people in a bar or club, on a subway, walking at night—anywhere. They all wake up uninjured, though. Who do you think could be doing it?"

Hanna sighed. "I have no idea, but I hope they catch the creeper soon. It's been going on for like three months, right?"

"You don't drink, do you?"

She blinked. "Before twenty-one? That's illegal." She took off her fluffy earmuffs and handed them to him. "You're clearly cold." Annoyed by his hesitation she stabbed, "You know I'm right."

He acquiesced, pulling his hands out of his pockets, his right lagging behind his left. "They're so warm. Are they real fur?" he asked, putting them on.

"Faux," she chimed back. She rewrapped her scarf higher to cover her ears. The wind picked up. She hunched her shoulders and buried her nose in her scarf. They walked side by side, hands in their jacket pockets. Surgite University soon came into view. The stone walls, iron gates, and abundant oak trees indicated the warmth of the campus library was not far off. Relief filled Hanna as she passed through the archway to the formerly verdant forest she had called her home since last August. In winter, the lawns, reduced to patchy scruffs of dull green and languid brown, endured against the cold. Otherwise vacant winding macadam walkways toured them past the academic buildings and yet more oaks.

At the hub of the branching pathways stood the expansive library. A brick patio was laid just in front of the entrance. Wooden benches encircled a rhododendron, ever green, even in winter's short days. Hanna stopped at the benches and slung her backpack down onto an empty one in the deserted courtyard. She retrieved her student ID to open the library door.

"You're a *neko jita*—a cat tongue," she called over.

Theo stopped, visibly confused. "What? You haven't mentioned that before."

"We learned in Japanese class that people who can't eat or drink hot things are called cat tongues. *Neko* is cat and *shita* is tongue, but it becomes *jita* when it's in combination with another character like neko."

"You really like studying Japanese, don't you?"

"Hai!"

"You're going to declare Japanese as your major?" he asked.

She giggled, brandishing her ID card. "Yep. I've made up my mind. Sticking with your philosophy major?"

"Yeah."

"I think that's cool. You love wisdom and seek the truth. You'll be busy," she said but reminded him, "Don't forget to send me that selfie we took together."

"I won't forget you asked me."

Her hand swiped her ID card through the reader and the door's lock clicked. Theo pulled it open and gestured her inside. She merrily obliged, enjoying this warmer Theo.

Beige was the only color of the entire library. The carpet, the bookshelves, the ceiling panels, the painted walls, the desks, the computer monitors and tower cases, the window frames, the cardigan of the information desk attendant—all beige. The sunlight that could reach inside offered some other tones of beige, but the fluorescent lights soon blended everything into the same shade. Only the books dared to wear colors not beige.

A few students spoke in hushed tones by the entrance. The first floor housed many volumes, but did so between broad beams supporting the mezzanine just above it. The labyrinth of the first floor was often overlooked in favor of the open space and tall ceiling of the mezzanine. Hanna led Theo to a secluded row of desks on the first floor, safely out of sight of the mezzanine's curious inhabitants. Scores of books hushed all sound except that of one nearby student's pencil scratching madly away at his notebook. She placed her backpack on a desk and gestured Theo to take the desk adjacent to hers.

Hanna whispered, "How long can you stay?"

"My train isn't for another hour," he replied, sliding off her earmuffs and producing a small journal from his pocket. The combination lock on it intrigued her.

His presence comforted her. Her textbooks overwhelmed her. Lurking in the darkness of her backpack were chapters that brought ambivalence and problem sets that menaced her. Visions of studying together with Theo last year sprung to her mind: the patience in his explanations, the discipline with which he kept his classroom notes, those calculating hazel eyes able to astutely identify questions for a text undetected by her. Hanna's heart ached at her imaginings ending. Theo went to college in the city now, had moved there too with his father from New Jersey last June, and could only see her on dates—far less frequently than she desired. These realities were suffocating. Her red spiral notebook stared back at her, unopened. She opened it to her classroom notes. It offered no solutions.

Hanna stole a glance at him. He sat leaning forward, presumably writing in the journal he brought. She had never seen it before. The divider between their desks obscured him. The intimacy of the library would surely draw out his honesty. She looked back at her colorful classroom notes. Incomplete translations of song lyrics filled the side margins in cyan. Vocabulary words littered the top margin in magenta. Details of recently discovered Japanese songs crowded the bottom of the page in periwinkle. She pulled her music player out of her puffy jacket, put in her ear buds, clicked on the music player, and slipped off her jacket and scarf.

Soft rock and roll, dancing to Japanese lyrics of summers gone by, poured into her ears. A conjugation table took shape on the newest sheet in the tome of her notes. Appropriate choice of pen color engrossed her as she alternated to distinguish the correct conjugations of the example verb. Producing this from memory was simple. Documenting it neatly required concentration. Theo tapped her shoulder and she looked up behind her. Notice of his approach had escaped her. She pulled out her ear buds and he asked, "I'll see you again next Saturday?"

"Yes, of course," she beamed, twisting back to face him while seated.

"Good," he replied derisively. "Too bad you won't remember."

Hanna stared back at him. "I . . . don't follow," she said, concerned.

"You're kind of figuring it out, but not fast enough. Of all the versions of you I've seen, this one was getting close."

Anguish and shock mixed on her face, suddenly caught by an uncomfortable flush of hot blood. She attempted to stand but his icy hand on her shoulder forced her back into her seat.

"I didn't expect us to get this far. I was sure you'd leave me by now," he murmured, one hand palming her skull. He swiftly turned her to face her notebook.

"Theo, what are you doing? We're in public!" she whispered, alarmed under his hand.

"I almost want you to figure it out," he said, void of feeling. Just as she felt a small wooden object press against the bare nape of her neck, his whisper came, haunting and dead: "*Shio.*"

TWO

"NOT AGAIN."

Hanna opened her eyes and scrambled to recollect the scattered fragments of her attention. How long she had been sitting idly escaped her. Music seeped out of her still-running ear buds, strewn out before her in the tranquil silence of the library. Her half-finished conjugation table demanded its remaining contents. She put her ear buds back in, slid her chair closer to the desk, and resumed filling out the table. She groaned to herself, "I really need to stop spacing out."

A trading card bookmark guided her to the contents of tomorrow's class. Eagerly, she opened the book to tackle memorizing the lesson's vocabulary. Seeing that she already knew most of the words bolstered her confidence—at least for tomorrow. The little white music player continued bathing her with saccharine Japanese lyrics about love. Her lists of vocabulary grew as the player marched steadily to the album's end. Her gliding pen drew out more homework answers while her feet tapped softly to the music, her flats hardly making a sound against the beige carpet. Nearby, the student's marathon pencil charged its way down the page and onto the next. Hanna's cell phone buzzed, bearing a message. She flipped it open as another came, greeting her frown.

"Where r u?" the first one said, "in library?" the second. Hanna asked why, to which Emma rapidly answered, "Study. U forgot?" Hanna knew Emma was typing another.

"In lib," Hanna's thumb spelled onto her phone's minute screen by its number buttons. As soon as she pressed send Emma's third message came. "Broc come 2?"

Hanna grimaced. "Ok," she tapped out and pressed send, knowing their arrival meant abandoning the quiet areas of the library. She collected her academic tools and placed them back into her backpack, donned her jacket and scarf, and headed for the entrance. The student writing madly stopped and peered at her vacant desk. She noticed his bewildered look.

Were my ear buds too loud again? she thought. Several bookshelves down, his hushed voice called behind her, "Excuse me. You dropped these."

"Oh, thank you," she whispered, taking her earmuffs from his outstretched hand.

Turning back to the entrance ahead, the soft fur shot a recollection through her mind. A vague feeling of noticing their absence in the cold wind pierced her memory. But when? She lamented her forgetfulness.

Beige bookshelves glided past her. The threat of more messages from Emma pushed Hanna's pace to the limit of decency in a library. Forced to yield to student traffic, she brusquely emerged from the catacombs into the spacious entrance. Just in view, she could already hear Emma's booming voice.

"Yeah right!" Emma said. She led Broc through the library doors. The mezzanine easily heard her.

"I'm telling you it's true," Broc replied calmly. You can get high off running."

She faced him. "There's no way just running around could actually make you feel good. Running sucks. It's painful."

"You should give it a try?" he said, sounding unsure.

Emma's head jolted back as she retorted, "Careful what you're implying there, champ."

"I didn't mean it like that or anything!" he replied, panic hastening his high-pitched retreat.

The help desk attendant scowled at them. Hanna mouthed, "I'm sorry," to the attendant and mutely waved hello to her friends. Emma's dark hair was pulled back in a tight ponytail. Her shoulders were tense under the weight of her backpack, bearing thick textbooks explaining the natural world. Broc carried just one workbook.

"Look at you, all dressed up. Skirt, earrings, and all," Emma quipped.

Hanna quickly recognized the disparity in their attire and removed her earrings, saying, "Oh, yeah. Sorry." Why was she wearing the earrings Theo gave her? All possible answers perplexed her.

They headed for the designated study area where voices could be raised freely. Exiting the beige, the party of three passed through a bridge of glass and steel connecting them to the newest addition. A small café that had recently been erected in the hallway tempted them midway. Enervated students were often caught like flies at its sumptuous glass counter. Darkness had already overcome Sunday's fading daylight.

Emma walked beside Hanna and asked, "How'd it go with biker boy? Did he ride here?"

Confusion shook Hanna. Only memories of an uneventful solitary afternoon came to her. Sky, windows in a café, thoughts turning to pressing homework, a beige carpet, solitude, loneliness —memories that would be ambivalently filed away to fade away.

She raced to answer, "Oh, terrifically!" in an ascending pitch. "He took me out to an Italian restaurant, a late lunch, and we went around town and went shopping . . . and I walked him, or, um, we walked together, I mean, to the train station. We said goodbye and stuff—yes, that's what happened. He's busy with Lincoln and all, and then I got here—well the library here. I was studying and—"

"Okay, okay," Emma interjected. "I don't need the whole play-by-play."

Hanna hastily drew breath. Remorse stung her. Why would Theo forget about their date, and how did Emma know they even had a date? Hanna recollected visiting the café alone, walking back to the library, and studying Japanese. Lying was an impulsive but easier solution to cover for Theo's apparent transgression. The idea that she had somehow forgotten their date crashed into her contemplation. Why had Theo not called then? *There's no way I could have forgotten I had a date with him, is there?* she thought.

Flatly, Emma continued, "Well, it sounds like you had fun. Just be careful where you go. Ya know, those abductions in the news and all."

Hanna gave an acknowledgment but caught Emma shooting an incredulous look back at Broc, quietly following behind them. Hanna heard no audible reply but guessed he gave a knowing expression to her as he often did.

Emma resumed, "You missed out. My brothers' birthday party was epic, by the way—all planned by yours truly. Bowling-arcade-pizza epicness." She pointed at herself haughtily.

"It was really fun, Hanna. You would have had a great time," Broc added.

Hanna remained silent and aware of the painful gap in her memory.

"Do you have your calculus stuff?" Emma asked.

"Yeah," she answered, drifting away.

"Did ya do it already? I tried the first two and couldn't figure it out."

"I haven't started it yet."

Hanna kept her eyes on the groups of students ahead. Clusters of students had already huddled around tables. Some would stay well into the night, until the library closed. They arrived at an open table and soon their textbooks and notes spread across it like battleplans. Their pencils and banter chipped away at the problems. Broc had brought his accounting homework. Ostensibly, it was his sole task that evening.

Emma interrupted his studying. "Hey," she barked. "You took this last semester. Do you remember this one?"

Emma slid her notebook across the smooth gray tabletop.

Broc caught it and examined the exponential word problem. His pencil calmly untangled it. Realization of why Emma had invited him dawned on his face. He slid the notebook back. Emma's expectant look prompted him to expound, "It's asking you to write a function that describes the exponential growth in the word problem."

"But how do we do that?" Emma pleaded. Hanna was struggling too.

"The population grows ten percent per year," he said, disappointment deflating his usually chipper explanation. "You just kind of write down a table of what the population is each year, then notice the difference. Then you try out a bunch of functions until you find one that describes the population growth."

Hanna stared, confounded. Emma looked to Hanna and back to Broc, mouth agape. He joked, "If you could see the looks on your faces! Emma, you're premed. You should get this."

"I just have to get through this," she said, correcting him.

"Same here. General education requirement," Hanna added, giving a cheeky grin.

Broc rolled his chair closer to Emma. Hanna was already sitting close on Emma's other side. He explained the solution in detail. The two girls listened intently.

Emma declared, "Thanks, Broc. Whew! I need a break," and stood up to stretch.

With his attention focused solely on Emma outstretched and

yawning, Broc said, "Have you been to the new café here? They just opened it this semester."

Even through a sweatshirt, Emma could easily show off her figure. Hanna wondered why she had to boast like that in front of him. Her stretch lasted a second beyond necessary.

"I haven't been yet. Do you think it's good, Broc? Should we eat there tonight, right now?" asked Emma.

He meekly avoided her piercing stare. "I don't know. I ate there once. It . . . was nice. They had sandwiches and pretzels."

Hanna exclaimed, "I love pretzels! Let's all go when we're done with calculus."

Emma monitored Broc's reticence, then concluded, "Bueno. I'm taking a stroll."

She sauntered off, and he rolled back to his accounting homework. His pencil skittered nervously across his notebook. Hanna could not resist asking, "Do you like studying with Emma?"

Broc looked up innocently. "Um, yeah. Calculus is whatever, but it's a chance to hang out with her." Emma ambled in a wide circle around the now-crowded study room.

"Ask her out," Hanna blurted.

His pencil dropped along with his composure. "I mean, I would but I . . . it's not that simple. I don't want to risk messing up our friendship."

Hanna spotted Emma on her return already and hurried to whisper, "She likes video games. Ask her brothers what she has. She plays one with guns on the internet in our dorm."

He nodded gratefully as Emma returned to her seat and resumed the battle. Packs of students hammered at problem sets, ruing their procrastination. Sometimes a chance raised voice would rival the volume of one of Emma's choice exclamations. Sandwiches and pretzels did come several solved problems later when they migrated to the hallway café. Emma sat across from Hanna, as she often did, to facilitate the conversation. Broc stood frozen until Emma beckoned him to sit next to her. Broc eventually warmed up to sharing stories of the soccer team. Hanna listened intently, giving exuberant reactions. She felt it was the only way to thank him for helping with calculus. Emma complained that she was tired of soccer stories.

Homework finished, Emma thanked Broc, and the two girls departed the library. He waved back at them from the table. Emma's confident stride bolstered Hanna's courage as they passed the recently placed warnings for students to "buddy-up" and avoid walking alone at night. Their comradery while walking back to the dorms warmed them against the frozen darkness. They never strayed from the well-lit pathways. By the time Hanna remembered to ask Theo about their supposed date, it was already too late.

Unresolved thoughts kept Hanna from restful sleep. The glaring red numbers of her alarm clock kept reminding her how tired she would feel. Taking calculus at eight in the morning was no longer an admirable idea. Recalling how Emma had recommended they take the class together roused her fully awake. She could not let her down.

Only two minutes remained until both of their alarms would blare their sirens. Hanna threw off her heavy covers and disarmed hers. She knew the blast of Emma's clock radio was about to play the greatest hits of yesteryear loud enough to rouse adjacent buildings. The linoleum floor panels chilled her feet. She quickly changed from her pajamas, wincing at the thought of Emma's alarm.

Sure enough, it sounded. Emma swore loudly, groping for her clock radio. She smacked the snooze button on the alarm, which had lain on the windowsill since August. They readied themselves for the day together, careful not to wake their suitemates further. This had become their morning ritual every Monday, Wednesday, and Friday.

The dining hall welcomed them from the dreary dawn. Emma rushed to the pastries. Aromas of pungent coffee drew Hanna to her first stop. A large breakfast did not appeal to her, and she carried her light tray to a table in the mostly empty dining area. Emma brought back her tray, making full use of their meal plans.

Emma spoke first. "Hey, why do ya always take the messed-up muffin? You know you don't have to."

"If I don't, no one will. It deserves love too. It didn't choose to be that way."

Emma's disdain colored her objection, "It's a muffin, Hanna."

"Hey, can you remember things, like what you did a couple weekends ago?" Hanna asked, changing the subject.

"If it stands out. I don't really expect myself to commit everything to memory," she said coolly between bites.

"Do you . . . I don't know . . . space out and not really remember how long you've been somewhere?"

"Nah, I haven't been hit in the head repeatedly like you."

Hanna objected to Emma's uncouth attempt at humor, to which Emma replied, "Okay, jeez, calm down. That's not a new thing for you."

Hanna shook her head, saying, "It seems to be happening more lately," then decided to go for it. "You don't happen to remember what I told you before my date with Theo yesterday, like what we were planning to do?"

Emma looked at her, exasperated. "Hanna, I don't remember your pregame commentary about your date."

"It just kind of slipped my mind . . . that's all. I'll ask him about it."

"Who, Two-Wheel Teddy? Do what you want, but I don't know why you still go out with him. Lots of couples break up after high school. It's not like there's a lack of options here."

"Theo's different."

"And rich."

"That's not it."

Emma chomped away, not finishing her bite, before adding, "I wish I could get a rich husband. I wouldn't have to deal with calc, chem, or bio." She swallowed her bite and added, "It's either one of those or the pole. Ya know, Hanna, you could make good money."

"Don't be lewd," Hanna said, annoyed. Emma pretended to laugh. She changed the subject, saying, "Chem and bio are kicking my ass with the labs and all. Half the kids who declared premed are out already."

"Do you think you'll stick with it?"

"Well, with this whole 'mortgage-meltdown recession' caused by Wall Street, I have to become a doctor. It's guaranteed work."

"Do you enjoy it?"

"Guaranteed work, Hanna. I don't have to enjoy it. I want enough money that I don't have to worry. If I can't hack it as a doctor, I'll have to do something grand to pay back these student loans." Emma caught Hanna staring blankly at the misshapen muffin on her plate.

"Ya know, if you actually ate your food, the wind wouldn't be able to knock you over."

Hanna gave no reply. Emma resumed, more sincerely, "Say, you really like Japanese. Are you going to be a translator? Are you finally going to declare a major?"

"I don't know. I haven't decided yet."

"Not going the teacher route?"

"It'd make my dad happy. My mom says I need to make money."

"What about teaching English in Japan? Don't they make more?"

"I think so. I'd be okay moving to Japan and living there."

"Permanently?"

"I don't know," she replied, her voice trailing off in search of tender memories.

"Japan is a long way from New Jersey. You sure you want to leave us all behind?"

Hanna let the conversation stall. Emma leaned toward her.

"Hey, don't worry about it, kiddo." She grinned and added, "We have plenty of time to figure it out."

Hanna thanked her for the encouragement. Spirit buoyed, she made short work of her remaining breakfast and rushed Emma with evident enjoyment. Emma complained and consumed her fit-for-a-glutton plate. They grabbed their backpacks and made for class.

Calculus offered little respite. Emma sat next to her in the drafty classroom. The professor sifted through the available chalk to identify an outstanding specimen. He settled for the least mediocre choice. Their homework sat in the pile by the professor's desk. Hanna glanced at Emma's open notebook. She knew the incompleteness of her notes would result in Emma asking Hanna to study with her. Hanna looked back to her own textbook. The folded corners of the pages upset her. She smoothed them. The curled pages stacked neatly, restored to their original form, but still bore the creases of their previous owners' neglect. It brought her solace to comfort this ignored, pitiable object. She thought, *I bet it remembers how it got its creases.*

Focusing on the lecture was a sufficient distraction. Only black ink graced her notebook pages, save for Emma's occasional comments in red. When Emma would lose the logic of the professor's explanation, she would slide her notebook to Hanna. A large question mark cued Hanna to transpose the missing link of logic to Emma's notebook. Hanna had enjoyed the same service from Emma's notes.

Fifty minutes seemed all the class could bear before collapsing in either fatigue or despair. The professor merrily told them about their next class and assigned textbook problems. Emma swiftly waved goodbye and was off to her next class. Hanna, too, left the classroom but in no rush. She slipped through the now-crowded hallways to the exit and stepped out into the January sunlight.

Forgotten piles of snow hid in the shadows cast by the great L that was Surgite's mathematics building. Salt crunched under her leather boots. She raised her face toward the sunlight and closed her eyes. Weak but still present, its warmth drew out of her a longing for an embrace—his embrace. A day seldom passed without her thoughts visiting him. What warm memories of Theo she could find were her lighthouse. His quick insight and thoughtful approach would surely draw these fragments together into a cohesive explanation. Someday, these unexpected lapses in her memory would become a distant but intact memory.

Her phone buzzed. Her hand flew into her puffy jacket pocket to answer. She flipped it open and the name that appeared raced her heart. She pressed the green button and said, "Theo?"

"Hey."

"Hi!"

"Do you have a minute?"

"Of course!"

"Would you like to go out this weekend? Whatever time works for you. I haven't seen you since Christmas break."

Helpless, alarm gripped her. She had no idea what he was talking about. Questions regarding her hazy recollection of Sunday raced to her attention. Looking up at branches, a café, studying in the library, her backpack heavy with books, but where was Theo? Had it really been a month since they last saw each other? She stammered, trying to piece back together memories of her January. She fumbled out, "I . . . but Emma . . . did we go on a date yesterday?"

"No. I called you on Saturday to say we had to reschedule," he said, his measured voice reassuring. "Sorry I had to cancel. I messed up and forgot my dad asked me to help deep clean the apartment. It really needed it."

Memories of Theo telling her he lived alone with his father came to her. Vivid images resurfaced from the murky pool of her memory: sitting together on a bench, leaves in the wind, his candor, the pain of saying goodbye. She clung to them. "Hanna?" his voice reached out. She did not realize she had stopped walking.

"What's happening to me?" she asked of him and the world.

"It's just a couple of things slipping your mind. It happens to everyone," he emphasized in a comforting tone.

"I guess you're right," she said, wanting to believe. The distinct void in her memory refused to be ignored. This was not just forgetfulness. Resolve welled up in her. She lived away from home now. The responsibility of protecting the sanctity of her mind was apparent. If it truly was amnesia, she had to verify it. The idea of doctors, tests, psychoanalysis, and the disappointment on her parents' faces for having "a problem" wracked her confidence. She quickly recalled afternoons spent in Theo's apartment. His father was often out on weekends. Those memories were intact. Emma's contradicting question about how their date went seemed out of place among her solid memories of Theo. Yearning to search for clues about her broken memories with Theo sprung forth.

"So?" His word hung between them with a touch of impatience. Warm Theo was fading.

"Will you help me remember?" she asked, pained innocence coloring her question.

"What do you mean?"

"These gaps in my memory, I don't know why I have them. They keep popping up. Can you help me find them? I feel like I'm losing my mind."

"Let's talk about it in person this weekend."

Rekindled hope hastened her answer. "Yeah. Where should we meet?"

"How about lunch in the city this Saturday?"

"Sure. What time?"

"Penn Station at eleven?"

"Okay."

He went silent. Sweat moistened her vicelike grip on her phone. The faint static of a connected call continued. Apprehension arrested her curiosity as she fought to ask another question.

Just a moment later, she heard, "Goodbye, Hanna," and then silence. She flicked her phone closed, making a dull clack, but her phone was quickly open again. Her thumb frantically jammed the arrow buttons to summon the recent calls screen. There it was: Saturday; incoming call; Theo—eleven minutes.

THREE

HANNA COUNTED THE DAYS. The sun rose and she impatiently waited for it to set. The sun set, and she demanded it rise again already. Classes sufficiently dragged her attention away, but languid moments of tedium or exhaustion clawed her thoughts back to the recent gaps in her memory. By Wednesday, she gave in and called Theo. No reply. An hour later, he returned her call only to reaffirm that they would talk that weekend. Friday afternoon saw her absentmindedly strolling the sunny campus with Emma and Broc. Questions for Theo preoccupied her. Emma avoided discussions of weekend plans.

Saturday morning, she stood on Greenberm's icy train station platform. The ticket machine reluctantly complied to her touch. She inserted her debit card knowing she was spending her dining allowance on just the tickets. It was the first time in a month and her mother did not need to know. She peered down the tracks, waiting alone on the platform. The other passengers sheltered in the meager station. *Better to stay away*, she thought. Catching the leers of older men was never pleasant anyway.

A stillness blanketed the platform, broken only by an occasional sweep of stinging wind. Out here, she could easily detect anyone's approach—or so she kept reassuring herself. A bird took off. She shuddered.

Silence resumed its reign, and her mind turned to the recent abductions. Nobody had confirmed a modus operandi of the abductor. Some victims had reported disappearing during the day, some at night. Some could not recall exactly when. Some were at clubs or bars, others out walking. One was in her own apartment. None had identified an assailant. Most victims were young women. They all reported no injuries and no evidence of sexual assault but did report feeling exhausted or weak. Surgite's girls' dormitory had a mandatory meeting on every floor about the disappearances. Hanna had not imagined college life would include these sobering occasions.

A familiar chorus of steel, engine, and wheels came to her ears faintly from the distance. The horn greeted her next, then the headlight beaming under the heavy clouds above. Passengers soon vacated the station for coveted spots in the ambiguously forming queues. Hanna knew where to stand but remained away from the clusters of coats bemoaning the cold. She monitored them, her hand clutching her phone in her jacket pocket. She boarded nearly last.

The train stirred to motion, and she took an empty row of seats. Saturday morning did not draw a large crowd, especially just over an hour out on a local train. She set her petite black backpack down beside her. Its stylish buckles and smooth leather gave her pride. She turned it to hide its signs of wear and opened it for her umbrella. Digging through the assortment of potentially useful items she had haphazardly accumulated, she realized her umbrella was missing. Was it even socially acceptable to use an umbrella in the snow? Hanna gazed out at the barren forests between stations. Her already tired reflection stared back at her in the train's window.

Daydreams of being at the restaurant with Theo staved off

consternation and intrusive thoughts of the mounting tally of lost umbrellas in her life. At least none of the victims reported being abducted on a train. A message buzzed her phone, reading, "Where are you?"

"On train?"

"You're late."

Hanna grew flustered. She stabbed the phone's keys to type, "I thought 12?"

"11," he wrote back, cutting her. Could he not offer some conciliatory words? She sent words of apology and he merely conceded that he would wait. In her reflection on the window, the cheery polka-dotted bow on her hairband mocked her dismal expression. Japanese lyrics from her music player came to her rescue. The train grew more crowded with each stop. The barren forests gradually morphed into unwashed concrete edifices and gas stations. Snow began to fall. "Please, no delays. I know you can do it," she softly pleaded as the train's trot graduated into a lope and next a gallop into the darkness.

The dive into the tunnel indicated New Jersey was behind her. An unthinkable number of gallons of Hudson River water were above her now. The train effortlessly pushed through the blackness. The conductor strained to mask his contempt for the tedium. Passengers began stacking at the doors. The terminal stop came just a few minutes behind schedule. Hanna was grateful and messaged Theo apologetically yet again. He had instructed her once to not message him such updates, citing some cost for receiving text messages. She was dubious, but mostly acquiesced. She departed the train onto the well-lit underground platform and adopted the brisk pace she reserved for the city. It had recently become her pace everywhere. Up the stairs, she found Penn Station crowded, as usual.

The ascent always invigorated her: stairs up from the platform, more stairs up from the waiting area, yet more stairs up to the street. She accelerated onto the gusty sidewalk, weaving between the unyielding currents of pedestrians. Some stared back at her as she rapidly searched for him.

Theo stood in the unending traffic not far from the station steps. His scarf meandered in the wind like an impatient child. His hair swayed like wild grasses; its color reminded her of twine. His ears were pink, but his black wool peacoat looked cozy. It matched his black jeans. Studying the screen of his cell phone, he wore his usual grave countenance. Webpages glided by his thumb, bringing information to his astute eyes which caught her approach. His brow and lips relaxed into a relieved smile. She relished her effect. They greeted, she apologized, and they set out for the restaurant. She kept close to him, comforted by his shrewd watchfulness. Nobody could sneak up on Theo.

Walking beside him, she asked over the city's cacophony, "Is it far? Did we miss our reservation?"

"It's not far. We didn't need a reservation."

Hanna became aware that her attire may not have met a dress code she quickly envisioned.

"What's it called? I hope what I'm wearing is okay," she said.

"The Fair and Debonair," he answered flatly. "They won't care."

She began, "With a name like that . . ." but stopped her rebuttal. He would have specified if it truly were a concern.

Her raised nerves calmed as she walked beside him. Noticing his scarf uselessly flapping in the wind, she called over, "Aren't your ears cold? You can borrow my earmuffs if you'd like. You can't imagine how warm they are."

"No, and I know how warm they are."

"You do?"

He cast her a stunned look for a moment, before answering, "You let me borrow them back in December. You must have forgotten."

Another memory gap struck her. She felt the vigor draining from her footsteps. A sinking feeling came to her stomach. "I guess you're keeping to your word to help me," she said, feigning a nonplussed response.

No reply. They came to a stop. She realized her jaw was clenched.

Snow gathered on her earmuffs as they waited for the crosswalk light to change. Nonchalant vigilance guided his footsteps as he led her across the crowded streets and sidewalks. Hanna admonished herself for not checking the cross traffic too. Times Square came closer, with its unending lights. Theo ignored the colorful displays and swiftly led her to the entrance of a hotel. Passing under the lavish awning, then through the spacious revolving doors, the hefty walls of stone shut out the city's clamor at once. Theo brought her through the marble and granite lobby to ornate elevators. He summoned one almost instantly and they boarded with a few other patrons and guests. As they waited for the fiftieth floor at the back of the elevator, he reached for her hand at her side. Fingers like ice met hers, but tenderly, and she reciprocated his touch.

The doors opened to reveal the Fair and Debonair Club. Dark wood panels morphed broad daylight into evening. Luxuriously padded booths encircled patrons hidden in their own worlds. Expansive glass, fortified by steel, gave an ample view of the adjacent cityscape just beyond the snow-covered outdoor patio. A few patrons took pictures of themselves on the much warmer side of the glass. Many wore suits and graciously ordered drinks for their guests. Soft jazz smoothed relaxed conversations into a tipsy harmony. Hanna forgot about the streets below entirely. Theo advanced to the reception and acquired a table.

Once seated at a plush booth, they removed their jackets. Hanna slid next to him immediately. Her shoulder pressed against his bicep in his crisp collared shirt. She lazily opened the menu.

The prices made her blush. "Theo, you don't have to . . ." she began.

He sat up, saying, "You're right. I don't," and started sliding out of the booth.

"Hey, wait! Come on, don't be brash," she exclaimed, grabbing his wrist.

"Why do you say things you don't mean?" he asked, pulling his wrist out of her grasp.

"It's called being nice. You could learn a thing about it sometime."

"I guess I could," he reflected, before adding, "I appreciate your candor. I just don't . . . I struggle seeing people's invisible rules."

"It's alright. Maybe I should be more clear. I've known you long enough that I should know this by now."

"Thanks," he said sincerely.

The waiter came and Hanna ordered through Theo, who brusquely summoned a ginger ale for her and a cranberry cocktail for himself. She enjoyed the softer tone he often reserved for her. Warm Theo was not around enough, though. She could not forget what she came here to ask.

Better to gauge his temperament first, she thought before asking, "Hey, Theo, you don't mind ordering for me, do you?"

"No. You seem to enjoy it."

"Even though you don't really, I don't know, enjoy ordering or making small talk with waiters . . . or anyone?"

He leaned his elbows on the table. "I hate the pretense. This is a monetary transaction. I am obligated to pay a socially acceptable tip as insurance against future damage on repeat visits. Their superficial conversations won't change the outcome."

"Do you wish all restaurants had robots instead of people?"

"Yes, actually," he answered, intrigued. Desire tugged on Hanna to continue the conversation, but she returned to her premeditated question.

"Before I forget," she said, "I wanted you to help me with a gap in my memory. I was talking to Emma, and she was under the impression we went on a date on Sunday. But when we talked, you said we didn't. I don't remember you calling to cancel."

"When did I call you on Saturday?" he calmly asked.

"I don't know."

"Go check your phone."

She obliged, drawing her phone from her jacket lying next to her. He casually sipped his cranberry cocktail, shrewdly checking on her clicking away. The familiar Saturday call from Theo appeared. "Eleven forty-seven p.m.," Hanna read aloud. "God, we talk late."

"I think you never mentioned it to Emma. I told you about that café in our call. I recommended you try the mocha. You posted a picture of yourself on Friend Link."

"I did?"

Theo produced her Friend Link post on his phone. Hanna saw herself in the café looking back at her through his expensive phone's larger screen. A tepid smile and tilted head indicated her usual pose for photos. Her visible arm made it clear she took the photo. Eight at night on a Wednesday seemed a reasonable time to post. Confusion mixed into her impulse to yell at herself to log in more frequently. Classmates were always gossiping and organizing get-togethers for more things to gossip about. Her notifications piled up. Capitulating to Emma's constant prompting, she had finally made an account last September, but it just added to the growing demands on her frayed memory.

She read aloud her own words accompanying the picture: "Just me and my coffee! A mocha with double cream, sugar, and whip cream today." The mug of said mocha was just visible in the bottom of the frame. Supportive comments from her Japanese class friends already accompanied the photo and noted her stylish attire. Theo's lilac earrings on her ears caught her attention.

"I guess I did go alone," she concluded, yet wondered aloud,

"But that's so weird. I remember the café, I think, and I remember the mocha. Sometimes I can't tell if I'm just making up that I remember something. I hate letting a good conversation stall. People are mostly willing to keep a conversation going. It's like a skill that isn't taught but somehow expected of everyone. Do you ever feel like you make stuff up when people ask you to remember things just to have something to say?"

"No," Theo answered, observing the passing waiters. Hanna's eyes became unfocused, splitting her drink into two blurs. Their bubbles rose to the surface and their inevitable fate. Theo pulled her from the trance when he continued, "But I can understand why you would feel compelled to say something. You can read people's reactions. You can sense their mood and when the conversation prompts a reply." His eyes met hers. "You're good at it."

"You really think so?" she asked, hope rendering her vulnerable.

"You're the only person I can talk to," he answered, bashful sincerity lowering his voice.

Hanna pulled his arm against her and closed her eyes. Theo's relaxed hand rested politely on his own thigh. She held him for some time, until he asked for her order. The waiter stood patiently unaware. Hanna released Theo and told him to order the least expensive sandwich, which he relayed to the waiter. Theo opted for chicken tenders despite the opulent choices. Alone with time, Theo caressed her hand under the table. She welcomed his revitalizing massage and returned his touch. He paused to ask, "Why do you tell little lies?"

"What do you mean?" she asked quizzically.

"Like complimenting someone when it's unmerited or telling someone they don't have to pay for something when you expect them to pay."

"It's part of being nice. They're not quite lies because lying requires a deliberate intention to obscure the truth. They're more like little exaggerations that have become socially acceptable. We accept it because most people like it and it doesn't hurt anyone."

"Isn't that immoral? Doesn't it hurt the truth?"

"I don't know? Truth often ends up a victim in social interactions. We judge the morality of lies by their consequences. Lots of people don't want to be alone. Sometimes an innocent lie can do more good than harm in preserving a relationship."

"What stops you from lying to me?" he asked, giving a piercing look.

"There's no need. You have no pretenses about you. I can be myself around you."

"And others?"

"Maybe sometimes I get carried away."

"You like playing with that fire?"

She struggled to verbalize her thoughts, her pauses drawing Theo discreetly closer. "It's . . . not playing but . . . more opening up to possibilities. The nuance deserves more consideration."

"Do you remember when we went ice skating?" he asked abruptly.

She shrugged, pursed her lips, and looked to the side.

"Central Park?"

He was met with a confused, "When?"

"Both in January."

Hanna's eyes returned to his, then fell to his defined Adam's apple. "I vaguely remember ice skating, but not with you. I can't recall if it was recent or when I was a kid. I remember the trees in the park not having leaves. The air was cold, but that could have been home too. Maybe it was with my dad? It's just these disassociated images prompted by you asking. I could just be making them up, honestly."

Theo leaned on the table, deep in thought.

Hanna peeked up through her bangs, her hands clasped tightly together on the table. "I don't know what's wrong with me," she said, her voice cracking like autumn's leaves, desiccated and fallen. "I forgot a month of our dates. I even forgot posting on FL—my earmuffs too. I'm a mess."

Hesitation gripped him. Caught by something, he simply took her hand and asked, "Are you okay?"

Her throat tightened and she fought the feeling that tears would well up. "Not really."

"Does your school have a doctor's office? It might be worth visiting."

"I suppose. I've never been."

"You're not forgetting anything else? Are your studies okay?"

"Yeah, school's fine."

"Friends and family?"

"Sometimes I wish I could forget."

He sat back. "If it's just me, I can take it. I'm sure there's an explanation we're missing. It may just go away." She sat back too and leaned against his firm bicep. She drew his hand onto her lap, the restaurant an afterthought. His knuckles rested on her stockings and khaki shorts. He failed to conceal a shudder, and his grave composure was reduced to timid excitement.

"I don't want to forget you, Theo. What would I do without you?" she said.

Another pause strangled him as if he were smothered by regret. Then he shook himself free.

"What's something you're looking forward to? Probably not midterms," he asked, raising a new subject.

"Going back to Japan one day, I guess."

"More short term."

"I don't know. What are you thinking for Valentine's Day? It's only a week away," she asked, returning his hand to him.

Theo nodded pensively. The pause prompted Hanna to add, "Whatever you like, really."

"I need to come up with something memorable."

"No pressure. It doesn't have to be a big deal."

"What about a Japanese photobooth?"

"*Really*? You know where one is?"

"Yeah, there's one in a karaoke place here in the city."

"I think that's a great idea! Do you mean like ones with the automatic filters?"

He looked down at her, no longer slouching. She attentively held his eye contact as he replied, "Yeah, and it prints them out at the end. It's called something special in Japanese. Doesn't it start with a P?"

"*Purikura*," she answered, perking up. "We had a whole class about it in Japanese. It's mostly for junior high girls but it's fun for dates too." Her brow wriggled into a furrow. "I could swear I was telling someone about this recently."

"You'd enjoy figuring out all the Japanese instructions," he was quick to add.

"You know me so well," she replied with an endearing smile.

"How about it?"

Her face lit up. "It's a date." She reached for her drink and tried to slyly catch his reaction, but her hair, seemingly black in the dim restaurant, obstructed her view of him.

Their exquisitely arranged meals arrived, to Hanna's delight. She devoured hers shamelessly. Afterward, Theo asked her why she took the pickle off his plate.

"You don't like pickles. It'd be thrown away otherwise."

"But do you actually like pickles?"

She bit into its crispy cold flesh. "Not really, but it breaks my heart to see it ignored." Theo seemed unsure of her logic.

Time was easy to forget in that place. At Theo's request, Hanna elaborated on her knowledge of purikura machines and her cherished memories of Japan. Before she knew it, two hours had passed in their conversations, punctuated by furtive caresses when the staff and other patrons were finally out of view. Discussing their next destination, she voiced her first impulse: "Why don't we go back to your place? It's been a month since we could hang out there."

Theo messaged his father and they prepared to depart. An anticipated ding chimed from his phone. Theo's father would not be back until dark. A second came notifying Theo that he would have to find his own dinner. Theo neatly wrote out his signature on the credit card receipt. Hanna dared not look at the amount.

Theo led her back through the grid of streets now dusted in snow. Twenty-five blocks of frigid wet sidewalks and impatient cars did not bother Hanna. They made their way south at a merry pace. Broadway brought them past famous landmarks, which Hanna always admired. Theo's eyes never diverted from the route. They turned onto a quieter street, and soon the buildings morphed into meticulous stone and well-washed brick. The muted colors of fabric awnings indicated which ostensibly modest building housed his father's lavish apartment.

He took her past the velvet ropes outside. The chestnut doors swung open, pulled by dutiful attendants. Inside, the receptionist greeted Theo by name from behind his marble desk. He feigned to recognize Hanna, and Theo offered the minimum utterance in reply to pass unhindered. Theo's cold hand pulled Hanna to the elevators, past the fireplace and large mirrors. Hanna remembered the chair in the elevator, which she had found queer. This was the only elevator she knew that had one. A quaint hallway of hardwood floors met them when the doors opened. Two apartment doors stood on opposite sides of a table holding a vase of fresh camellia flowers. Anticipation harried her heart as he calmly unlocked and opened his door.

"My God! It looks like a hotel," escaped her lips.

"Hand me your jacket," he replied.

She gave him her backpack, jacket, and earmuffs. Hanna stepped into the inviting living room and took in the tranquil scene.

Natural light poured through the floor-length windows, revealing a snow-covered patio outside. A tastefully off-white and decadently high ceiling matched walls reflecting wondrous light throughout the spacious room. The sofa and chairs sat comfortably on a lush carpet. Pillows on the couches and chairs posed for their imaginary portraits. At the far side of the room hung a television buttressed by two bookshelves, and sitting opposite was a plush loveseat where Hanna and Theo had spent most of their time previously. The curtains were impeccably drawn and tied in neat bows. The apartment was tidier than it had been on her previous visits and much quieter without his loquacious father around.

"I'd love it if you could make us some coffee," she chirped, leaving her boots by the door. Their metal buckles, aggressive rubber soles, and distressed black leather looked out of place in his peaceful abode. Theo nodded and disappeared to the equally bright adjacent kitchen. Sitting on the sofa, she heard the sounds of a coffee machine she imagined well exceeded the cost of her entire outfit. Theo returned, gently setting a mug for her on the table, its sweet, creamy aroma rising to her cold pink nose. An ice cube floated in his. He sat beside her. They looked ahead, watching the snowfall accumulate on the patio.

"Why are you taking calculus?" came his voice, gently piercing the quiet.

Off guard, she replied, "Wait, what?"

"Calculus one. You mentioned it earlier," he clarified.

"Oh, it's just a math requirement for graduating."

"I'm sure there were other easier courses."

"There were. Precalculus or the history of math. Lots of liberal arts majors take history."

"So why are you, a Japanese major, solving integrals?"

"I haven't decided that yet."

"Oh, right," he acknowledged, slightly startled.

"But you're probably right. I'll choose Japanese. And who knows? Maybe calculus will be useful later?"

He raised his mug to his lips. The ice cube had mostly vanished into the blackness.

She took in the snowfall but could sense his incredulous look. "For Emma, honestly," she admitted. "She has to and asked me to take it with her. Eight in the morning was the only time available for both of us."

"You didn't have to be in the exact same class."

"She wanted me by her side."

"Why help her? She's your roommate and friend, but what do you gain?"

"My friend is in need. How could I say no?"

"Is it worth the effort?"

"I don't feel like I'm paying. Or if I am, then I don't expect anything in return."

"You don't . . ." he began, but stopped himself. He watched her holding the steaming mug to her lips. No smile graced their gentle curves. Brilliant light off the snow illuminated the hue of her chestnut irises. Rosy flush painted her cheeks behind her hair, reaching just below her jaw. He softly brushed her hair behind her ear. Revealed were her lilac earrings, dangling by their short silver chains.

"You would really do that for her and expect nothing in return?" he asked.

She set her coffee down and faced him. "She's my friend. Sometimes you help people because you have hope for them. Sure, there might be nothing in it for me and I might end up selfishly wishing she would thank me more, but life isn't a transaction. Sometimes things work out in ways you can't foresee. You just have to trust that you should do the right thing."

Gray rings colored Theo's eye sockets, which were shadowed by his sculpted brow. His discerning hazel eyes stared intently back at her.

"Suppose you really can act selflessly," he said. "You are doing this expecting nothing in return. You do this because you have hope for her future?"

"Yes," she answered nervously. He was up to something, but she enjoyed his patient attention.

She feared a rebuke as he continued, "You're saying hope is required for altruism."

"Yes, I suppose."

"Where does that hope come from?"

Hanna cupped her coffee mug on the table now. "I don't know. Hope is a feeling. It comes from your fundamental view of the world. It could come from your belief in God, or from examples of people's humanity you've seen. Some people draw hope from their life experiences, like when a parent made a sacrifice for them and they can believe that someone of that character would do the same."

Hanna heard him softly say, "Go on." Shocked, she looked over. He was silently sipping his coffee, focused on her. The often-thin ice of his attention had seemingly grown thicker.

She ventured further out, saying, "Hope is cultivated. People often say something gives them hope, and I think people need that. But some people don't want hope and enjoy watching the depravity of mankind like it's some kind of twisted show. They suddenly want hope, though, when they need it for themselves, like hoping some problem goes away. But even for that, they're still counting on someone in some way. Hope, wherever we can find it, strengthens the bridge to believing in people and ultimately believing that life is worth living."

"Where does that hope in people come from for you?"

"You're really going all out," she said, deflecting him, but his countenance and posture displayed genuine interest. She continued, "You, actually. If someone as emotionally deaf as you can learn to be nice, then I think anyone can be less of a jerk."

He laughed. It startled her, but his understanding grin met her spooked glances. Hanna giggled and he playfully shoved her shoulder. Lips curling mischievously, her hands impulsively darted to tickle his unprotected ribs. Violent convulsions contorted his off-guard body, and he ended their engagement by grabbing her wrists. Forcefully, he pinned them on the sofa cushion between them. She marveled at the tempered strength coursing through his arms.

Hanna looked up and Theo's sudden kiss met her lips. She pressed her lips against his, tasting the bitterness of his coffee. Her wrists released, she embraced him, resting her cheek against his to whisper, "I like you."

"Your cheek feels like a pancake."

"I thought philosophy majors also read poetry?"

"They do, but—"

"Just make time for me," she interrupted, then kissed him to block a reply.

The snowy silence was broken only by their escalating passion —their coffees and phones a distant memory. She pushed him back and he released her from his embrace, although he was easily capable of preventing her escape. That surge of fear always made her yearn to return to him for the thrill of his reserved touch breaking free. She sauntered to each window to release the curtains, one by one. Darkness gradually hushed the room. Theo patiently watched her, unable to contain a smirk. Hanna playfully pulled each ribbon, releasing the curtains. His full attention was a delight.

"I don't like sitting all twisted," she pouted, returning her hands to the sturdy support of his shoulders. She permitted his grip to pull her to kneel beside him. Being the fire of his passion frightened and intoxicated her. Crippling shame came too, but his patient and caring caresses were nevertheless exhilarating. Nobody knew what transpired between them except Him. Could He not forgive these cherished moments of innocent pleasure? Theo's long fingers nearly encircled her waist. He pulled her into a kiss as if to say *I need you.*

She straddled his lap.

"The front door is right there," he softly reminded her.

"You said your dad won't be back until dark."

He looked away in consternation. Another calculation. Flush

with heat, she pulled off her sweater, and his attention returned like reconnected electricity. He studied the colorful heart patterns on her T shirt, focusing on her petite bust. She grasped his hair and rested her forehead against his. His hands took her hips, then moved to her thighs, caressing her stockings. She felt him fondling the button of her shorts. The lock on the front door clicked.

FOUR

PANIC ASSAILED THEO. His father's voice called out his name as the door swung open. Theo's heart leaped to his throat. He felt Hanna spring from the couch, nearly crashing into the table. He sat up in a rush of nausea and dizzy shame.

His father stopped abruptly. "That explains why you didn't answer your phone."

"It's so nice to see you again, Mr. Jansen," Hanna announced loudly to the ceiling. Theo watched her pace in a frenetic circle, compulsively smoothing her colorful shirt.

"It's great to see you again too, Hanna . . . was it Popov, I believe?" he heard his father ask.

"Yes, sir. Popov," she promptly answered. His dark suit and beige overcoat looked perfectly at home on his broad shoulders. Hanna's sweater in Theo's shaking hands, less so.

Mr. Jansen quipped, "I hope I wasn't interrupting anything."

Theo cleared his throat and croaked, "We were having coffee." He looked his father in the eyes.

Mr. Jansen asked, "In the dark?"

Hanna impatiently tugged her khaki shorts down to their natural position and crumbled into an armchair. She stared at her feet.

Theo's father calmly opened the curtains and announced, in his usual boisterous voice, "Awful snow today. It just keeps coming. My client decided to cancel at the last minute. Of course, you would have known all of that if you checked your phone, Theodore."

He gave no reply. His father continued to the next pair of curtains. "I see you took Hanna to the Fair and Debonair. How was it?"

"Wonderful, sir!" she exclaimed. "We got a booth, and the sandwiches were tasty and the view was fantastic."

He grinned in the bright room. "That's great. I'm glad you enjoyed it. I've taken many clients there and never had a bad time. It's nice to have a dependable place not too far."

She rushed to say, "The apartment looks great too. It's immaculate."

"Oh, that was mostly Theo. He went redline cleaning this week. It's damn near like a hotel."

While he finished the last curtain, Hanna gestured to Theo for her sweater. He tossed it and she hastily put it back on. Mr. Jansen took the vacant armchair across the coffee table from Hanna. Theo meekly observed him. His formidable frame commanded their due attention.

"Well, I didn't have a chance to eat, and my plans are shot. What do you say I take you both out to an early dinner?"

"That's very kind of you, Mr. Jansen," she began, "but I should probably get back. The trains might be delayed in the snow. Plus, I promised to have dinner with my roommate and her friends."

The addition of the needless fabrication puzzled Theo. Its presence was harmless and undetected by Mr. Jansen, but lingered with Theo. Her visible discomfort and wholly flushed face were apparent to both of them. Theo concurred, "It's probably best if she goes back."

"Theo, get your phone and check the train schedule for delays,"

Mr. Jansen ordered. Theo swiftly obeyed and Mr. Jansen turned to Hanna. "I could drive you back if you'd like."

Theo saw her waving her hands dismissively and overheard, "No, no, I'll be alright. You don't have to trouble yourself. I'm sure the trains will be fine." Sweat glistened on her pink temples, visible by her yet-again-adjusted hairband. Theo liked the bow on it.

In the hallway, Theo tore open the closet door and snatched his phone from his coat. Its screen mocked him: "missed call (2)—Dad." He dismissed the notice and fumed, then turned his attention to navigating the web browser. No delays, or at least nobody bothered to update the website. Collecting Hanna's things in his arms, he peered over his shoulder. His father and Hanna were out of sight, discussing King's prep and her high school career there. Hanna was good at small talk. Theo admired that.

Theo's hand surreptitiously reached into Hanna's puffy jacket pocket. He pulled out her phone and opened it. No messages to dismiss—good to go. He went to her sent folder and clicked down the list. There was her message last Sunday reporting, "On my way." He deleted it. He summoned the recent calls screen and located the familiar eight-minute Saturday call from him. He noted the incoming calls from Emma, her mother, names he didn't recognize, and his second call. Returning to the home screen, he gingerly closed it and slipped it back into her pocket.

Theo returned bearing their coats, her earmuffs, and her backpack. She pounced up and snatched her belongings as he reported, "Looks like no delays yet. I'll walk Hanna to the station."

Mr. Jansen was already standing, prompted by Hanna's standing.

"Albeit brief, it was great seeing you again," he said cordially.

Unsure what to do, she reached out and shook his hand and heartily replied, "It was great seeing you too, sir."

His firm handshake seemed to condone her choice, until he casually remarked, "A little formal, don't you think?"

She winced, retracting her hand, and fled for the hallway. Theo scowled at his father in disapproval, but Mr. Jansen carried on unconcerned. He called over, "Theo, a word." Theo approached his father as he heard the distant bathroom door close. Her footsteps hardly made a sound. It was hard to keep track of her sometimes.

A lustrous silver business card holder rested between his thumb and fingers. It popped open to display a single card bearing Mr. Jansen's scrupulously chosen font, color, and design, presenting his professional contact information. "Tell her to give this to her father; he's a Latin teacher at King's. You didn't know?" he said, his voice lowered to just above a whisper.

"Trying to sell your cigarettes to teachers? You going to send in one of your sales guys? Are you insane?"

"You owe me. Teachers are busy people too. He can smoke in his car."

Theo seized the card and dispatched it into his pocket.

"Still the same mousy Jersey girl, huh?" his father said coolly. "You are just going to ignore the bounty at your doorstep?"

"Yeah, you'd know a lot about picking through the city's wreckage."

"Don't be spiteful. Just be more careful—maybe not the living room. Check your phone."

"Hasn't stopped you."

His father did not dignify his comment with a response. Theo hammered on, "They don't look old enough to be my mom."

"They are not your mother," he snapped with mounting frustration. His father felt compelled to add, "You should see other girls. Don't get hung up on one, even though I'm shocked this one puts up with you. You're young. Enjoy your freedom."

Theo fired back, "You're right. I should see other girls. Mom liked it when you did that."

Exasperated, his father said, "Dammit Theo, we talked about this. You say hurtful things just to say them. Why?"

The sound of water running through the pipes ended their

exchange. Theo turned away as his father pocketed the business card holder. "And Theo," he said to his back, "wipe off that lipstick."

Theo angrily rubbed off the lilac with the back of his hand, enjoying the pain from his overresponse.

Hanna returned, smiling and composed. Her angular face and sharp nose had returned to their usual porcelain color. She had reapplied her lipstick to her small and unremarkable lips, now somewhat conspicuous. Her innocent eyes needed no embellishment. Theo found them endearing just as they were. Her uneven application of nail polish to her short, jaggedly cut fingernails, though, bothered him. Her hands moved like music while she spoke, and he found himself again caught in their spell. She made for the door and briskly put on her boots.

A final round of obligatory goodbyes ended the clumsy affair. Feelings about his father boiled up in the silent elevator. A nascent sentence from Hanna attempted to reach his unconcerned ears. It died, along with her voice. *You should have stopped her. You should have checked your phone. You don't deserve her*, he thought. The words sounded in his head like the city's frequent sirens. Diffidently, the elevator doors shuffled out of his way, and he charged outside. Snowy air soothed his burning face.

"Theo, wait!" he heard her shout behind him.

"What?" he asked, stopping.

"Are you okay? What was that? What did he say?"

Turning to her, he saw genuine concern and lack of accusation. Her lips were parted but they almost always were. Sighing, he answered, "He just told me off for embarrassing you. That's all."

"Oh—" Her voice stalled, but she continued, "It was my fault, really. Sorry for the trouble."

"Let's forget about it. I'll walk you back."

Snow had crept into everything. Business and leisure alike pressed on despite the slippery slush menacing everyone. Afternoon darkness seeped into the city. Her voice reached out again, this time, while they waited at a stoplight.

"Theo, how did your dad know we went to the Fair and Debonair?"

"He gets an email every time I charge my card."

"He wasn't mad or anything?"

"No. He recommended it."

"Give him my thanks."

A walk signal urged them to movement. Penn Station was not far. Theo would take her to the glowing monitors in the waiting area and spot her train on the list. He would thank her and sneak a kiss onto her expectant lips, and she would wave him goodbye. He knew Hanna savored these rituals. Theo gladly obliged. Hanna concluded, "I had a great time today. Thanks for taking the time to help me remember."

Theo nodded. Disappointment suddenly stung her expression. Hanna told him, "Shoot! I forgot all about the coffee you made for me. If it's still there, don't waste it. Drink it for me."

"I will," he affirmed, and she heartily waved him goodbye. Irritated by the din of the station, Theo raced up the multiple befouled staircases. *Repulsive*, was his only thought about the people sitting on the stairs. Drawing his phone like a weapon at the top, he rapidly called a contact and raised the smooth glass screen to his ear. A callous voice answered, "So?"

"It worked."

"Really? You made sure?"

"Yes. What did I just say?"

"Did you confirm the duration?"

"Yes. Three weeks erased."

"Selective amnesia," the callous voice wondered aloud, "who would have thought?"

Theo maintained his pace, weaving between the clots of obtuse pedestrians. At a crosswalk, he refused to stop moving, instead crossing the street to avoid pause. Theo jabbed, "Are we meeting or not?"

"Sure. The shop, as usual. I can do . . ." the voice faded from the phone and returned, "I can do eight a.m. on Sunday. Bring the knife. That's all." Silence made Theo dump his phone into his pocket. Mr. Jansen's business card touched his fingers. He took it out, tore it several times, and threw the shreds at a nearby trash can. They scattered in the snowy wind.

Nothing greeted him as he opened the door to the apartment. No coffee mugs remained on the table. His gaze lingered on the emptiness. Theo headed for the kitchen, where he expected to find his father. There he was, sitting at the table intended for dining but often repurposed for work despite his home office in the adjacent room. Sunlight had a way of drawing people out. Focus etched his brow into a defined groove, his laptop open before him and cell phone in hand. Theo could not remember the last time more than one person ate there.

Theo asked, "Where did you put our coffees?"

"I dumped them. They were cold."

Stillness enveloped Theo. His mouth felt sealed shut, his tongue unwilling to form another word. No emotion held the muscles in his face.

"The car needs to go to the dealership for state inspection. You could take her over sometime this week. I don't think you have class on Thursday," his father said. His voice sounded far away.

"Friday, and I still have morning classes," Theo corrected, turning to the snow outside.

"Right. Thursday was last semester. I'll call the dealer and make the service appointment then," he affirmed.

"Sure," Theo replied.

His father produced a small planner from his pocket. Its fine leather and accompanying weighty metal pen in his confident hands resembled an image out of an advertisement. Theo watched the wind whip the helpless snowflakes about the city. Maybe the lucky ones would land on a building top and die in the sunlight. The majority would land in the filth of the streets below, dying instantly. He wondered about the ones fortunate enough to land on Hanna's earmuffs.

Noticing the building silence, he asked his father, "Was December the last time we talked?"

Silence. He looked over and his father was holding his phone to his ear. Exuberantly, he greeted a client's call and began a conversation about cars. For directing sales at a global tobacco company, he did not discuss the substance and its adverse effects very much. Theo slinked off to his room.

Door closed, he sank into his desk chair and slouched in the darkness. A chartreuse light blinked rhythmically on the computer tower under his desk. Black painted his bed, dresser, and book-cases, neatly crammed with volumes. The white walls were the only hope of reflecting light in his room replicating a void. He reached for the switch on the small desk lamp he favored to the much brighter overhead light. A miniature model jet fighter on his desk glimmered in the yellow glow.

Pulling the keyboard toward him, he jolted the mouse to awaken the machine. Fans stirred to life. The blinking light shined solidly. A login screen replaced the blackness of the monitor. With unfocused eyes, he quickly typed an often-changed password. Pages of maps and news came back to life. He moused the cursor to an open document of innocuous notes. After a quick scan of where he had left off, he saved it yet again and closed it, then closed the pages one by one.

A new blank web browser window popped up. Navigating to a map of the city, he checked the door, and then opened his top desk drawer. Taped to the top of the inside was a small key, with which he opened a larger bottom drawer in his desk. Beneath a pile of motorcycle magazines in that drawer was another banal key, which he took over to an inconspicuous book wedged into the stacks on the bookshelves. Unlocking the book revealed it was not a book at all, but a clandestine box. He gingerly placed it on his desk, careful to preserve the silence. A voluminous stack of notes bearing his cursive penmanship sat inside. He sifted through them, carefully preserving their order. Reaching the layer of relevance, he extracted the thin stack and spread the notes across his desk.

He picked up his crudely drawn map of the city. Red crosses brought unsettling color to the otherwise monochrome map. The crosses made no pattern. Studying the map on his screen, Theo scrolled to the dealership where the car was scheduled for an upcoming service. His cursor then traced a route from his apartment to the dealership, making several stops along the way. Ink hastily recorded the names of nightclubs and venues in his notes. He consulted the map of red crosses and put a star next to one of the establishments. Leaning back in his chair, he rubbed his smoothly shaven chin. This was an easy one. He could use the car. His father would not notice the odometer, just any scratches on his "Mia," but the dealership's report would show the odometer reading. He jotted down several plausible excuses. He circled two.

He sifted through the box again. This time, he pulled out a small journal. A combination lock on the side prevented entry. With the three dials aligned to read, "134," he opened it. Detailed notes flipped past him until he reached the unwritten pages. He copied the words bearing colons on the previous page to a new one: "pickup," "drop off," "duration," "intended recipient," and "full or directed." His pen halted above the five colons. Slowly, he answered two but was unable to fill in the rest. He wrote, "translation" off to the side. How hurt Hanna had sounded when she said, "Not really," came to his mind. He could not shake the memory. He added, "Hanna's amnesia" under "translation." Pensive, he ruminated for some time, forgetting the door again. Hearing his father's footsteps pass by made him expediently return everything to its resting place.

Those three unanswered colons lingered. He changed to athletic clothes. Maybe answers would come with sweat. He slipped out of the apartment and down the elevator to the building's fitness room. Not a soul there. He boarded the treadmill. Its beeps assured him that the escape of physical exertion was coming. He put on his headphones and let stories of revolution and rebellion shouted over rock and roll flood his ears.

FIVE

"NO PRIOR HISTORY OF MEMORY LOSS?"

"No, ma'am."

The counselor's cold voice equaled the chill of the examination table Hanna sat on. Calculus class, just an hour prior, felt far more inviting than this. Hanna stared at her own knees, avoiding the counselor's interrogative frown. Her pen hastily scratched the paper on her clipboard. She resumed her volley.

"History of drug use?"

"None."

"Are you sexually active?"

"No." Hanna's eyes darted away, as she remembered stolen afternoons at Theo's apartment. She weighed asking, "To what extent?" but the next question came.

"Do you smoke?"

"No."

"Do you drink?"

"No."

"Are you eating well?"

"Yes."

"Migraines, seizures, confusion, stiff neck, or vomiting?"

"No."

"Do you play sports?"

"No."

The counselor scratched her batch of answers onto the clipboard. Hanna wriggled on the table, regretting the visit. At least her parents would not know. Alerting them about an ailment affecting her studies remained a poor decision.

"Have you had any surgeries?"

"No."

"History of neurological disorders?"

"Not that I'm aware of."

"Do you have trouble committing things to long-term memory?"

"I mean, that's why I'm here."

"What can you not commit to memory?"

It was nice to receive an open-ended question. So many closed questions in quick succession buried Hanna's hope of cooperation. "That's what I wanted to explain—like, how I felt. When I go out with my friends, well, one friend in particular, I see him and then sometimes after, I can't remember the details. I can remember the day and going out, but just not anything about him."

"Have you experienced trauma to the head?"

"No," Hanna answered defensively.

"Have you experienced traumatic events in your lifetime?"

"No."

The counselor retreated to her clipboard and Hanna to her memories of Theo. Vivid recollections easily surfaced. It was only at his prompting that she recognized there were gaps. Hanna heard the wheels of the counselor's chair roll her away to a computer. The keyboard pattered like raindrops at the counselor's rapid touch. The raindrops continued as she concluded, into the screen, "We're not equipped to handle patients of this nature at this facility. I'll need to refer you to a specialist."

I'm sitting right here, Hanna thought, but it all seemed hopeless. The counselor turned and faced her. "We'll need a blood test for a baseline. You may also be deficient in a certain protein necessary for memory function. You seem to be experiencing difficulty forming new memories. These are possibly symptoms of anterograde amnesia."

Hanna's mouth felt dry. She felt her pulse in her temples and chest. She did not hear the next words from the counselor, however many there were. *Anterograde amnesia* repeated in her mind. The counselor's impatient tone brought the examination room floor back into focus.

"Can you hear me?"

"Yes."

"You mentioned you play a musical instrument."

"Yes."

"Have you learned anything new recently?"

"Not really."

"Can you still play songs you already learned?"

"Yes."

"That may be a good way to test your implicit memory."

"Do I have dementia?"

The counselor frowned behind her spectacles momentarily, then answered, "That's a broad category. Early-onset dementia usually occurs between ages thirty and sixty. At eighteen, it would be exceedingly rare. A genetic predisposition is also present in many cases, and you have not indicated a family history. So again, rare."

Anxiety suffocated any reply from Hanna. Her boots felt like anchors on her dangling feet. Passively, she heard the counselor conclude, "We may need to do an MRI, which we don't have here at the university clinic. I'll have to refer you to the hospital for that too. You'll need to make an appointment with them. Your next step is to get your blood test, which can be done here at the phlebotomist's office."

The counselor carved her pen into her pad of blank prescriptions. Hanna heard her phone buzz in her jacket pocket. *What now?* she thought, staring at her hiking backpack and puffy jacket on the empty chair in front of her. There were still classes to get through. Noticing the counselor ordering her to take the prescription from her outstretched hand, she took it and stared. The counselor's handwritten "anterograde amnesia" assessment condemned the document as shameful and frightening to Hanna.

She feigned to hear the counselor's concluding remarks and readily complied with her instructions to leave. In red ink, she penned on the prescription, "when I'm with Theo." She slipped it into her jeans' pocket. Outside the office, she put on her jacket and backpack and rushed to the exit of Surgite's sports and recreation center. Shoving the glass doors out of her way, the frozen air swept against her burning face.

Hanna ran. Her lungs strained for more air under the sudden exertion. She cut through the empty campus as if late for class, her backpack violently swaying behind her. She charged through the snow-covered lawns between the neatly shoveled macadam trails. The brick rectangle of the student center building was within sight.

Arriving at the doors, she ripped one open. An alarmed student yelped and stepped back at her violent ingress. She apologized and tried to regain her composure, walking inside. A handful of students milled about the wooden tables and matching chairs. They meekly noticed her belabored breathing and politely ignored her. She spotted her target and took a deep breath. The soft carpet muffled her footsteps advancing toward the rotunda, an extension built just off the main hall. No doorway marked her passage into the sunlit room. Its semicircle of windows allowed light almost all day and its tall ceiling had a pleasing acoustic effect. She sat at the bench and slipped off her backpack, letting it drop with a thud against the carpet. Giving a quick scan of the room, she gingerly pressed the keys of the grand piano.

Warm notes ascended in rhythmic harmony. Her fingers, diminutive but deft, spread to just barely span the octave. Her experienced hand continued the harmony while her eyes scanned the room. No complaints yet. She brought to life a melody she had known since childhood, and her boot reached for the pedal. Blending the keys, she closed her eyes, raising then lowering her boot to gently transition to the next measure. Relief swept her. She wanted to cry out. *She remembered.*

Hanna stopped abruptly. Withdrawing her right foot, her left darted to the damper pedal. Her fingers raced to summon the next song, played in a hushed and sped-up manner comical to all but the player. Relentlessly, she tested her memory, playing through songs just long enough to confirm her solid recollection and then dashing to the next. At her accelerated pace, she tore through her collection, spanning more than a decade. To the students chatting in the common room, it sounded like an irresponsibly late rehearsal. To Hanna, it was blissful assurance. Satisfaction gradually eased the frantic testing. Yesterday's studying came to mind. An otherwise unremarkable Sunday spent in the library and her room, she now cherished in vivid recollection.

Her phone buzzed again. Emma had messaged twice, now asking, "Where r u?" Typing out the inevitable saga felt tiresome. Hanna pressed the call button and raised the phone to her ear. Two rings later, she heard Emma's salutation, "Where you at, girl?"

Feigning a chipper voice, Hanna answered, "In the student center. What's up?"

"You missed a cool party Saturday night. I know, I know. I already told you. Well, I just had an idea. You might hate me, but I want to explain in person."

"Building up the tension?"

"It's . . . well . . . let's just say there's a fifty percent chance you'll hate me."

Air rushed out of Hanna's nose. "Only fifty?" she tossed out.

Emma pressed on, "Trust me, it'll be good for you. Can you just wait there at the student center? I'll be right over. Are you at the piano again?"

"Yeah. I'll wait here."

"Okay, cool. On my way," she acknowledged and hung up.

Hanna returned to the faux ivory. Morning sunlight danced through the branches outside, tickled by frozen wind, and splashed on the fine maple finish of the grand. Her hands returned to the keys. Seeking escape, she closed her eyes and brought to life one of her creations. Gracefully, she drenched the room in a wistful waltz, pining for unachievable joy. She swayed, absorbed in the notes, retarding the end of each section before building again to the next despondent drop. On the final chord, she held her legato keys and struck a single root key to conclude the performance to herself.

Applause met her ears. Startled, she opened her eyes. The chatting students cheered and grinned at her acknowledgment. Hanna cheerfully waved, but sheepishly hid her countenance in the keys. Motivation to summon another song did not come. Her fingers pressed keys aimlessly, still remembering the inebriating applause. Emma's approaching voice chased her hands away from the instrument.

"Spin me a tune."

"Hi, Emma."

"Hi, friendo."

Hanna slid over on the bench and gestured Emma to sit next to her.

Emma plopped herself down with the grace of a falling pear. She began, "So, um, last Sunday, did Theo stand you up?"

"Our date? No, of course not," Hanna answered through hazy recollection.

Emma sighed. "Neither of us are going to enjoy this, so I'm just gonna come right out and say it."

Concern drained the mirth from Hanna. Emma drew her laptop from under her arm and placed it on her thighs. Having just escaped panic, Hanna regretted the feeling rushing back so soon. Emma remained silent as she logged into her Friend Link account and pushed the cursor to the tiny icon of Hanna's beaming face on the screen. That Hanna in September was so carefree. There, at the top of Hanna's infrequent posts, was the one in question. She turned her laptop, which was missing a key, to Hanna, who saw herself in the café looking back at her through Emma's fingerprint-dotted screen. Her tepid smile and tilted head greeted her once again.

"Was there never an Italian restaurant that day—or even Theo?" Emma asked in a low, stern tone. "Did you really have to lie to me?"

Alarmed, Hanna said, "Wait. Slow down. What do you mean, 'lie?'"

"In the library last Sunday. You supposedly came back from your date with Theo and met Broc and me for calculus. You said you two had been to an Italian restaurant. Now you went to the café alone, ordered a mocha, and took a selfie? And posted about it? Are we keeping secrets now? Why couldn't you just be honest? If you didn't want to come to my brothers' birthday party, you could have just told me."

Hanna tried to give a reasonable answer, saying, "It's . . . that's not exactly what happened. I was caught off guard and must have mixed up some details. I had been spacing out in the library and —" but Emma cut in, "I don't need a speech."

Hanna pleaded, "You didn't have to bring it up like this. Just listen for a second."

Emma remained resolute. "No, you listen. We avoided talking about this all day yesterday, but I can't let it stew. They're twins, Hanna. They always only get half a birthday each. And they turned twenty! You've come to their party eight years in a row—hell, helped me put together a bunch of them. This is the first time we can hang out every day since middle school, and now you're putting crap like this between us? When I found out you were going to Surgite, I was ecstatic. It helped me make my final deci-sion. I thought we'd be besties like the old days—not hiding stuff from each other. Not lies."

"I didn't lie."

"Yeah, you did. Don't act like I didn't catch you. You told me you had a date with Theo. Sure. I get it. Fine. But that turned out to be a lie, huh?"

"That's just how you ended up seeing it. If you saw it through my eyes, you'd understand."

"So you admit it, liar."

Hanna stood abruptly. "Don't talk to me that way."

"Then don't lie to me," Emma barked, shooting a cross glare.

Hanna sharply drew breath for her pounding heart. She refused to look away from Emma's choleric brown eyes.

Emma broke the standoff, closing her laptop, and, in a dejected murmur, said, "Call me selfish or whatever. I thought we were best friends."

"We still are," Hanna protested.

"Look at yourself."

Hanna realized her clenched fists were beginning to sweat. Her whole body was rigid, poised to retaliate.

Emma shook her head. "Best friends don't lie to each other. Best friends don't bail on each other for no reason."

Hanna sighed, her pounding heart back in her throat. "You're right. They don't. I did and I'm sorry. I panicked because I couldn't bring myself to say Theo had canceled late the night before, citing some lame excuse. I didn't want to do that to him in front of you and Broc. Call me selfish too but I wanted to protect him. He—"

Emma jumped in, "Like he needs it."

Hanna's fist slammed the piano. The haunting echo smacked the formerly cheerful students in the distance.

"There's that temper of yours," Emma remarked at the familiar scene.

Hanna closed her eyes and breathed deeply. Darkness shut out Emma but let the shades of her childhood anger taunt her in unwanted recollection. Seconds passed. Exploding felt inevitable. Time doused the flames, suffocating the oxygen of Emma's scorn.

"I apologize," Hanna said, assuming a tempered tone. "He asked me to try the mocha there when he canceled. I got dressed up and took a selfie and, I guess, posted it on FL too." Hazy recollections of Friend Link's reoccurring reminders to verify her identity upon logging in swirled up. The website fought the convenience of logging in from a library computer, which she did frequently. She raced through it, impatient with its pestering questions. The laptop was burdensome to lug around.

"Not cool," Emma remarked brusquely.

Silence resumed between them. Hanna took the seconds afforded to her by Emma's patience. Sunlight danced past the piano and onto the carpet. A stain marred it—anything to look at but Emma's choleric eyes.

Sighing, Hanna said, "I know. I won't blame it on being forgetful or anything. I'm sorry."

"What if you took a break from seeing him?"

"I couldn't do that to him," Hanna answered defensively.

"He's driving a wedge between you and your life here. Listen to me just a teeny bit."

Hanna sighed again. "Okay. I'm listening—I really am. I promise."

"Don't go into the city!" she implored. "Don't see him for a bit. Get your bearings back."

Exhausted, Hanna crumbled onto the bench beside her. "Why? I've seen him every weekend in January . . . I think." She paused before concluding, "This last time really stood out in my memory. He's sweet."

Emma grabbed Hanna's arms. Even her hands could mostly encircle them. "You can't even keep straight when you've seen him. I feel like you've missed some red flags."

"Like what?" Hanna retorted, shrugging out of her grasp. Dejection returned to Emma's expressive face. Hanna took a deep breath and instead asked, "No, really, I'm listening. What red flags have I missed?"

Emma smirked. "Actually, there's a pretty fun game to find out. Saturday night, there was a dorm mixer. Everyone trying to pair up for Valentine's, ya know? I was bored, so I went with the other premed girls. It was a red-flag-green-flag party. Red means you're taken. Green means you're single. You're supposed to carry a flag or wear a shirt that's green or red to indicate your status. The red flags got bored and started listening to the conversations of the greens and would wave their red flags when somebody said something questionable. It devolved into a kind of gameshow. The greens started taking it a little hard."

"Where'd you get a red flag?"

"I grabbed one from the basket." Realization flashed across Emma's face, and she added, "That's not the point. The point is, why don't we play the game with you? I'll get Broc and we'll ask you questions about Theo and wave the red flag as appropriate."

Hanna replied a flat, "No."

Emma hastily answered, "Come on, you owe me this. Let's call it making amends for lying. It'll be like old times."

Hanna paused, feeling that anger swirling again. Emma gave her a few more moments. Hanna rested her chin in her hands. "Okay, but don't make it weird."

"Deal," Emma answered, satisfied.

"Why Broc?"

"He was there at the party, so he knows the rules. In fact, we may have been involved with starting the whole red-flag fiasco. Premeds are such squares. We're not going to ask you anything too personal and it's important to have an outside perspective."

"Okay. When do you want to do this?"

"This afternoon."

"Fine."

Emma stood up, invigorated. "Bueno. I'll let him know. Soccer practice doesn't start until four anyway."

Hanna stood too and retrieved her abandoned backpack. "What time is it? I should probably get to Japanese."

"Ten till noon. Run."

Exasperated, Hanna exclaimed, "I won't forget this afternoon. Talk later. Bye!" Running again, she heard Emma's halfhearted jeer. Hanna's Japanese language classmates saw her burst through the classroom door and throw herself into her seat seconds before Sensei arrived. Hanna frantically produced her books in the front row, knowing that if she were called, she could rely on herself to give a sufficient answer. In fourth-semester collegiate Japanese, though, her ability to "wing it" was quickly becoming insufficient. Her classmates chided her for her tardiness, for which she apologized.

Sensei enthusiastically conducted the class in an energetic salutation, and then led them straight into the daily vocabulary quiz. Turning in her quiz early as usual, Hanna wrote, in the margins of her notebook, "Don't forget to record your new memories." Class slipped by without her noticing the time. Only Sensei's return to English at the end aroused Hanna's concern.

"Do not forget, the video project will start tomorrow." The clock indicated the allotted time for class was over, yet no one dared move. She concluded, "This will be a great chance to show your abilities and have fun," and, in Japanese, said, *"Well, that is all for today."* The class enthusiastically gave their farewell salutation and were released. For being just marginally taller than Hanna, Sensei commanded her pupils with an imposing presence.

Class dismissed, Hanna resumed her cardio challenge, running back to the dormitories for her laptop. A Boethius paper was due in her medieval literature class in less than an hour.

Printing required transferring the document to a USB stick and running the stick to the sizable library printers, which ate up all the coins she could scavenge. She always submitted papers like this. Hanna never paid much attention to the now dozens of files and pictures scattered about her desktop. The printer sang its productive song as her finger impatiently rapped on it. She smacked a staple into the thin stack bearing her name and resumed the running.

Seated in the sleepy classroom, her stomach protested her oversight, giving a prominent growl as she slid off her backpack. The back row never judged her.

Halfway through the class, she realized she would not be called on. Submitting her paper was enough today. The pain of its grade could be endured later. The professor took full advantage to elocute ad infinitum on concepts in the text unseen by Hanna and all of the students save for one. Nobody liked him much. Hanna languidly took notes, enjoying the bright colors of her pens. The sudden surge of students standing up alerted her that class was over. Her phone immediately started buzzing in her pocket. She flicked it open, and Emma's messages showed on the screen, instructing her to return to the piano right away. Broc could not be late for soccer practice.

Why does it have to be spread out? Hanna thought as she ran back through the frozen forest. Chatty crowds of students migrated about the campus. Birds exuberantly sang for spring atop barren trees. Hanna felt like collapsing, but reached the student center's piano. Emma and Broc flanked it. They were joking with each other in their infectious good spirits. Neither sat on the piano's sunlit bench. "Oh, hey," Emma beamed, turning to her.

"Hi, guys," Hanna said and plopped onto the bench.

"Hi, Hanna," said Broc, cheerful as ever. He met her eyes earnestly. "Thanks for doing this for Emma."

"It's for the best, right? I heard you guys had fun at the mixer?"

"Yeah, it was a great time," he replied. Broc was a good boy with a round, innocent face occasionally vexed by acne. His green eyes never seemed accusatory, but nor were they ever invigorating. His hair was never combed atop his somewhat large skull, bearing a face that appeared too compressed to be called charismatic. His strong frame always carried just a little extra weight, but he was the kind of wholesome boy Surgite put on their website homepage as a private Christian university focused on fellowship and high graduation rates, while vigorously warning students about the dangers of premarital sex.

"Come on, Hanna, let's not hog the piano," Emma chided and beckoned her to an empty table. Monday afternoon did not draw a crowd. Broc and Emma sat across from Hanna. Emma held two little red flags. Handing one to Broc, they each put theirs flat on the table.

"I believe the first question should go to Broc, as our honorary guest," Emma announced.

Hanna slid off her backpack, folded her arms, and leaned back against the insufficient padding on her wooden chair.

"*Alllright*," she replied in a playfully drawn-out tone, "let's have question number one."

Broc laughed nervously at the sudden pressure. Emma prompted him, "Any day, champ."

"What's his name?"

"Theo."

Emma's red flag shot up.

"Oh, come on!" Hanna rebuked. Emma laughed. Broc relaxed his shoulders and joined Emma's laughter.

Emma lowered her flag and said, "Next one is mine." Hanna crossed her legs.

"Is he older than you?"

"Younger by like two months."

Both red flags stayed down.

"Back to you," Emma told Broc, jutting her chin at him. Broc considered his next question momentarily.

"What's his hobby?"

"I guess, exercising."

No red flags.

Hanna added, "And spending time alone on his computer."

Broc meekly raised his red flag. He looked over at Emma's lowered flag and quickly lowered his. Emma smirked. "So what do boys do alone on their computers, hmm?"

Broc hid a cheeky grin. Hanna hastened to clarify, "He plays some online game and has, like, friends in a guild."

Emma said, "Okay, okay. Let me think."

With the rhythm established, they traded asking questions.

"Does he smell good?"

"Always."

No flag movement.

"Does he have friends?"

"Not that he's ever mentioned."

Emma snatched Broc's red flag and shook them both like maracas. Broc deftly plucked his back, and Emma resumed the game.

"Does he have a Friend Link account?"

"No."

A red flag from Emma shot up, but Broc argued, "It depends. Not everyone needs one."

Emma nodded. "Yeah, but I'm still giving it a red flag because he can never update his relationship status. Your turn."

Sudden realization picked at Hanna.

"Is he on his phone all the time?"

"No."

No flag movement.

"Does he call you?"

"Almost exclusively. He avoids text and email."

Broc's red flag twitched, then rejoined Emma's flag, flat on the table.

"Does he offer to pay for food on dates?"

"Yes, but he doesn't insist."

No movement from the flags.

"Does he kiss on the first date?"

"Well, yes, but we were already classmates before we started dating."

Both red flags stayed down, but Emma said, "I suppose he

wanted to be clear he was interested in you, but he might also just be pretending to take things slow."

Hanna replied, "Theo's not like that. He gets really fired up about debating philosophy, though." Broc chuckled and Hanna added, "He's really sweet when you get to know him. He doesn't talk much at first. You have to get past his tough outer shell."

Emma perked up. "Why don't we meet him? I only saw him once at the Halloween party last year. I don't think he even took off his helmet."

Hanna began a reply, but Broc cut her off. "Oh yeah, he was wearing all his motorcycle stuff. I bet I can find the picture on FL."

Seconds later, Broc turned his phone screen to her. Halloween Hanna stood next to Theo dressed in his black leather racing suit. The armor added formidable width to his somewhat-lacking tall, taut frame. His full-face motorcycle helmet obscured much of his countenance, save for the eye port, unobscured by the raised tinted face shield. A rare smile was evident in his eyes. Hanna's own smile radiated as his arm wrapped around her. Witnessing herself, Hanna blushed in recollection.

"I remember that," Emma jumped in. "You dressed up as a Japanese high school girl because he made you."

"*Suggested!*" Hanna squeaked.

Emma returned fire, saying, "We were supposed to go as fellow communist dictators. I had the fake mustaches and everything."

"You called me Comrade Popov all night anyway and snuck a hammer and sickle sticker onto my jacket," Hanna lamented.

"You're Russian. I'm Cuban. It would have been perfect."

Broc retracted his phone as Emma noted, "I'm pretty sure that's the only photo of him on FL, and you can't even really see his face."

Feeling cornered, Hanna snatched one of the red flags from Emma's idle hands. "Broc," she said, "Who's your crush?"

Petrified, Broc's agape mouth was unable to articulate an

answer. Hanna chortled devilishly and continued her interrogation. "Is she older or younger than you?"

"Younger," he answered carefully. Neither red flag moved.

Emma eagerly chimed in, "Ooh, yes. Let's play."

"I should get going to soccer practice," he announced.

"Alright, alright," Emma said. "Funny how quickly that devolved into a 'tell the truth' game," she quipped as he graciously hurried off.

Broc out of sight, Hanna asked, "Do you get the feeling he's holding back? Like he's actually interested in you?"

"We hang out and all," Emma said listlessly. "Not much in the way of surprises with him."

"Surprises can be fun."

"He's an open book," Emma said dismissively. "That Theo, though," she continued, her voice picking up a shiver of wonder.

"I feel like I know him well."

"Do you really?" asked Emma.

A sickening doubt churned in Hanna's stomach.

SIX

"YOU'RE GONNA GET US KILLED!" the girl from the nightclub screamed next to him. Theo pressed the accelerator pedal farther. His father's car downshifted into a roar.

"What are you doing! A *hundred*?"

"One hundred twenty-four now," he said calmly to his loud guest in the passenger seat. The headlights of the contender's car beside them faded back into the darkness of Long Island. Spotting the yellow traffic light ahead, Theo gently pressured the brake pedal with his foot.

"Why aren't you stopping?" she yelled.

Theo gradually applied more pressure and the coupe's lengthy hood bowed to the traffic light. He eased off the brake and the car returned to rest just before the line. The contender screeched a car length past the line. The driver's window rolled down and Theo heard frivolous shouting. Theo watched the opposing traffic light turn yellow.

"Not again! You're not gonna race this guy?" she protested.

He scoffed. "We're going in a straight line."

"Just take me back to the club!"

Green light—Theo released the rage of the eight Italian cylinders. They shot forward, and first gear was finished already. His guest grabbed the supple red leather of her door's bracing handle. She loudly cursed him. The contender's headlights pulled closer. Theo spotted the green light ahead, but the much slower traffic presented complications. His lane was blocked. This night's competition could use the shoulder. Entering the intersection, he swerved into the opposing traffic lanes.

"*You're nuts!*" she shrieked. One light. That's all he had to clear in the opposing lanes. He unleashed the car's full power. It was pleased. The tachometer had long yearned to tickle its highest numbers. Their competitor fell behind. The headlights in front of them swerved to make way. Theo returned his foot to the brake pedal and engaged the car's forceful engine braking. He eased them back onto the correct side of traffic at the next intersection. Looking over his shoulder to merge, he saw their challenger shoot ahead and noted his loud guest's baffled expression.

Theo noticed her bare legs. Her party dress left much exposed. This would be easy. Theo clicked the signal stalk behind the paddle shifter and brought the silver coupe to a restaurant's quiet parking lot. Little traffic pestered this part of Long Island at midnight. Spotting the lights of an open gas station ahead, he slid the car into the blackness behind the restaurant and killed the headlights.

"Let me out, you lunatic!" the loud girl demanded. He turned to her. His father's car offered an intimate setting between its two doors. Its spacious back seat was inviting on any other occasion.

"What are you afraid of?" he asked, irritated. "That you'll die having never known happiness?"

"You really are insane! Forget it. I'm getting out here and calling a cab."

"You aren't, but your quiet friend will."

Terror drained the color from the girl's face. Theo's window descended as he drew the sheathed knife from his coat pocket. In the black of night, the inky lacquer and dark fabric handle were impossible to make out. A miniscule guard, called a tsuba, barely interrupted the gently curved handle-to-sheath flow, concealing a capable blade. He swiftly slid his thumb under the belt loop at the sheath's top. Holding the sheathed knife out the window, he raised his thumb and the belt loop popped up, giving an affirming click. His loud guest gasped.

Violet light burst from the knife to the size of a person. Black lines within it rapidly materialized a young woman in a party dress floating prostrate under his hand. Immediately, she fell to the ground with a limp thud. Theo retracted the sheathed knife back into the car. Having released the quiet girl from the club, he looked into the eyes of the now-petrified loud girl and asked, "You don't believe in ghosts, do you?"

Her hand shot for the door handle.

Theo thrust the wooden sheath's tip against her bare thigh. Rigid tension locked her in place, eyes unfocused. Theo retracted the sheathed knife and pressed it again to her uninjured leg. Violet light leaped out, encircling his victim with snaking black lines. In merely a second, she was gone. Theo dropped the knife in the empty passenger seat, grabbed the purse stowed under the seat, and threw it out his window at her quiet friend. She struggled to her feet as he maneuvered the car back to the road.

"You idiot," he said to himself, picking up the westbound direction. Just over an hour back to the nightclub. A one-hour amnesia charge was not ideal, but good enough for a salvaged attempt. Convincing this loud drunk that he lived on Long Island and her quiet friend was on her way for the last hour had been exhausting. He focused on the road ahead.

Mia, as his father was fond of calling the car, purred pleasantly and roared on command, her electronics subtly correcting the driver's inadequate preparation or inexperienced execution. She needed little prompting to display her prowess. At the speed limit, she was comfortable and maneuverable but maintained an eager readiness for more vigorous input. Theo turned on the CD player. His father never used it, instead taking unending phone calls. *What a shame to ignore her*, thought Theo. An image of Hanna playfully closing the curtains flashed from his memory.

Theo nodded his head to the succulent sound of the synthesizer pouring from the speakers. For not being a motorcycle, her rear wheels broke traction just as easily. She did not forgive careless mistakes. Theo reset his foot on the throttle as Mia's traction control system also cut power. Theo enjoyed Mia staying under his control. Occasionally, the thrill of handling something that could escape his grasp, though, called to him. The lights and steel of his preferred bridge spanning the East River indicated the evening was coming to a close. Just two more things to do. Manhattan always looked boundless from the Queensboro Bridge, spilling past his peripheral vision on both sides—an entire island of yet more life tucked underneath midway. New York promised him tantalizing possibility and dismal reality like no other place could.

Traffic was usual in the city, Theo lunging red light to red light. He put the sheathed knife back into his coat pocket. Even behind tinted windows, it was not worth the risk. Fortunately for him, navigation was never complicated in midtown. Turning onto the soulless street of the nightclub, he parallel parked.

Mia's still-running engine purred expectantly. He clicked off the CD player. With one last look in each mirror, he drew the sheathed knife from his coat pocket, slipped his thumb under the belt loop, and leaned far over the passenger seat. The blade itself did not have to come out for these operations. It sat safely idle inside the wooden sheath while Theo employed the sheath's malignant functions. He pulled the door handle, lifted his thumb, and pushed open the car door.

Violet light returned and the black lines rapidly twisted into the shape of his loud guest. He never knew which way they would materialize. This time, she landed facing the seat. Her disoriented body arched her spine backward before she regained full consciousness. Theo seized the interlude and shoved her out of the car. She plopped onto the sidewalk. He tossed her purse out behind her, yanked the door closed, and drove away. Theo enjoyed the last few straights and turns the island's grid offered, despite Mia's boredom.

He nosed into the residents-only parking structure just a block away from his father's apartment. Well-lit concrete pillars and exotic cars that never saw redline glided past him. The echo of Mia's motor in the enclosed space pleased him. He confidently returned his father's car to its designated spot. Adjacent were his father's two motorcycles. Their modest covers hid striking figures. Theo shut off the engine and inspected the cabin for any evidence but saw none: just immaculate red leather. No cleanup was always good. He returned to the empty apartment.

Darkness greeted him. He tossed the key into a basket and left his shoes by the door where Hanna had left hers. At the kitchen sink, he scrubbed the black X marks drawn on the backs of his hands by the bouncer at the nightclub. Being clearly denoted as underage for drinking sometimes served as a useful conversation starter with older women, even if their comments were mostly derisive.

Drunks were easier to capture but no bar would let him in. Strip clubs proved similar. Maybe they could tell he was not there to spend money. Restaurants were too well lit. Cameras infested drugstores, supermarkets, gas stations, street corners, alleys, and especially banks. Nobody wanted to get stabbed in a bank—or anywhere really. These five boroughs had eight million people crawling around them and he could not find one to capture unseen. The subway stairs offered brief opportunities, but the risks were extreme. Concerts and raves sufficed. Finding one on a Monday night was tricky, but Manhattan proved resourceful. Those girls would look at his car and assume drugs were next. Without the car, patience was critical. An accomplice would make things easier— especially a girl.

Theo shut off the water, dried his hands, and retrieved his cell phone from his desk. He pursed his lips at the missed call from

Hanna. Had he really been gone five hours? Her answering did not seem likely at two in the morning on a Tuesday. The glass screen went dark, and Theo turned on his desk light, took out the sheathed knife, and drew the blade. Its gently arced single-sided edge feigned modesty before his fascinated eyes. Its appropriate weight could not escape his envisioning its intended use, though the sheath had seen all usage so far. The black steel blade and its true abilities remained unknown. The red Japanese characters engraved at the blade's base mocked him.

Theo carefully placed it near the model airplane he had made with his father years prior. His stare lingered on that sleek fighter jet, then at the expertly crafted black wooden sheath. *That artisan was far superior to me in planning and careful execution*, he thought to himself.

At least it was charged, albeit just for an hour, and it would store that charge until he used it to inflict amnesia on his next victim. So far, at least, he had not noticed the charge dissipating over time. Whoever made this tool had designed it well. Neither Theo nor the man who gave it to him knew who made this artifact or even how. It unsettled him to think who would. He resheathed the knife and left it on his desk. His father would not be back tonight. The women he dated seemed desperate for company on Monday evenings. Theo did not bother remembering their names. He just stayed out of their way.

Theo awakened his computer and returned to the familiar screens. Opening a new web browser window, he navigated to the message boards of the only game on his computer that he permitted a desktop shortcut. He clicked to the random forum and started a new thread. He posed the questions, "Where do you ask girls out one-on-one? Why do they always have a friend?" At least he would get a few replies before the moderators took it down. Maybe one of his guildmates was online. They were active most nights, inviting him to play with them to tackle high-level dungeons requiring a dedicated team. Theo's participation had waned recently. He repeated the question on an unrelated forum. Comparing the differences often revealed more.

Theo followed his steps to bring out his notes. The results of this evening's sortie had to be documented. He pulled out the relevant sheets from the stack and added two red crosses to his hand-drawn map. He filled in observations around the name of this evening's nightclub and chronicled his mistake of assuming his target, the quiet one, would follow him to the car alone. Though she was inebriated, he ignored her mumbling about her loud friend. He had been lucky this time.

To help channel his frustration, Theo obstinately adhered to his standards of penmanship. He charted his subjects' consciousness and plausible memories from each of their perspectives. The hard part was releasing the victim undetected, to avoid using the resulting amnesia charge on them.

Combination entered into the locked journal, he flipped to the most recent blank page. All five colons had answers except "duration." He wrote, "one hour." His pen stopped above the two choices still uncircled: "translation" and "Hanna's amnesia." Arthur, the man who bestowed the responsibility of charting this knife's ability, already made translating the characters on the knife his next task. At their meeting on Sunday morning, he had stressed that he was eager to move past this testing phase. Hanna's amnesia would have to wait. Pangs of regret arrested his pen from circling "translation." Why was she so caring? Could she really be that sincere? He had never met anyone as loving as her. He hesitated, but he could not stop the rush of thoughts. She only liked him when he bought her things. She was using him. She would never accept him and what he was involved in. She would leave him. She was only happy when she had attention. Deep down, she was selfish like everyone else.

Theo opened his desk drawer. There sat the bottle of antidepressant medication. He stared but closed the drawer. Not tonight. December had seen him give up on them. No reason to be an even bigger failure and go back on that. Therapy had not been helpful last fall. His father blamed it on his new school. The therapist blamed Theo for not cooperating. Theo blamed himself. He folded his arms on his desk and rested his head on them.

You're going to mess this up too, he thought. He closed his eyes for some time and opened them, feeling heavy sleep coming. He sat up and circled "translation." Once this was over, he could disappear—just a little bit further. Hanna would never forgive him, but nor would she remember him.

Theo shook his mouse to awaken his monitor and clicked to refresh the forums. Disbelief pushed up his eyebrows. More than fifty replies on each met his widened pupils. He scrolled through them. Both boards converged on the assumption that he had no experience picking up women. That was true. He scanned for leads.

"Dating sites, dude. Try one."

"Have you tried chloroform?"

"Girls flock in groups for protection against weirdos like you."

"You have to make it through their committee. No date unless you pass a panel interview."

"Step one: be attractive."

"Just look over her shoulder in the supermarket checkout line and tell her you have the same bank. What a coincidence. Conversation started."

"How old are you? Go to bars. Lots of divorcées looking for companionship."

"Get a name. Stalk the hell out of her online. Learn her routine. Pretend to bump into her at the gym or something when you know she's alone."

"Dude, just be fit, clean, tall, rich, and funny."

"Go to mixers if you're still in college. If you don't have a personality, buy one."

"How fast can you run? Maybe you can pick off the slow ones from the herd."

Expectantly, he clicked to refresh again. One of the threads had already been deleted. No sense in continuing. This was enough to start. He could ask his guildmates for their ideas tomorrow. He recorded select answers, then carefully stowed his notes and prepared for bed. Lastly, he tucked the knife up inside the box spring under his mattress. "*Oyasumi*," he whispered to it. Above his covers and blankets, he lay there in his clothes and coat. He closed his eyes and drifted out of consciousness.

Consternation kept knocking him awake. By four, he had slipped under the blankets. Sick of reaching for his phone to check that only another hour had crawled by, he rose at seven. In the hallway, he caught himself in the mirror. Wearing the same clothes to school would attract attention. He prepared to depart for class while pondering his next attempt to charge the sheath's amnesia power. News channels were running stories about disappearances. People were on alert. This was not going to get easier. He plucked Tuesday's notebooks and texts from his bookshelf and set out, having eaten little.

Walking to the subway station, he drew his phone. Heavy clouds above threatened precipitation. *It better not rain*, he thought. He slid the screens to his brief contacts list and called Hanna. It rang twice and then he heard her melodic voice.

"Hi!"

"Hey."

"Sorry I missed your call last night. I have a favor to ask."

"Oh, no, not a problem. You must have been busy. I wanted to ask you a favor too."

Theo and Hanna both spoke at the same time. He yielded. Her timid voice broke the silence with, "What were you doing last night, if you don't mind me asking?"

"Playing Demon World Online."

"I guess you do that a lot."

"Fun things are fun."

The coquettish rush of air out of her mouth sucked away his attention. He imagined her parted lips.

"So what can I do for you?" she asked. It killed him when she spoke with such innocence.

Infected, he let the eagerness show in his voice. "I want you to translate some Japanese. It's for one of my history classes. It's not required or anything, but I figured you would enjoy the challenge and I would gain some insight. It would mean a lot to me."

"I'd love to! You don't even have to ask. Is it a quote or a speech or something?"

"Engravings on a sword."

Hanna's ecstatic squeak pierced his ear. He pulled his phone away, but her voice rushed back like a child on a swing. "It's not some kind of historic sword, is it?"

Theo replied, "I suppose. It's in a museum. My history professor has a connection with them. It's a long story. He's helping with a text-book." Surely, she would be horrified by the actual knife. Would she even believe it possessed such unholy power? He added, "I'll bring you rubbings of the engravings. I can show you on Valentine's."

Hanna replied, "Well, it could take some time, depending on how long the engraving is. How about you come to Surgite on Saturday? It kind of ties in with the favor I'd like to ask."

Theo paused outside the subway stairs. He started around the block. "Go on."

"So there's a video project for my Japanese class. We're gonna divide into groups today and make a script and all that. The printout says we can assign nonspeaking roles to anyone—like extras in a movie. I was wondering if you'd be in my video? Hope-fully, we can shoot this Saturday."

"How many people will be there? What do I have to do?"

"Just ride your motorcycle," she said bashfully. Hanna quickly filled Theo's silence with qualifications, saying, "I mean, maybe not like fast or anything. We might film it starting up or something.

It'll probably just be Emma and myself; she can help me with the camera work. You can have fun with it."

Neither of his father's motorcycles belonged to Theo, but he was permitted to ride the smaller of the two since getting his license. His father would be grateful that he took care of the car's service appointment. Dealing with just Emma would be manageable.

Theo must have lingered too long in thought, because Hanna broke the silence with, "Not a big deal if you can't. I hope I'm not bothering you. I figured it would be an easy character for you to portray. I think my group will go with this idea."

"Sure. What time on Saturday?"

"Oh my God, really?" Her voice rose like daybreak. "I have no idea when we'll shoot. I'll let you know later today."

Enthusiasm crept into his imperative, "Let me know when you can."

"Will do!"

"I have to get to class."

"Oh, right. Me too."

"Bye."

"Bye, Theo."

He lowered his phone and descended the sordid subway stairs, humming a festive tune.

SEVEN

RAIN PATTERED on Emma's little pink umbrella in Hanna's hand. Emma let her borrow her spare on the promise she would not lose it. Emma had faith in her friends. Hanna marched alone through the muddy puddles of the campus walkways. She looked up at the brick and stucco forming the dignified walls of the building housing the political science and economics departments. Professors would often complain mid-lecture about "that other department here" and tout their superior approaches.

Hanna stowed Emma's umbrella and pulled open the great wooden doors. She entered what plausibly could have once been an estate. Chatting students loitered in the large entrance. She walked to the classroom determined not to forget her mission. The newly added tiny green journal in her backpack would fortify her memory. The investigation of its contents was sure to yield results. This had to become a habit—especially by the time she saw Theo. Getting him on camera would make an undeniable memory too. She just needed memories that were sure to stand out.

The boy in the back row lounged in the empty classroom. Hanna took her seat two desks over and thought, *I have to do something*.

She cleared her throat. "Hi. My name is Hanna. What's yours?" she said in a chipper tone.

"Steve. Nice to meet you," he replied automatically, disinterested and haughty.

Hanna set her backpack down and leaned it against her leg. She took out her notebook and asked, "What's your major?"

He confidently pushed his long blond hair out of his eyes. "Poli-sci, prelaw. My mom's a lawyer so I pretty much have an in."

"That's exciting. Surgite has a good law school," she remarked, opening her notebook.

"I'll probably go elsewhere. Can't be a big fish in a little pond."

More students filed into the classroom on that soggy Tuesday morning. Hanna captured Steve's name in her notebook, cognizant of his watchful eyes. He flipped through his textbook unamused by its contents.

"Do you have an interest in international law or East Asian studies?"

"I just have to take the LSAT."

Hanna rapidly recorded his answer in the margins of her blank page. She chose an orange pen, thinking it hardest to read from a distance.

"What brings you here?" he asked, twirling his pencil in his fingers.

"Oh, I'm a Japanese major. I figured some supporting coursework would be important if I can study abroad in Japan. Hopefully, I can take classes in Japanese while I'm there. Already knowing some of the material, or at least being familiar with it, would be a huge advantage in breaking through the language barrier."

He yawned, then asked her, "Can I borrow a piece of paper? I forgot my notebook."

Hanna returned to her notebook and peevishly tore out the last page.

"Thanks," the blank page compelled him to utter. Hanna recorded this latest exchange. Her eyes darted over to him reaching for the highlighter that had rolled off his desk. "He's one of those that just highlights textbooks—hadn't noticed before," Hanna rapidly scrawled. She bit her bottom lip at her stenographer's pace. *Time to test a different subject*, she thought.

"Have you seen the news about those mysterious disappearances? You know, the ones with the victims that all come back with amnesia?"

Steve straightened from his slouch. "You didn't see the most recent headline? Some girl went to a club in Manhattan and the next thing she knew, she was out on Long Island. She managed to wander into a gas station, otherwise she would have frozen to death."

"When did this happen? Was she okay?" Hanna asked, concerned.

"She was fine. Whoever it was must have realized she wasn't what he wanted. That's what you get for going out to clubs. Girls need to be more careful."

"It wasn't her fault. She was probably kidnapped or drugged," Hanna stated with rising indignity.

"Whatever," he said dismissively. "All she could remember was a silver car driving away when she came to."

Hanna nodded, transcribing the morsels of details. She titled the section "The Long Island Incident." Steve did not lack charisma, with his long hair, muscular frame, letterman jacket, and expensive jeans, but his cocksure demeanor was sickening like oil. Discreetly, she recorded these facts until the professor finally arrived. Six weeks Hanna had sat next to this Steve. Today she learned he had a name. They constituted the entire back row. The lecture started.

East Asian political theory was vast, but this professor kept these early weeks focused on World War II. In her notes, Hanna patiently recorded the facts, opinions, and anecdotes of this professor, who had lived in Shanghai, Fukuoka, and Taipei. His lectures turned more into personal reflections when he recalled his excursions to Manila and Nha Trang. She pitied his asides, which were neglected by the unamused students. He carried on unaware and assigned them a research paper. Some students began loudly storing their notebooks and standing up at the clock's strike of eleven fifteen. The time for his stories had run out.

Hanna stood up and knocked over her backpack. Realization brought her back to her paltry desk. She produced the tiny green journal and assiduously transposed the facts about Steve and the Long Island abduction from her notebook. In time, this tiny journal would reveal a lapse in her memory. Japanese was next. She stowed her journal and notebook, stood up, and slung her backpack over her shoulder. A feeling of reluctance had caused her to keep her puffy jacket on around Steve. She slipped out into the traffic of the hallway. As she put in her ear buds, she felt a hand on her shoulder. She gasped and turned around.

"It's me again," Steve announced.

"It's rude to sneak up on someone," Hanna snapped through frayed nerves.

He gave her a reassuring smile. "Are you a reporter for the school newspaper or something?" he asked, his tone nicer than before. "I saw you taking notes about me earlier."

She gasped again, covering her mouth. So much for calming her nerves. "I . . . uh . . . I didn't . . . I promise I'm not spying on you or anything."

His usual sneer returned. "No. It's not a problem. I know I have an effect on girls."

This was not at all what she had envisioned. "I'm trying to make new friends. I'm kind of forgetful, like really forgetful, actually, so I figured I'd introduce myself and make a new *friend* today."

Her added stress on "friend" would hopefully dissuade any further advances.

"That's cool," he remarked. "So I'll pick you up on Friday at six?"

"*What*!" Hanna exclaimed. "No. I'm seeing someone."

He took out his phone. "Interesting. What's your number? I'll text you mine. We should meet up some time to talk about the upcoming paper for class or something."

She replied, "On a not-date? In a non-dating way? As friends, right?"

He flicked his hair away from his eyes. "Sure."

Hanna surrendered her phone number, judging the request vetted enough. She could not remember the last time she had made a new friend. If he called it a date, she could just abandon the enterprise. Otherwise, it was still a good opportunity to make new memories for the journal. She chastised herself for not having planned this out better.

"I need to get to Japanese. See you Thursday."

"See you around," he acknowledged ambivalently.

Hanna headed outside. Japanese was her only class that was five days per week. It earned her an extra credit hour, but Surgite must have been the only university that made both first- and second-year Japanese five days a week. Knowing Sensei, she must have pressured the Modern Foreign Language Department for years to bolster Surgite's Japanese program. Studying abroad was Sensei's most suggested goal for students. Hanna had heard stories that she helped students get jobs with Japanese companies in New York. She demanded excellence in the face of student apathy. Most of them were just taking a language requirement. Sensei was building a legacy.

Hanna took the front row of Sensei's classroom. Many of the students knew each other from first-year Japanese. Hanna was the only freshman testing in. Eddie, by far the most proficient student, hosted a forum, which crowded around his desk. He shared news of updates about anime season renewals, new releases, and polls about favorite characters, all straight from Japan. Hanna often joined the conversation, unable to ignore the nearby crowd. Seeing the same students every day reminded her of how much had changed in only a year.

Sensei's arrival signaled the students' return to their seats. They enjoyed Sensei's discipline as if they were in high school. She merrily obliged playing this part and often merely pretended to scold them. Hanna's classmates described the relationship as tongue-in-cheek.

I bet Eddie would know how to translate that, Hanna thought, sitting back down after the greeting. Today's vocabulary test was not her concern. The students handed them up and Eddie, seated just in front of Sensei's podium, collected them. She took them, set them aside, and proceeded immediately to the next task.

"Please turn in your workbook sheets for pages twenty-seven and twenty-eight." A flurry of workbooks opened around her. Hanna's face burned in shame. She swallowed hard and stared at her textbook. She had completely forgotten. The green journal had consumed her. Left out, she limply passed along the stack of other students' workbook pages to Eddie, who gladly delivered them to Sensei. Eddie's own carefully completed pages graced the top of the pile. Hanna focused on Sensei's explanation. Maybe it would distract from the silent scornful judgment of her peers.

"Today you will divide into groups for the video project," said Sensei. "You will work together on writing a script and submit a first draft by this Friday."

A collective groan wafted from the students.

"Just a first draft," Sensei insisted. "The final draft will be due next Tuesday. You will have another full week to film and edit after that. Film anything you can imagine but still is reasonable to shoot and edit in very short time. All of you must speak on camera for at least thirty seconds. As I mentioned, you may use extras, as long as they do not speak. Please keep the total duration under two minutes. I enjoy reviewing your work, but want to make sure I can give the proper time to critique each one." She smartly tugged the lapels of her olive jacket. "Questions?"

Nearly every hand shot up. Some students just blurted out their questions, their imaginations running wild with possibilities. Hanna's optimistic hand had shot up too, but she quickly retracted it in the unfolding melee. Sensei restored order answering rapidly and graciously, then divided them into groups. Excitement ran through Hanna. Sensei always divided the groups by skill level. Each group had one high, one low, and one middle. Her algorithm was apparent to all. Hanna listened eagerly for her name as she called out the groups. At last, she announced, "Group three will be Jonzu-san, Torassu-san, and Popovu-san."

Disbelief shook Hanna as Eddie Jones stood up just two seats over in the front row. Quiet acceptance came next. Hanna was slipping. Katie Truss grabbed her notebook and traversed the classroom from the far corner where the film majors huddled for protection against Sensei's pelting questions like penguins in the Antarctic. Eddie helped Hanna rearrange their desks into a triangle.

"Popov-san, are you *genki*?" he asked earnestly, taking his seat. Hanna's voice struggled to stamp out her envy as she replied, "Yeah, doing great."

Katie, void of emotion, slid into her seat. An uncertain silence lingered between them.

Hanna put on a chipper voice and burst out, "My friend has a motorcycle. What if we base our video around it?"

Katie laughed. "What? That was out of nowhere."

Eddie asked, "Is it Japanese?"

"Yes, in fact, it is. It's a blue sport bike, if I remember correctly. I talked to my friend, and he said he's okay to ride it here this Saturday. I thought it would be really cool and unique. We could come up with some kind of script around the bike. Like maybe there's a mysterious vigilante biker that nobody can catch, we're all discussing it, and he shows up."

Katie's face twisted asymmetrically. "That's great and all, but just some guy on a motorcycle seems boring."

"Uncatchable mysterious vigilante biker has been done," Eddie mused aloud. "It's cliché. I've read it before."

Hanna wilted under their criticism. Eddie quickly added, "It's not a wholly bad idea, but we don't have to go with the first idea we think of."

Hanna did not offer that she had been formulating the idea all day. Memories of its multiple revisions in her imagination now conjured morose self-judgment.

"I'm sorry. I know I jumped right out with this. If you guys think you can work with it, great. Maybe the vigilante thing is dumb. It would mean a lot to me if the bike could stay, though."

Katie leaned forward. "It's an interesting idea, for sure, but I don't know. It's kind of limiting, don't you think? What if we did something like a retro noir film? Or really make use of the camera and shoot a horror scene? Think of the lighting effects we could try. I have so much I never get to use for fun projects like this."

Hanna forced a compliant smile. "Sure. Retro noir, horror movie, whatever you want to shoot." Then she added, "But on a motorcycle?"

Derisive laughter came from both of them. Katie snickered. "You really don't give up?"

Hanna unzipped her jacket to vent the suffocating heat. The wood grain of her desk seemed an easier conversation partner. It beat meeting the vicious eyes now trained on their injured prey.

"You really want this friend and his motorcycle in this video, don't you?" Katie asked with unbridled curiosity.

Solemnly, Hanna said, "It's a rare . . . opportunity. It would mean a lot to me and would make for a memorable video."

Eddie nodded in silent sympathy.

Katie asked, "What do we get?"

"A great video. He also goes to Lincoln," Hanna said, her voice cracking.

Katie perked up at the mention of his school.

Seizing Katie's interest and Eddie's passive silence, she added, "I'm sure he has a connection in the film school there. He's pretty social." How much further down this hole until Hanna hit bedrock?

"What's his major?"

"Film," she answered, instantly regretting the lie.

"Okay, sure. I think we can work with this."

At least this was guaranteed to be a memorable event with witnesses. There was no way she could forget this, or if she did, too many people could corroborate their stories. Hanna rationalized to herself that freshmen change majors frequently, so the lie about Theo's major was more like a liberal stretching of the truth.

Katie continued, "Okay, we can make this work, but what about Eddie?"

"I'm okay with the bike, even if it is a little funny as the monster in our horror film," he piped up. "A sport bike would look pretty out of place in a retro noir film. I wonder how to say 'time travel' in Japanese? That might look cool, actually. I'd like to handle compiling the script, if there are no objections."

Hanna looked earnestly at her two classmates. "Then I think we're in agreement?"

"Sure," Katie concurred. "Just make sure the talent is on time."

Eddie dramatically flipped open his notebook. Drawing his mechanical pencil, he clicked it twice, declaring, "I will write the first draft. Ladies, lend me your strength. Give me your ideas."

Katie groaned. "Oh God, we set him off."

Hanna leaned back, exhaling. The remaining minutes of class evaporated with the rain droplets on her backpack. Her thoughts returned to her memory loss. Theo could not escape her catalogue of details. Pinning down her memories would surely reveal a gap. Eddie and Katie bantered about potential dialogue. Hanna wrote, "Film shoot," in the margin of her notebook. What if the amnesia victims could get together and discuss what happened? Maybe sharing their stories would yield a clue.

Unaware of the time, Hanna looked up and class was ending. The students returned their desks and gave an energetic salutation for Sensei. Eddie and Katie immediately returned to Hanna to exchange contact information.

As Katie departed, Hanna decided to ask for another detail to fill out her journal. "Hey, Eddie, why do you care so much about Japanese?"

He collected his pencils into his messenger bag and explained, "Oh, you know, I guess I can't help it. I've always wanted to go to Japan. I'd love to see a real manga studio and talk to the artists, the writers, the interns—heck, anyone that would talk to me!"

"I'm sure you could swing that during a study abroad," Hanna replied.

"I just love the art style and . . . just . . . man, it would be so cool," Eddie said, his nerdy voice taking on yet more enthusiasm. "I think it'd help my own manga too."

"Your own?"

"Oh, well, it's nothing really," he said, poorly feigning bashfulness, "but I'm working on something. It's just a few sketches, some illustrations, some story concepts, and stuff like that. It's about a runaway slave in the Antebellum South who gets sent to modern day by time travel into some big city, maybe LA. He has to find his way back but also decide if he even wants to go back. I'd draw it like a manga, and he'd run into a beautiful Japanese woman who tells him about how the whole world changed and people fly in airplanes now and can talk on handheld phones with people on the other side of the planet just like that, but at the same time some things didn't change."

"Wow. Where'd you get all that?"

"I dunno. Do you wanna see some of my sketches?"

"That's great, Eddie, but—" she deflected noticing the time, but he readily produced notebook pages of hand-drawn characters anyway. The most heroic one, obviously resembling himself, stood out, and she asked, "He's not based on you, is he?"

"No, I think Jimu-san is totally different than me. He has dreads. I don't."

Her eyes continued to a buxom parasol-wielding Japanese woman in a crassly cut-down kimono. Hanna gave a disapproving look.

"Ah, *shimatta*," he acknowledged.

"Anyway, I hope you get to go to Japan and draw your manga, Eddie. You do your best."

He grinned and asked, "Are you going? I'm going to study abroad next year in Niigata. You have to apply for it, like, now if you want to go. Surgite also has a study abroad in Tokyo."

"I mean, I want to, but it's expensive, isn't it? I'd go if I could get some scholarship, probably just for a semester. Are you going the full year?"

Eddie answered, "Yeah, and there are plenty of *baito* opportunities there. I'm sure you could get an *eikaiwa* gig to help pay for it. That's what I plan on doing, but a miraculous baito at a manga studio would be awesome too."

Hanna paused, lost in thought. Explaining her grades to her parents would already be a struggle. Asking them for yet more money to study abroad while her sister was applying for colleges would be impossible.

"Think about it," Eddie said. "Who knows what adventures are out there? College is short. Think about where you want to be next year. It'll be here before you know it."

She meekly agreed and followed him into the hallway before asking, "Did you see a pink umbrella in the classroom?"

Eddie cackled. "It's in your backpack! How'd you miss that?"

Hanna slid her pack around to see Emma's umbrella still tucked in the outside pocket. She reciprocated with feigned laughter. "Oh, yeah. How could I forget?"

Anxiety surged and left her weak. Disappearing was her only desire. Having passed her slowing footsteps in the busy hallway, Eddie shouted, "Coming to lunch? The anime club is meeting up."

Hanna drifted to a stop. "Not this time. Maybe tomorrow."

Eddie waved goodbye. "Well, okay. *Jya, mata ne*," he said merging into the sea of traffic.

An open bench under the hallway's bulletin board saw Hanna dig her tiny green journal out of her backpack. She scratched in her newfound observations. Japanese history class at two thirty had yet to be recorded. The plethora of details begged the question of which ones were important enough to remember. Faltering under the weight, she sketched a tiny sweater unraveling, its thread spiraling down the page. The details of the video shoot were surely important. She started there. As she transposed the notes, she solemnly remembered why she had started this journal.

Familiar, expressionless faces passed unnoticing, uncaring. Hurrying to classrooms through the worn hallways, did they truly know where they were going? How many felt discarded like details deemed unworthy to remember? How many were near tears? What were the chances if she shouted happy birthday, one would turn and say thank you? Maybe Sensei could see this and chose to persevere with a well-disciplined lesson. Empathy was impossible without experience, but how could you live someone else's life? Hanna hung her head and finished the entry in the now-deserted hallway. As her purple ink neared the end of the page, she penned the final question: "Where do you want to be next year?" Her pen hovered above the page in the silence.

"Happy and safe," she wrote.

EIGHT

THEO APPROACHED the student center Hanna was describing and ended their call. Silence blanketed the empty tables inside. Various offices along the room's edges sat dormant, their lights and services off for the weekend. Theo spotted her seated at a table alone. She hummed a tune with crossed legs, her boot bobbing along. A tiny green book lay open on the table. Her pen moved purposefully. Hearing his approach, she looked up cheerfully and an excited shiver ran through him.

"Hi!"

"Hey."

She embraced him tightly. Her warm touch was bliss after the long ride. Theo reciprocated with his free arm, his other holding his helmet. Feeling her sage sweater again reminded him of the apartment.

"Thank you so much for coming today," she said. "You look great! You wear all of that gear well. I have so much I want to talk to you about. I started keeping a journal to spot any gaps in my memory. I want to show you, but I guess we don't have a lot of time today."

Theo caressed her warm cheek with his thumb. "Bring the journal tomorrow. We'll go over it together when we have time."

She nodded, trusting and doubtless.

Hope colored her face, and she quickly took her seat, gesturing him to sit beside her. "So let's start right away on the translation. We're supposed to head over at ten to film. That gives us just over an hour," she affirmed, closing her green book.

Theo set his helmet on the table and produced the folded papers bearing the four rubbings of the knife and its sheath. He handed them to her eager hands and sat down rigidly in his armored jacket. Opening it was too risky around her, considering the real knife and sheath were concealed inside, affixed by makeshift straps he had sewn in. It blended in well at his side, and to Hanna's undiscerning touch, it felt like a rigid part of a hard and complicated heated touring jacket.

"It's getting to me," she began, "this whole amnesia thing. I find myself worrying about it a lot, like it's a chronic condition." She met Theo's concerned look with her own. "I should pull myself together, shouldn't I? I shouldn't be dumping all of this on you."

Theo blinked, focusing on his helmet between them. Guilt strangled him, leaving him unable to produce a word.

Hanna turned her attention to the inscriptions, admitting, "I can't read these."

"What's wrong?"

"The characters are tiny," she answered, reaching for her round spectacles.

"I didn't know you needed glasses," said Theo.

She turned to him with adorably magnified eyes. "Too much time in the library, I guess. My parents got them for me. I think they're kind of dorky."

"They look nice," Theo remarked.

"You really mean it?"

"I wouldn't say so if I didn't."

"Aw, thanks," she said in a rosy blush. "You're in a good mood today. It must be the weather. That first warm day in winter usually draws people out and gives everyone a good mood. Today might not be that day, but I just know it'll come. It's usually late February anyway."

"The characters, Hanna. What do they mean?"

Hanna returned to her task. Theo patiently watched her examine his work from earlier that morning. The knife felt oppressive in his jacket.

"Did you take these in crayon?" she asked.

Confused, he replied, "They're legible, aren't they?"

"Theo, this is intricate. It's someone talking, but, like, in an odd way . . . like a poem. I think I can do it. One of these words is even written in calligraphy. I might have to ask Sensei about that. It'll take more time than I thought."

"How can I help?" he asked eagerly.

A perplexed Hanna met his eager attentiveness. "Well, um, actually, you can help with the dictionary part. Here, let me get my laptop."

Down she reached for her laptop from her backpack. "I figured I would need this," she said, placing it before them adorned with many colorful stickers. She prescribed such cheer to everything she touched.

"You'll help me make a list of the vocabulary. Let me see . . ." her voice trailed off as she opened a digital Japanese-English dictionary. She consulted the engraving and careful reproduced a drawing of the character on the screen with her mousepad. Murmurs about a stroke order contorted her formerly eager face and she redrew the character until the desired one appeared.

She wrote the character on the inscription page and slid it to Theo.

"Could you copy down the definition and how to read the kanji from the screen? While you do that, I'll find the next kanji I don't know and work on how the sentence fits together."

Theo nodded. She followed up with, "What color is your bike again? Blue, isn't it?"

"Yes."

"Then you get the blue pen."

Gradually, they untangled the engravings, one on each side of the sheath and one on each side of the knife. The single word of calligraphy, located on the pommel, remained undeciphered. Theo recorded the dictionary entries, forming a glossary between them. Her translation attempts filled the papers. Theo had taken four blank sheets from his father's printer. The rubbings occupied a small space in the center of each. English followed the first line, saying, *"I am falsehood. Bestowed in me is power,"* joined by Hanna's attempts at the remaining words.

When she paused to rest, his voice reached out, "How do you say amnesia in Japanese?"

"I don't know. Come to think of it, that is a word I ought to know," she answered, perplexed.

"Does this dictionary work both ways?" Theo asked, pointing at the screen.

"Sure, it does," she answered and leaned in front of him to type. A sweet aroma rose from her soft hair, close enough to kiss. Unsure, Theo remained out of her way.

She returned to her seat and met him with a grin. *"Kioku soushitsu,"* she said in her practiced accent.

"How would you say, for example, Hanna's amnesia?"

"Hana no kioku soushitsu, but you might want to put something on the end of '*Hana,*' like '*chan.*' *Hana* is a homonym for flower or nose in Japanese. The kanji are different, and Sensei tells me the pronunciation of *Hana* as a name is different, but I can't really tell. If you just said, '*Hana no kioku soushitsu,*' though, the context would make it pretty clear you're talking about a person."

"Can you write that down for me? The best way to say Hanna's amnesia?"

She merrily obliged but asked, "What is this for? It's kind of relevant to me, don't you think?"

Ignoring her question, Theo asked, "How would you say a

person, for example, if you were telling someone to think about someone, or remember them? Can you just use their name?"

"That's a good question," she mused. "I suppose you'd want to add '*no koto*' after their name to make it clearer. I keep hearing Sensei do it. If I were talking about you to someone else, I could say, '*Shio no koto ga suki da.*'"

"What does that mean?"

She giggled. "It means I like you."

He resisted cracking a smile. "So if I said, '*Shio no koto,*' that would be clearer?"

Her pupils widened to marbles. "Yes. *Shio* is the closest approximation of Theo in Japanese since they lack the *th* sound found in English. *Shio* is also a homonym for salt. So if the listener didn't know the context, I could be saying, 'I like salt' if I just said, '*shio ga suki da.*'"

"Have you ever forgotten about salt?"

Confusion bent one of her eyebrows. "I mean, I know I'm forgetful, but that's such an odd question, isn't it?"

"Let's move on," he replied hastily. "Can you write the 'Shio no koto' phrase too?"

Again, she merrily obliged, but sighed.

"I miss this."

"What?"

"Working together like this. It reminds me of King's."

"We weren't even dating back then."

"Don't you know what a crush is?"

The buzz of her cell phone stole her away. After an enthusiastic greeting, she politely moved her conversation to the windows. He watched her go, catching the pleasant movement of the floral embroidery on her jeans. Alone at her laptop, he drew a USB memory stick from one of his pockets and monitored her. Hanna was giving instructions about the video shoot. Theo inserted the memory stick into her laptop. He calmly copied the picture of her in the café onto her computer. Disgust at her indifference or incompetence to organize her files briefly interrupted his task. Removing the memory stick, he pocketed it unnoticed.

"No, just come pick me up and we'll all drive over together. Theo's with me. He has to ride the bike over. He can follow you there," he heard Hanna saying as she came closer. She ended the conversation and hurried back over to find Theo studying her translations.

"Sorry I lost track of the time. Broc is driving his minivan over here to pick me up. He's going to take Emma, Eddie, Katie, and me to film in the park."

Agitation surged in him. "You said it would just be Emma."

She sat beside him. "I'm sorry, Theo," she said, assuming a consoling tone. "I didn't mean to bother you like this. It's true I said just Emma, but as we got closer, we actually finished the script and decided we'd shoot the whole thing at once. Eddie and Katie are in my Japanese class. They're nice."

Theo shook his head and asked, "I'm supposed to follow this Broc?"

"You don't remember Broc? Remember the Halloween party last year?"

"There were a lot of people there."

"He's friends with Emma. Anyway, it's not far."

"Fine," Theo stated flatly and folded the translations.

"Wait," Hanna interrupted, her hand grabbing his. "Can I work on them more? I know I can do a better job with a little more time."

The warmth and softness of her unforgettable touch blocked his attempt at risk analysis like alcohol to synapses in the brain.

"Can I keep them until tomorrow?" she implored.

Self-loathing strangled his voice. *Stick to the plan, Theo*, he reminded himself, but instead a meek, "Okay," escaped him.

Hanna hopped up, excited at her chance. Theo pulled his helmet toward him in defeat while Hanna energetically gathered her possessions. Theo's helmet and gloves were back on as Hanna put on her puffy jacket and backpack.

"No earmuffs?" he asked through his helmet.

She frowned. "I forgot them."

Hanna led him outside to the access road that traipsed through campus. A silver minivan waited patiently. The driver rolled down the window and waved. Hanna greeted him as "Broc" and instructed Theo to follow him to the park. Theo nodded and headed back to the parking lot.

Theo fired up the bike again. Broc's minivan gently turned around and waited for him up ahead. Theo gave the bike a dash of speed to approach. Through the back window, he saw their animated discussion. The minivan pulled away as the passengers inside bantered and pointed at him. Had they never seen a motorcycle? This was just his father's two-hundred-fifty-cubic-centimeter-engine bike, or two fifty. Theo wondered if they would respond differently if he took his father's Italian bike, housing four times as much engine displacement. Hanna's friends were acceptable at this distance. Theo followed the minivan with the dented rear bumper. Sunny roads auspiciously carried them to the fields of a nearby park.

Theo parked beside the minivan and immediately regretted it. The party poured out like hounds and quickly encircled him. Unsure of what to do, he shut off the engine and remained seated. Their voices shot out. Their judgmental faces danced about him in and out of his view. Theo kept his helmet on and face shield down. Hanna emerged last from the depths of the minivan, and she disbanded the circle and said, "I'm so sorry about that. I guess they got a little carried away."

Theo silently nodded. Hanna's flustered face turned rapidly to introduce everyone.

"That's Eddie and Katie helping Broc unload the camera equipment. They're in my Japanese class. Katie is a film major and might talk to you about it. Broc is friends with Emma, and we met him last September. He's a business major and on the soccer team with Emma's brothers."

Emma stood by the minivan, already madly typing on her smartphone. Hanna continued, "You wait here. I'll come over when we're ready. We'll shoot your parts first."

He closed his face shield. Hanna helped the party arrange their equipment in the empty field. A man walked his dog in the distance. February was an odd time to film a motorcycle. Theo sighed, set the bike on its kickstand, and removed his gloves and helmet. Alone, he reflected on how to erase Hanna's worries. He would get the translations back tomorrow—better to wait. Cool zephyrs swayed the grasses and his hair equally. His helmet sat on the gas tank. Hanna's chipper instructions moved her group to swift action. The paper in their hands flapped in the wind as they enthusiastically read their scenes aloud. Cheery commentary and crass humor often interrupted them. They joked. They laughed. Their conviviality was embarrassing. They did not appear as educated adults at all. Theo clutched his helmet tighter on his blue motorcycle.

"Hey, spaceman," he heard beside him. Emma stood there, her pink trench coat lazily undulating in the breeze. Her hands, buried in her jacket pockets, held it somewhat closed against her bleached jeans and snug sweater. Theo gave no reply.

"It's fun watching Director Popov on her debut film, huh? This has nomination potential for best supporting actor." She laughed at her own attempt at humor. Theo despised that.

He observed her shifting her weight from one foot to the other, checking his cold face for signs of life.

"Cozy in that getup? It's got a real 'climb Mount Everest' vibe to it."

Theo wondered what was the point of this unnecessary small talk.

"Hanna was right," she said. "You don't talk much."

"What do you want?"

"Excuse me?"

"You're talking to me because you want something."

"I don't remember you being like this back in October."

"I don't remember you giving a damn about me back in October."

She turned around and swore through an airy laugh. At least she would leave him alone.

Theo pursed his lips when she returned, barking, "You think you can just talk to people like that?"

Theo met her incredulous stare with an appraising look. He did remember her. Hanna talked about her frequently but never mentioned her bushy eyebrows. Her bombastic voice etched itself into people's memories. He recalled her vapid attempts at humor on Halloween too.

"Hello? You there?" she asked.

"You want something. Why not just start with that?"

Her eyebrows angled into a cross glare and her agitation boiled over into a low, "*Grrrr.*"

Theo resumed his reticent gazing of the fields.

"You ever talk to real people? Like, not through a computer screen?"

He reflected on the intentionality of her implication. Theo heard her swear in frustration and he strained to qualify, "Fine. I'm not trying to be hurtful. Let's just communicate."

"Okay then," she said. "Hanna's been dating you for, what, seven-ish months? She's my best friend so I wanted to . . . ya know . . . say hi and get to know you a little."

"You want to judge me."

"No, and do you have to be so literal all the time?" Palpable silence prompted her to continue, "I'm noticing a trend here. Look, be nice to Hanna. She's adorable and maybe even a little naive. She says you're a good guy somewhere deep down. She sees something in you."

"You can only tell a person's character by their actions."

"Well, right now they're telling me you're an asshole."

"Yes, I've heard that."

"You don't care?"

"Not really. People's perceptions aren't necessarily truth. The truth is out there regardless of anyone's perception of it. We just have to open ourselves to the possibility that the truth exists outside of ourselves and can be known. It's that truth I seek. The pretenses of socializing just get in the way."

"So you're on some kinda quest for it? Maybe that's why you're a philosopher."

Silence again. Theo wondered how much more of this he could endure. Hanna looked so happy in the distance with her team.

"Well, chief? Hanna told me you're pretty passionate about that kind of stuff. Ya know, truth, the meaning of life, and all that. Not gonna share a little on your views, Mr. Elusive?"

"You don't care."

"Yes, I do. Everyone does," she retorted. Theo stared ahead. Emma stood adamantly next to him. She softly swore again but did not move. "What if you look and don't find anything?"

"Then I can either accept the absurdity of life without meaning or develop faith in a transcendent power."

She mumbled about his grave tone and added, "So what, Hanna cares about that stuff too?"

Theo answered, "Yes, actually."

Hanna faced them and called for Emma. "Coming, Lord Hanna," she shouted back, running to the group. Theo got off the bike with a heavy sigh, set his helmet on the ground, and waited for Hanna's instructions. They finally arrived after there had been enough time for him to inspect his motorcycle twice over, consider possible optional parts, and take time to simply admire it.

Hanna ran over to him, apologizing and explaining his role.

"So just get on the bike, pick it up off the stand, and turn it on?" he confirmed.

"Have some fun with it," she added between labored breaths.

Filming was tedious work. Emma kept demanding Theo reset and wait for her and the camera. Theo kept demanding Emma have the camera ready because he was not going to start the engine that many times. Hanna nervously relayed their terse messages to each other. Broc sat quietly with Emma's laptop in his minivan's open trunk. After several arduous takes, they reviewed together on the laptop. Theo stood behind them, gathered at the back of the minivan, crowding to see the footage. The bike looked good on camera too. After a handful of reshoots, they were done. Theo returned to his bike and patiently watched Hanna trot off to film her dialogue with Eddie and Katie. Emma exuberantly ran away from Theo to operate the camera for them. Broc resumed his role as laptop bearer, heading out with less alacrity. He eventually retreated to his minivan.

Broc emerged and curiously approached Theo.

"Hey, um . . . in case you didn't know, Emma posted a picture of you on Friend Link."

Theo looked over at Broc's eager but timid face. Broc held out his smartphone, showing her post. Hanna stood next to him sitting on the bike. Her blurry hands gesticulated wildly as she explained something to Theo with apparent care. Theo's helmet blocked much of his response, save for the rapt attention in his eyes. Broc's scratched minivan constituted the background.

Broc added, "I heard you don't use Friend Link, so I wanted to let you know."

"She tagged me as Mr. Elusive?"

"I guess because she doesn't know your full name."

Theo returned to leaning on the bike's seat.

"I'll be over here if you need me. Cool bike, by the way," Broc said, returning to his minivan. The party wrapped up shooting shortly after. They raucously reviewed the footage on Emma's laptop. Theo knew he was surely not invited. The minivan's door slid open and Hanna popped out.

"Hey, we're all done with filming. We're heading back to campus."

He acknowledged her, put back on his gear, and climbed onto the saddle. Hanna joined him. His heart jolted feeling her sudden embrace against his back. Wrapping her arms around him, she exuberantly said, "Let's go back to campus."

"No. You don't have a helmet and you'll freeze," he shouted through his helmet.

Trembling, she stiffened behind him. "It's not that cold, is it? I'll be fine. Just ride carefully."

Theo turned on the bike, clicked the gear into neutral, and fired up the engine. He looked back at his passenger and shouted, "You're brave to stay."

She grinned.

"Put your feet there," he ordered. The toes of her boots groped for a foothold but failed. Theo reached down and grabbed her ankles to place her feet on the foot pegs. She complied, still trembling. Theo backed the bike out and faced the long, straight, empty parking lot. Emma raised her phone for a picture. A mention of Friend Link briefly passed Theo's ears. He ignored it despite Hanna commenting on something.

"Hold on," he shouted back to her. Theo clicked the bike into first gear and leaned forward. Hanna's embrace followed him and tightened with anticipation. He let out the clutch lever and twisted the throttle as far as it would go.

Hanna screamed like a wooden train whistle. The engine reached the top of first gear, and he clicked into second for more speed. Running out of parking lot, he engaged both brakes and descended from such brazen foolery. Hanna was shouting as he turned around back toward Broc's minivan. All four of them were now outside watching them. Theo clicked the bike back down into first gear and repeated the rapid acceleration. This time, he pushed it to the top of second gear over her elated screams, before braking. They overshot

Broc's minivan by several car lengths, reckless adrenaline pushing him. He braced himself against the handlebars, fighting the weight of his passenger. She unintentionally, and quite uncomfortably, pressed him against the machine under the hard deceleration. Far more calibration was required to accommodate the unfamiliar weight of a passenger. Safely stopped, he clicked the bike into neutral and called over his shoulder, "Too cold and windy, right?"

"Oh my God! This is amazing! Yeah, the wind is crazy!"

"The helmet helps. I wear earplugs on the highway."

He leaned back against her tense body. Her grip remained vicelike.

"What do you think?"

She gasped. "It's like a roller coaster! You have to take me for a ride sometime." He brought her to Broc's minivan, this time stopping well within his estimate. Emma quipped loudly, "Well, that explains it," as Hanna got off the motorcycle. Broc returned to his minivan, grinning. Katie and Eddie laughed nervously, seemingly unsure of what they had just witnessed.

Hanna laughed in unrestrained joy, watching him on the motorcycle. Broc told Theo to follow him back to campus as Katie and Eddie took their seats. Emma stuffed an elated Hanna into the minivan and closed the sliding door. Theo closed his face shield and followed Broc back to campus. This time, he watched Hanna's silhouette ebulliently retell the experience. Theo chose a parking spot a comfortable distance away from the minivan and shut off his machine. He popped off his helmet as the minivan deposited its garrulous passengers.

Eddie came over first. Inspecting the front forks, he asked, "Was it made in Japan? Does the VIN start with a J?"

"I don't know," replied Theo.

Eddie knelt beside the front tire saying, "Do you know where the VIN is? Sometimes it's in the front."

His head twitched like that of a cat locating a sound. Theo

joined Eddie in the search. Broc's voice came next as he said, "How do you get a motorcycle license? Does it take long?"

"You go to the DMV," Theo answered. He continued the search with Eddie disappointed he did not know the location.

Hanna's melodic voice answered Broc, "Theo got his license last September just after he turned eighteen. Once you're eighteen, you can take the written exam and then just take the riding test at the DMV."

"You thinking about riding?" Broc asked eagerly.

"Oh, no, not me, but Theo told me all about it."

She remembered, he thought, feeling a warmth in his heart. Hanna suddenly jerked and gasped. Theo looked up, concerned. "What's wrong?"

"Goddammit," she answered, peering at a student approaching her. His relaxed stride resembled more of a strut. He wore an incessant leer and his hands remained in his pockets. He vacillated between eying the motorcycle and gawking at Emma. Except for the high school jacket, he could easily blend in at the nightclubs in the city.

"Who's that?" Theo asked.

"Steve."

NINE

HOW? was the sole thought turning in Hanna's mind. Steve sauntered closer on the salty pathways, encroaching on her world, his stare shifting between the group by the minivan and the group by Theo's motorcycle. Hanna rushed forward to greet him, intercepting his path to Theo.

"What brings you here?" she asked.

"Saw the bike pic of you on Friend Link. I figured you'd be here when you came back."

"What picture?"

"The one Emma just posted. You didn't see the video too?"

"Wait. You know Emma?"

"Yeah, we're friends on FL."

Anger burned in her veins. Emma had not mentioned this despite Hanna mentioning Steve to her. Another confrontation seemed inevitable. Emma should have asked before she posted. Who knows who else had seen it? And the video too? Hanna remembered her sister was on Friend Link.

"I'm guessing that must be him there," he surmised.

"We're dating," she spat.

"Really? Looks like you have competition."

Hanna spun around to see Katie deep in conversation with

Theo, who kept stealing looks at Steve. Hanna froze. The whole film shoot had suddenly become a terrible idea.

Steve sneered. "I wonder if what they say about film girls is true?"

Hanna took this as her cue to change the subject. "Where did you meet Emma? How long have you been friends?"

Unphased, he ignored her questions, instead surveying the gathering before him. Sordid, base, shameless—he eyed Hanna like a dog.

"You're cute when you're angry," he quipped.

Hanna's eyes narrowed and her mouth opened in disbelief.

He pressed on, "Come on, you're not actually going out with racer boy?"

His hand reached for her shoulder. She ducked away, disgusted, her clenched fists burning for a target. That lecherous hand of his retreated, unphased, and he continued approaching the motorcycle. Hanna looked back at a vigilant Theo watching the scene unfold.

"Hey, you must be the biker," Steve said loudly to Theo and the males around the bike. "I saw the video on FL."

His cocky head jutted toward Emma, and he added, "Emma there does good camera work."

Emma, hearing her own name, looked up from her smartphone.

"Oh, hi, Steve," she called with a wave. His chin rose briefly as a salutation.

Hanna darted over to Emma, by the minivan. She turned casually and said, "Wow, you gotta see how many comments this already has."

With vitriol, Hanna whispered, "When the hell did you meet *Steve*!"

"I don't know, maybe at a party this semester?" Emma answered ambivalently. "Or was it last semester? We're not even like *friends* friends. I met him once and he added me on FL. After like five or six hundred, it stops counting."

Hanna hoarsely whispered, "There are only like two thousand

students at this school! That's including the law school and seminary!"

Emma raised her hand. "Slow down, Captain Killjoy. What are you on about?"

Hanna said, her chest pounding, "How much of Surgite saw me on the bike? My sister is on FL! She's going to see me on a motorcycle without a helmet!"

"Relax. No one will care by tomorrow," Emma said. She turned her cracked smartphone to Hanna, who saw herself screaming ecstatically on the back of Theo's blurry motorcycle.

"By the way, you're at over a hundred comments on the riding video alone. The still shot has over one hundred fifty."

Hanna wailed unintelligibly and demanded, "Don't just post pictures of me or Theo without asking!"

Emma recoiled in disbelief. "Really? Coming from you? It's not like you asked me before you told Broc I play video games."

The blow brought her to a bewildered silence. Emma snapped, "Or did you forget that too? Broc told me all about how you mentioned it in the library."

"No, I remember. Why is that such a big deal?" Hanna asked, sincerely trying to bury her offended aggression.

"What if I wanted to keep it on the down low? Now every guy on campus is gonna feel entitled to me playing with them. What if I just want to enjoy the game, huh? Why do you think I never play online with a mic?"

"I . . . had no idea."

"Well, now you do. You're so naive sometimes," Emma snapped before turning to a friendly shout behind her. She yelled back, "Look at you, scoreless try-hards!"

She turned back to Hanna, "So apparently, my brothers saw the post too."

The twins were walking toward them. What Emma had in curvature they had in muscle mass. Their broad shoulders gave prominent shape to their soccer jerseys, each bearing their surname, Camagüey. Their biceps appeared sculpted from marble. Their legs looked capable of lifting Theo's motorcycle—maybe Broc's minivan—momentarily. The whole family was blessed with exceptionally charismatic teeth, which flashed frequently in their banter.

Emma joked to their cordial faces, "All dressed up for the ball?"

The shorter of the two came forward. "At least we get invited to one. Where's Broc? Practice is gonna start soon."

Emma folded her arms. "Gawking at Theo's crotch rocket."

Their heads turned in unison as they spotted Broc in the throng around Theo. Victor Hugo, the older of the two, said, "I was always thinking about getting a bike."

Luis, the younger, shot back, "It takes real guts to throw your leg over one of those."

Theo turned away from Steve and jammed on his helmet.

"I think ya boy's making a break for it," Emma chided Hanna, who rushed to Theo's side.

"Theo, wait!" she exclaimed before he fastened the chinstrap. Eddie and Katie retreated to a safe distance, while Emma's brothers plucked a distracted Broc back to his team duties.

Steve laid a hand on the motorcycle's handlebar. "What? It's just a two fifty. All I said was I've ridden my dad's cruiser, which has a way bigger engine. No need to get all worked up over your scooter."

Theo fixated on Steve's hand.

"Go ahead. Fire it up. That stock pipe will sound like a sewing machine," Steve taunted.

Ire overflowed into Theo's fists, which gripped his gloves. Sensing danger, Hanna turned to Steve. "I think Theo has to go and you probably do too."

Steve kept an aloof look. "Whatever. My convertible would smoke this girl's bike anyway."

"Where is it parked?" Theo asked, calling his bluff.

Hanna's head snapped to Theo.

"In the commuter lot on the other side of campus. I'm heading there now," he answered, walking past him, their shoulders an inch from contact.

Theo thrust his key into the motorcycle, watching Steve depart without so much as a wave to Emma. Alone by the bike, Hanna hastily approached Theo.

"I'm so sorry about that. Steve's not a friend. He's just in one of my classes. I met him just this week. I guess he saw the post on FL."

"It's not like Friend Link is for friends."

She waved her arms out in exasperation. Theo fired up the engine, saying, "It's too crowded here with 'your people,'" irritably gesturing at the crowd by the minivan.

Pointing at Katie, he added, "That girl thought I was a film major. Why?"

The group congregated by Emma, loudly discussing the abductions. Her brothers boasted what they would do to the assailant.

Hanna took in Theo's anxious look. "I kind of fibbed about your major to convince Katie you should be in the video." With increasing remorse, she added, "I may have also said you had connections at Lincoln's film school."

Theo threw his leg over the motorcycle and stood above the seat.

"You didn't have to lie."

"I had to get you in the video."

"Why?"

"So today would be memorable and I wouldn't forget. That's why I decided to meet Steve earlier this week. That's why I started my little green journal. I can't ignore my amnesia. I have to do something about it. Hopefully, if everything stands out and I write it all down, it'll be super easy to spot a gap."

Theo tried to reply but trailed off, choked by dejection.

Hanna continued, "I worry about it constantly. What if I get abducted and come back with amnesia? This little green journal would be the only testimony." Her expression soured. "Testimony of how much of a screwup I am. Why was I so naive to talk to Steve in the first place?"

"When was the last time you spoke to him?"

"Thursday in class."

"Morning?"

"Yeah. Why? I won't talk to him anymore."

"You wouldn't mind him forgetting about you?"

"No, not at all. I'm sure he will. I told him we're dating." Hanna's eyes grew wide.

"You're not going to race him, are you?"

Theo shook his head and gently gestured Hanna to step back from the motorcycle. Instead, she embraced him, clinging for support. His gray motorcycle jacket had a coarse outer shell and many hard contents sequestered in its many pockets. She felt the armor on his back and slid her hands up to his shoulders, now granted heroic proportion. His armored pants and boots completed a look of intense preparation.

"It's exhausting," she began. "I'm scared, Theo. I'm scared I'm going to forget."

He offered no reply.

"I have so much to write in my journal today. Good things— things we did together. Remind me to bring the journal tomorrow. I have to show you," she told him.

Inside the helmet, over the noise of the idling engine, amid her friends nearby, she spotted his grave expression. Then, with a sudden shiver, he nodded and agreed.

"Ride safely," Hanna offered and placed a peck on his helmet's chin bar.

"Get a room!" she heard Emma shout as her brothers joined in with whistling. He patted the top of her head, sat on the bike, lifted it off its kickstand, and took off. The bike's front tire lifted off the ground briefly as he irresponsibly shot past them, out of their view.

Hanna stuffed her tense, cold hands into her jacket pockets and sighed. Katie's approaching voice turned Hanna back toward the minivan, where Eddie also stood.

"A philosophy major, huh?" Katie said sarcastically.

Crippled silence was all Hanna could offer.

"Whatever. Just don't forget your part of the write-up."

Katie inspected Hanna for some trace of guilt. With disdain, she turned, saying to Eddie, "Come on. Let's go."

Eddie compliantly followed but called back, "The bike was cool. See you Monday."

Defeated, Hanna answered, "Yeah. See you," distracted by the rising buzzy shriek of Theo's motorcycle launching across the main road.

"I'm sorry," Hanna said, her feeble voice addressing the cold ground. Fatigue pervaded the vacuum left by their departure. A sudden urge to cry tinged her eyes and nose. She resisted and instead focused on the lively farewells between Emma and her brothers as they piled into the minivan. Emma wished them well. Broc backed out of the spot and pointed his vehicle, full of Emma's siblings, at the far side of the parking lot. The dented silver minivan drifted at an unremarkable speed past her. Hanna gave a meek wave at their cheerful faces through the windows, either untouched by sorrow or adept at concealing it.

"Ya know, that bike is pretty quiet actually. It's kinda stealthy —like a ninja," Emma said approaching her. Hanna lacked the energy to respond.

"What d'ya want to do for lunch?" Emma asked.

"A nap."

Emma snickered. "Oh, come on. What's wrong?"

Hanna looked up. Emma offered her backpack for her to take.

"You forgot this in Broc's minivan," said Emma.

Imminent tears blurred her view of Emma. She closed her eyes and took her backpack containing her translation of Theo's important inscriptions. A sob shook her and Emma embraced her, asking, "Hey, kiddo, what happened?"

Hanna's arms remained at her sides, enwrapped by Emma's. Her backpack's loop handle cut into her hand, which was straining against the weight of her laptop and notes.

"Why am I so forgetful? It's like I really do have amnesia," Hanna said, pressing her cheek to Emma's shoulder. She tried to swallow back her sobs and struggled against the teary contortions of her face. Emma's unanticipated warmth and embrace assuaged her sobs. Emma took Hanna's backpack from her and slung it over her own shoulders.

"Come on. I'll buy you lunch."

Hanna walked beside her friend. She wiped her cheeks with her frozen fingers. "Just don't post anymore pictures of me on FL. I don't need even more to write in my journal today."

Emma replied, "Sure thing, captain, but don't worry about it. Like I said, everyone's gonna forget about this in, like, a day or two. It'll get buried in all the pictures of people's lunches."

Consternation welled back inside of Hanna. Emma continued her banter unaware. Hanna played along.

All through their sandwich lunch, Emma marveled at the unfolding drama of the two posts. A sickening feeling that Hanna's sister Lily had already shown the post to their parents soured Hanna's mood further. Theo's translation still hung over her, but Emma's repeated attempts at humor raised Hanna's appreciative spirits back to an industrious level.

Back in the dorm room, a boisterous Emma retired to her laptop on her bed. Hanna sat at her desk.

Exhaustion cajoled her to give up, but she remained seated in her unforgiving chair. She rummaged through her backpack for the green journal. Her shoulders ached as she began her newest entry. Black ink filled in a brief account of the translation work and her conversations with Theo. No detail of the video shoot escaped her—especially the painful aftermath with Katie. In a final effort, she recorded Steve's departure and the Friend Link posts. She wrote, "Share with Theo," at the bottom of the page, then dropped her pen and let the journal's pages spring back closed.

Pulling off her glasses, she pressed her hands against her face in the room growing dim. She took out Theo's inscriptions and her laptop and resumed her work. Whether a poem or song, she could not discern. She consulted the dictionary again and again. A faint possibility that Theo wrote this tickled her imagination. But how would Theo know such words as "bestowed" in Japanese? The sun sank farther toward the horizon.

"Is that your abduction-watch journal or are you really studying on a Saturday?"

Hanna looked up through her glasses at Emma leaning on her desk.

"Theo asked me to translate this inscription for a class."

Emma smirked. "Is it a love poem?" She clasped her hands together on her bosom. "Oh, my extolled Hanna. Tis thine eyes—"

Hanna interjected, "No, it's like extra for one of his classes or something."

Emma folded her arms. "So now you're doing his homework? What next, his laundry?"

Hanna retreated to her work. "I don't think it's homework," she said and read aloud.

> *I am falsehood. Bestowed in me is a power of death and something. The memory of taking life with this becomes truth for the entrapped. A murderer but not the truth is trapped in here.*

"And something?" Emma asked, her brows raised.

Hanna sighed. "It's just a placeholder. There's more about witnessing there I haven't figured out yet. And there's a whole other line too."

Emma whistled. "That's some hardcore nerd stuff. Sounds to me like you're helping him watch one of your Japanese cartoons."

Hanna winced. "Anime are not cartoons." Then she murmured, "You wouldn't understand." Emma ignored her gripe, flicked on the overhead light, and dashed back to her bed.

From the other side of their desks, Emma shouted, "It looks like the premed girls are having a house party tonight. We can walk over. Wanna come along?"

Hanna considered the offer, before replying, "I don't know. I need to finish this. I'm kind of tired."

Emma countered, with boisterous charm, "Don't worry about his inscription thingy. You'll have plenty of time. You already finished most of it, right? Take the rest of the night off. You ever try not studying on a Saturday night, nerd?"

Hanna accepted her valid points.

Emma carried on, "It won't be scary or anything. The square premed girls invited the equally square premed boys. There might be impure thoughts—maybe even dancing. It could escalate to, ya know, things your speed, like hand holding and head pats."

Hanna softly retorted, "Emma, stop."

"Say, what speed are you going with Theo?"

"Emma!"

"Fine, jeez, okay. I wasn't being serious anyway," Emma replied, throwing her hands up in mock surrender.

Glad Emma finally backed off, Hanna returned to her laptop and navigated to Friend Link to inspect the fallout from the motorcycle incident.

Both posts had reached every corner of the campus. The photo's numerous comments were mostly benign. The video's comments followed her grim expectations. Shame drenched her as she scrolled through the dozens of comments. Emma had failed to mention that more than half had predictably scolded her for not wearing a helmet. Even their calculus professor commented about her lack of helmet. Was that not a violation of some university policy? Hanna raced her cursor to the privacy settings and hastily switched everything to the allowable maximum. She searched for other ways to make her account as private as possible. Steven Chatsworth's friend request sat expectantly in her notifications. She declined it and resolved to finish Theo's translation.

The single word of calligraphy sat perplexingly unsolved. In vain, she stared at it yet again, its secrets above her deficient wit. She opened the chat messenger in Friend Link. Clicking Eddie and seeing he was online too, she messaged him, "Hey, what do you know about Japanese calligraphy? Could you decipher a word?"

She patiently waited for a reply.

Nothing—not even the indication he was typing. She returned to the translation and kept checking the screen. No answer released it from stagnation. Much-needed rest implored her to stop. At last, Eddie gave a curt, "Not really." His green icon retreated to a dormant gray and he was gone. Abandoned, Hanna simply wrote the meaning of the one tiny character she could identify: *say*. The meaning of the second remained out of her grasp. She closed the Friend Link page.

By dark, she had untangled the final line. Her eyelids hung heavily. Emma had finished her shower and Hanna heard the whir of her hair dryer. Hanna softly read aloud the final line of the inscription, "Released from here is amnesia to clear the memories for falsehood."

I have no idea what that means, she thought sitting back in her chair. These pieces connected somehow, but her weary mind could not piece them together. That word "amnesia" demanded further investigation. Rapidly flicking the pages of her green journal, she read her entry about their conversation. *Why would he give me a translation about amnesia? Why would he ask me how to say amnesia in Japanese? What is he trying to tell me?* She reached for her phone.

Emma's face popped around her desk. "Hey," she peeped. "Is this too much?"

Hanna's neck strained to turn.

Emma stood proudly in a formfitting coral party dress no parent would ever permit their daughter to wear. Its meretricious length and strings for shoulder straps left an unsavory amount of her olive skin bare. Her long brown hair was curled into soft voluminous waves framing cheeks painted to resemble what Hanna could achieve with little effort. She held up a pair of matching high heels with a shrug, inviting Hanna's opinion.

"I don't think the Lord would approve."

"Too much," Emma concluded, swiftly retreating. She called over, while changing, "So how about it? Come along. Have some fun. Back me up."

Hanna closed her laptop and neatly folded Theo's inscriptions. "Aren't we supposed to be careful about going out at night?"

"Why do you think I'm asking you to join me?"

"How far is it?"

"Two or three blocks from campus. That last abduction was forever ago. There are cops and campus security all over this place on a Saturday night always looking to bust us for underage drinking."

"There won't be alcohol there, right?" Hanna asked with mounting concern.

Emma's tornado of activity stopped on the other side of the desks. "No, not at all. You coming along?"

Hanna consulted her green journal. "It's only been like five days since the last abduction."

"So bring your pepper spray and we'll fight him together."

Emma popped around the corner again, this time in a cyan floral sundress of a more modest length. "I'm not going to spend my freshman year missing out," she said.

With sudden realization, Hanna asked, "It's because Valentine's Day is tomorrow, isn't it?"

Struck, Emma jerked her head in a nod. "Detective Popov strikes again. Not all of us have a date tomorrow."

Emma fled back to her side to escape the conversation's sudden turn. From her side of the divide, she continued, "Everyone around here is either too scared to ask me out or the ones that do are creepy jerks. I'm too young to have to lower my standards." With playful cruelty, she added, "Like you did."

"Hey, come on. I gave him a chance."

"How many more chances are you gonna give him?"

"He's shy. You probably didn't get through to the real Theo. He likely didn't say much."

"Oh, he doesn't talk much, alright. You weren't kidding when you said he has no friends."

"Right? He didn't have any in high school. Don't you feel bad for him?"

"Can't he just buy them?"

"Come on, now. It's not like he just wants to surround himself with sycophants—not at all. He needs someone who can talk to him on a deeper level."

"Certainly not what most guys are looking for."

Hanna rested her chin on her hand in recollection. "He has such a fire about him. When it comes to asking what life is about, he's not just idly letting it slip by. He approaches it with a, how to say, like a cavalier bravado of not just accepting the world how it is presented to him. Theo isn't afraid of anything."

"If that's how you see his flat affect," Emma said bluntly.

Hanna's phone buzzed and she snatched it, flicking it open. A rare text message from Theo updated her that he had returned home safely. Hanna's frown melted away. Sympathy to help her friend welled up.

"Hey, I'll come along."

Emma reappeared instantly. "Really?"

"Sure. Hopefully they won't bring up the motorcycle thing."

"Do my eyebrows look bushy?"

"Not really? What do you mean?"

Emma darted off again, saying, "Theo kept looking at them."

Hanna called Theo. Her hopes sank with each ring, until the automated voice mail message played. She sighed and hung up, her amnesia unforgotten.

Emma reappeared, shaking her head. "Oh, honey, you're not going like that. Don't you have anything more fun?"

"I have some skirts. I could wear my leather jacket and . . ." Hanna looked up to find two thin, curved lines where Emma's eyebrows had been.

"Did you shave off your *eyebrows*!"

"What? I drew them back on. Now they're not bushy."

TEN

"IT *TALKS*!" a bewildered Theo said. Hanna pressed her body against his in the photobooth. They stood facing the camera and saw themselves on the screen just below it. A sentence in Japanese illegible to Theo came up in bold pink letters. A pleasant Japanese woman's voice reiterated the instructions, which Hanna interpreted, saying, "Quick! Close your mouth and push your fingers against your *hoppe*."

Theo frantically asked, "What even?" as a countdown appeared. It snapped the first picture while Hanna pressed her index fingers to her cheeks. New instructions appeared. She hopped excitedly.

"Okay, um, it says line up with your friend like a *dango*."

The countdown began anew. Hanna stood in front of him and leaned her head against his chest. Theo's heart rate rose.

"What's a … a *dango*?" he asked.

In rebuke, she squeaked, "Don't talk!"

The screen held her enthralled as it revealed new instructions. To his annoyance, she practically shouted, "Put your hands open, um, open, um . . ." The countdown reached one as she finished, "… above and below your face!"

How the pictures would show anything but him looking clueless, Theo could not surmise, but Hanna was having the time of her life. She hastily drew breath to shout the next instructions. There must have been an option she had chosen to disable reviewing each photo, instead opting for the frantic quiz version. She took his collar, turned him to face her, and vigorously pulled him into an embrace. Her turtleneck was incredibly soft. She smiled at the camera, Theo realizing too late that the machine had likely instructed him to do so.

"This last one is free choice. You decide," she said gleefully. The timer appeared. He took out his cell phone and held it as if to take a selfie. He pressed his lips to hers, enjoying their unprepared tenderness. The machine's voice resumed, likely telling them the session was concluding. He pulled away and opened his eyes— hers wide open in pleasant shock.

"I hope you're not full of too many surprises," she joked, her short breaths rushing past her parted lips. Theo joined her in reviewing the photos on the unimpressively small screen.

Hanna giggled. "You didn't look into the camera much," she said. Theo withheld his retort in favor of her pleasant humming. The machine printed their photos. She continued, "I hardly have any pictures of you. I think these will be a great way to remember our first Valentine's Day."

Theo unlocked his cell phone again, the incriminating picture from the café still saved on it, but clicked its screen black in frustration. She zealously showed him their completed purikura pictures.

"They're pretty small," he said seeing himself bemused in every photo but one.

"It has to fit them all onto one sheet, silly. I think they came out nice."

Theo smiled. "I think so too." He picked up their jackets.

Hanna handed him his copy. "I suppose it makes sense you'd

find a purikura booth in a karaoke place. I can't wait to sing next," Hanna remarked, leaving the booth with him. They took in the dark lobby of the establishment. A Japanese woman stood behind a counter casually reading a magazine as she patiently awaited their approach. Popular music, occasionally interrupted by authentically Japanese advertisements, poured through unseen speakers. Muffled singing could be heard down the hallway leading to the modestly sound-proofed rooms. Hanna called out, "How many times did you say you've been here?"

"Just once. I came here on a Friday," he answered for a marveling Hanna.

"And you sang in Japanese?"

"No. They have songs in English too," he replied before asking, "One hour okay?"

She nodded, her lilac earrings jostling. Theo brought her to the front desk and repeated the same words he used last time. The woman filled a small plastic basket with two microphones, two toy tambourines, and the paper check on a mini clipboard. She pointed him to the same room as last time and once again instructed him of the checkout procedure with unfaltering politeness. He led a mystified Hanna, who said, "Who'd think this little piece of Japan would be hidden in the middle of New York City?"

"This place comes up on any online search engine," Theo said, opening the door to their booth for her. She passed by him chirping, "There's more than one?"

Inside, a large television screen hung on the wall facing plush seating that formed a U around a square coffee table. It played a loop of advertisements for new albums, singles, and upcoming tours of what the television claimed were popular artists. The whole room was no more than two motorcycles long by one wide. A telephone receiver hung on the wall in the corner.

Hanna took in the room. "It's exactly how I remember it," she said.

Theo took his seat. "Did you go often when you were in Japan?" he asked.

"Just once, but I remember it vividly," she answered, sitting close beside him. "My dad took me. He tried to sing a couple songs in Japanese. He never learned to speak the language. They were popular tunes we must have heard dozens of times in those two weeks. We found all of the kids' movies' songs in English. That was fun, but I was all over the place and kept trying to play with the machine. I guess that's what happens when you take a nine-year-old to karaoke. My mom and sister had no interest. I never stopped talking about it. My dad never took me again."

Noticing her lowered countenance, Theo offered the tablet for entering songs.

"Oh, no. You can have the first song."

Theo switched its interface to English and summoned the first song. He was drawn to her outfit choice: periwinkle turtleneck above a tartan skirt and knee socks.

The music started and Hanna twitched with surprise. "It's louder than I remember."

Theo took a microphone from the basket and clicked it on.

"Oh my God! I haven't heard this in forever!" Hanna exclaimed.

The dreamlike music video of the song's live performance unfolded on the screen. Lyrics appeared. Theo sang, taken by the lyrics of a hell-bound sinner.

Peace. Sorely missed, he reveled in it. Alone, it did not come, but now in the presence of a wanted audience—his secret audience of one—he could not help himself. A song which he had long enjoyed in secret, he sang for her "Demons." In the tempo his calculations receded. Focus and prediction were no longer weapons. Hanna clapped and shouted, "You're amazing!"

Theo carried on, the shackles of reserve falling off. Intrusive thoughts of the knife caused him to miss a note. Guilt festered like an infected wound. The last words disappearing, he clicked off the microphone and picked up the tablet Hanna had forgotten about.

"Wow!" she chirped, giving hearty applause.

"It's easy if you don't judge yourself," he said.

The upbeat drums and guitar of his next selection thundered through the speakers, startling Hanna again. She watched Theo stand up to the splash of synthesizer.

"What is this?" she asked, but the lyrics appeared and Theo dove right in. Hanna bobbed her knee along. Her hesitant hand picked up the second microphone but merely held it. Theo closed his eyes as he hit the repeated words of the final refrain. He overheard Hanna's unamplified voice joining the vocals of the electronic rock tune.

Theo returned to his spot to Hanna's cheers. *Would she question why I picked a song called "Policy of Truth?"* he thought to himself. The tablet had not moved.

"You won't sing? Are you not having a good time?" he asked while the screen returned to its quieter loop of advertisements.

Hanna scrambled to answer, "I will! . . . I can. I haven't thought of one yet." She avoided his inquisitive stare.

"You can make mistakes. Don't care what other people think. Sing in Japanese if you want."

Hanna seized the tablet and poked the stylus to its screen. A song name in English flashed onto the screen. She stood. Hanna's voice filled the room like morning light from a curtain at last drawn back.

In the short rest after the song's intro, Theo prodded, "English?"

Joyous laughter bloomed in her voice as she said, "I don't care what you think!"

Theo grinned.

The last lyrics of "Simple and Clean" faded from the screen. Hanna raced to enter another song in the interlude. Surprise filled him when she swung the tablet into his hands. Her next song started, and so did her enthusiastic voice. Unenthusiastic singing was dreadful; half the fun of karaoke was getting into it. Another entry by Theo flashed onto the screen. As they traded songs, remorse kept digging into him. Hanna called over to him multiple times, saying, "Do you remember this one?" or, "I remember this one." Sometimes the guilt would nearly push him to answer. *Yes! You played it for me in Central Park,* he shouted in his mind.

The wall phone rang. Theo answered, extending their session another hour and ordering a plate of crispy chicken tenders.

After another quick hour of trading songs, the wall phone rang again, their session coming to a close. They paid and left, Hanna still marveling from the sidewalk at the banal edifice that housed such a magical place for her.

Just erase her memory of the translation. Get it over with, he thought before asking, "Why don't we review your green journal at my place?"

She grinned and nodded, her steps nearly turning to skips. Their stroll through Manhattan, polluted by tourists, gave Theo time to think. He entertained her aimless conversation until she mentioned Surgite's spring break.

"That's the same as Lincoln's," Theo said in acute realization.

She burst out, waving her hands, "Oh my God! We have to do something! Our spring breaks line up. That's like destiny!"

A signal prompted them to resume walking. He said, "We could go to a Japanese tea ceremony. I read about them when I was looking for karaoke places. You have to reserve a spot."

"Come to think of it, I've never been to one. Sensei dedicated a whole class to it one day. I'll ask my mom if she could deposit some money into my account. I'm sure she'll include a little extra for something like a tea ceremony. It's educational," she said, drawing her phone from her pocket.

Hanna mashed out her message to her mother while Theo guided her through another crosswalk. Hanna only glanced up to spot him. Where they were going did not enter her concern at all—just that she was following him.

Theo continued, "We could sing karaoke again. I could find a Japanese restaurant too."

She pocketed her phone and took his bicep in her hands, exclaiming, "That would be lovely!"

Theo genuinely smiled at the prospect and led her into his secluded apartment.

"When is your dad coming back?" she asked, leaving her flats by the door.

"Tuesday."

"Tuesday?"

"He's in Orlando for the three-day weekend," he answered, leaving his shoes beside hers.

Her brow rose. "Oh, right. Tomorrow is some holiday, but Surgite still has classes."

"Presidents' Day."

She glided past him to take her usual spot. "I always forget about that one," she remarked in mock defeat.

Theo stood behind her on the couch. They gazed out the window at the late afternoon clouds commuting past the lackadaisical February sun. He took off his coat and placed it beside her backpack. She did the same. He placed his hands on her shoulders and began a mollifying massage.

Feeling the details of her defined shoulder blades and clavicles, he continued the circular squeezing motions as her muscles melted. His fingers worked their way to her supple nape and found their way underneath her turtleneck's collar. *Not exposed enough*, he thought. His hands migrated to her spine, feeling her vertebrae through her turtleneck. Catching the outline of her bra was unavoidable.

Hanna mumbled, "You're good at this." Her bare thighs between her socks and skirt grabbed his attention, but were far too risky for contact with the memory-erasing knife. How to get her distracted enough? Her hands sat in her lap plainly in her view. Turning his hand to a fist, he pressed his knuckles into her back. She moaned. He stopped.

"Harder."

"Really?"

Hanna nodded and muttered a playful, "*Mmm-hmm,*" to which he replied, "Let me get something that might help."

Theo made for his room where he grabbed a small bottle of lotion and the knife. Upon returning, he handed her the bottle and kept the knife in his back pocket. She read the bottle's poetic description aloud while Theo surreptitiously drew the knife. He scrutinized her preoccupied hands. How to get them out of her sight? Suddenly he pulled her into a kiss and her startled hands shot out, groping for context. He stabbed the sheath into her hand and managed to say, "*Hana-chan no kioku soushitsu.*"

Her grip on the couch remained stern. Her tongue ceased its expressive work. Her pupils dilated in her expressionless eyes. Momentarily, her mind was blank and muscles tense in their last action. It worked. Theo deftly slipped away and slid the knife under the couch. He stood near Hanna, now in a daze, the bottle of lotion having fallen into her lap.

"Did you say something?" she innocently asked, turning to him. Theo halted his advance. He had forgotten to prepare a substitute phrase. Answering, *"Hanna's amnesia"* again in Japanese would defeat the point of having just erased her memories of it for the past month. The amnesia charge from capturing Steve the day prior would be wasted. His dry mouth ventured the first words his mind procured.

"I . . . said . . ." he stated with growing pauses, "*Hana-chan no . . . Shio.*"

She giggled.

"You tried to say you're mine?"

Theo nodded, sitting beside her. "Yeah . . . yes"—he cleared his throat— "I did."

Her miraculous smile drew him closer. Maybe God did exist. Verifying the extent of her amnesia was next, though he could not resist Hanna's adorable beauty.

Hanna perked up. "I finished the translation you asked for." She dug through her nearby backpack and handed the pages to him.

"Emma invited me to a party last night with her premed friends. She didn't want to go alone. We stayed out way too late. I did the best I could on the calligraphy."

The sheath's amnesia was like a scalpel. Hanna's memories were otherwise intact. Her recollection of them remained smooth and uninterrupted. Only noticing the absence of particular ones would instigate an investigation. The mind's network of associations and linked memories, though, remained dangerously unpredictable. He flipped through the pages, contemplating what other memories would be beneficial to delete. Steve had been trapped in the sheath for slightly past twenty-four hours. There would still be enough charge to erase Hanna from Steve's recent memory. He could take care of that once she was back at Surgite.

"Do they make sense? Are they good enough?" she asked, leaning close to him. Theo spotted the word "amnesia" in her translation. It surprised him unpleasantly. Maybe the inscription represented instructions after all, like Arthur had suspected.

"Yes," he was obligated to say. He glanced up. Just a few inches away, an alluring Hanna watched him through her bangs, her parted lilac lips and rosy cheeks at once startling and rousing Theo. He looked back at the incriminating word in the translation but could not help stealing another look at her.

"I copied the translation into my journal too. Would you like to see? We can go over it together. I write about you all the time." He looked at her blankly. She added, with disappointment, "But by the time we finish reviewing it, I'll probably have to go back."

Why did she have to copy the damn translation into her journal? he thought.

Flustered, he stood up and said, "I'll put these away first. Would you like coffee?"

She shrugged indifferently. "Sure."

Theo escaped to his room and stuffed the translation into his desk. Next, the kitchen saw him making coffee and plans. She remembered the journal and why she had come here. The impetus for starting the journal had just been deleted from her recollection. Another fabrication was needed. He could overwrite why she had started the journal. Her amnesia would be a nonexistent memory and she would carry on unaware.

"Hey, um, Theo?"

Hanna's soft call spun him around from the coffee machine. On the threshold she stood, bashful and uncertain. "I was thinking . . . about how there's not enough time to talk about my journal. In fact, I was thinking how I really . . . well . . . like to just spend time with you. It's already five o'clock. Your hands must be magic, because, after that massage, I feel like a huge weight's been lifted off my shoulders."

Seeing her relief brought him a novel feeling of joy.

"So, anyway, what I'm saying . . . what I'm thinking about . . . well, what if I stay over? Just for the night?"

Theo felt arousing trepidation for the first time in his life.

"Here? With me?"

She nodded and stepped closer to Theo.

"You look so surprised. I hope I'm not imposing."

Theo shook his head. "No, not at all. I just never thought of the possibility."

Hanna stepped into his unprepared arms. "I feel like all of my worries are gone when I'm with you. We'd have more time to hang out. You could show me your room."

Realizing the implication of her stay, he said, "I'll have to skip my guild's raid tonight."

Another giggle escaped her.

"But sure. You can stay. Decaf instead now?"

Hanna smiled in his arms. "Actually, I'm kind of hungry."

Before he could answer, his phone buzzed angrily in his pocket. He stepped back and his stomach sank at seeing the phone number. He swore and stated, "I have to take this. Make whatever you want for dinner."

Hanna fumbled a reply. He tore past her, heading for the balcony, shouting back, "The whole kitchen is yours. Help yourself."

Call accepted, he remained silent, yanking open the sliding door to the gusty patio. "Get somewhere you can talk," Arthur's callous voice commanded. The sliding door slammed behind him, and Theo raised the phone to his ear in Sunday's dusk.

"What?"

"Did you get the translation?"

"Yeah, but we agreed I'd give it to you tomorrow. Why are you calling me now? I'm busy."

"You? Busy on Valentine's Day?"

"Yes, actually."

Arthur cackled audibly. "How much did you pay her?"

Irritated, Theo remained silent.

"Read it to me now over the phone."

"Already? We're not even done testing yet."

Fear shook his hand trying to open the sliding door again.

"Getting cold feet?" Arthur asked, his voice steady.

Back inside, Theo spotted Hanna in the distant kitchen up on the counter to reach a high cabinet. Arthur did not relent while Theo snatched his coat from the couch and tucked the knife inside it.

"Did you take care of the translator?"

"Yes. He won't be a problem."

"Excellent," he answered, clearly pleased and eager. "No problems with testing?"

Entering his room, Theo replied, "No." He quickly stowed the knife in its den under the bed, dropped off his coat, and snatched the translations.

He asked, "Did you find out anything about The Makers?"

"That myth? Total fabrication," Arthur said with conviction.

"This had to have come from somewhere."

"Who cares? It's not like they're coming to take it."

"You're not the one out here using it."

"The cops are a greater concern."

A bewildered Hanna watched Theo storm back outside to the dim porch. Theo shivered in his button-down shirt. Admiring Hanna's thorough work, he said, "I'll only read this once."

A clatter of motion came from Arthur's phone, then his voice returned, saying, "Proceed." Theo read aloud slowly.

Falsehood I am. Bestowed in me is a power of death and to write its testimony. Memories of taking a life with this become truth for the trapped. Trapped in here is the murderer but not the truth. Released from here is amnesia to clear the memories for falsehood.

Theo added, "And there's a note that the single word of calligraphy on it means 'say.'"

Arthur whistled. "I guess your connection to the Japanese side of your family came through. You said your grandfather on your mother's side was Japanese, right?"

"Are we still meeting Wednesday?" he asked, pocketing her translation.

"Fine. Same spot and time," Arthur said callously.

Theo sighed. "Are we done?"

"Afraid she's going to run away?" his snide reply came, slithering through the phone. "Try tying her up."

Conceited laughter rushed Theo to hang up. He turned around. The sight scared years off his life.

Hanna stood, knife in hand, just on the other side of the door.

Her ghostly pale face judged him in the darkness. The door to his bedroom hung ajar in the far hallway. Theo grasped his chest, knees buckling and heart thundering. It was too painful to meet her stare. Possible explanations for the weapon swarmed up like hornets. He wanted to shout and destroy the pathetic reflection of himself in the sliding glass door—any outlet for the compounding self-loathing.

Hanna pulled open the door, calling, "Theo! Are you okay?" and rushed to his side. The chef's knife in her hand glinted in the city's lights.

"Oh God, I wanted to ask what salad dressing you like but you were on the phone and so I waited just a little, but then you turned around so suddenly."

Theo rose back to his full height, struggling to steady his voice. "You scared me."

Hanna stepped back, scrutinizing the knife. "I guess I shouldn't have brought this. I'm sorry."

"Let's forget about it," Theo answered through labored breaths.

"Who were you talking to? It seemed pretty intense," she said, following him back to the kitchen.

Theo leaned on the counter for vital support. "It was the history professor. He needed the translation right away."

Hanna resumed slicing a tomato, its red pulp spilling onto the cutting board. "I'm glad I could help," she replied before finishing the salad and adding, "Why don't you have a seat? You look ill."

"What did you decide to make?" he asked, taking a chair.

She erupted into a swirl of apologies and admitted, "It's just … all of your food is so nice and … I don't want to ruin it."

"You can't cook?"

"Theo, don't be mean," she said.

"It's alright. I should have some leftovers," he said, heading toward the refrigerator. They resumed their domestic work in newfound fervor.

A pause in their dinner preparations left him the chance to

inspect her journal. Hanna dutifully kept watch of the warming pans.

It was a detailed account. Its early pages catalogued meeting Steve. Theo read them intently. Hanna's disgust was evident. Personal observations peppered the factual accounts, with most sections ending on notes to share with him. Particular attention was given to times, dates, and details about him. A copy of the engravings was taped inside. Some records were ramblings, but the most recent entry turned particularly despondent. He spotted a tiny "help me remember" scrawled below "you are broken, Hanna." A knot clenched in his stomach. Perhaps she forgot she had written that. Theo closed her journal. Not long after, Hanna brought over their dinner, humming a cheery tune.

It had been a long time since the table had accommodated a guest. His father's liaisons never cooked. Theo fled into the city during such occasions. Across from Theo was his father's empty chair. Hanna sat beside him and made their plates.

"So, what do you think of the journal? There's no way I can forget what happened now. I've been keeping it religiously every day."

"Yeah," he said, as if awakening from a trance.

Hanna poured him the tea he had made. "Maybe we're both tired," she commented.

Theo hastened to his first bite of the featureless salad she had prepared. Until that day, he had not known the extent to which a salad could be so uninspired.

"It's good," he said, meeting her eager look.

"Really?" she asked, a lamb in his hands.

"Yeah."

Maybe he did not have to erase her memory in the end. Maybe he was wrong to have resigned himself to her inevitably breaking his heart. Theo sat up, refocused and casting aside distracting thoughts. He handed her the journal, saying, "It's a very thorough record—just five days but already a consistent habit. I think you'd have no trouble identifying if you had been abducted and came back with no memory."

She stared quizzically, her cheeks rounded by the leftovers he had not planned on sharing.

"Remember when you told me that's why you started this journal? It was at the end of the film shoot."

He watched her rapidly process memories behind her perplexed expression. Theo's own notes bore testimony that she had mentioned abductions as the second reason to keep her journal. He wished this second reason would supplant the primary reason of her amnesia, ending her investigation. His decision to make this move so haphazardly irked him.

Hanna blinked twice. Theo felt like the salad would come back up. She looked right at him. "Oh, yeah. Those abductions are scary. I wrote about the Long Island girl in my journal too. Did you see?"

Relief flooded him. The unholy power could be trusted. His shoulders untensed. "It's interesting to read how you see the world," he said. "The first entry is about your East Asian politics class. Tell me about it."

The journal occupied their conversation, Hanna recalling, in detail, her banal adventures. Theo listened attentively. At first it was penance, but gradually he felt himself creating conversation as he became touched by her infectious mirth. Theo could not have imagined the joy he felt discussing Hanna's calculus crusades over shared leftovers. Hanna savored her clear recollection and Theo's dutiful help in recalling their shared memories. Theo shared how he found the purikura booth during his solo karaoke experience. Her chin rested on her interlaced fingers. Enraptured by his story, her foot occasionally brushed against his leg under the table. Her lilac lipstick had worn off, her sleeves were damp from preparing their meal, and dark rings colored her eyes. One of her knee socks had slid down and was now merely a sock. Still, he longed to get closer. Why had he not thought to erase her memories of having amnesia earlier?

Night arrived, pulling its blanket over the city.

Hanna yawned, then said, "It feels so late. What time is it?"

"Five past seven."

"It would be pretty silly to go to sleep this early, wouldn't it? How early do I have to wake up to make it to campus by eight?"

"Probably five."

She whined about her fate, but Theo felt his phone buzz again. An email greeted him, asking, "Where are you?"

Recognizing his guild leader's name, he stood. "I need to tell my guild I can't do the raid."

Hanna flashed a thumbs up. "Take your time. I'll clean up."

Theo headed to his room, distracted by imagining a life together with Hanna. Closing the door, he sat at his desk. The computer came to life and shortly displayed an online telephone program. He accepted the invitation to his guild's group call. The lively voices of his guildmates came through his headset.

"Dude, what took you so long? We're getting ready and you aren't even logged on yet. You still need to spec. It's holy themed," came the rapid voice of the guild leader. Three other rancorous voices added their disapproval of his tardiness.

"Guys, I can't join."

Questions raged until Theo interrupted them with, "I have a date."

They paused in shock.

"With a real girl?" the nervous healer asked.

"Yes."

The boisterous monk said, "Come on, man, why do you think we made the Valentine's Day raid in the first place?"

The guild leader lamented, "Four years we've had this raid on Valentine's Day. You can't bail on us."

"Do you have pictures of her feet?" asked the necromancer.

Theo retorted, "What? No, and I'm sorry. I really am."

The nervous healer asked, "Can she do that thing girls do where they take off their bra without taking off their shirt?"

Theo said, "No, I won't ask her that. I'm serious," but paused deep in thought. "That can't be possible. There's no way . . . Regardless, she's here and spending the night."

They all gasped.

"The Grand Inquisitor has ascended. Maybe we should be glad for him instead of envious," marveled the nervous healer. All adamantly rejected his suggestion. Theo wiped the sweat from his brow.

The guild leader cleared his throat. "Now listen. Being a Grand Inquisitor is a major responsibility. Bailing on a raid with no warning will require recompense. The guild requires a sacrifice."

Growing impatient, Theo said, "Sure. What?"

A pregnant silence gripped all. At last, the guild leader said, "Does she have a sister?"

"Huh?"

"Cousins?"

"I don't even know."

"Hot friends?"

"I guess?"

"*Bingo!*" he shouted. The other three cheered the guild leader's decisive victory. Theo accepted his charge to introduce one of Hanna's friends to the guild and said goodbye.

The boisterous monk shouted, "Wait! Tell us how you met her. How'd you do it? Please say you didn't tell her what you think about tipping."

Concurring voices bolstered his request.

Theo replied, "She started sitting with me in the cafeteria about a year ago. She kept trying to talk to me, so eventually, I started listening to her."

Multiple voices urged, "Then what?"

His impatience growing, Theo answered, "I don't know? I did some research on small talk and started working out. It all just happened."

The necromancer chimed in with, "Yeah, sure, but where did you find the will to get out of bed like that?"

Theo replied, "From Hanna, honestly."

The boisterous monk jumped in with, "How'd you get her to sit with you in the first place?"

Theo blinked repeatedly. "I . . . don't know. I have to go," and hung up. The guild's judgment weighed on his steps as he returned to the kitchen, until he saw Hanna. She stood washing the dishes. He placed his hands on her hips and rested his chin on her shoulder.

"Thank you."

"No problem," she chirped. Her hair smelled like a department store. Losing focus on everything but her, he held her as she finished washing the last knife.

"It's been a long day," she said, turning around against him, "Can I use your shower?"

Theo answered, "Sure," and she took his hand and walked him to the bathroom. He hesitated at the threshold, but she pulled him, flashing a siren's smile. The scars on his body immediately leaped to mind. Hanna did not know. His expression turned bitter. The knife still had to be hidden better too. She waited for him patiently. There again was that feeling of peace washing over him he only felt while alone with Hanna. His shoulders relaxed and he breathed easily.

Theo said, "You . . . go first. I'll find you a toothbrush."

Hanna looked up, confused, but understanding softened her furrowed brow. "Okay. Could I borrow your pajamas?"

Theo politely agreed, his imagination stirring. Hanna set about her shower, disappearing behind the closed door. Theo returned to his room for the knife.

"You can't see this part," he said, bringing the knife back to the living room. Kneeling, he continued, "Hey, keep an eye on Steve in there. Make sure he doesn't wake up. I'm going to ask you to erase his memory tomorrow. You would like Hanna, or *Hana-chan*.

She speaks Japanese, *nihongo*. She could talk to you . . . someday. She's nice. You would be friends."

Emotion choked him as he said, "Anyway, I can't believe she's sleeping over. Thanks for erasing her amnesia. You did a great job. *Yoku dekita*. I have to shower next. She doesn't . . . can't know our secret. We'll talk more later. *Oyasumi*." He tucked the knife under the couch, overhearing Hanna's jubilant singing from the shower.

ELEVEN

HANNA REMEMBERED her first hug with Theo.

HER LOQUACIOUS FRIENDS surrounded her at the senior prom. King's Prep had converted the gymnasium into a colorful bombastic swirl of music, teenage inhibition, and hormones. Hanna had not announced a date that evening. Her friends gossiped loudly about the evening's unfoldings. Gaiety filled their voices. The dances picked up and Hanna's participation waned further in the conversation. Hanna stole a look at her buzzing phone. Was he really there?

She dipped away from the bouquet of girls, a violet plucked. Hanna threw open the gymnasium doors and rushed down the empty hallways, hampered by her prom dress. Faster, she struggled, until she ripped open the doors to the echoey stairway. On the landing below, she saw him alone. She remembered how prim his school uniform always looked: his navy jacket neatly squaring off his shoulders, his crisp shirt and slacks never bearing a wrinkle. She seldom ironed her own uniform to such perfection. Theo abandoned his usual pensive frown making him often appear older than he was, unable to hide his amazement.

"There's glitter on your eyes."

"I thought you'd like it."

"I do," he said, ascending the stairs.

She tucked her phone away into her tiny clutch. He reached her on the platform and softly said, "I heard you decided on Surgite."

Hanna nodded, finding herself stepping closer to him. Everyone gossiped about how he had gotten into Lincoln.

"You're not going away?" he asked.

She shook her head. He pulled her into a tight embrace. She stood in his arms, her own useless at her sides. Unsure what to say, she simply breathed into his shirt, his cheek pressed against her hair. He smelled so good.

"Congratulations on Surgite."

"Thanks."

"Would you like to dance?"

"Yes," she answered breathlessly.

Theo took her to the moonlit gardens of King's. She swayed with his guiding steps to tender piano from the smartphone in his breast pocket. Other couples refrained from interrupting their unforgettable memory. His father had let him borrow the car. He drove it like he owned it. The grumbling silver coupe swept them to her favorite diner, where she enjoyed sandwiches together and wearing his jacket.

Laughter, candid discourse, and reflection played like a soundtrack to admiring his decisive demeanor. The boy who gave up speaking in class, whom classmates ridiculed behind his back and teachers feared the worst from, who commuted on his bicycle alone every day no matter the weather, was, in fact, quite charming. And he was her secret all to herself.

He brought her back by eleven, Hanna completely forgetting the time. He helped her create a plausible fabrication to her parents for why she returned without her friends. In the darkness of his parked car, he leaned over and kissed her anticipating lips. He watched her run off to her front door several houses down. She stole looks back at him. A day after graduation, they were dating.

———

HIS WHOLE ROOM smelled of him. Lying now in his bed at his side, Hanna relived that day in June. She savored the brief moments of consciousness between stretches of desperately needed sleep. The warm air blowing from the apartment's vents made a heavenly harmony. The heavy blankets of his bed sheltered her from the degrading hailstorm of existence outside.

They had talked long into the night. Other, less intellectual activities had occurred, too, between their conversations. He insisted the lights remain off and kept his long sleeve shirt on. Several times, she had awoken too excited to sleep or uncomfortable between him and the wall. His twin bed had obviously not been chosen to accommodate a guest. She rested her forehead against his arm in the serene darkness and drifted back to sleep.

The alarm sounded. Theo snatched his phone on the nearby desk, silenced its ringing, and sprung from the bed. "Where are you going?" she asked as he opened the door. He disappeared, leaving a painful absence. Hanna collapsed into its warmth.

Some minutes later, Theo woke her. He sat on the side of the bed dressed and already wearing his coat.

"Hey."

"Come back to bed," she whined.

"We'd both fall asleep."

She yawned and sat up. Sleep called her back. She resisted, opting for any conversation to hold her from collapsing into his inviting bed.

"I've never slept with a boy before," she said, rubbing her eyes.

"Neither have I."

Hanna stared blankly. "I've slept in the same bed with my sister."

"How was that?" Theo asked with uncertainty.

"She yelled at me for kicking her in my sleep. Why are we talking about this?"

"I don't know."

At least he was trying. Theo was finally open, indulging her questions and making earnest conversation. Leaving here would mean leaving that Theo. She feared he would regress to being Mr. Elusive. Emma had already called her last night, asking her whereabouts. Neglected homework, too, demanded her attention. Hanna climbed out of his bed and stretched in front of him. She looked back to catch Theo's reaction, but instead was caught in his sudden embrace.

There ended up not being enough time for breakfast. A kiss felt appropriate at the door, but he made no opportunity for it. The illuminated sidewalks carried their determined steps back to the station. Commuters had already begun their treks. Stores began their opening routines. The federal holiday seemed irrelevant to the city that tired, but never slept.

Theo followed her farther than the station's monitors. The surveillance cameras on the well-lit train platform saw them facing each other. Just off the platform was the abyss of tunnels snaking their way out. The open doors of the train waited impatiently. The heat from the train car felt a cruel imitation of Theo's warmth.

"When will I see you again?"

"I don't know yet. I'll call you," he answered in the deep, sonorous voice she admired. Theo checked his watch. "Almost time."

Hanna pursed her lips and viewed the grimy train. A piercing rush of air burst from its airbrakes. Cantankerous passengers hurried by them. She held his cheek in her hand, feeling the rare stubble of the nascent beard he never grew.

"I don't know what I'd do without you. It's getting so hard to say goodbye," she told him.

Theo pulled her into a kiss, tenderly held her in it for a moment longer than she expected, then turned away. She boarded the train and took an empty bench.

"Am I falling in love?" she asked her reflection in the window.

His kiss lingered in her memory long after the train pulled away into the blackness of Monday morning. Each time the train slowed, she briefly revived to spot the station, but with waning vigilance. Dawn shined through the train's scratched windows. Her head dipped involuntarily in a doze. She slouched lower and leaned her head against the hard plastic of the train.

I'm just resting before class, she knowingly lied to herself. No new passengers boarded the train. All was quiet. The few passengers in the car were busy appearing busy. Theo had concurred with her assessment that none of the abductions had occurred on trains. She remembered the softness of Theo's pillows only an hour prior.

A passenger kicked her outstretched foot in the aisle. Hanna shuddered awake, embarrassed and frightened. Catching sight of the familiar station name, she bolted off the train and down the station's stairs. A few cars populated the commuter parking lot. A yellow convertible caught her attention amid the crowd of sedated monotony parked around it. Surgite University was not too far, but, moments ago, would have been another two hours away had she remained asleep. The clock on her cell phone told her she was heading straight for calculus. An appreciated granola bar from Theo made for breakfast. Crashing through the classroom door, she took her usual seat, panting.

Class began but Emma was nowhere. Hanna feigned a chipper voice and asked for a sheet of paper from a nearby student. He obliged, graciously shocked at the female attention. She scavenged a pen from her backpack. Still no Emma. Hanna focused on the blackboard's equations.

After the lesson, with nearly festive intonation, the professor informed them about their upcoming midterm test. The clock indicated the students' imminent escape, and he bid them all good luck.

Just outside, Hanna called Emma, who immediately answered, "Where the hell are you? Are you back yet?"

"Slow down. What's going on?"

"Broc and I got interrogated by the cops. They're coming for you next," she barked.

Hanna gasped. "Oh my God! What happened?"

"Steve disappeared. They think it's connected to the Long Island abductions. Broc and I are the last known witnesses. Just get over here and I'll explain."

"Where are you?"

"In front of the dorms. Again, where the hell are you?"

"Calculus. I'll be right there."

Hanna hung up and ran. Weary student traffic lumbered along. She darted between their anemic packs. The panic in Emma's voice pushed her to alert consciousness. The cold air filled her lungs, oxygenating the blood thumping through her. Emma stood up ahead at the empty picnic benches by the girl's dormitory. Broc held a lighter's flame up to a fresh cigarette in her mouth.

Meekly, Broc said to Emma, "You really should stop."

Emma took a deep drag. After her exhale, she shouted, "When the cops think I abducted someone, I'll have a damn cigarette!"

Emma's cigarette shook in her hands; its distinct odor pervaded the conversation. She smirked. "Same clothes as yesterday, huh? Ya weren't kidding. You actually slept with him."

Hanna raised her hands in exasperation. "It was getting late! What was I supposed to do? It would have been more dangerous to come back than just stay the night. You said so yourself!"

Broc looked away, embarrassed by the subject matter.

Emma continued, "Well, I hope you had fun, because the cops are coming for you next. They ran us through the ringer about an hour ago. Spoiler: you don't get to say no."

"Jesus!" Hanna exclaimed. "That early?"

Emma grimaced. "They say the first forty-eight hours are the most crucial in a missing person's case. Unlike other abductions, Steve has rich lawyer parents who are probably twisting arms to get the cops moving. And it's not just the campus police wannabes —Greenberm's finest are handling this. Funny how they went after my brothers and me first."

"Oh no," Hanna said, realizing the gravity of the situation. "When did he go missing?" she asked.

Emma ripped a quick drag on her cigarette before continuing, "Apparently, his parents filed a missing person report early Sunday morning when he didn't come back home. Nobody saw him after the video shoot. His stupid yellow convertible was last seen in the commuter lot."

Recollection shot through Hanna. "I saw his car at the train station this morning."

"What?" Emma and Broc both yelled.

"Yeah. A yellow two-door convertible," Hanna confirmed.

"Aftermarket exhaust? Tinted windows? Lowered? Fender flares?" Emma asked in staccato.

Hanna replied, "I didn't get a good look, but how many canary-yellow convertibles could there be here? I should tell the police."

Emma scoffed. "Easy for you to say."

A confounded Hanna asked, "What do you mean?"

"Sure, just walk right up to the cops. Talk to them like it's no big deal."

Realization dawned on her as Emma added, "God, you're so naive sometimes."

Exasperated, Hanna asked, "But they interviewed Broc too?"

Emma retorted, "He has a minivan and the pictures on FL place him at the last known location of Steve. Duh, he was a suspect. But they took one look at him and knew he didn't have what it takes."

"I'm standing right here," Broc said, slightly indignant.

"Light my cigarette. It died," Emma ordered.

He complied, leaning closer than before to ignite the cigarette held by her red lips.

"I'll let you know how it goes," Hanna said. They offered no reply, preoccupied with the flame between them. Hanna rushed over to campus security.

The plain brick building was nestled close to the large parking lot by the athletic fields. Surgite's emblem adorned the building. Hanna pulled open the door to the modest lobby.

Save for the university emblem hanging on the wall, it could have been a waiting room of any doctor's office. A locked door loomed beside a receptionist's counter, shielded by clear plastic. Two police officers stood talking in the lobby in hushed voices. They stopped momentarily, taking notice of Hanna's unannounced presence. An officer sat viewing a computer monitor behind the receptionist's counter. She met Hanna's apprehensive look.

"Can I help you, miss?" the officer asked. Hanna's stomach felt twisted in knots. Her hands trembled and knees felt poised to buckle. Meeting the officer's interrogative stare, she could not shake an intense feeling of guilt.

She approached cautiously. "I don't know what to do. I have information about the disappearance of Steven Cha . . . er . . . I forgot his last name. The Steve that went missing."

The officer leaned forward in her creaky chair. "You have information regarding the case of Steven Chatsworth?"

"Yes. I saw his car at the train station."

"Miss, he was already found earlier this morning," the officer replied bluntly.

"Really?"

"In his car at the train station, in fact. The case is resolved."

"Oh. What happened to him?"

"That's a matter of an open investigation," the officer said, her voice taking on dismissive authority. "I'm unable to share that information. Are you a friend of his?"

"Yes," was easier to say than no.

Hanna thanked her but was made to give a statement on record before leaving. The two officers watched her exit before resuming their conversation. Outside, Hanna retreated across the stale green lawns into the gardens near the university's central mansion. The abductions had been going on for months now. Steve was a fellow student—albeit not a fond one. Fear for her own safety gripped her.

Alert, she quickly took in her surroundings: tranquil perennials in a garden complacently awaiting spring. She folded her arms and frowned. Emma and her brothers did not even own a car. Even without one, how and why would they knock out Steve and drag him away just to bring him back? Was there a ransom? Did he do something? No plausible motive came to mind. Eddie and Katie did not even know Steve and they both lacked cars too.

"Eddie also isn't exactly in great shape. It'd have to be someone pretty strong," she told the ground. They would probably never talk to her again anyway.

Broc . . . she wondered, but nothing added up. A sparrow fidgeted in eager hops on a nearby bench. Theo's motorcycle raced past her mind's eye.

"Yeah, like he could abduct anyone on a motorcycle," she murmured to herself. The thought to call him lingered, though. They talked about Steve right before he left that day. Theo did pass the commuter lot.

But Steve's car moved from the commuter lot. There's no way they would both go to the train station without saying a word about it to each other beforehand. Or did he meet him in the commuter lot first? Then what? They drove to the train station and Theo took him into the city, but that leaves his motorcycle behind . . . unless he's working with someone?

Her green journal hungered for this new information. She could not forget why she had started it either. Hanna headed back to her dorm room, where her journal devoured her rapid scrawling. At least her memories were safe. She changed to jeans and a sweater.

Hopefully, nobody else had noticed the evidence of her overnight adventure. There was still so much to do that day. Hanna set out to face her classes.

In Japanese class, Hanna kept her eyes on the blackboard and her notes, but, with the surety of gravity, would catch Katie and the film majors leering at her. Hanna grew uncomfortable. Sensei ended class but their whispering persisted. She informed Eddie she had finished her part of the write-up. He curtly acknowledged and left.

Her medieval literature lecture cast a soporific spell on her. The toll for having stayed at Theo's came into focus. The students formed small discussion groups. She prayed it would not be too evident she had not done the reading.

Nightfall saw Emma and Hanna safely inside their dorm room. An unsaid pact had formed between them. They texted each other as soon as their classes ended. They returned to the dormitory as soon as possible. They dined together exclusively, and their short walks between campus buildings were filled with surveillant glances at their surroundings. Hanna lay on her bed, clasping her phone. Theo would surely return her unanswered calls. Sleep pulled on her eyelids. Maybe the ringing would wake her.

Emma sat at her desk, swearing every minute or so. She slapped her hand on the desk, startling Hanna.

"Oh come on, Broc!" yelled Emma.

"What did he do?"

"Grenaded me."

Incredulous, Hanna let out a breath. "Wait, he blew you up?"

"Well, duh. We're in the same match."

Hanna ventured the four footsteps around their desks to Emma's side. Hunched over her laptop, her left hand commanded its keyboard and her right, the mouse. Disorganized piles of graphs and charts sat waiting to be filed into her binders. Magazines featuring muscle-clad actors, makeup advertisements, sex advice, and celebrity gossip lay intermingled in piles of science textbooks of staggering value. Out of place was the camouflage rifle in the hands of a dark-clad commando on her laptop screen. She kept him in constant motion, occasionally allowing him to pause to inspect the dilapidated warehouse he patrolled.

"Is it just you and him?"

"No, it's two-on-two. He's on the other team this match. Sometimes he taunts me and tells me where he is."

"Broc? How?"

"Oh, he's pretty bold when it's just text. We have a chat open," she said, pointing at a tiny box in the corner of her screen. Hanna watched it, but no message came.

She asked, "Do you play on the same team too?"

"Sometimes."

The words "basement hallway" popped up in the chat window. Emma's commando whirled around and sprinted down a staircase. Suddenly, he stopped and peered around a corner. Bullets screamed past him, and he wavered, one having spilled his blood. Emma made her commando throw a grenade while backing up the stairs. Its explosion was just audible through Emma's headset. Her commando rushed back down the stairs and turned the corner, blasting his rifle. A dusty guerilla fighter rushing toward her fell in agony. The text "hungryman69 gunned down brytsyde" was displayed on the game screen as Emma shouted, "*Ha*! You thought I'd back off!"

"You call yourself 'hungry man?'"

Emma grinned widely. "Nobody knows you're a girl on the internet," she said and resumed patrolling the warehouse.

"Isn't it nice he plays with you?"

"Part of it's guilt. I was kind of mean to him today. I don't want to be, but he's such a doormat. God, I wish he'd just get a spine. I mean, sure, around my brothers I get it, but he never really shakes off that scared rabbit look."

Another message from Broc popped up, and Emma changed course immediately. Emma's commando ran straight down an empty hallway but slowed. She said, "He's behind me. He wants to stab me instead of just shooting me . . ." Her voice trailed off as her commando held out a grenade.

"Isn't that going to . . ." Hanna began, but the explosion on screen answered her question. Emma cackled victoriously at the sight of Broc's guerilla fighter also perishing in her martyrdom blast.

"See, sometimes you can't let them know you know."

"But you died too."

"I was dead anyway, but I got him good."

Reflecting on his clandestine approach, Hanna asked, "You don't think Broc had anything to do with Steve disappearing, do you?"

"No, he definitely didn't," she answered, firing her weapon after a sprinting guerilla fighter.

Hanna asked, "Who could it have been?"

A preoccupied Emma tossed out, "I dunno. I just want it to stop."

The buzzing cell phone in her hand interrupted Hanna's reply. Hanna flipped it open, saying, "Hang on. It's probably Theo."

Dread filled her as she read the tiny screen.

"Hi, Mom," she greeted, opening the door.

"Hi, sweetie. I hope things are well?"

"Yes, they are," she answered, stepping out into the dormitory hallway.

"Are you in the dorms?" she asked in a pleasant tone.

"Yes."

"Oh, and I just know you're studying hard?"

It had been a while since she heard her mother's saccharine Carolina accent.

"Yep. As always."

"I talked to your father about the Japanese tea ceremony, but first I want to bring up something I just saw on the news tonight."

Steve gave a snide smirk in Hanna's memory. They both knew what this was about, but her mother was going to ask anyway.

"You mean the abduction on campus?"

"Why, yes. It's just awful, isn't it?" she answered with sweet concern. "They interviewed that poor boy, and he came back all cold and shivering. The last thing he remembered was two days prior. He has no idea where he was or who took him. Isn't that just absurd?"

Hanna winced at anyone feeling pity for Steve. He must have made the most of the camera's limited scope. "Did the news say if he was hurt?" Hanna asked flatly.

"He had a busted lip and reckons he was somehow drugged and must have hit the ground," she answered, "but not a soul can explain why he woke up in his car or why he had driven to the train station."

"That's crazy."

"Oh, it was bizarre," her mother said. "They were saying campus security reviewed the surveillance footage and saw him driving his car out of the commuter lot Saturday afternoon. Who would forget that? The whole thing has put everyone on edge. I heard they are fixing to start an investigation involving New York City too, seeing as he was parked on the side of the tracks bound for New York."

Hanna realized her mother's trap was set. She fumbled a reply, saying, "Well, they don't know for sure the abductor is in the city. There have been incidents all over the tri-state area."

The trap was sprung. "Well, I find it a little unsuitable for you to be going into the city during all this. I know how much you love Japanese culture, but a tea ceremony with friends can wait. Why, the Good Lord knows I'd be worried sick if you were in the belly of the beast with some deranged devil on the loose."

Her mother's change in tone signaled that there was no room for debate.

Hanna asked, "So can I go anywhere for spring break?"

"What's your friend Emma doing? I'm sure you two can go somewhere once you finish your homework. I'll be picking you up from campus after your last midterm. You can help me clean up the tomato beds and help your sister study for her SAT subject tests."

"But Mom, I'm doing fine. I don't need to study all spring break," she hurled back at her.

"You had a little trouble last semester, which is okay being your first semester away and all, but you seem distracted. Your father and I want to sit down and do a little check-in. You need to think of what you're going to do this summer too."

"But—"

"You really ought to focus on your studies. Think of your future," her mother insisted with noticeable force.

"Okay, I will," she answered obediently.

"You stay safe now. Stick with Emma. I'll call you tomorrow."

"Okay."

"Bye now."

Hanna flicked her phone closed and sighed. She walked back down the empty hallway, catching the curious faces in the communal lounge one last time. Her heart ached as she remembered Theo's embrace just that morning. She reached for her key but realized her grave error. As she knocked on her own door, she accepted that her forgetfulness was never going away. She leaned her forehead against the wall in defeat. In that still moment, she hated herself.

"Darn doors needing pesky keys," Emma joked, opening it for her. Hanna slipped past her and, once seated at her desk, began a new lugubrious journal entry.

Emma called out, "Hey, uh, since you're probably an expert now, how does he kiss?"

"Who, Theo?"

"No, Santa Claus. Who do you think?"

Hanna wistfully thought back to the train station that morning and answered, "Like it's the last time we ever will."

TWELVE

ARTHUR'S STARE bore into Theo.

He repeated, "Give me back the knife."

Theo reached into his jacket pocket, keeping his eyes on him. At his desk, Arthur leaned forward with anticipation. Noontime sunlight cut through the blinds of Arthur's office window. Behind Theo, the door and shades to Arthur's office were closed, shutting out the rustle of customers browsing his store's alternative medicinal remedies. No part of visiting Arthur was ever comfortable. Taking one last look at the door behind him, Theo pulled the sheathed knife out and placed it on Arthur's desk.

"It's unremarkable, really—just a tiny Japanese sword. Nobody would suspect a thing. My research tells me it's called a *kaiken*: a dagger for self-defense or suicide carried mostly by women in feudal Japan. In modern times, it's a trinket reserved for ceremonies. It's often tucked into a woman's kimono and kept in a modest wrap to conceal that it is, in fact, a weapon."

Arthur inspected the black blade that appeared ashamed for being so visible in the daylight. "But like you said, we've only tested the sheath," he continued.

Placing the knife on his desk, he scrutinized the skillfully crafted sheath. He poked the sheath's tip against his desk: nothing but an impotent thud. He touched it to his keyboard and the side of his computer monitor.

"Only works on people, huh?"

"Correct—only bare skin."

"Only living?"

"I haven't been able to confirm that," Theo replied indifferently.

"Be convenient if it could. Does it work separate from the knife? Does the knife have to be in the sheath?"

Theo looked away from Arthur for the first time. "I don't know. I've never used it without the knife in it."

"Does it lose charge over time?"

"Not that I can tell. The longest I've waited between charging it and using it was only eight days. I don't know if it could hold the charge months in advance or indefinitely."

"And the charge time corresponds to the resulting amnesia?"

"Yes."

"One hour of charge erases one hour of a person's memory, right?"

"Yes, if using unguided amnesia. Once charged, touching the end of the sheath to anyone will inflict them with amnesia. They'll forget everything up to that point for however much charge it has. If you guide the amnesia by specifying something, then it will erase the target's memories of that particular concept, thing, or person. I observed about one hour of charge will erase a day's worth of memories of that concept, but I suspect it varies by how many memories the person has of that concept. If you erase something that the target doesn't have a lot of memories of, then it should keep erasing farther back."

"And you can't control where or when it erases memory. It just does?"

"Yes. The moment you touch it to someone, it erases from that moment back as far as it can go."

"And how do you guide it?"

"By saying, in Japanese, what you want to erase when you touch the sheath to the target."

"Has to be in Japanese?"

"Yes."

"It ever talk back in Japanese?"

"No," Theo responded after a brief pause.

Arthur hung on his apparent subterfuge. "I'm serious. Have you ever heard this thing speak? I've heard from at least one source that this might have a mind of its own. That's why I told you to try talking to it in Japanese."

Theo resumed his tempered monotone, saying, "No, I've never heard it speak. In my observation, it can only hear keywords for amnesia. There's no indication it's sentient."

Arthur weighed Theo's words but abandoned the inquiry.

"Can you use the amnesia charge while someone is trapped in it?"

"Yes. It just starts charging again from that point," he replied, remembering erasing Hanna's amnesia with Steve trapped in the sheath.

"Interesting. You tested all of this?"

"Yes, multiple times."

"Ever on yourself?"

"No."

"Really?" Arthur asked with surprise.

"I couldn't risk trapping myself inside it."

Arthur shrugged. "A reasonable precaution. But you could erase anything? As long as you could say it in Japanese, right?"

"Yes."

"You ever have it fail? Ever say something it couldn't figure out?"

"I only picked clear concepts. I won't risk exposure by attempting to erase something overly specific or complex."

"What's something you specified?"

"The target's recollection of their own amnesia."

Arthur frowned, speculating why he would have needed to do that. Theo's pulse surged. He had revealed too much. Arthur continued, unaware or uncaring of his struggle, "You never wanted to erase one of your own memories? Something traumatic? Something embarrassing?"

Silence sufficed for an answer.

Arthur pressed on, "So it can't hold multiple people?"

"No. If someone is in there and you touch the sheath to someone else it will just inflict them with amnesia."

Arthur scrutinized the blade's engravings and asked, "And you tested all of this on your friends?"

Theo's eyes darted around, searching for conviction. "Yes, by interviewing them afterward."

"You interviewed them?"

"In roundabout ways. I had to use people I knew so I could ask about specific memories. I discovered that a lot of memory is dormant until prompted. They didn't notice their amnesia until sometime later after I had erased something specific. Something related would prompt them to remember. Unguided amnesia was harder to explain, since a one- or two-hour gap in someone's immediate memory stands out. I only tested that a couple of times but was able to explain it away."

"And they never found out?"

"I had it planned out well," Theo answered in monotone.

Arthur remained silent, judging Theo.

Theo grew defensive, saying, "We have a device that can erase people's memory. If someone ever suspected they had amnesia and it was connected to me, I'd just erase their suspicion. Even if they did catch on, they would never believe this witchery is real."

"You say you planned things well, but the news is running stories about abductions. People are on edge, looking for some assailant—especially that kid in New Jersey. You attracted a lot of attention nabbing the son of a federal judge. Cable news got wind of it and has been running the story every night. There's a federal investigation open. Kind of exciting, wouldn't you say?"

Theo wiped his sweaty palms on his jeans. "I trapped him Saturday afternoon in his car at Surgite University," he said, his voice as steady as jelly. "There were no witnesses. I moved his car to the train station so it would look like he went into the city. He wasn't—"

"What were you doing at a small Christian college in New Jersey?" Arthur interjected.

"That's where I took care of the translator."

"You were caught on camera, by the way. Nicely done, I say," Arthur said.

Dread left Theo's mouth dry as Arthur typed on his keyboard. He turned his computer monitor to show the news story's video. There was Steve's convertible from the surveillance footage covering the entrance to Surgite's commuter lot.

Theo rushed to defend himself, saying, "That's why I wore his jacket. You can see only my arms through the windshield."

"How did you get his jacket off?"

"Victims are stunned and delirious for a few seconds when they come out of the knife," Theo recalled ambivalently. "By repeatedly trapping and releasing someone, you can keep them stunned. His car's rear seats were secluded enough."

Arthur chortled. "Well, if it works, it works. You should have put the top down. That would have been more fun." He turned his monitor back and asked, "Did you take the train back into the city?"

Theo lied, "Yes," omitting his journey back to Surgite for his motorcycle, through the university's forest preserve. According to campus security, his motorcycle and its rider entered the lot once and left the lot once.

"When did you bring this kid back?"

"Early Monday morning, back in his car. I erased his memory

with the remaining charge." An associated memory of kicking Hanna's foot to wake her up surfaced.

"Why'd he have a fat lip when they found him?"

"There . . . was a struggle on Saturday."

"Liar. You socked him Monday morning, probably before he regained consciousness."

Theo glared back at Arthur.

"Don't act like you didn't," Arthur scolded. "If there was a struggle on Saturday, that busted lip would not have been fresh. We know that people trapped in the sheath are going somewhere. They are asleep and time is passing wherever the hell they go, but they are somewhere. The blood would have been dry and the swelling reduced, if it had happened Saturday."

Theo had no defense. Arthur's cutting voice brought his attention back. "This Steve kid didn't remember anything while he was trapped, obviously, but how much of his memory before his abduction did you erase?"

"It was unguided amnesia, so the same duration he was in the knife, but minus the charge used to erase the translator's memory. It was about fifteen hours of charge. Fifteen hours back from about two o'clock on Saturday meant he effectively forgot everything that happened that Saturday."

"Convenient, isn't it?" Arthur remarked. "The sheath knows to delete a victim's memory starting before they enter the sheath and are unconscious."

Arthur leaned forward and inspected the knife on his desk. "Who could have made this?"

Theo did not answer. Arthur resumed his interrogation with, "The release is in the sheath's belt loop?"

"Yes, it moves. Pulling on it releases a trapped victim instantly and randomly."

"Randomly, you say?"

"They don't come back the same way every time. Wherever

they are coming from, it looks like black lines are carrying them out of a hazy white and purple light."

"Do they come back hurt?"

"No, just worn out. I believe the sheath is drawing power off them somehow and that's what supplies the energy for the amnesia."

"During your testing, you charged this and released those people without using the amnesia on them?"

"Yes," Theo answered, wiping his sweaty palms on his jeans again.

"Well, you'll have fun now running around abducting people with the authorities on alert—at least near that college in New Jersey," Arthur said, keeping up the tempo as if sensing his weakness. "What if you pull the release with nobody inside?"

"Nothing happens."

Arthur pulled the belt loop to no effect.

"And finally, what does the knife do?"

"Nothing, possibly," Theo said.

"No, it does something," Arthur asserted. "It has to. The inscription says right on it that the person trapped inside will take the memories of taking a life. I'm thinking we need to have someone trapped inside the sheath and then use the knife for real."

Theo fidgeted uncomfortably. "You mean kill someone?"

"What else is a knife like this for?" Arthur asked, fed by Theo's anxious expression.

"Test it," Arthur commanded.

"I can't do that."

"Why not?"

"It would be complicated."

"You want to know the truth behind this, don't you?"

"Yes."

"You have what it takes to find out, don't you?"

"Yes."

Arthur's eyes, those wild eyes that hooked into their prey, bore into him again. Theo stared back into them, refusing to show weakness. Twisted creativity lurked in that mind. Images of knives plunging into necks were circling behind those eyes, prominent and unobscured by Arthur's short-cropped hair. Arthur broke the standoff by picking up the sheath. He casually tossed it to Theo, who frantically caught it.

"Test the sheath without the knife. I'll keep the knife here and think of something." Arthur stowed the knife in a locked drawer in his desk and put back on his shop apron.

Arthur escorted Theo out of his office and through the shop's clutter of tables. Browsing customers and the spry part time cashier took little notice of them. Theo zipped up his jacket, the sheath safely hidden inside. "Next steps," Arthur reiterated as Theo passed through the door onto the gusty sidewalk.

Alone, Theo exhaled and wiped the sweat off his brow. A text message from his father updated him, saying his service appointment at the motorcycle dealership was still on time.

Nothing from Hanna greeted him. They had spoken Monday night when he returned her call. Their spring break plans were canceled. Tuesday, she called to discuss Steve's mysterious disappearance and the increased security on campus. Today, Wednesday, she texted him early to say she was not sure when their next meeting could be.

I knew this would happen, he thought. She had grown tired of him. Spending the night probably erased her esteem for him. Their affair had run its course. He had called her that morning about seeing her, but she declined, citing midterms. Thoughts of the inevitable end of their relationship clawed at him. He fired up the motorcycle.

Riding through the winding shaded streets of Tarrytown, Theo's mind worked on Arthur's problem. *I could just catch and release someone in their sleep. They'd never know and that would test if the sheath worked separated from the knife. I'm done testing the amnesia. I know how it works.* The only person he could see sleeping, though, slammed the door in his mind's eye, saying she was busy. Dread for their relationship sickened him again as he merged onto the highway and plunged toward Manhattan.

Wednesday's two classes were already done. Other than homework, all that remained was driving Mia to the motorcycle dealership in New Jersey to pick up his father. Inevitable traffic slowed his return. A car behind him seemed to mimic his every move. Was it the same car as earlier? He cursed his forgetfulness. He rushed the motorcycle back into the parking garage near his apartment. The car following him was gone. Theo hurried through parking the motorcycle and stowing his gear in Mia's trunk. He reached for Mia's door handle. A voice behind him called, "It's a shame, really."

Theo violently turned to locate the voice. A tall figure stepped out from behind a resident's parked car. Theo reached for the sheath.

"Relax. I just want to talk. I know Arthur," the man added.

Theo's hand remained clutching the sheath inside his jacket. Taking two steps closer, the tall man continued, "And I believe you do too."

Theo watched him raise his hands to show they concealed nothing. His expression was pleasant and professional.

The man said, "I didn't mean to surprise you, but it looks like you are leaving in a hurry. I wanted to introduce myself. I'm Greg."

"You followed me?"

"It's unfortunate, but the only way I could reach you away from Arthur. I'm parked outside. Arthur is unaware of this conversation, just as I was unaware of you until recently."

Greg gingerly lowered his hands back to his sides. Theo remained tense. Greg said, "I understand Arthur has you running errands, researching a Japanese knife, one that's all black and inscribed with some kind of mysterious wording. Is that correct?"

Fear surged in Theo. Greg filled the silence with, "Do you actually have the knife?"

Taking a steadying breath, Theo fought to stay calm. "How do you know Arthur? What do you want?"

"I work with Arthur in his store. I'm his business partner and he's recently let me in on his secret project. Quite the venture," Greg answered. He stepped closer until he was just a couple paces away.

"There. Now we don't have to raise our voices," he said in the garage's artificial light. Theo monitored him as he explained, "Arthur wants to use the knife's power to make a true otherworldly product and experience in our Memory Therapy line. Yet he has you slinking around in the dark abducting people? Turning them into amnesiacs? Is it true that it makes them disappear in a flash?"

Theo held his dry, unsteady tongue.

"Don't worry. Arthur's already told me. I want to know why he's having you do these abductions."

"It has to be tested."

"Do you really want to be risking your life like this?"

Theo remained silent. Greg prompted him with, "You don't fear The Makers?"

"How do you know about them? Arthur said they aren't real."

"He is under the impression they are just a superstition, but I don't think so. Where else did that knife come from? Power like this doesn't just drop out of the sky. What if they're real? What if they find you?"

Theo studied Greg's troubled, almost caring, expression. Greg continued, "Do you have the knife?"

"No. Arthur has it," Theo answered, but hurled back, "How long have you been selling trinkets with Arthur?"

"I used to manage a bookstore up the Hudson, but met Arthur one day and he told me about the lucrative world of alternative medicinal remedies. He bought some books from me, kept coming back, and mentioned he was looking for a business partner. I joined him. Antiaging crystals and creams kept our lights on, but Arthur really found something this time."

"Where did he find it?"

"I wish I knew." Greg wore a pleasant smile and continued, "But what I do know is that he's found something real. What I want to know is what you want."

Invited by Greg's understanding expression, Theo said, "I need to know where this power came from and why. If that leads me to The Makers, so be it."

Greg assumed a censuring posture. "You wouldn't want to look too hard. From what I've heard, you'll end up at the bottom of a river."

"But killing people is complicated. It creates evidence. It raises questions. People notice," Theo replied earnestly.

Greg chuckled. "People notice. No wonder Arthur picked you."

It occurred to Theo that Greg may have easily been twice his age. His overgrown stubble and relaxed demeanor befitted a benevolent bookshop owner. Greg spoke in a caring, familiar tone.

"We're talking about a secretive society of unknown size and unknown means that could have existed for centuries. They could have other unworldly items or could pull the right strings to make someone's murder remain negligently unsolved. That's assuming there's just one secret society. There could be more. We just don't know."

Theo found himself nodding in agreement before quickly raising his guard again.

"Look, I shouldn't keep you any longer. You're probably already late to wherever you're going, and my car is probably getting towed. I just wanted to introduce myself. You're not alone in this. You can talk to me in confidence."

Greg reached for a handshake.

An icy sense of foreboding settled in Theo's gut. His shoulders tensed.

"Never follow me again," said Theo.

Greg nodded. "Of course. That's perfectly reasonable."

Theo inspected Greg's extended hand before hesitantly reaching out with his own. Greg's handshake was warm and affirming.

"I'll see you around," he said, turning for the exit, but stopped. He faced Theo and raised his finger, saying, "Just one more thing."

Theo met his inquisitive look with his own.

"You're young. You don't want to get wrapped up in this. What about your family? Your friends?"

"There's nothing for me here," Theo answered bitterly.

Greg nodded and left.

Theo sat in Mia's driver's seat and closed the door. He stuffed the key into the ignition. Several strained moments passed. Only his labored breathing broke the silence. His heart pounded. His fists shook. His anger exploded.

"*You idiot*!" he roared at himself.

"You could have died!"

He pounded his fist against the passenger seat.

"You didn't even realize you were being followed!"

His fist turned to himself. He yelled, through gritted teeth, "You were completely unaware!"

Theo stopped, hearing only his frantic breaths. He grabbed his skull and tried to crush it. He yelled incoherently and slammed the steering wheel. Then stillness. Self-loathing for his childish outburst followed.

Theo started the car. Reassuming his composure like donning armor, he calmly adjusted the center mirror and drove out of the garage.

Sunny weather and light traffic graced his drive to New Jersey. Expectation for some call or message preoccupied him. Nothing came. Mia executed his inputs with predictable poise. He exited the highway knowing he would be late. The thought to abandon the exit and remain on the interstate tempted him. Farther down its open lanes was Surgite. He fantasized about seeing her, but instead continued onto the local road to the dealership.

A few other riders impatient with winter had also journeyed to the dealership. His father's Italian bike stood out in the crowd. The undertail exhaust, lipstick-red fairings, uselessly low windshield, toylike painted frame, and aggressively low handlebars demanded attention anywhere the bike went. Mia's silver curves looked modest parked next to it.

Theo walked inside to find his father embellishing track stories with the dealership staff. Theo wondered what the point was. His father caught his approach and bid farewell to his hapless audience.

"What took you so long?" his father asked in a jovial voice.

"Traffic."

"None on the bike—smooth riding all the way here."

"There was a car accident," Theo answered in a dejected mumble.

Mr. Jansen led his son back outside to the car. Theo surrendered Mia's key and his father carefully stowed his colorful riding gear in the trunk. He took the driver's seat. Theo crumpled into the passenger seat, exhausted. His father whipped Mia back onto the road and merged onto the interstate with gusto. Mia was pleased. Cruising back to the apartment, his father asked, "You seem down. Hungry?"

"Just tired. Midterms and all."

"I remember those not so fondly." He chuckled. "You'll do fine if you don't overthink it."

"Dad," he asked, "When are we going to ride together? You said we would when we got the two fifty."

His father's plastic smile dropped. He regripped the steering wheel as if unsure of himself. "We will, Theo. This spring," he said, feigning sincerity. "I'm getting my bike inspected—new tires too." He repeated, as if to convince himself, "We'll get out there.

I'll have my bike back this weekend. We'll figure something out. I mean, it's still February."

He listened to his father's words—words he had heard before. Every time he had asked, he received a similar answer. It struck Theo to ask just one more time before he never asked again.

THIRTEEN

HANNA DEPRESSED the piano's key. Its sole note cried out in the silence of the empty living room. Spring break was passing uneventfully in her family's home. Her mother had made her abscond from Surgite the Friday afternoon spring break began, whisking her away in the family SUV. Chores were not Hanna's delight. Her sister, Lily, would come back from King's and slink away to her room. Her father came home after dinner, sought solitary shelter from the three women in his life, and left before Hanna awoke. Hanna was keeping holiday hours. The rest of the household maintained their punctual routines. Her mother assiduously kept a full schedule despite her recent spell of unemployment. Only the cat, affectionately named Koushka, was grateful for Hanna's unoccupied attention. Mostly, Hanna just wasted away in her room checking her phone and procrastinating her homework.

In the quiet of Wednesday afternoon, she played a single minor chord. Its somber declaration darkened the empty house. Her green journal sat on the piano's sill. Her unbroken memories for the past two weeks had been consistently unremarkable. Since coming home she had only spoken to her family, Emma, and had some chance interactions on Friend Link. In the absence of her university life, she found herself clicking through the traveling updates or partying victories of her spring-breaking classmates. It sickened her how much time she spent doing so. The website's consistent reminders for her to verify her identity upon logging in irked her. Hanna speculated she had logged in from Surgite's library computers too often and confused it.

Frustration suspended her listless playing. *Why can't I play something beautiful and perfect?* she thought. She banged another minor chord. The upright piano's strings resonated through the entire house. The piano had often been useful for discovering such untold feelings. A mirror just showed the cheery face her parents had inculcated her to show the world. It was rude to inconvenience others with one's problems.

Hanna scowled at the nearby window. The neighbor's snowy lawn drenched in sunlight mocked her. Stabbing a song to life, her right foot pedaled her adaptation of the metal tune into a vigorous creation. Just a three-chord harmony, but she summoned their agony. Harder, she pressed on the keys. Faster, her right hand added returns to the root key. Deeper, her head moved with the tempo. Improvisations of the melody blossomed. She added flourishes and hammered expression from the keys.

"Mom doesn't like that music," a judgmental voice said next to her.

Hanna yelped, thoroughly spooked. Lily stood next to her.

"You're back early," Hanna replied, flustered.

"You can hear it from outside," Lily coolly remarked, dropping her backpack on the carpet.

Seeing her sister in her own school uniform from just a year prior still befuddled Hanna. Lily sat next to her, nudging her over despite their similarity in size. Lily's expertly painted fingernails assumed the upper half of the keyboard. A touching flurry of notes poured out of the piano. Raised an octave, they resembled transient gusts of a snowstorm crafting its snowflakes into an ethereal veil.

"Franz Liszt, 'Un Sospiro.' I get it," Hanna said, unimpressed. Hanna waved Lily's hands away and assumed control of the lower half of the keyboard. Like a cloud pulled over a sunny day, her despondent notes pooled into the house, drowning the joy from it; the Popov living room was transformed into a wake.

Lily protested, "You hold the notes too long. Quit adding so many grace notes."

Hanna stopped and answered, "'Prelude in E Minor' is meant to express pain."

Lily's hands assumed their place on the keyboard again. She budged Hanna farther off the bench and took control of the entire keyboard. Ire roused the keys, producing a tempest of violent outcries. Her notes swirled like hornets. The song roared at Hanna, who feigned disinterest at the veritable Gatling gun of fire from Lily's hands. Lily missed a key. She reset and attempted again, only to fail again. With a frustrated grunt, she withdrew her hands and abandoned the effort.

Hanna assumed a casual tone, saying, "Yes, we all know you can play Chopin's 'Etude Opus Ten, Number Four.' You don't have to show off all the time."

"It's about perfection," Lily declared, burning the keys with her stare. Hanna nudged Lily back to her side and took the entire keyboard. In sweet passion, she brought to life a cherished song: Mozart's "Turkish March." She skipped ahead to the tune's festive concluding measures. The living room morphed into a celebration as she drilled the keys in allegro joy. She returned to the ending measure but withheld the melody. Her sister watched in anticipation. Hanna closed her eyes and let the wind of her passion take the sail of the melody.

Lily grabbed her right hand midflight.

"Stop changing it! 'Turkish March' doesn't go like that!"

Hanna flashed a devious grin and played it as a ragtime tune. Lily stood and yelled, "I'm telling Mom!"

Hanna ceased her torture and said, "Alright, alright, but what's the point of music if not to express your heart?"

"Just express what the composer wrote. The sheet tells you how to play it."

"Not completely—you know that. There's always a little interpretation. Why not expand on their ideas?"

Lily lounged on a nearby chair, twirling her similarly dark but longer hair. "If you wanted to do that, do it with your own songs. They're all the same anyway."

Hanna burst out, "*Have you even heard them*!"

An unphased Lily left her question unanswered. Hanna skulked in the silence—the keys unperturbed by her shrill eruption. She began an unsteady harmony. Clemency reverberated back through the keys and His path of forgiveness dawned on her. The unsteady harmony found its way to a long-remembered hymn. The notes rejoiced singing His praise. Hanna's shoulders retreated from their tense shrug. Lily soon joined in her choir voice. Hanna concluded the brief praise and Lily remarked, aloud, "*Spasi gospodi lyudi tvoya.* Grandma would be happy."

Hanna began the hymn again, but an improvisation took the melody in a new direction.

"Ugh. You always change it and make it like all your songs," Lily spat.

Hanna dropped the melody but maintained the lento harmony, saying, "The heart has many facets. Each song is a mix of emotions, never just one. Sometimes bittersweet is just the beginning of seemingly contrary emotions happening all at the same time. Something as nuanced as love, for example, would require a whole concerto to touch upon just one expression of it. It pulls you. Your heart aches and you wish it would stop. It hurts, yet it hurts to ignore it too. It's scary how much it could hurt you, but nonetheless, you're drawn to it."

"You always talk like things are so grandiose and dramatic," Lily said dully, adding, "There's a hole in your jacket, by the way."

Hanna turned to see Lily folding back the end of her sleeve, showing the torn silky material.

"It's just the liner. Nobody can see it," Hanna said, returning her attention to the piano.

"Mom says we're not buying new school uniforms. I have to keep this through senior year too," she said, pouting. "Stupid hand-me-downs."

It'll pass, Hanna thought to herself. The living room grew still, until Hanna felt the cat brush against her legs. "Aww, Koushka," she and Lily both said while Hanna petted the cat's arched back. She reached for another pet of Koushka's magnificent coat, but she sauntered off to Lily, who flipped closed her cell phone and uncrossed her legs. The cat jumped up onto her lap. Hanna looked on with jealousy.

"Mom must be coming home soon. We're gonna look at schools this Friday," Lily smugly announced, scratching behind the purring cat's ears.

"Can you drop me off at Surgite? I could go back early."

"We're not going there. I know I can do better—most of King's could."

"You know I got an academic scholarship at Surgite. It's like half off and in-state."

"Again, most of King's could," Lily fired back sardonically.

Hanna frowned. "Why are you such a brat all the time?"

"Look in a mirror."

Hanna heard the white SUV pull into the driveway. She watched her mother step out of the inoffensive car, with its rounded edges, soft curves, and unremarkable driving experience. Learning to drive in it had been taxing but difficult to remember, like a bad dream not ending in mortal peril. She thought of the stark contrast between it and the motorcycle in her life. That egg on wheels was her only way back to Surgite, save for some miracle that her father could take her back earlier than Sunday afternoon. The family was fond of reminding her about the dent she put in its rear bumper. It had been predictably christened "Hanna's Dent."

Their mother came through the front door. The cat leaped off

Lily at once and Lily called over, "Mom, Hanna's messing with the classics again."

Koushka swirled around her, crying imploring meows for food.

"Won't you play nice with your sister, Hanna? We haven't seen you in two months," their mother said, placing her keys on the kitchen counter. Lily swirled around her, now joining Koushka in cries for food. Hanna grabbed her green journal and escaped to her room. Emma would be over shortly.

Theo had requested Hanna's help in asking Emma to play with his guild. "Just once. That's all," he had emphasized to Hanna over the phone on the Wednesday that had been lambasted by midterms. That was the last time they had carried a conversation. A week had passed since. Hanna paced her humble room, phone and journal in hand. She tossed the disheveled pile of notebooks and colored pens on her desk onto her unmade bed. The walk from Emma's house was not long.

After meeting Emma at the door and Emma graciously greeting Mrs. Popov, she took her friend back to her room. Lily and Koushka evaporated at the presence of guests. Mrs. Popov offered Emma sweet tea and pie, but she politely declined on the pretense that such a reward was only appropriate after she completed her homework with Hanna.

"Your mom's gonna make me fat," Emma said behind Hanna's closed bedroom door.

Hanna giggled. "She's just encouraging you to make me study."

"Welp, too bad because first we gotta play video games with Theo's imaginary friends."

Hanna clicked her tongue in disapproval.

"It sure was nice of him to buy the game for me," Emma remarked, placing her laptop on Hanna's desk.

"He takes his game seriously. I think his guildmates are his only friends," Hanna reflected aloud, sitting on her bed.

"Isn't that kind of sad?" Emma asked, plugging the ethernet cable into her laptop.

Hanna's phone was already back in her hand as she answered, "I know, right?"

It showed no updates. Hanna sighed. "His silence is getting to me. He hasn't called me back all this week. I wonder if he's okay."

"Where did you leave things with him?" Emma asked, opening her laptop.

Hanna watched Emma boot up the video game. "I told him we'd meet at Surgite after spring break. I want to show him my green journal again. It was fun talking about it together last time. He sounded really down after I told him I couldn't go into the city. Then I got busy with midterms. Then spring break happens and he can't come here."

"I take it you're still keeping him on the down low?"

"They'd just yell at me if I told them about him," Hanna said in defeat. "Focus on your studies," she said, imitating her father's deep voice.

"He should understand that. He has midterms too," Emma said, clicking her mouse.

"I was looking at the possible grades I can still get based on my midterms. The margins will be pretty slim to keep my scholarship."

Emma turned to her from Hanna's chair. "Are you sure a simple conversation with him wouldn't clear this up?"

Hanna sat on her bed, holding her knees to her chin. "It would if he'd answer. He gets moody like this sometimes. He disappears and overthinks things. He says actions convey more than words anyway, but what am I supposed to do?"

"You can't stop thinking about him, huh?"

"I'm human, Emma, and my condition is need."

Emma turned back to her screen. "Well, he'll remember Valentine's Day and come back. You two seem like you've been going steady for a while now." She noticed Hanna's lack of reply and offered, as a change of subject, "Plus there's still a whole second half of the semester to go. There should be plenty of time to work on your grades."

"Yeah. It feels like a job," Hanna said, having never held one. Trapped by thoughts of a cold and distant Theo, she carelessly chose her words. Only Theo would demand such precision.

Ignited, Emma said, "See, wouldn't it be great to have an athletic scholarship instead? All my brothers have to do is play soccer to keep theirs. They can't believe I treat studying like it's my job."

Hanna nodded. "Totally."

The talk of jobs made her recall her mother losing her book-keeping job in December. Uncertainty about affording Surgite came into focus, though her mother would never discuss the subject directly. A wave of despondence pushed her spirits lower.

"Demon World Online," Emma said, her boisterous voice ending Hanna's trance. Looking at the title screen, she read aloud, "A boundless realm of mystic adventures, blah blah blah." Emma clicked through the screens, mumbling, "Just let me make a char-acter and get on with it. Oh God, they're making me choose a side."

"Make sure to pick the one Theo's guild is on," Hanna cried out.

"Okay, which one?"

"I don't know."

"Well, then, ask him."

"I told you he isn't answering. I hate calling someone and they don't call back." Hanna continued, sounding wounded. "He hasn't answered since Friday."

"I'll just pick one and if it's wrong I can remake the character," Emma said, pleasantly moving past the larger issue.

Oblivious, Hanna said, "It hurt to call him and cancel our spring break plans. He sounded so . . . like I was breaking up with him. I tried discussing the abductions and my parents' decision, but he suddenly had no interest. He withdrew further the last time we talked, giving pretty much one-word answers. Something's bothering him."

Hanna stared at the lilac earrings on her nightstand. Emma broke the silence with, "Hey, Juliet, I'm in. What's his guild's name?"

Hanna lay on her back with her hands behind her head. "I forget. I should have written it down. Can you look up players?"

"Yeah. Shoot."

"Look up Ray. R-A-Y-G-U-N-Z-Z. Ray is the guild leader, apparently," Hanna said, remembering a conversation she had with Theo. He spelled it out the same way for her. She missed his professorial voice.

"Not Theo?" Emma asked, typing as directed.

"He's some high-ranking official in it. I don't get it, but it sounds important."

"Heh. Boys." Emma chuckled. "Ooh, things are happening. He's inviting me to his party."

Emma put on her headset. Hanna put on her spectacles and watched Emma's screen intently from the safety of her bed. Emma's red demon sorceress stood in a sunny glen teeming with wildflowers. Before her stood four other players, suddenly still at her presence.

"That looks like all of them. They're just standing there," Emma said, perplexed.

Hanna leaped from her bed. "Oh my God, is Theo there?" She rushed to Emma's side and held her face close to the laptop's screen.

"I don't know. I can't hear anything. Is this thing on?" Emma answered, adjusting her headset. She glanced at Hanna. "Ew, you still wear those uggo glasses?"

"Theo likes them," Hanna said while interpreting the screen's copious game information.

Emma asked, "Don't you know his in-game name?"

"No, just that he's a Grand Inquisitor, whatever that means. Put your mouse on them. Does it say their title? Isn't there a chat box? Why can't you hear them? You accepted their invitation, right? Is your mic on?"

In feigned anger, Emma shot back, "Slow down! I started playing this five seconds ago."

Hanna exclaimed, "Come on! He could be here."

Emma opened the menu. "Alright, alright. Let's see . . . uh . . . there. That's who's in my party." She scanned the names in the menu and burst out laughing.

"What? What is it?" Hanna asked, confused.

Emma's whole body convulsed with hearty laughs. She struggled for breath. Hanna looked for clues, but to no avail. Emma saw the screen again and howled in great fits of laughing squeaks. She smacked her hand on the desk and Hanna demanded an explanation. She wiped away tears and pointed to the usernames on the list.

Hanna stood up in disgust. "Oh, come on. Really?"

Coming down off her euphoric high, Emma whined, "Ah, cheese and rice, I'm so sorry. It's beyond stupid. I mean . . ." She began another sentence but could only wheeze.

Hanna shook her by the shoulders and Emma asked, "Those are really his friends? Death Grip On My Blank? Clapping Cheeks two-four-seven? Two-D-G-F-Four-Me? He hangs out with these guys?"

Anger tensed Hanna's sweaty hands into fists. "You're sure Theo's not on that list, right?"

Emma shook her head. "Goddamn, I haven't laughed like this since I met Broc. Nah, there's no Grand Inquisitor in this list. I like the Descended Necromancer, though."

Hanna and Emma spotted a message on screen. "Necro, say something! They like you!"

An embarrassed hush fell over them. Hanna's face burned with shame. Emma was a nice shade of tomato as well.

Another message appeared with the name *DeathGripOnMy_* before it. "What? You'd laugh harder if you saw me in person?" it said.

Hanna stared, both repulsed and intrigued. Emma covered her mouth, suppressing giggles.

"So he's not there," Hanna said, heading for her bed.

"Wait! Wait! Come back. They're talking now."

Hanna trudged back and held her ear close to Emma's headset. She faintly heard an argument. Outraged voices rebuked Ray for not speaking first.

"Hey! Easy there, deputy," Emma bemoaned to Hanna who was leaning her head against hers. Hanna's mouth hung open as she strained to hear the heated conversation.

A shout came through: "But you were supposed to talk first! That's what we decided."

Another voice, presumably Ray's, answered, "You all just sat there in silence too!"

"We had no idea there'd be two of them," a new player vociferously chimed in. "Dude, the first thing I heard on my headset was two girls arguing so I stayed on mute! We were all waiting for you to say something. What the hell do we do now?"

One moaned, then said, "The flowchart I made is scrap now. All that planning and we blew it in the first few seconds."

"Like always," another said.

A cantankerous voice stated, "We'll have to modify the script. We can stay here in the Valley of Achelous, but the parts about items just for her isn't going to make sense anymore."

"Guys, we can roll with this. Act natural," Ray said, taking control.

They all fell silent. Hanna kept her head pressed to Emma's, struggling to comprehend that these nervous voices were Theo's compatriots. Emma began a tepid, "Er . . . guys . . ." but was interrupted by a sudden voice, saying, "Both girls are breathing on the same mic."

A second voice followed immediately with, "God, I wish I were that mic."

Another rushed to say, "I still can't believe there are two of them."

Emma shot back, "Ew. Back off, mouth breathers."

Hanna interrupted their exchange with, "Hey, um, hi."

All four voices answered, "Hi," in a simultaneous ripple. Still unable to believe what was happening, Hanna carried on, "Do any of you, um, know where Theo is? What's his username?"

"Theodolite one-three-four," several voices chimed back.

"You sound like angels," said a different, nasally voice.

"Aw, thank you," they replied in unison.

Several concurring voices joined to bolster the assertion while one endured a fit of coughing. He muted his microphone to conceal his escalating struggle for air. Hanna looked at Emma, wondering if their response had inflicted something upon him. Emma shrugged and looked back at the screen.

Hanna pressed her head against Emma's. "You guys haven't seen Theo?" she asked, concerned.

"No," Ray said, a natural leader to this crew. "He hasn't been online recently."

"Isn't he usually?" Hanna asked.

"All the time, really. He's max level in the current game and has all the best gear and items. He's never missed a raid . . . except once. We invited him here today too," Ray answered sincerely.

Another voice added, "We still can't believe he got two of his girlfriend's friends to join."

"Oh, really?" Hanna said in sudden realization. "What does he say about his girlfriend?"

"No, no, no. No, you don't," Emma cut in. "Hanna here is Theo's girlfriend."

They all gasped.

"Hey, I'm here too, ya know," Emma barked.

"You can yell at me if you want," one of the voices pleaded.

Hanna pulled her head away in amused disbelief. Emma looked at the screen, enjoying her captive audience. "So, uh, what do you want me to yell at you about?"

Hanna returned to her bed and the notebooks scattered on it. The green journal on top hungered for another entry. Instead, she took her purple pen and sketched the beginnings of a plan.

"Hey, they're giving me a ton of free stuff. I have, like, way OP items now," Emma called over gleefully.

"Yeah, they seem nice. Gross, but nice," Hanna answered, busy with her plans. Time was running out.

Emma's one-hour session had been extended to two. Hanna heard Emma answering their pleas for her to join another time. She teased them with the possibility and finally logged off. A much-needed review of calculus followed. Emma kept her word.

At her departure, Mrs. Popov insisted she take some of her homemade pumpkin pie. Emma graciously accepted it.

Outside, on the front patio, Emma said, "Hey, um, don't drive yourself crazy over Mr. Elusive. If anything, you seem more focused now."

"Do you really think so? Do you think I'm less forgetful?" Hanna asked nonchalantly in the evening light.

"I dunno, maybe? You keep that journal now. That helps, I'm sure. It's like you were losing your mind when you were seeing Theo every weekend."

Hanna frowned, gloom shadowing her previously cheery disposition.

Emma backpedaled, waving her hands, "Don't think too much about it. No big deal, right? You were probably just under a lot of stress."

Hanna rubbed her chin. "Do you think I should bring my journal with me every time I see him now?"

"If you think it'll help."

Hanna said, "Okay, I will."

Emma saluted her and departed. Hanna returned to her room,

where contemplation awaited.

She began pacing. *It's true*, she thought, *I seem to be less forgetful. Is it just a coincidence that I haven't seen him recently? I haven't had a random episode of forgetfulness like last semester.* Hanna stopped her pacing. She snatched her green journal and flipped to its early entries, which became magnified by her spectacles. *The abductions have been bothering me, of course, but why do I remember going to the campus clinic? I can't remember why.* A scan of the early pages revealed nothing about the campus clinic. Her memory drew the building, the cold nurse, and her sprint to the piano. But what was it about? The discussion in that examination room escaped her recollection.

Further, she flipped through the pages. Almost every one bore a comment or reminder to, "Tell Theo."

"Share with Theo."

"Don't forget."

"But why? What was I trying to tell myself?" Hanna asked aloud to her silent, empty bedroom. Her stuffed animals gazed back at her quizzically. She lay sprawled out on her bed. Theo's was softer. *We went over my journal together the last time I saw him. I know I wanted a record if I ended up abducted somehow,* she thought. She flipped to the entry regarding that evening together. Then her pupils widened. Faster, she read the pages. Briskly, her hands swept to the next page of her jagged handwriting. Again, she tore to the next page. She sat up.

Her pupils narrowed on the entry from their evening together. *Why do all the entries after that day have nothing about telling Theo? But all the ones before are covered in reminders to tell him? I told him about everything and then just forgot? Did I tell him about the clinic? Is Emma right that I was losing it when I was seeing him all the time?* Hanna's heart worked fervently in her chest. Her jaw found itself clenched, her brow, pressed into an interrogative arc. Hanna flipped open her phone: still nothing from him. He would know. A passionate gumption stirred her to motion.

She made for the kitchen, where she found her mother starting preparations for dinner.

"Mom, I was thinking I want to go back to Surgite early—like, tomorrow."

Her mother cocked her head back, confounded. "But why, sweetie? You have everything you need here. You brought all your books, didn't you?"

"I can't concentrate here. I haven't gotten nearly as much done as I thought I would."

Her mother nodded. "You have been sleeping in a lot."

Hanna seized the foothold. "Maybe Daddy can take me back tomorrow on his way to work? It's on the way, isn't it?"

Her mother shook her head. "Not exactly. And we still need to sit down and talk about your grades and what you're doing this summer."

"Can we talk about it tonight?" Hanna asked eagerly.

Her mother turned from her cutting board, knife in hand. "I say, aren't you in a hurry?"

"I just want to study hard and do the right thing," Hanna said, washing vegetables for her mother to cut. *I'll win with kindness,* she thought.

Her mother paused her industrious dicing to say, "I suppose we could if your father isn't working late again."

Hanna nodded, sure of victory.

Clearly eavesdropping, Lily entered the kitchen and said, "*Ya goloden,*" in a thick accent. *Did she have to say she's hungry like that,* thought Hanna.

Her mother shot back, "Y'all are insatiable. And why are you talking like your grandmother's visiting?"

Lily swung another sentence of Russian. Their mother surrendered the last of her homemade pumpkin pie.

"*Spasibo,*" they both said, each taking their winnings and bowing away.

Evening could not leave fast enough. Hanna played the dutiful daughter, helping her mother finish dinner preparations, though she was mostly relegated to cleanup. All three Popov women gravitated to the front door, hearing Mr. Popov's gray sedan pull into the driveway. The modest single-story Popov house was full of wondrous home cooking when he unlocked the front door at seven thirty. Hanna ambushed him first, having the most to request. He looked softer and pudgier than Hanna remembered. Having two teenage daughters had taken its toll on him. His time was brief and precious. She brought up her early return to Surgite immediately, to which he answered, "No. Why?"

Hanna pressed but he dismissed it, deferring to her mother. Mrs. Popov approached, demanding a review of Hanna's semester. Hanna agreed that the review should happen right away.

Mr. Popov adjusted his round spectacles and rubbed his black-and-white scruff of a beard.

"I suppose we could discuss it after dinner," he said.

Dinner passed with Lily's successes dominating the conversation. Hanna cleaned up afterward and found Lily cheerfully recounting her recitals at King's to their father. He enjoyed her stories of triumph and accomplishment. Hanna dragged him back to the table, where her mother was waiting. Lily disappeared to her room, where Koushka lounged, unamused.

Sitting beside her mother, both of their arms folded, it dawned on her how much she resembled her—save for that unforgettable accent.

Across from them, Mr. Popov began, "We should probably think about what you'll do this summer. There is also the matter of your grades."

"She's not studying enough. Tell her she needs our help to focus," her mother implored.

"I can't concentrate here. I need to go back to Surgite tomorrow," Hanna insisted.

Mr. Popov's eyebrows rose at the opening arguments. "I'll put on some coffee," he said solemnly.

FOURTEEN

WAVES LAPPED against the jagged coast. March's unforgiving wind pinned helpless seagulls against the sky before sweeping them away. Dawn's light beamed like an insult. The grass had given up waiting for spring and resembled a patchwork of beige and hopeless green. A couple walking their dog pretended not to notice him. Theo sat on a platform of stone amid dozens of similar perches. Next to him rested his helmet. It stared blankly across the Sound at Long Island. Behind him meandered a walking path through an oft-traveled wood. The saltwater not far below looked pleasant: gentle, gray, and capable of swallowing people whole. They could disappear in it. Nobody would know.

Artificial, he thought. *Those waves could never carve these boulders. The sand over there is trucked in. What a lie it is.*

The thought drew a smirk out of him.

"Like you can talk," he mumbled.

Speaking was an effort. He had not done so for several days. Sometimes he reminded himself he still could, even if just to himself. The relentless natural beauty pacified his gloom. Come spring, the town would require residents to show purchased tags for access. Nonresidents were simply not welcome. The resident he knew flashed in his memory. Six years had passed. He wondered if he would even recognize her.

Probably her voice, he thought.

A seagull landed nearby, demanding food. He waved it away. It refused, hopping closer to his stone precipice.

"You know what you want. It's easy for you. Your brain is so small," he said to it. The seagull twitched and shrieked. Upward it soared. Theo watched it ascend.

"You're free but can't even appreciate it," he said in parting.

Theo picked up his helmet. He held it before him looking at its nonjudgmental face. His reflection morosely greeted him in its tinted face shield.

What do you really want?

A longing wrenched his heart. His hands returned the helmet to the stone. He reached beneath the armor of his jacket to a hidden pocket.

Silly faces. You're pathetic, falling for it, Theo thought, staring at the five pictures of Hanna and himself from the purikura booth. Seeing her smile eased his lips into their own gentle curve. She had posted it to her Friend Link page. Reading the speculative comments made him want to reply in her defense about this Mr. Elusive—her Mr. Elusive. Only the fact that he was logged in as her stopped him. He resolved to minimize logging in, especially given that she may notice the remote access, but found himself checking it frequently anyway.

Then how do you tell her? he asked himself.

Theo pocketed the photograph and felt the sheath in his jacket.

How do you tell her who you are?

A thought to cast it into the unforgiving waters below called to him. Memories of Greg in the parking garage crushed the fantasy. "They'd find me—then her," he mumbled.

Theo imagined the gray waters swallowing him up.

She'd cry a lot but eventually move on.

"Would she, though?" he asked himself. Theo covered his eyes with his icy hand. *Why'd you let this happen? You messed it all up —just like your cello.*

Theo had been counting on their inevitable break up. Nothing mattered last autumn. Why she stayed remained a mystery. Why he wanted to tell her about the knife confounded him more. He remembered how sweet she looked lying next to him, propped up on her elbow. She waited on his every word, biting her bottom lip or leaving her supple lips parted, ready to breathe sugary replies.

The recollection momentarily lifted his despondent trance. How Hanna said she liked the way he smelled struck him. It was the only compliment he had ever received. Then she cast him aside. Unneeded, she shut him out and told him to stay away. Again, his mind replayed their conversations that night. Again, he critiqued his own words. The memories brought nothing but agonizing shame. He had surely driven her off. Again, he stared out at the Sound. What was there to talk about? She held up the abductions as an excuse. Her actions were clear. Deciphering her words would be a burdensome exercise in false hope. Their relationship had gone through throws like these before. Each time Theo expected its demise. Again, the idea to explain everything crossed his mind.

"So I'm supposed to tell her about all this? And somehow she'd keep the secret?" he asked the Sound. It rolled more lackadaisical waves in reply.

"Or will you do nothing just like before?" he asked himself.

Theo stood. The wind insisted on pushing him to the ground. He refused. Resolve began to cure in him. A cloud meandered in front of the sun. Theo drew his phone and inspected his recent calls screen. Windy swells buffeted him. He called but was relegated to her voice mail.

"Hi! I'm sorry I missed your call. I must be busy right now," her cheery voice greeted. He imagined her many attempts before choosing one that balanced the imperative with an apology, both maintaining amicable nonchalance. "But please leave a message after the beep and I'll call you back as soon as I can," her prerecorded voice continued.

So many had heard this message. Did any hear her words? Or did they just impatiently wait for her to shut up so they could unload their message, frustrated by her inability to answer. Theo ended the call just before the beep. Hanna meant it when she said she would call back as soon as she could. Giving a last look at the Sound, he scooped up his helmet and began the trek back.

The blue motorcycle carried him off the gusty peninsula. Bird-watchers stared him down as he rode the empty one-lane roads through the patchy forests. Frequent scatterings of sand diluted his enjoyment, but he appreciated the motorcycle's ability to shut out distracting emotions. He crossed a narrow bridge. The stacked granite composing its walls would tear into his bike and leg at the slightest mistake. He accelerated, unphased, watching it pass with detached curiosity. Unassuming homes blended into the trees and bushes that feigned aesthetic appeal but were planted to fortify privacy from prying neighbors. Hanna would faint at the home prices.

Theo diverted down a side street. He did not know precisely where she lived now. He overheard his father say the town name some years ago. Since getting the motorcycle, he disappeared to this place occasionally on quiet mornings. He would roll down residential streets hoping he would somehow spot her out on a walk or maybe in the garden. She loved her flower gardens. He wondered if she still did. The street bore no fruit. It was added to his collection of streets that had failed him. He loathed this private ritual of his. He passed a house giving off unexplainable familiarity. "Hi, Mom," he said from the safety of his helmet.

The buzz of his phone slowed him. It was likely his father chastising him for taking the bike out. Salt still crunched in the roads. The blue two fifty had recently become a blue-and-white two fifty. Cleaning it would be a good, distracting chore. His phone buzzed again. Two messages seemed odd. Then another. Theo pulled over and took out his phone.

"In car with mom," the first said.

"Convinced parents bring me to Surgite," the next.

"On way there," the last.

Theo's heart raced.

"I'm on my way," he wrote back.

A few seconds later, a smiling face came as her answer, and he was racing back onto the main road. He plotted a direct route.

"Dammit!" he shouted, remembering his unfinished business with the sheath. Another abduction could not make the news. It would scare Hanna away. A couple of red lights gave him enough time to draft a new plan. He swore at himself for telling Hanna he was on his way and tore onto the highway. Ignorant traffic clogged up viable lanes. Theo twisted for all the speed the bike could muster. The cars witnessed him moderately move past them. He aimed himself at the city. Hopefully, this errand would be a brief matter.

Activity brimmed in Uptown even for a chill Thursday. Theo parked the bike at his university, stowed his helmet in his backpack, and hurried onto the campus. Lincoln was never empty. Even during spring break, the university produced a steady swill.

Too many witnesses, he thought, crossing the majestic courtyards.

Magnificent pillars marked the most important buildings existing mostly for ceremony now. Theo headed to the comparatively humble brick-and-stone classrooms—the marble inexcusably garish for an edifice for adjuncts to lecture undergraduates. Up the monochrome stairwell he climbed to a carpeted hallway. He pulled on the handle of a classroom door only to find it was locked. Back outside in the terraced patios, he surveyed the campus buildings for a viable location.

The auditorium caught his eye. It would likely be empty. He swiped his student ID card for access and headed for the stage. He yanked on the door, expecting it to be locked. To his delight, it swung freely, his overexertion causing him to stagger back. Darkness poured over the copious ascending seating encircling the stage at the bottom. A few of the stage lights far above shot lazy white beams, giving the auditorium a glow of warmth. Theo wondered if she would freeze. A quick inspection of the room yielded a vague assurance of no witnesses. Theo ran up the shadowy stairs into the seats and looked back. *No, it'd make more sense on the stage.*

Theo took the empty stage. He drew the sheath and knelt. His breathing became shallow and unsure. With a determined inhale he pulled the belt loop on the sheath. Out burst the black lines and misty violet light. A girl in a red dress and dark coat materialized instantly and smacked the stage face first. Theo realized the stun had already worn off while his hands, scared and clumsy, fumbled the sheath back into his jacket. The girl rose slowly on her elbows and knees, her long hair draping around her face. Theo knelt beside her. "Oh my God, are you okay?" he asked, assuming his most cordial voice.

Her head jerked. Emotions raced through her face—predominantly alarm. Theo hurried to recapture her attention with, "You passed out. You woke up and are not hurt."

She stared back at him, clearly out of it. "An' who'r you?"

Theo lowered himself to her level as if speaking to a small woodland creature, "Remember me? I'm Mike. We met at the concert last night. We're at my school."

Maintaining a pleasant smile and tone taxed him.

"Who?"

"You already asked me that."

"Where on earth am I?" the girl asked, regaining her voice and footing.

"Lincoln University," Theo answered, forcing another smile.

Just keep her from panicking. I can't waste the amnesia charge, he thought.

Another reported amnesiac abduction would be disastrous.

Theo stood by the girl, who was teetering like a newborn fawn. She took in her surroundings, blinking furiously. The empty auditorium felt protected from the outside world. Sensing her smoldering anxiety was ready to erupt, he adopted a childlike tone, saying, "You're okay. You were not abducted."

Her head jerked and nostrils flared. She retreated a step.

Theo's heart was back up in his throat. "No, really. In the news, there are all of those abductions, but you're fine. In fact, other than the passing out and hitting your head part, it was really uneventful."

Her eyes narrowed. Theo surmised those may have been normal occurrences for this young woman. She surveyed him.

"You say we met last night, huh? What's my name?" she tossed out.

"Sara," Theo answered confidently.

"What was the DJ's name last night?"

Theo promptly answered. Scrupulous note-taking brought him pride in moments such as these. Sara brushed her hair behind her heavily pierced ears. Theo caught the tattoo on her wrist. She adjusted her duffle coat and inspected its pockets. She smoothed her dress and rapidly assessed the contents of her purse.

Theo filled the terse silence with a helpful, "I paid for our subway fair to get up here. I was showing you my school and then you passed out and hit your head."

Concern would not leave her expression. Theo's hand crept for the sheath.

"This far uptown? And I just blacked out?" she pondered aloud. Seconds trudged along in the accumulating silence. Theo opened his jacket. Her eyes remained trained on his hands. He watched them. Pinned by her stare, Theo felt the need to distract her with, "Sorry I didn't catch you. The stage did, though."

She chuckled, but resumed her glower.

Theo held his hands out to his sides. Her eyes rose to meet him as he tried to convey trust. "Why don't we go outside? Fresh air is nice," Theo offered.

Sara remained alert. "The last thing I remember is talking to you outside the rave, I guess. Maybe I did have one too many drinks, but . . . did I really spend the night out with a . . . You sounded older last night."

Theo nodded and decided to stretch the truth. "The rave was fun. We went to a bar after—restaurant, I mean, and had a long conversation about living in Manhattan."

"I'm from Staten Island."

Theo crossed his arms to match her pose. "I may have forgotten some details too. It's been a long day . . . night."

Sara leaned on one hip. "I've done some dumb stuff in my life, but this is bizarre."

Theo waved his hands in a supplicating gesture. "It was a great time, though. Why don't I take you outside and finish the tour?"

She bought his lie with a "Sure. Why not?" despite him abhorring his own delivery. Back through the hallways, he led this Sara, who asked, "Why are you wearing . . . what are you wearing?"

Theo turned back. "Motorcycle gear."

She followed him into the sunlight. "You got a motorcycle? How'd I miss that?"

"It's parked nearby. Let's take a look?"

Sara swore at the brilliant daylight. "No, it's fine. I believe you. You're an idiot for having one of those deathtraps," she added.

Peeved, Theo ignored her. At least she was not panicking anymore. Assuming the role of a tour guide, he pointed out Lincoln's mighty academic buildings, imitating the orientation tour he had suffered through last August. She paid him little attention, instead looking about often and rummaging through her purse.

"What year are you again?" she asked, interrupting his tour.

"Freshman."

"*Undergrad?*"

"Yes."

"Holy cow, I drank a lot. What did you say you were studying?"

"Philosophy."

"What a waste."

Theo guided her back to the subway stop, closing the tour.

"You seemed older last night. That dance floor was so dark," she kept saying, no matter what conversation he attempted.

Growing frustrated, he shot back, "How old are you?"

She stopped on the sidewalk next to him.

"Didn't anyone ever tell you it's rude to ask a girl's age?"

He answered, "No," with such definitive conviction that she laughed.

She eventually surrendered on the subway, sitting next to him. "I'm twenty-four and in grad school like you kept saying you were. I'm getting a master's in psychology. You're young. You still have time. Don't throw your life away on philosophy."

Their subway car jostled them beside each other. She still smelled of alcohol and flicked through her cell phone every few seconds. Cynicism had worn away her genuine smile. Bored and fearful of her believing this was not a date, Theo continued to throw himself at her.

"Do you like doing the same things over? If you could go to the same concert twice?"

"What's the point in that?"

"Do you feel bad when you lose a memory?"

"What kind of a question is that?"

"Like how you forgot what happened for the past few hours."

"It's not the first time. I've blacked out at parties before. Never with a kid I just met, but I guess even drunk me realized you're not a bad one."

"Do you feel like you lost a part of yourself, losing those memories?"

"Does it matter? Why are you asking like it's life and death?"

Theo fell silent. The conversation was turning predictably

bitter. The subway doors played their dirge at each stop. He rested his forearms on his thighs for some reprieve from the hard plastic seat. Seeing this Sara only made him feel worse.

"What if it were? What if your life depended on your memory?" he asked.

She stood and waited by the subway doors. "Look, you seem nice. Weird, but nice. It was . . . last night was fun, I guess. You don't have to, like, bring me back home or nothing. You on spring break too?"

Theo met her eyes. "Yeah."

"Why don't you hang out with your friends? Relax a little? Take it easy," Sara said, assuming a nicer tone. Grand Central Station's platform was shuffling into view.

Theo stared at the filthy subway floor.

"See you around," she called over her shoulder and disappeared into the crowded station.

Safely alone, Theo exhaled deeply and messaged Arthur, "Works fine," to which he received a simple, "Good."

The whole subway ride back, he planned what he would say to Hanna. Finally at the motorcycle, he called.

One ring played and, "Hi!"

"Hey."

"Oh my God, where have you been? Where are you now? Are you on your way?"

"Hey," he repeated wearily at her barrage.

"You sound exhausted. Are you okay?"

"No."

Hanna was silent for a moment. "I called you. I kept calling you. You didn't pick up," she told him. "You can call me anytime," she added.

Theo sat on the motorcycle's seat. "I was thinking about what's important in my life. I needed some time to think. I probably waited too long to call you back."

"It's okay. I probably called you too many times," she said with the magnanimous sympathy only her heart was capable of. Theo watched the passing traffic. Wind swayed the barren branches of the struggling trees in the city's cracked sidewalks.

"What did you find is important?" she asked in his silence.

"You."

Hanna's effusive breaths played through the tiny speaker in his phone. He envisioned her face flushed and hands clasped together.

"I miss you. I need to see you," he admitted.

"Yes! I miss you too! I have to see you!" she responded.

"I will be late. I'm leaving for Surgite now."

"I'm in my dorm. Call me as soon as you get here."

After a brief pause for consideration, he added, "I have something I want to show you. It's a surprise—nothing dangerous or anything."

Without hesitation, Hanna replied, "I can't wait!"

A plan taking shape in his mind, Theo gave a heartfelt, "Goodbye."

FIFTEEN

"WHAT DO I DO?" Hanna yelled through her helmet. She gripped the motorcycle's handlebars. Just ahead of her, the muddy rut of the parking lot's edge threatened to swallow her and Theo's bike whole. She held the bike's two levers in panicked uncertainty, keeping the bike precariously stopped. Her toes barely kept the bike balanced.

"How do I back up!" she shouted, frantically searching for Theo. Unable to remove her hands from the levers, her fright-induced foggy breaths clouded her helmet's face shield.

"Let go of the brake!" she heard him shout behind her.

"*What*! I'll roll into the ditch!"

"I got you. Just keep holding the clutch lever," his voice assured her.

Terrified, she relaxed her right hand. To her surprise, the bike magically resisted gravity and the parking lot's slope. She began rolling backward, away from danger. She gave a delighted cry. Theo was pulling the bike away from her poor decision. Back on level ground, he flicked the handlebar's red switch, shutting off the engine. She shook her cramped hands, sore from gripping the levers.

"Sorry I almost lost your bike."

"It's okay. You learn through experience."

"How do you back up?"

"With your legs."

"What?" she asked, perplexed.

"There's no reverse on a motorcycle—at least most of them. If you get stuck like that, downhill, you just have to pull yourself out of it an inch at a time," he explained.

She rested on the bike's gas tank and let out a defeated moan. Theo asked, "Would you like to try it again?"

Hanna snapped upright. "I won't let you down."

Afternoon sunlight splashed in orange bars through the meandering broom ends of tree branches above. Surgite on respite gave no interference to their private lesson.

Theo's recalcitrant frown softened. "Go ahead and start the engine. Get the bike up into third gear, then come to a stop mid-turn without passing me and downshifting back into first. Keep your eyes up like we practiced."

"You trust me? What if I crash?"

"Don't think about it."

They both lingered on the scratched handlebar end and mismatched clutch lever.

"What's its name?"

The question puzzled him.

"You haven't named it?" she pressed.

"No."

"Then we'll have to come up with something," she asserted, cheerfully returning to the task at hand. She lowered her face shield and clicked the handlebar's red switch to prepare for ignition. The fuel pump whirred its song of readiness. Hanna's face rose to meet the road. Theo took his position in the turn and Hanna pressed the engine's starter button. It buzzed back to life.

"Clutch in, click into first, look where you'll go, and gentle, gentle out," she coached herself aloud from inside the helmet. "Gentle, gentle," she repeated, releasing the clutch lever. The bike rolled forward and gradually engaged its first gear. Moving, she twisted the throttle and a thrilling shiver raced down her spine.

Wind swept past her. The parked cars and trees of the lot blurred in her peripheral vision. The needles on the motorcycle's display sprung up. Theo had told her to ignore them. Approaching the far turn, she clicked the bike up into second. A great lurch indicated her clutch handling still needed work. She pressed the handlebar and the bike leaned into a delightful arc. Like her bicycle in middle school, Hanna swept the two wheels through the turn. Several prior attempts had not been as smooth. Back where she had started, Theo stood watching her with folded arms. A twist carried her out of the turn. She clicked into third and her heart palpitated. Did he really trust her?

Mid-turn he stood observing her rapid advance. The memory of her previous attempt intruded on her concentration. Going wide seemed a far better option than ramming Theo. She shook off the unwanted memory and raised her eyes. Looking past Theo, she jerked the bike into a hasty turn.

Downshift, front brake, rear brake, Theo, don't fall! The thoughts stampeded through her mind, barely able to process the sequence. Her hands and feet smashed the motorcycle's controls to complete the inputs in time. Unable to process it all, she nearly did not recognize she was safely stopped mid-corner beside a grinning Theo.

"Oh my God, I did it!" she squeaked.

"Yes! Yes, you did," Theo said, elated. His tone had changed. The vulnerable tenderness of spring's first flowers touched it.

She stood to embrace Theo but felt a sudden violent weight on her left leg. Forgetting the kickstand, her whole body was pulled down by the motorcycle hurtling toward the pavement. Desperately, she grabbed the handlebars to save it. Stumbling and struggling, she miraculously found the weight of the motorcycle supported.

Theo grunted. "Get off!"

Holding the motorcycle with all his might, Theo shook, supporting it.

"Get off!" he repeated from under her. She jumped off and he righted the machine.

Burning with shame, Hanna burst out, "I'm so sorry! That was stupid." She pried open her helmet's face shield.

Setting the motorcycle on its kickstand, Theo's chest heaved cloudy breaths. He rested his hands on his knees, sweat beading on his ruddy face. He forced out the words, "You can't . . . forget . . . the kickstand."

Hanna gazed, dumbfounded, at the panting Theo before her.

"I'm really sorry. I really am! Are you . . . mad at me?"

Theo stood to his full height. She pulled off her helmet and set it on the ground like he had. "What you did was careless, avoidable, and irresponsible," he said, using his professorial voice.

At some point, while seeing him almost crushed under the bike, she had begun to expect a rebuke like this. She winced at his raised voice.

"This is not even my bike; it's my dad's."

Hanna tensed up, expecting that the worst was yet to come.

Theo tempered his breathing. "But . . . I'm glad you're not afraid. Maybe one day . . . we can ride together."

"Really? You're not mad?"

He regained his composure. "No. You like motorcycles. Just don't do that again."

She embraced him, the stress melting away.

"There are actually two bikes," Theo said with a rare sentimentality.

He let her go. "This is my dad's second bike. He has a red one that's much faster. We were supposed to ride together. He helped me a lot through high school. We spent time together. But once I graduated, he disappeared into his work and the city. I hardly know him now. I guess he did his time. I had this foolish idea that I would take his red bike and you this one. We would ride together."

He laughed derisively. "Why am I suddenly telling you all this? It's pathetic, isn't it? This spoiled rich kid is so lonely with his toys and nobody to play with. Wouldn't the world be better without him and—"

Hanna interjected, "Theo, don't!"

Wind surged past them in erratic buffets. She stepped closer to him. "Don't do that to yourself. There are people that care about you. I care about you. I don't know how, but maybe we can ride the two bikes together one day."

He stood motionless. Hanna was just a pace away. "Why don't we eat dinner? It's getting dark. Let's talk it over," she offered.

Pained silence buried his voice. Their two helmets stared confidently up at them.

"It *is* getting dark," he admitted. "We can eat and then I'll head back."

Concern filled her. "Isn't it scary? Riding in the dark?"

"I'm not afraid. I can handle it," Theo answered resolutely.

"What if we go back together?" she suggested. "We can eat in the city. There's still some light left."

Theo's hands moved to his pocket for his phone. Hanna picked up both of their helmets and awaited his reply. She liked the contrast of the black matte finish on hers to Theo's glossy white helmet. It matched her leather jacket.

Several messages later, he reported, "My dad's out tonight. He's not around much anyway. He'll be back tomorrow."

She handed him his white helmet. "Then we'll just have to sneak in some karaoke tonight."

Theo took it with earnest appreciation. They climbed onto the motorcycle together. His own backpack and armor obstructed her touch. Still, the bike forced intimacy between rider and passenger. After a brief stop at her dorm for some overnight items, Theo took them off to the dusky highway. His programmatic inputs kept the bike at a predictable pace through the traffic. She tried to limit clacking her helmet into his. Rush hour made the early journey a low-speed endeavor. Hanna marveled at the previously unknown view of familiar sights.

His world was full of fascinating danger. Cars were monstrous and moved about in a cacophony. Trucks were terrifying. The icy wind howled around them in an incessant drone. She stared into the blur of passing road below. *A fall at this speed could be fatal*, she thought, too amazed to process the fear. Her heart pounded and would not relinquish its furious work. A chance bug caught in the headlight's beam appeared as if a vanishing snowflake. The thought of snowfall made Hanna feel sick. She inspected the clear night sky above for reassurance. The machine's headlight yawed noticeably in turns. Theo leaned with the machine and his helmet's movement telegraphed his upcoming action. His whole body was preoccupied with running it.

She learned to move with him. His body would press against hers in uncompromising shifts and adjustments. He ignored her completely. Hanna wondered what he thought about the undeniably intimate contact. *Annoyed, probably*, she thought as her helmet once again clacked against his. Bracing herself from falling into him when they decelerated remained a developing skill. How she longed to speak to him, alienated yet so close. The bike never lurched, unlike under her previous command of it. They gracefully advanced through traffic. Her thighs shivered in her jeans. How Theo made this journey routinely amazed her. His expert navigation of the tolls and bridges awed her. The Holland Tunnel was thick with traffic that ran like molasses. Reaching the city, her body hung on his for support—tired, frigid, and unashamed of their sensual pressing.

Theo rolled to a parking garage she recognized, near his apartment. He brought them to a parking spot half-occupied by a covered motorcycle. Beside it, the familiar silver coupe was parked. They disembarked, her ears ringing. Theo inspected the tires. He rubbed the tire's edge and sighed.

"How do you survive the cold?" she asked, still wracked by occasional shivers.

"The heated jacket and gloves help, but mainly I've just gotten used to it."

He set about taking his bike's cover out of the coupe's trunk. It occurred to Hanna that he carried a key to his father's car. Hanna took off her helmet and surveyed the concealed second motorcycle. She ran her hand along its windshield, feeling the contours of the mysterious figure underneath.

"Do you want to see?" Theo called out.

"Is it your dad's?"

"Yes."

Theo pulled off the cover. The striking red motorcycle posed elegantly for them.

"It has much more power than what we just rode. He takes it to the track. It's modified."

They stood silently marveling at the red motorcycle, bored being relegated to just stationary admiration. Theo covered the bike again. "He wouldn't even notice if I took it out," he said curtly.

Hanna said, "I'm sure he still cares about you. Has it always been like this?"

Any expression drained from Theo's face. "I manage."

"I'm sure he has some way of showing he cares. You could have parents like mine. The only way they show they care is by telling me to study. They sacrificed so much for my education. Now look at me . . . struggling at Surgite."

"Some of that's my fault."

"You don't have to blame yourself. It's mine. My parents don't even know I'm here. They think I'm catching up on my studies— even if it is spring break."

"At least you're honest," Theo remarked, taking her hand.

"I'm really not. I'm a horrible person," Hanna replied in monotone.

They stood hand in hand, gazing at the two covered motorcycles.

"Why do you hide us from your parents?" he asked.

"At this point, because I'm in too deep," she answered helplessly. "I could argue it's understandable for a girl like me to slip away from her protective family to ride motorcycles with her Mr. Elusive. What a dumb teenager thing to do. My parents want the best for me. They always say so. That doesn't include dating. They think the best for me means studying, graduating, getting a good job, and all of that. My mom says I can get married once I have a career. She thinks God will just teleport Mr. Perfect to me. My dad would love it if I met a teacher—even more if I became one. They don't see that I'm just human and need to be loved. Everybody does."

The echoes from the parking garage resonated around them. A car drifted in the distance, searching for an open spot. The air was thick and warm. Concrete, steel, machines, and artificial light captured them. The forlorn figures of the motorcycles sat under their oppressive covers. They headed to his father's apartment together.

Undisturbed darkness greeted them. Theo set about neatly storing their motorcycle gear. Hanna left her boots by the door and made for the familiar kitchen. She ferreted through its flavorful contents. A search concluded that a wonderful chicken meal was possible. Theo suggested a Japanese dish called *oyakodon* and set about preparing it. As with the motorcycle, he set about his task unused to company.

"Parent-child dish," Hanna translated aloud. "Chicken served with eggs. It's kind of sad, don't you think?"

"I don't think about it."

"You cook a lot, don't you?" she asked, watching his methodic work from the kitchen table.

"For myself. I'd starve if I didn't," he replied, sauteing the chicken.

"How do you know when they're done?"

He kept his attention on the sizzling meat. "Sight . . . smell."

Theo opened a cabinet and reached for a glass. Hanna spotted a half-full bottle of liquor on the top shelf. Excitement, dread, curiosity, and concern all churned in her. The steadiness in her voice failed as she asked, "Is that your dad's gin?"

"Most of the time," he answered, filling his glass with water.

"You shouldn't act like it's cool or something," she said tartly. "It's a crime at our age."

Theo made no response.

"I've never tasted gin," she added.

"It tastes horrible."

"How do you take it?"

"Cut with water."

"Does your dad know?"

"No."

"You keep it a secret?"

"Why'd you point it out anyway? You're not a stranger to keeping secrets," he said, gesturing to the apartment.

Shame tinged her cheeks. "I'm such a hypocrite."

"You're not as much as you think. You don't forget what you've said." He handed her a glass of cold tea. "Your memory is actually quite good."

"How do you know how good my memory is?" she asked, taking the tea.

An anxious expression seized Theo, but he played it off, saying, "No reason."

Hanna envisioned Emma waving two red flags like maracas. Theo retreated to the counter and finished their meal's preparation. "We have some time while the rice cooks," he said, disappearing to the living room. He returned holding a deck of cards.

"Would you play a memory game with me?"

An intrigued Hanna agreed and watched him set the cards between them on the empty kitchen table. A vast grid of facedown cards formed. Theo flipped one in a corner, then a second one in another corner, and returned them to their face down positions. He gestured Hanna to take her turn. She picked two cards randomly and set them back. Theo scored the first pair, recognizing a match from her cards.

Hanna mentioned during her turn, "Sorry about your second helmet. Some of my makeup wore off on the chin bar pad thing. I can clean it for you."

"I don't mind. Nobody uses that second helmet. I don't know why my dad has it."

Hanna selected two more cards. Theo took another pair.

"Well now it has lilac lipstick on it. It's more snug than I thought. I could kiss the pad just in front of my mouth."

"They do that. What color lipsticks do you have?"

Hanna's mind ventured through the bins of her long-term memory, a few short-term card locations falling out along the way. "Some reds, of course, some darker reds, black, and the lilac you gave me. I never would have thought I'd like it."

"Did you think you'd look asphyxiated?"

She stifled a chuckle. "No, but I suppose the thought did cross my mind."

Hanna's hand meandered above the cards as if able to discern their concealed contents by proximity.

"All makeup is deception," she noted plainly. Theo leaned forward in apparent intrigue. Taking a pair of cards, she elaborated, "It's not who we really are. Lips are simple on their own. We want to dress them up—give them hope of being noticed. We're willing to lie about it because it's not really hurting anyone. In fact, it's helping."

Theo softly countered, "It's not really a lie. There isn't an intention to deceive. I know your lips aren't actually purple. You just want to make them memorable."

She countered, "For sure. But like in other things—not lipstick but maybe lying about one's age, for example—once you set the wrong memory, you have to keep it up. The lie becomes truth for that someone."

Realization flashed across Theo. "What if you could change someone's memory? When you tell a lie, you're altering someone's memory. That deviation, that altered fact, becomes a part of their recollection. If undisturbed by the truth, it can lodge itself in the fabric of their memory and become truth—but just for them. There is only one reality that happened. A lie is a departure from it. When you lie to someone, you're effectively creating an alternate reality in their perception. It's clearly false. It no longer matches what actually happened, but it exists, thereby bringing it into reality. It requires care and attention to preserve. Truth is eternal, unconcerned with perception. Falsehoods require tending, much like a garden. If left unattended, they are eventually discovered and die."

"I mean, yeah," she said, unsure of his intent.

He gestured to the cards. "Take these cards, for example. Your memory is holding the location of one or two of them."

"Hey, more than that," Hanna protested playfully.

They both looked at the disparity in their captured pairs. Theo carried on, "To move one of the cards without you knowing would be lying. To remove a card and simply tell you it was never there would also be a falsification. You would call it immoral, wouldn't you?"

"Of course. Messing with someone for no reason is cruel."

"What end would justify altering the cards?"

"If my life depended on the game, I suppose."

"Would you ever forgive someone for altering the cards if losing the game meant discovering something incredible?" Theo asked, his voice strangely sympathetic.

A sinking feeling seized her stomach. "You're not seeing someone else, are you?"

Theo twitched. Startled by her question, he answered, "Hanna, you are amazing—full of compassion, beauty, curiosity, and life. My heart is set on you."

Hanna gasped and covered her mouth. Theo stared blankly at the cards. His plain language was as forceful and refreshing as the March wind.

"My gosh, Theo, that's sweet of you," she breathed through a smile. Theo mumbled some words but failed to complete a sentence. Hanna wanted to chastise herself for getting swept away in his conversation. She could not forget the main reason she came here.

"But it's funny you bring up altered memories."

Shock grew his pupils to black marbles in his hazel irises.

"I was looking through my green journal and noticed something. It has many notes reminding me to tell you what I wrote down. We talked about my green journal on Valentine's Day, I remember that, and then, strangely, there's nothing. There's not one note to share with you after."

Theo avoided her eyes. "We talked about it. The abductions were the reason you started the journal. I don't see why notes to tell me would continue after telling me about it on Valentine's."

"Don't you think it's at least a little weird?" she suggested. He gave no ground. Hanna's own face fell into a frown. "Do you notice if I'm less forgetful when I'm not with you?"

Theo's brow contorted. "How would I notice that?"

Hanna realized her error, saying, "Look, I know I've been keeping this journal because of the abductions. The Long Island incident and Steve testify to that. What I can't piece together is why I have this hunch that I am more forgetful around you."

Theo observed her patiently. Calculations tempered his mood, which had moments prior been lush with excitement. "It's true you have been keeping the journal because of the abductions. I don't think you're more forgetful around me. It's just easier for you to catch little things you normally forget. You scrutinize our dates too much."

"That's not . . . I wouldn't call it that," she said.

Theo hammered on, "I saw something in the news that they have a suspect. I bet the abductions have stopped."

Hanna mused, "I wonder if they identified him by his car."

No response.

"The reporting about Long Island mentioned a black car," she said deliberately.

Theo corrected her at once with, "It was silver," then locked up.

"You're right. It was silver," Hanna conceded.

Theo's prompt correction hung between them.

"You know, it's funny how we remember things differently sometimes," she remarked coyly, holding a card between her fingers. "I remember going to the university clinic some weeks ago. Over spring break, it just popped up in my memory. The thing is, I can't remember why I went. There's nothing wrong with me— at least as far as I can tell."

She looked Theo dead in the eyes. "Do you know why I went?"

"Are you quizzing me?"

A sinister grin crept across her face.

"Because I recommended you should go."

"Why?"

"You mentioned you were concerned about your weight . . . and not eating."

"Oh." Hanna gulped, hearing him bring up the matter. *Did I really share that? I haven't struggled with that since junior year,* she thought to herself.

Theo leaned forward on the table. "I . . . you must have forgotten you mentioned it."

"I think I lose my mind when I'm with you," she said aloud.

"You don't have amnesia or anything like that. You're just a little forgetful."

Both sides relinquished their counters. Moments passed effortlessly in their shared reticence. Hanna tore through her memories. So many conversations with Theo contained revelations about her true feelings. He always listened patiently. Sympathy touched her heart, raw from the thought of a forsaken Theo, practiced in solitude yet still so considerate to her plights, dreams, and fears. She dove deep into the pool of her memory, swimming through the blackness for when she shared that with him.

A delightful song beeped from the steaming rice cooker on the counter. Theo pressed the button, ending its triumphant tune.

"It's Japanese, isn't it?" Hanna called out.

"It was my mom's," he nearly whispered.

She joined him at the rice cooker. Its worn buttons bore authentic Japanese text marred by use. Its fragrant steamy contents made Hanna's mouth water.

"Do you always make rice this way?"

"It's most familiar to me."

"It looks like you've used it since forever."

"Since the divorce."

Theo joined the rice to their meals. Hanna studied him carefully. This was the first time he had mentioned the divorce since they met. She could not quite discern the emotion he bore, but she felt invited to ask, "Do you talk to her? Your mom?"

"I ruined our relationship when my parents split up. That was six years ago. I was the reason. She would visit on and off after the custody battle. We haven't spoken since the move."

Hanna fell silent beside him while he solemnly made their plates. "She's an alcoholic now, living with her parents in Connecticut. That's what my dad told me. We don't see her side of the family anymore either."

"I'm sorry," she said, helping him set the table.

"It's not your fault. You didn't know," he replied, sitting beside her.

Dinner lacked conversation. It did not matter with Theo. Such expectations had no bearing one-on-one with him. Hanna found it liberating. She broke the silence to praise him for his expertly made oyakodon. Theo thanked her and explained the recipe.

In the quiet over their empty plates, he said, "We talked about eating disorders back in January in Central Park. You mentioned it in passing."

"I guess I forgot."

"It must be stress or something."

She sighed and rubbed her temples. "I hate it, Theo, feeling so fragmented. I should write this all down in my green journal. Will you help me remember?"

A rare warmth of understanding softened his features.

"I will," he answered as if a vow.

After cleaning up, she found herself back in his inviting arms. His demeanor had become disarmingly sweet. At ease, she asked, through a languid blink, "What do you want to do? How about karaoke?"

"You're tired, aren't you? We don't have to go out," he said checking his watch. He brought her to his room and suggested they watch a movie on his computer. Theo sat at his desk. Hanna sat on his bed and watched him click through the folders. She imagined him sitting there like that every day and every night— alone, his father out, his mother unreachable, his classmates grateful for his absence, his friends offline, wasting away in his room. Hanna hopped up and joined him as he scanned the library on his screen.

"I want you to know that," he said, meeting her eyes, "it means the world to me you came here today."

"Me too," she said, wrapping her arms around him. Yet it was not adequate for the ache in her heart. She assessed the space behind him. Hanna climbed on and sat between him and the back of his chair.

"What are you doing?" he needlessly asked. Her legs hung on either side of him. She leaned against his back just as she had done on the motorcycle. Theo settled into the unforeseen arrangement, eased by her warmth.

She nestled against him, enjoying his soft sweater. He chose a film and asked, "How do you introduce yourself in Japanese again?"

"A *jiko shoukai*? Like this," she answered and brandished her practiced Japanese self-introduction.

Theo replied, "*Shio no koto ga suki desuka?*"

"*Hai!*"

THEO AWOKE. Beside him lay a deeply sleeping Hanna. Curled between him and the wall, she warmed his bed to serene comfort. In her arms, she clutched a pillow just as she had held him earlier. Only the chartreuse lights of his computer's languid blinks illuminated the void of his room. Just audible were her soft breaths under the gentle blow of the heater. Her hair spilled across her face and graced her bare shoulder outside the blanket. Dread seized him.

Theo reached for his phone and spotted the time: three thirteen antemeridian. Recently, it was rare that he slept through the night. The unexpected warmth had woken him last time too. His serendipitous return to consciousness meant a task easier to accomplish.

It feels so wrong, he thought, slipping out of his bed. Familiar darkness cloaked him in the living room. He reached under the couch and took the familiar sheath.

"*Midori no nikki*," he whispered to it. The words haunted him. There were moments he could forget what he had to do. The situation and its consequences, though, always came back to him. *Inescapable*, he thought, practicing those words for "green journal" Hanna had taught him earlier. He returned and saw Hanna still fast asleep, an innocent contour beneath his blankets. Guilt tore through him like a fissure.

Theo paused, the sheath in his hand poised to strike her. Did he have to erase the journal? Was she that close to discovering the source of her amnesia? Here she lay, defenseless in his own bed.

Once she finds out, she will leave me, he thought. *But erasing her journal will end her investigation. I hope I can find the words to tell her someday.*

That word bothered him.

Hope.

It enraged him.

What hope was he allowed to have?

Theo's fist grew tight around the sheath.

Erase yourself. End it. You don't deserve her.

Obstacles and impediments flooded his mind—namely that the sheath was not charged nearly enough to erase the entirety of himself from her memory. Theo's anger turned on himself.

She still knows about the translation. You couldn't bring yourself to delete that memory. You told Arthur you did, said his mind's voice. Yet, there she was. Even missing memories, she still admired him through the fragments she presumed were the whole.

It was never supposed to get this far. I should have left long ago, rang in his mind. *I need to delete her visit to the clinic now too. What kind of a charge would I even need for that? Should I delete that now and erase her journal later? The clinic visit was probably an isolated event. I need to read her journal to make sure.*

Hanna moved.

Theo's hands shot behind his back. Her leg spastically kicked under the blankets. Theo's heart pumped in frightened thuds. Hanna clutched the pillow tighter, returning to a much-desired slumber. Theo's hand returned to its treacherous position. He pressed the sheath against her bare shoulder and whispered, "*Midori no nikki.*"

An unmoving Hanna continued dreaming peacefully. Theo fled

the scene, taking her backpack out of the room. He hid the sheath back under the couch and shamelessly rummaged through her possessions for the green journal.

She will have no memory of bringing this here, he thought, taking the journal and hiding it next to the sheath. He returned her backpack to her memory's location. Slipping back under the blankets beside her, he lay there in pained rumination about the trajectory of his life.

———

HANNA FOLLOWED Theo into the bookstore. Tucked at the base of a skyscraper, the alcove of Japanese books, media, and souvenirs welcomed them.

"I thought of a fun nickname for our helmets," she called over. "I couldn't think of one for the bike, but I came up with something cute. What do you think it is?"

"Don't ask a question only you know the answer to. It's annoying."

She pouted. "You're no fun."

No response. She wondered if this was the same Theo that had given such tender caresses earlier. Hanna had felt the sinews in his neck and shoulders in the secluded darkness without removing his shirt. She had rested her head against his chest hearing the excited beats of his heart. She savored their conversations in the intimacy of a shared bed. Theo's undivided attention had been a treat.

Joylessly, she delivered, "Salt and pepper."

Confusion played across his face.

"Your name in Japanese, Shio, is a homonym for salt. Your helmet is white. My helmet is black. Black and white—salt and pepper."

Nothing. Theo was mute. Hanna wondered why his demeanor had soured. Perhaps he had not slept much. That was her fault too. Theo led her to the second floor's rows of authentic Japanese texts.

The store was nearly empty on that unassuming Friday morning. He paused, the first good look she had gotten of him in the daylight, having hardly spoken over breakfast.

"Oh no! One of your eyes is bloodshot. Did you sleep okay?"

He rubbed his eyes. ". . . yes."

"Did I keep you up? I'm sorry. Is something bothering you?"

"I'm just . . . tired. That's all."

Theo pointed at the countless books neatly stacked on the shelves. "These are the novels you wanted to see," he said. Many kanji surpassed Hanna's ability in their titles alone. Her cheeks ignited with embarrassment.

"These are pretty dense. They'd take me forever. I don't think I could do it. How much Japanese can you read? You can speak it, right?"

"Just a little," he said, picking up a book. "Just a handful of basic words and phrases . . . conversational stuff my mom taught me. I can't read any of this."

Hanna stepped closer. "Conversation is a start. I bet you're pretty good. You've never mentioned how much you can speak."

"Why bother? It just creates expectations and disappointment."

"Did she speak Japanese at home?" Hanna asked softly.

He reflected, "Not really. Never with my dad. She told me I should be bilingual. She wished she had taken it more seriously. She only visited Japan once or twice a year. We never went as a family."

Theo glanced at Hanna, noticing how close she stood. His eyes darted for a different subject. "She wanted me to learn the kanji. She said that was the most important."

He sighed. "I never did."

Hanna eased a book from his hand. "You still could. We could study it together. I could help you."

Theo shook his head. "You can already read novels. I can't even write my own name."

"It's never too late to start. You could take a class next year."

"Don't you register for classes soon? Registration for fall classes at Lincoln opens in a couple weeks."

"Shoot! I forgot," she answered, carefully returning the book to the shelf. "Gosh, I always forget little stuff like that, but don't think I forgot you promised to tell me your middle name—your mother's maiden name."

He took her hand. "Come on, Dido. I'll show you the DVDs."

She reeled back. "*How*?"

"You must have forgotten you mentioned it," he replied, pulling her along.

Theo toured her past the shows and movies in their prim DVD boxes. Still, her flustered mind raced to retrieve the memory of mentioning her middle name. How did he know it if she had never told him? He began a new conversation, pulling her attention away.

"There's this friend of mine who is Japanese. She lives in Japan and doesn't speak English. We talk online sometimes."

Hanna suddenly felt woozy. "Who is she? How long have you been talking to her?"

Theo faced her. "No, it's not anything like that. She's older than us. She has a job. She's a friend of my history professor at Lincoln . . . in a way."

Hanna lowered her sweaty hands.

Theo continued, "Sometimes, she likes to practice her English, but she doesn't know much. It's . . . kind of painful to talk to her. I was thinking about how you could talk to her. I could introduce you. You'd probably be friends."

"Sounds like fun! When can we talk?" Hanna's voice leaped out in the hushed aisles.

Theo grew excited. "She talked about visiting last time we spoke, but she can't."

Hanna's curiosity stirred. "Why can't she come to America?"

"Her job is . . . difficult. That's what she says, anyway. She doesn't know how she can get time away from it, but I didn't really understand what she was saying."

Theo looked into Hanna's eyes. She stared back, unsure of his intent. His expressive eyes lingered, causing hers to widen in anticipation. She broke away and laughed an airy, "What?" to the floor.

He took her hand. "I'll let you know when she's ready to talk."

Hanna followed his tour of the store's enchanted treasures. It concluded with his offer to buy her a book. Theo intently listened to her explanation of the children's picture book she chose. No judgment polluted him. She marveled at the Japanese sentences adorning its watercolor illustrations and avoided reading the receipt Theo had tucked into the pages.

Once outside, distracted, she walked beside Theo along the city's crowded sidewalks. She stuffed the receipt into her jeans' pocket hastily, not reading the price.

Not long after, they found themselves back in the familiar karaoke booth. He volunteered the tablet for her to choose the first song. She snatched it from him with immature abandon.

"You act like you're so full of secrets. Don't forget I have some too," she said, taking off her jacket and backpack. He merely gave a pleasant expression. Hanna searched the tablet's library for her most obscure selection first. Theo was due for a lesson in humility. She chirped a jovial, "Yay," when she found it.

The song loaded and Hanna delivered the opening salvo in a thick accent. She opened her eyes during the song's first rest, when Theo shouted, "You speak Russian too!"

"Just a little," she said, coyly soaking up his disbelief.

Hanna had him. He marveled at her delivering the memorized lyrics of "Ya Soshla S Uma" effortlessly.

She scoffed. *Dido, huh? I'll show him*, she said in her mind. Lily could have done better, but she did not sing songs banned by their parents. Hanna's hips swayed and voice burned to the synthesizer and guitar's fiery work. Once the song ended, she clicked off the microphone and sat beside Theo.

"You were pretty worked up. What's the song about?"

"Rebellion."

"It's okay to let it out."

Hanna's heart soared. She hopped back to her feet, taking the next song she had entered. The thundering rhythm and hailing guitar swept her into a melodic tirade long enjoyed in secret. Her voice crackled in the growling shouts that funneled her ire. Cathartic bliss filled her. She roared the lyrics and shot back to the melody her lungs gave their all to sing. The conclusion of her chosen song "Happy?" sent her breathlessly back to the couch, where Theo had been singing along and loading another song.

"I'm sorry I cussed," she said.

"It was in the lyrics," said Theo.

"I know."

"I also know one from this band," he added, turning back on his mic. Another song Hanna recognized began its stampede through the speakers. Only the metal channels carried it. Theo's voice changed. He sang the opening lyrics' frustration then pivoted to a pained melodic shout. Such vitriol came so easily to him. The hairs on Hanna's neck bristled with fascination and concern. She joined him in the second verse. He stood. She stood with him. Hanna's tender heart pounded. The final lyrics saw their unrestrained singing giving life and form to unbridled rage. The couch welcomed back their panting, sweating bodies.

"Some duet, huh," she joked.

"Yeah."

"You sing those words so sincerely," she said. "Why did you pick a song called 'Forget to Remember?'"

"No reason," he answered insouciantly.

An image of Emma waving a red flag again came to Hanna. She found herself enamored anyway, watching him click through the tablet's library. *Why am I like this?* she thought. But her self-reflection was interrupted by the buzzing of Theo's phone. He suddenly froze and reached for his jacket beside him.

"I have to take this," he said, taking his call out of their booth.

Alone, Hanna collapsed on the couch. The plain beige ceiling tiles stared down at her in a pacifying manner. *He bought me gifts. He fed me. He taught me how to ride on his motorcycle. He let me stay over. He shared so much about himself and his mom. Now he's letting me scream my lungs out in karaoke. All I want is to spend more time with him. And yet he keeps acting weird. Who is he talking to?* she thought, reaching into her jeans' pocket for the receipt from the bookstore.

How much was that book anyway? she thought as a second folded paper came out stuck to the receipt. She sat up, unfolding the weathered page. It appeared to have been inadvertently sent through the wash. How long the folded page had sat unnoticed in her pocket escaped her. She read its contents and gasped.

"Oh, God."

The beating of Hanna's heart apexed to a panicked drumming. Dizzying nausea blurred her vision. She swallowed hard. Leaning forward, she read the prescription in horror. "Anterograde amnesia," she whispered.

"When I'm with Theo," her own handwritten note bore.

Memories rushed back. The green journal, the clinic, the café, Emma's observations—the newfound discovery snapped the recollections violently into place. The prescription slipped from her shaking hands onto the table.

"No . . . no," she whispered, and could only repeat her stultified utterance. Her limbs felt disconnected. She remembered his tender expression the night prior as he lied about the clinic. *It wasn't about my eating disorder at all! If that's not why, how the hell does he know about that? Did I really tell him and forget?*

Rage seared her face.

No! It's this amnesia! It has to be!

"But why? Why do I have amnesia? And only around him?" Through gritted teeth, she fumed, "How is he doing this to me!"

Curtailed breaths rushed past her dry mouth. She thought, *My *green journal! Where is it?* and searched her backpack, finding only bitter disappointment. Throwing her backpack on the couch, she stood clutching her head.

"I can't remember. Where is it! Why can't I remember! The last memory of it is in my dorm," she whispered, her cheeks growing hot. The karaoke booth's television played its cheerful advertisements. An impulse to throw a microphone through it stirred her. She snatched one from the table.

He can't see me like this! If he really is erasing my memory somehow, I need to catch him in the act. I can't tip my hand. He can't get away with this, she thought, peering out the glass of the booth's door. She set the microphone down, loaded three songs, grabbed her backpack, and called Emma. She kept her phone tightly pressed against her ear and exited the booth. She spotted a cordial Theo returning with a basket of fresh chicken strips. She passed, giving only a wan smile.

Emma greeted her with, "Ya know you could text? It's spring break. I could've been asleep."

Hanna paced the dim hallways of the karaoke establishment. "Hey, what are you doing?"

"Squeezing garlic out of my face. Why?"

"Do you remember if I said if I'd bring my green journal with me to the city?"

"I don't know. What journal? Yeah, I think."

"The journal I started because of the abductions!" Hanna shouted, her voice shrill. "Did I or did I not!"

"Yes! Yes. Goddamn, calm down."

Her throat tightened as she struggled to ask, "Do you want to go on a double date later today? Could you ask Broc?"

"Slow down," Emma said. "What's going on? A double date outta nowhere? Do you want me to go into the city? I'm still at home! You texted you're with biker boy. Are you still there?"

Before Hanna could reply, Emma added, "Oh, and, uh, Broc and I aren't a thing."

"Ooh . . . that never happened?"

"It's complicated. We had a long talk. We're still friends."

"Poor Broc."

"We're still friends! He'll be alright. He values our friendship too."

"Could you bring him as a friend?"

"Actually, I have a date," Emma boasted. "I met a guy named Chris. He's a senior, a business major, a friend of a friend kind of deal—gonna land a job real soon, beefy arms, but none of that's important right now. You sound kind of panicked. Where are you?"

"I'm with Theo at the karaoke place. I'm fine," Hanna lied, "and just had this thought to go on a double date."

"Yeah, but . . . I'd have to ask Chris if he's even up for something later today," Emma said, still sounding skeptical. "My whole family's going out to dinner tonight. I probably can't make it."

Hanna whirled around to pace the hallway again. Emma filled the silence with, "What's really going on?"

Hanna groped for an explanation. A plausible fabrication sprung to her mind. "I think he's cheating on me."

Emma shouted, "Whoa! Theo? There's competition?"

"Please! I need your help."

"Okay, okay. What can I do?"

"I need to catch him in a lie. I get all mixed up when I'm with him. I'll explain more when I'm back on campus. When are you coming back?"

"Tomorrow."

"What time? Could we have a date on campus tomorrow?"

"Hanna, you're throwing a lot at me all of the sudden. Accusing Theo of cheating is a big deal. Did you think through how you're going to do it? Do you have evidence? Do you know who the girl is? Do you even want to know? Does he know you know? If not, keep it that way. You shouldn't blow your cover until you're sure you can nail him and really make him hurt for what he did."

"Please," she implored. "That's why I need your help."

Emma let out a capitulating sigh. "Alright, but you owe me after this."

"Done."

"I'll see what Chris says."

"Can you ask him right now?"

"Jeez, now you really are being pushy."

Panic whipped Hanna. "I know. I'm sorry. This is all really sudden, but I have to get to the bottom of this."

"Alright, alright. I'll text you in a bit," she said and hung up. Hanna returned to the booth, which housed a concerned Theo.

"What happened? What's wrong?" he asked.

"I . . . um . . . just remembered about a big assignment I was supposed to be working on with Emma. She's gonna text me back. I need to go back to Surgite right away."

"Ah," he said, dumbfounded. "But we were having a good time, weren't we? Was it something I said?"

"Yeah, no, we were . . . I don't know. I'm sorry I forgot about this." Her voice was hollow. She added, "Emma texted me and I really should have written this down. It's like I have amnesia."

Hanna monitored his response. Only helpless dejection.

"Do you know where my green journal is?"

He avoided any eye contact. "I . . . don't know."

Theo ended the despondent song she had entered, saying, "We could just go back."

Hanna remained standing. "We could."

The dead microphones between them caught their forlorn silence. Theo stood and courteously extended her jacket to her. She accepted it, keeping vigilant watch of him. They gathered their belongings, paid, and left—the basket of chicken tenders abandoned. Hanna shivered, succumbing to waves of anxiety as they walked back.

Stopped at an intersection, he asked, "Your assignment with Emma, is it somehow related to your green journal?"

Unsure, she asked, "What do you mean?"

"I just thought it might be somehow."

She caught his frightened look. *Something's wrong for sure. Why is he scared?* she thought, following him to Penn Station. *I need to make a plan. I need to make up some stuff I forgot and see how he reacts. I need to get away from him—I could lose my memory at any moment. Emma will be my safety net. She can remember for me. We'll get to the bottom of this.*

"Your next train is not for a while," said Theo in the commotion of the station. Hanna refocused on her immediate surroundings.

"Oh, that's okay. I'll wait."

"Would you like me to wait with you?"

"No," she said promptly. "You don't have to. You can go back. Emma's supposed to call me back about our assignment."

Theo's shoulders slumped. He blinked in morose disbelief, leaving an injured, timid boy.

"I don't understand. Again, I have to ask—was it something I said? Or did?"

Not wanting to expose herself, Hanna scrambled for the right words. "I just felt . . . uncomfortable. It's not your fault."

The lie stung her but differently this time. She wanted to scream the truth at him. What was he doing to her? Who else could it be? She drew her phone and absentmindedly flipped it open. Theo remained standing there doltishly.

"Goodbye, Theo," she said finally.

With one last look, he walked away. Regret began its caustic pervasion of her. She would never forget his pained expression.

THEO SAT ALONE at his desk replaying Hanna's abrupt departure over and over in his mind. *Why did she want to go back so suddenly? She was fine until karaoke. Something must have reminded her of the green journal. Or was it me? Maybe she's onto me, but there's no way she could figure out how I'm erasing her memories.*

The chilling phone call with Arthur during karaoke rushed back to him. Arthur had been particularly forceful, saying, "Trap someone you can interview after. No mistakes or witnesses. Meet me tomorrow at noon with the subject trapped."

Theo opened Hanna's green journal and frantically tore through its pages. Her uncouth handwriting had a charm. Hanna called him an hour later. Desperate, he picked up on the first ring. She invited him to a date at the coffee shop near Surgite. He agreed at once, exhilarated at a chance to redeem himself.

"What time?" he asked.

"Eleven," she answered listlessly.

"Can it be earlier?"

"That's the only time that will work," she said, sounding peeved.

Hanna was slipping away. The vast loneliness of his room bore down on him. He agreed to eleven o'clock, knowing there was no chance he could get back to Arthur in time. Would it really be her? Her tepid voice ended the call.

Theo paced the empty apartment, tender memories of the spaces she had occupied just hours prior gouging him. Arthur's words "someone you know" repeated in his mind, which seemed unwilling to solve the problem. He returned to his desk and wrote the names. The prospects were daunting and distressing. "Hanna" was circled.

He called Arthur, unable to conceal his feverish anxiety.

"Where is your house?"

"A little up the Hudson. Why?"

"I have to be at Surgite at eleven tomorrow. I can't change it."

"Surgite? Isn't that where your translator was?"

"Yes. That's where I'm getting the test subject."

"Why are you making this difficult?"

Theo gripped his chair. His breaths and patience had grown short.

"You asked for someone I can interview. I'm just doing what you said."

"Nobody at your own school?" Arthur asked.

"No. What are we going to do?"

"One final test."

SEVENTEEN

SUNLIGHT FILLED the verdant athletic fields. Birds belted their cheery songs. March's incessant wind had finally retired, leaving a gentle breeze. Surgite's soccer team performed their energetic drills in the expectant days of late winter. Emma's pink trench coat was open to the balmy morning. Hanna shivered in waves of nerves as she stood next to her. She pulled her leather jacket tighter against herself. They watched the team, Broc and Emma's brothers intermixed within.

"Boys are chaos, ya know?" Emma began. "With their ridiculous motorcycles and cars, their wild love poems and songs, their brash displays and pompous competition. It's laughable, almost pitiful, to witness."

She smiled wryly. "And yet somehow we end up giving in and saying, 'I need some man in my life.'"

Hanna glanced at her in concern. Emma continued, "What fun would life be without them? Maybe not all of us, but most of us are at least humored by their efforts. Our species would have gone extinct otherwise. They can be downright entertaining sometimes, and in rare cases of a special guy: completely enamoring. Maybe biology urges us to find them charming. That or it shuts out our rational fear of getting handcuffed to a fridge. Dating is exciting but exhausting. It's not the end of the world if you break up with him. Sometimes a girl's got to step off the dance floor and collect herself—get her thoughts together. There's a whole world of men out there without all this 'whatever is going on with Theo.' Isn't that nice?"

"I guess so. I don't like how I feel."

"How do you feel?"

Hanna breathed in the brisk air, filling her lungs. "Like I'm about to make a horrible mistake."

"If you ask me, I don't think Theo's cheating on you," Emma said, her voice reassuring. "He just doesn't seem like that kind of guy. Even if it doesn't work out, then no big deal. We're just animated skin bags of neurons and hormones. Move on. Play piano. Find a new guy or don't. Enjoy life."

Emma resumed watching the field. "So is he gonna show up on his motorcycle?"

"Yes."

"That might explain the whole leather-jacket-boots-gloves thing you're doing. We're going to talk to him at the café?" Emma asked nervously.

Hanna nodded. "I'm not going to do anything rash. I just want you to ask me about the green journal like we rehearsed. He said he has to meet someone right after. It won't take long."

"Theo's social now?" she asked incredulously.

"Something to do with his history professor—the one I did the translation for."

Hanna watched Broc out in the field. *Now there's a boy without issues*, she thought. Emma noticed Hanna's stare and felt compelled to add, "It's fitting he plays goalie—he never scores."

She chuckled at her own joke. Hanna was unmoved.

"Christ, Hanna, you look nervous," Emma said.

"I was too hard on him yesterday. I cut off our date and he looked like I ripped out his heart."

"Well, ya gotta do what's right for you," Emma replied, watching the industrious practice heat up.

They must have noticed their audience. Soccer balls were brazenly airborne. Unnecessary tackles were thrown. Even Broc's sprints displayed prowess, but Hanna remained distracted by thoughts of Theo. *What if what I want is to not hurt him?* She recollected Theo's honesty.

A miskicked soccer ball hurled toward a ruminating Hanna. Noticing far too late, she accepted her fate, cowering and wincing. Emma swiftly caught it.

"Hands!" a player shouted at her.

She kicked the ball right back to him with ruthless accuracy.

"Crack shot there, sport!" she shouted, upon the ball contacting his body.

He scuttled away to the jeers of his teammates. The team's captain, Emma's oldest brother, Victor Hugo, restored order.

"You there, space cadet?" Emma prodded.

"Hey, you can't inflict amnesia on someone, right?" Hanna answered, sharing the question on her mind.

"For the last time, Hanna, nobody can cause amnesia. Unless he's been whacking you upside the head, which I doubt, there's no way he's making you forget stuff. Your brain automatically dumps useless information all the time. You must have found your dates in January boring, so your brain chucked 'em. You don't have amnesia—you're just not as into him as you thought you were."

Even if Theo was somehow making her forget, how was he doing it? Why did she only forget things about him? Would he really do that to their relationship? If so, why? Emma's absence snatched her attention. Hanna looked about and spotted Emma in the parking lot, just beyond the team's view. A telling whisp of smoke trailed behind her.

Hanna chased after her. "What are you doing?" she asked abruptly.

"Like I said," she said, taking another drag, "you're makin' me nervous now."

Hanna snatched the cigarette from her hand, squatted down, and pressed it out in the asphalt.

"You know those aren't cheap," Emma fumed.

"Cigarettes are bad for you," she retorted, returning the crushed stub.

"You can't just butt into people's lives," Emma said, discarding the dead cigarette in a trash can, pursued by Hanna's punitive stare.

A motorcycle buzzed behind them into a nearby parking spot. Desire for the truth urged Hanna to rush toward him. Having only taken a few paces from Emma, she stopped, seized by apprehension. The sudden painful recollection of the previous day, then weeks, then months, flooded back. She spotted her helmet strapped to the bike's pillion. She watched him park and remove his helmet. A single day had aged him years. They locked eyes. He dismounted his bike, holding her apologetic look—Hanna forgetting her own innocence.

"Hey, dorkwad!" Emma shouted, sauntering past Hanna. Theo studied Hanna's helmet to avoid Emma's overbearing stare.

"Ya know where the café is?" she asked in a cordial tone.

"Yes," he answered.

Emma continued, "Bueno. When Chris gets here, we'll head over. We've been a couple times."

Theo asked, "What do you mean *we*?"

Hanna followed timidly behind Emma.

"What do *you* mean? Hanna didn't tell you? It's a double date."

Theo grabbed his helmet.

"Wait! Theo, please!" Hanna shouted. "I know I didn't tell you, but please stay. I'm sorry about yesterday."

"Are you?"

"I just . . . had to get my thoughts together. Please stay. We can talk it over after," she implored. Unresolved silence sat between them.

Emma grumbled, "Could've mentioned to me he didn't know."

"That makes two of us," Theo said, setting his helmet down.

Emma smirked.

"What does Chris drive?" Theo prodded.

"Oh, you'll know. It's a rich burgundy and has a huge spoiler. It's pretty intense," Emma answered smugly. She continued describing the car while Theo checked his watch. A piqued Emma relinquished her audience and checked her phone.

"You look worried," Theo said to Hanna, who stood nearby.

"You look tired. Did you sleep well?"

"No. You?"

"Me neither. Are you sure you're okay to ride the bike?"

"I'll be fine."

Emma broke their exchange with, "I bet I could ride that bike."

Theo glowered. "No. You could not," he said.

A growling exhaust gurgled in the distance. The angry burgundy four-door sedan advanced toward them. Emma waved it to park next to Theo as if guiding an airplane.

She laughed at her own humorous gesture, then said, "I crack myself up sometimes."

The driver stepped out. His jeans and hoodie fit tightly on his muscular frame. His hair neatly adorned a comely, defined face, handsome and bold—a veritable Adonis. Hanna spotted a pack of cigarettes in his car.

"Hey, babe," he said to an expectant Emma. She placed a peck on his stubbled cheek and lifted a foot doing so. She glanced back to catch Hanna's reaction.

"These your friends?" he asked genially.

"Yep. Hanna and Theo are joining us at the café today. They'll follow you on his bike."

"Nice to meet you," he said, extending a hand over the motorcycle for Theo's. Their firm handshake put Hanna at ease. When he turned for hers, she kept her distance and simply waved.

Theo said, "We should get going."

"We can all ride in my car if you'd like. There's plenty of room," Chris said, his politeness seemingly at odds with the tattoo on his wrist.

"No," said Theo, picking up his helmet. "I'm faster on my bike anyway."

"I don't think you know how fast this beast can go," Chris said through an airy laugh.

Theo put on his helmet. "I do."

Emma turned to Theo. "Alrighty, kids, we'll see you at the café. Try not to lose Hanna off the back," she said, giggling once again at her own humor.

Chris opened the passenger door for Emma and ushered her into his lowered chariot. Theo unfastened Hanna's helmet and handed it to her. She hesitantly took it. Theo reassured her the ride would be uneventful. Hanna cursed her unsure hands as she fastened her helmet. She climbed onto the bike, and they set off, following Chris in his garish car. Theo's warmth was familiar but empty. A brief ride down the hill into town, and she found herself swept along by the double date. The café's parking lot, Chris and Emma chatting about Theo's motorcycle, discussing the menu in line, ordering and getting a table—it all drifted past her.

Energizing morning light reached through the glass door. A queue of familiar faces flowed from the register just out of reach of her recollection. A garrulous Emma and Chris sat across from Hanna and Theo, their two helmets resting on the table. Only Theo kept his coat on. A sickening dread crept over her, keeping the surrounding voices alien. They spoke as if in a tongue she had once understood. All eyes were on her suddenly. They expected something from her.

"Oh, I'm sorry. What was the question?" she asked, confused.

Patiently, Chris said, "No biggie. I was just asking if you both ride motorcycles?"

"He does. I just started. He taught me a couple days ago," Hanna answered.

"Wow! That's really cool," said Chris, grinning widely.

Emma chimed in, "Yeah, she likes the bike, alright. She's gotta be more careful, though. One pebble in the road and she's gonna end up looking like raspberry chutney. Why d'you wanna drive something that could be taken out by a pebble anyway?"

"It'd take more than a pebble," said Theo.

Emma rolled her eyes. "She and speed demon here have ridden into the city together too."

"Really? That sounds pretty epic. How do you survive the cold?"

"I don't really know," Hanna replied, her voice adrift, her heart off balance.

What are Chris's flaws? she pondered, scrutinizing his benevolent smile. Theo made no effort to augment Hanna's answers.

"You're brave. An uncle of mine died in a motorcycle accident. I could never," said Chris. Shame bled through Hanna. Theo stared into his untouched black coffee.

"But I think it's cool that you two ride. More power to you," continued Chris. "What did you do in the city?" he asked innocently.

"I live there," Theo answered flatly.

"We went to sing karaoke," Hanna remarked. Chris was evidently wanting to continue the conversation, but Hanna shut it down.

"Hey, Emma," she said, her sudden volume surprising Emma mid-sip.

"Yeah? What's up?" answered Emma, catching her cue.

"Do you remember if I said I'd bring my green journal with me into the city?"

Emma answered her rehearsed, "Yeah. I do."

"Funny thing is, I can't find it," said Hanna, mindful of Theo's reaction. He tensed up slightly. Subtle, but she felt it.

"Where was the last place you remember having it?" Emma asked deliberately.

"I remember having it at home. Then it's like there's this gap in my memory and I can't find it."

Theo avoided her wounded stare.

"Oh, I lose things all the time," Chris interjected.

"Yeah!" Emma said, laughing. "Oh my God, I do too! I can lose a pen without even moving."

Chris picked up on Emma's enthusiasm. "I've done that too. And then you frantically look around and it's been right in front of you the whole time."

Emma returned his volley, swept up by his charm. Hanna watched Theo, who maintained his acerbic reserve. Eventually, Chris and Emma's laughter-filled banter died down, his hand having made its way around her waist. Emma's smile waned under his lustful touch, her mascara-heavy lashes blinking slowly with disappointed acceptance. She discreetly shrugged away from him.

"You brought your green journal with you when we went into the city," Theo said to Hanna in the available silence. "You left it in my room when you slept over Thursday night."

Sipping her sweet coffee, Hanna choked and angrily cleared her throat.

"Did ya leave room for the Holy Spirit?" Emma said, chiding Hanna.

Hanna rushed to say, "I can't remember bringing it at all. Emma remembers me bringing it, right? I told you."

Called to action, Emma perked up. "Yeah. The journal you started because of the abductions."

Hanna tested Theo, saying, "Really? Was that why I started it?"

Theo reached into his jacket pocket. "Well, it's right here," he said, mysteriously producing the green journal.

"Oh," was all Hanna could utter. Her jittery hands took it from his confident grip.

Emma gave an exasperated sigh. "You could have just started by saying you have it."

Theo retorted, "She hadn't asked for it yet. I was going to return it at the end of the date." He reached back into his pocket and produced her lilac earrings. He set them delicately on the table next to Hanna's mug.

"I forgot I gave them to you," she marveled.

"I forgot too," he said.

Hanna dropped them into her jacket pocket. Shaken, she thought, *I completely forgot about these, but he forgot too? Am I really just forgetful? Why would he make me forget about the earrings he gave me?*

"Hey, Mr. Elusive," Emma barked. "So what were you up to last night anyway?"

Theo could not escape. Chris and Hanna equally watched Theo in anticipation.

At last, he said, "I went home and worked on my history professor's project. It's been stressing me a lot. I worked out after and rehearsed what I was going to say during this date. That kept me up, along with the anxiety and regret over Thursday and Friday's dates. I was waiting for my dad to go to sleep anyway, so I ate at midnight. I didn't feel like moving or doing anything. I just … stared out the kitchen windows, remembering how the snow glows so bright, illuminated by the city's lights. It's like a comforting twilight. The beauty of it struck me, even in memory. I had a sip of my dad's gin and passed out around two."

They all stared equally in dismay. "It's how most nights have gone recently," he added candidly.

Hanna attempted to stutter out a response but failed. Emma softly swore to herself. The café's activity sounded much louder than when they had entered. Hanna wondered if Eddie or Katie came to this café—or, heaven forbid, Sensei.

Chris abandoned the dead conversation with, "Hey, Emma and I are going to get a snack. Want anything?"

"No, thanks," Hanna and Theo said in unison.

Emma rose with Chris and followed after him, explaining her friends' behavior. Hanna's heart ached. A couple now visible at a far table taunted Hanna with their enraptured conversation and saccharine touching. Theo leaned close to her and murmured, "You started your journal because of the abductions. Don't you remember?"

"I did? Didn't you ask me to start keeping one?"

"Really? You don't remember?"

"No," she lied.

"No—try to remember. You can remember, right?"

She gazed into his perturbed hazel eyes. "No."

"What about yesterday? What about your schoolwork? Can you still remember that?"

Seeing his concern mounting, she tested his reaction with, "Not really. I forgot about my calculus quiz."

"What did we do yesterday?"

"Went to the bookstore, then karaoke."

"And the day before?"

She remembered perfectly well what had transpired but chose to say, "I don't know. What did we do?"

"Are you asking me or testing me?" he said, growing panicked.

"I remember riding the motorcycle. Then it's kind of blank from there. Did we eat at a restaurant?"

"Oyakodon."

"Oh yeah! We ordered Chinese food. Then we went out to karaoke."

"No! No. It's getting all mixed up," he said, distraught.

Her thoughts unfolded rapidly. *Why is he so concerned about my memories? I change something and he's freaking out. It's got to be related to my amnesia. He must know something. How do I get through? How do I get him to reveal the truth?*

Chris and Emma returned, Chris declaring, "The brownies are really good. I got extras."

Obliged, Hanna took one. Theo's phone rang. He gave a terse greeting and slipped outside.

The three of them sat together. An understanding chuckle passed through them. Chris and Emma's relaxed expressions put Hanna at ease.

"Busy guy, isn't he?" Chris remarked.

"It's probably his history professor again. He's doing a special project involving the translation of inscriptions," Hanna chimed back, watching Theo through the window. He disappeared around the corner and she turned back. "I helped him with the translation."

Intrigued, Chris followed up at once with, "He goes to school in the city, I'm guessing?"

"Lincoln," Emma said flatly.

"Oh, dang," said Chris. "That explains it," he added in response to Hanna's quizzical look.

Emma sipped her tea. "Yeah, karaoke king here is a philosopher."

"He seems like an interesting guy, albeit a bit off," remarked Chris.

Theo returned, saying, "I should be taking Hanna back now."

Emma stood, her shoulders squared to Theo. "Hanna can stay if she wants. You can split if you have to. She can ride back with us. Heck, it's not a long walk."

"I'll go back with you," Hanna said, standing up. Emma looked perplexed—Theo elated. Hanna handed Theo his helmet and took hers. The prescription in her pocket gave her reassurance. *I have enough to confront him. I have my journal back,* she thought as they said goodbye and returned to his motorcycle.

"Why are your hands shaking?" Theo asked, donning his gear.

"Just cold," she lied through her helmet. A message from Emma buzzed her phone: "Theo slipping away. I talk to him 1-1."

How? Hanna thought. Theo fired up the bike and Hanna climbed on behind him. They rode back to Surgite in the powerful sunlight, the stinging wind lashing Hanna's exposed wrists and neck.

Theo maneuvered them to a secluded spot beneath the mighty oaks in Surgite's main parking lot. Snaking nearby were the pedestrian paths to the dorms. Chris parked some distance away. Hanna hopped off the motorcycle and unfastened her chinstrap, only to catch Emma flagrantly waving her arms from across the parking lot.

"What is she doing?" asked Theo.

"I don't know. Maybe she wants you to go over there?"

"She keeps pointing at me and waving her arms."

"Why don't you ride over and ask her?" Hanna suggested. Whatever Emma's plan was, it had surely started. Theo fired up the bike again and rolled down the parking lot toward Emma, still waving her arms. Alone, Hanna paced to collect her thoughts. This was it. The time to accuse was imminent. Answers were surely close, but her resolve was not. Theo was already coming back. He stopped beside Hanna and said, "She wants you to ride over to them. She said she wants to see you on the bike."

His lack of helmet surprised her.

"Right now? In front of everyone?" Hanna replied, unsure of Emma's intent. Balmy sunlight invited her to hop on the bike. At Theo's encouragement, she fastened her helmet, mounted the bike, and made a jerky start toward an ecstatic Emma and Chris. The soccer team spotted her.

"Whoo! Yeah girl!" Emma cheered, waving Theo's helmet in the air.

"You're a natural!" Chris shouted.

Hanna stopped the bike, set it on its kickstand, and popped off her helmet. Emma's voice rang out, "Oh no, honey. You gotta do it like this."

Emma jammed Theo's helmet onto her head, shouting, "Damn! He can wear this thing?" She gracefully slipped it off and gave an ostentatious swing of her cascading curls. The entire soccer team zeroed in on the show. Emma flashed a coquettish smile. Her brothers gave boos and downward thumbs. Emma came to Hanna and said, in a low voice, "Hey, you're, like, trained on this thing, right?"

"I mean, Theo gave me a lesson, but . . ."

"Can you ride in a straight line?"

"I think so."

"Can you take me back to him?"

Hanna recoiled. "Right now? In front of everyone?"

"Well, yeah. You're the expert here," Emma said, stuffing her head back into Theo's helmet. She climbed onto the pillion seat while Hanna donned her own helmet to much less fanfare. Hanna found herself unprepared for the sudden additional weight and movement of Emma's larger frame. Her proportions pressed against Hanna. The motorcycle sank on its suspension under the weight of a passenger. The gravity of the task at hand dawned on Hanna.

"You can fit on this tiny seat? Theo should get a real bike," Emma muttered.

Over her shoulder, Hanna growled, "Was this part of your plan too?"

Emma cackled. "Ah, no. I'm just messing around. But seriously, take me to Theo and then ride back here. Give us a few minutes. I'll get the truth out of him."

"What am I supposed to do?"

"I dunno. Just ride around. Theo ain't going anywhere as long as you're on his bike."

Emma wrapped her hands around Hanna's torso and shouted, "Onward, mighty steed!" Chris chuckled while Hanna lurched, taking Emma and the machine across the parking lot in uneven spurts of speed. Emma's flagrant swearing drew yet more attention from the team.

Once stopped, Emma dismounted with a skip and patted Hanna's back. "Hang on a minute, horsey," she said.

Hanna glowered while Emma yanked Theo's helmet off and tied it to the bike's pillion.

Theo scowled. "You smeared your makeup all over it."

Emma announced, "Hanna's gonna give Blue here a few test laps around the parking lot."

Theo's expression flickered between apprehension and anger. Emma addressed Hanna over the engine's hum, saying, "Go on, crack that throttle open," then winked at Hanna. It was the first time she had ever done so. It startled Hanna. She let out the clutch lever, pointed the bike back toward the burgundy sport sedan, and rolled on the throttle, trusting Emma's plan.

———

THEO FELT the sweat on his neck. Arthur would be there any minute. He was not leaving without Hanna. She had his motorcycle and helmet, there was a crowd of witnesses, and Emma had cornered him in the shade of the barren oaks. Her choleric brown eyes narrowed in on his.

"Look, Hanna's being weird and indirect. She's not tackling this head on. Real talk: are you cheating on Hanna?"

"No."

"Really? That's it? No? You gotta explain, buddy."

"No. I would never. All other women are vapid."

"Thanks, bastard."

"My point."

Emma laughed derisively. "Really? You've talked to all women? All the women in the world? Every one?"

He stared back at her.

"You're hopeless."

He offered no response.

"So you really aren't cheating on her?"

"No. Why would I? Everything was fine until karaoke yesterday."

Emma rubbed her chin, "Huh. Well then one of you's lying because she said this whole double date was because she thought you were."

"So that was two lies to get me here," Theo said, speared by the truth.

Pity and confusion played across Emma's expressive countenance before she resumed her usual pugnacious smirk. "Okay, then, tell me this. Hanna's convinced she is some kind of amnesiac. Poor girl doesn't realize she's just head over heels for you."

"She is?"

"How blind are you?"

"I mean, I didn't know she knew she had amnesia."

"So she does?"

His stomach sank. "I mean, no. I mean . . . I didn't know she had amnesia."

Stepping closer to him, Emma asked, "What's going on with this whole amnesia thing?"

Theo looked out over the parking lot.

"No, ya don't," she said, stepping into his view.

"I . . ." he began. He spotted Hanna tracing sloppy circles on the motorcycle. The soccer team cheered her on and gestured her to do a wheelie. She seemed so happy. The bike bucked into a sprint. Positive attention surrounded her—something he could never give her. Realization rattled through him. He opened his jacket, oblivious to Emma's ongoing interrogation.

Maybe there is a way after all, he thought. *Maybe I don't have to disappear from her life after this. Just one more test and I'll tell her. I'll find a way to tell her.*

"I never believed my relationship would get this far with Hanna," Theo said to his boots.

"What?"

"I've never told anyone this, but I've always wanted to fall in love. I was convinced it's impossible. Then I met Hanna."

He reached inside his jacket, watching Hanna ride in the

distance. He wondered if she could see the guilt on his face. He began a lento stroll behind the cars and spoke, waiting for Hanna to turn away from him. Emma followed closely.

"I'm beginning to think I was wrong. My treatment of her was perhaps irresponsible—testing her like a rat. I didn't believe anyone could love like she does. I know I can't. Yet, somehow, she cares about me. Maybe it's pity. Maybe she does for her own selfish reasons. But the more time I spend with her, the more I'm beginning to think she could actually love . . . well, me. I don't deserve it. I deserve to suffer this sentence to learn the truth."

Hanna veered away from them. Theo spied Emma's hands in her coat pockets. A chic scarf protected her neck and she remained guarded walking beside him.

"Why are you telling me all of this?" she asked nervously.

"Because I know you won't remember," he said, stopping behind a car blocking their view of the soccer team.

"Get outta here! What are you on about?" she retorted with contrived laughter.

"Would you believe me if I told you I've been erasing Hanna's memories?" he answered, stepping closer to her. She remained still. A black SUV loomed in the distance.

Just a pace away, Theo stood looking down at an anxious but steadfast Emma. His right hand reached for the sheath. Emma jerked to spot his hand in his jacket.

"What? You gonna pull a rabbit out of a hat? You do magic too? Hanna's in over her head."

"I don't know about her, but you are," he said, drawing her eyes back up to his. Hanna would turn around in seconds. Arthur was here. Emma was about to bolt. A tender memory of Hanna stabbed him.

Theo kissed Emma's glossy, sinful lips. Her hands shot out of her pockets. Her whole body went rigid, unwilling or unable to move. The smell of cigarettes and guilt permeated Theo. She stared back into his open, unfocused eyes.

"What the fuck are you doing?" she asked curtly into Theo's lips, her breath warming them. He slipped the sheath out from under his jacket and touched it to her exposed hand. Violet light made her merely a memory. Alone, he sighed and answered, "Ruining my life."

EIGHTEEN

HANNA SWUNG the bike around one last time toward Theo and Emma. Only a wheelie could satisfy the soccer team's sky-bound exuberance. Unable to do so, she buzzed by them one last time. *That's all the time I can give you, Emma. Hopefully you got some answers*, she thought, returning to them. She stopped in their previously occupied location. They were gone. An undertow of concern dragged her spirits lower.

"Maybe they're still talking," she mumbled in her helmet. The distant campus security building flickered in the sunlight spilling through the surrounding maples. The registrar's office soaked up the remaining daylight. There she spotted him. Theo backed away from a black SUV ominously turning around in the empty lot of the yellow registrar's house.

She gasped. "The abductions!" she said, slapping her face shield closed. A click of the gear shifter, a zealous twist of the throttle, a snap of the clutch, and she shot down the parking lot. Unforgiving wind stung her neck. She pressed on, down the empty road, and turned the bike into the registrar's lot. Hearing the familiar hum, an observant Theo spun around. The black SUV hurled past Theo and swerved to block off his escape.

"Run, Hanna! Get out of here!" he shouted.

The bike heaved to a stop under Hanna. The back door of the SUV flew open.

Hanna opened her face shield and shouted, "What's going on? Where's Emma?"

The SUV's driver spotted her.

Theo looked over his shoulder at the open door, then back to Hanna. Panic lashed his anguished face. He shouted, "Hanna, it's too late now! Take the bike as far—" but a man sprung from the SUV and grabbed him. Her frozen hands gripped the bike's two levers helplessly. Despite his struggle, Theo was dragged into the SUV. It roared off past Hanna. The driver's piercing eyes caught hers as they passed.

Released from her trance, gumption swelled in her. Her left hand released the clutch lever and the bike rolled. She jerked through the process of turning around and pursued the escaping vehicle—the alarmed soccer team an afterthought. The black SUV plunged into traffic. Hanna crouched low on the machine, gripping it with her entire body. A quickly narrowing opening in traffic presented itself. She burst onto the main road, catching the sudden horn of a car. Ahead, she saw the black SUV weaving through traffic.

Theo can't get abducted, she thought, surveying the cars ahead. The black SUV slipped down a side road. Hanna veered into the shoulder and found the throttle's maximum travel. Gravel and debris threatened destruction. A scream escaped her dry mouth. She snapped the throttle closed. Down past the cars she shot, their belligerent horns sounding her advance. She leaned the bike into the turn but vastly overshot. An approaching car in the opposing lane slammed on its brakes, narrowly avoiding catastrophe. Stunned, she shoved the bike back into her own lane with a determined grunt. The bewildered driver's indignant sign language needled her as she passed.

Unyielding fog encroached her face shield. The black SUV heaved down another turn. Hanna twisted for all the engine's might, but fear twisted it back. She and the machine hurled themselves toward another uncertain angle. Stabbing the brake, the front tire chirped on the cold asphalt. The entire machine lunged forward. Hanna panicked and released the brake lever. The rapidly approaching trees braced themselves for the inevitable. Squeezing the lever again in mortal terror, she hemorrhaged all her speed to make the turn.

Hanna's chest heaved. Her nose was running terribly, teeth chattering, and fingertips completely numb. She twisted for another lunge at the escaping black SUV. It roared down an entrance ramp onto the highway. "No! Dammit," she cursed, making one final attempt. By the time she took the ramp, it was gone. She cried out, banging up through the gears onto the highway, losing her target. The frozen wind was unbearable. The relentless din of engine, wind, and traffic assaulted her senses. Her fogging shield blocked her vision, now irresponsibly obstructed. The surrounding imperiled cars witnessed her tremulous gasp for speed in vain.

Hanna rolled off the next exit, hypothermic and unable to manipulate the machine any further. Lethargic inputs led her and the bike to veer off the road. Unfocused, she pulled both levers, losing speed and any hope of a safe return. She teetered into the grass just off the exit ramp. The wild greenery, unkempt and thorny, caught her next. Machine and rider found themselves toppled. She hoisted herself back to her feet, catapulted by instinct's vigorous pulse, and shut off the motorcycle napping in the underbrush. It was somehow intact. Ripping branches off her, she fought her way out of the flora back into the clearing. Hanna collapsed to her hands and knees, panting at the roadside, the staring man burned into her memory.

———

"WHO'S the girl on the bike?" Arthur asked, casually swerving through the highway's traffic.

"Take me back. This is all wrong," Theo demanded, peering out the back window for another glimpse at Hanna. Worry sank its fangs deep into him. Greg sat beside Theo, keeping a vigilant watch of him in the back seat.

Ignoring Theo's pleas, Arthur pressed on, saying, "Why did she follow us?"

Theo retorted, "I told you not to enter the campus. The whole damn soccer team probably just saw what happened."

"Who's the girl?"

"A friend. Not the translator."

"On your motorcycle?" Arthur paused, then continued, "It doesn't matter." He slowed to a speed comparatively modest to the velocity he had just forced upon the black box. "They'll blame it on the abductions. We'll have to lay low for a while," he added.

"I doubt any of them got the plate," Greg surmised.

Theo asked, "Why are you rushing? You could have just waited and met me somewhere else like I told you."

Arthur's face contorted into a snarl. "You had plenty of time. You waited until the last minute for no reason. We need to move forward, and Greg's on board now."

Theo's stomach sank. The day was not at all unfolding how he had predicted.

Greg explained, "Arthur's let me in on what you've been up to for the past few months. If he's telling the truth, then what we're about to see is most definitely not just another trinket. This Memory Therapy thing could be revolutionary. Think of the market potential."

"Sure," Arthur said callously, continuing to snake the SUV through the expansive highway. The cresting hills of trees and granite of northern New Jersey gradually morphed into New York's cliffs, blasted out for commerce's veins.

Greg turned to Theo. "Show me the sheath. Arthur's already shown me the knife."

Theo hesitated, but Arthur assented to Greg's demand. Theo carefully produced it from his jacket. Greg motioned for Theo to pass it to him. Arthur watched from the rear view mirror and said, "Not until we get to my house."

An apprehensive silence covered them for the journey's last legs. Theo beheld the steel structure of the Tappan Zee Bridge, knowing the intermission would soon end. On the eastern side, they shot northward along the river. Arthur powered his SUV down an undulating private drive until, at last, his modest abode appeared. He parked beside a small car Theo presumed belonged to Greg.

The three men exited the vehicle and entered Arthur's drafty house. They passed an unremarkable living room as Arthur led them to the basement. Theo became distinctly aware that Greg was keeping Theo in his sight. He wondered if the two men had forgotten they were actually a party of five. The wooden basement stairs creaked beneath their feet. Greg locked the door behind them and pocketed the basement's key. The unfinished cinderblock walls and water-stained concrete floor were complemented by a bare bulb for lighting and a single dirty window high up. A pole supporting the house stood in the center of the ominously empty room. Trash bags and cleaning supplies loomed in the corner.

Greg remained silent beside Theo. Arthur moved to the far side of the room. Next to him was a small table on which the knife and a pair of handcuffs sat. Theo remained behind the pole in the darkness.

Arthur asked, "You know the person you trapped? You can ask him clearly what happened after you let him out?"

"Yes. Why?"

Arthur held out the handcuffs to Theo. "Cuff him to the pole."

Theo took them with unsteady hands.

Greg's face paled. "What do you mean, let him out?"

"Show him, Theo," Arthur answered calmly.

Theo drew the sheath, knelt near the base of the pole, and pulled the belt loop. The violet light summoned her prominent figure and dropped her down prostrate. Her pink trench coat settled around her in the dust. Theo grabbed one of her wrists but missed the second, already groping for her surroundings. Arthur's hand lashed out for her other wrist and yanked it around the pole.

"You never said you could get girls like this!" Arthur exclaimed.

Theo clacked the handcuffs around Emma's wrists, which were quickly regaining their vitality.

Greg stepped back out of the light, marveling, "I'll be damned. No joke this time, Arthur, you found the real occult."

Emma moaned, returning to life. Her eyes opened slowly and took in her surroundings. She gasped for air and jerked her head up, only to realize she was trapped. Thrashing like a cornered animal, she stopped, spotting the man standing in front of her. Greg and Theo remained out of her line of sight.

"Hey, what's the big idea here?" she asked, sitting up against the pole. She continued pulling fruitlessly on the handcuffs digging into her wrists. Arthur squatted down for a closer look, his violating stare penetrating her jeans and blouse.

"Look at the figure on you," he remarked, snatching her scarf.

Her kick just missed him.

"Easy there. We're just going to run a little experiment," he said, walking back to the table. "See, you're going to take a nap. And when you wake up, you're going to tell us what you saw in your dream."

"Get the fuck away from me! Where am I? Where's Theo?"

"Behind you."

She turned and spotted Theo in the darkness. On the verge of tears and screams, she stared at him. "Why?" was all she could mouth.

"Just do what he says, Emma," he told her, losing his composure. Her panicked eyes darted to Greg and back to Theo.

"The rules are simple," Arthur said, pulling her attention back. "Tell us what you saw in your dream."

"Fuck you!"

"Or you die."

She let out an ireful scream, thrashing her handcuffs against the pole. Standing, she realized the futility of her struggle. She asked, "What the hell? What the hell am I supposed to remember?"

"Oh, it'll be quite easy for you to remember. It will be something you'll never forget. You might even call it"—Arthur picked up the knife—"a nightmare."

"Bag her, Theo," Arthur ordered. A quick touch of the sheath and her memory was erased. A second touch and she was gone. Black lines ensnared the disappearing handcuffs before slithering away from them. They clattered onto the concrete floor. Theo observed the peculiar event and noticed that Greg had been filming it on his cell phone's camera. "I can't believe this," he said, mouth agape.

Greg moved to Arthur. "You made it far, but your time's up," he said, his voice taking on a menacing tone. "You're no longer needed."

"What?" Theo asked, remembering that the door at the top of the stairs was locked.

"You've been played. I pity you, but not enough to stop," Arthur callously remarked.

Theo realized there were two of them. Even releasing Emma, he could only capture one. Sweat threatened his grip on the sheath. His heart hammered blood through him. He reached to pull the belt loop to release Emma, but his attention was diverted to Arthur.

With an exaggerated frown, Arthur said, "It's a shame, really, what that girl's about to see," and plunged the knife into Greg's chest.

An agonized scream burst from Greg. Theo froze. Greg's last

words were, "A . . . voice?" Theo struggled to catch his breath. Arthur pulled the knife out and sunk it deep into his chest again. The putrid sound mixed with Greg's frenetic yelling. A red glow briefly enveloped the knife. Again, Arthur sank the blade into Greg's flailing body, following him down to the unforgiving concrete slab. Theo blocked his own view, unable to witness the life pouring out of Greg. Several torturous moments later, Greg was a fidgeting mass, carved open. Arthur continued. Blackness encroached Theo's vision. He staggered and clung to the icy wall for support. He yelled just to hear his own voice—any sound but Greg's last.

At last, Arthur stopped. Theo continued looking away—darkness his only comfort. Sounds of keys jangling and Arthur unlocking the handcuffs pulled Theo from the abyss of fainting. Theo found himself at the top of the stairs slouched against the locked door, sweating profusely.

"We're not done," Arthur called calmly. "We have to ask the girl what she saw. We need a confession."

Theo banged on the door.

"Theo, we're not done," Arthur repeated calmly against the din. He stood at the bottom of the stairs holding Greg's phone in one hand and the knife in the other.

Theo yelled back, "What happened to cutting my wrist once while the victim's trapped! When did murdering Greg become a good idea!"

"It's alright, Theo. Greg didn't understand," Arthur said, his voice unnervingly calm. "We don't want to monetize the knife. I knew he was traitorous. I knew he'd kill you after me. He was never going to realize its true potential."

Theo looked down the stairs. Arthur wore a perplexed face. "You said you had seen this stuff before?"

"It's different in real life," Theo growled through strained respiration.

Dizzy, he fumbled to his feet as Arthur approached, pocketing

Greg's phone and producing the key to the door. He unlocked it and beckoned Theo to follow.

"This isn't anything like last time," Theo protested.

"Man up. There's work to be done," Arthur said, his callous tone resuming.

"How are we going to hide this?"

"Leave that to me."

Afternoon light seeped through the closed curtains of the trite living room. A table and two chairs cowered against the wall. Arthur ordered Theo to sit at the table. Theo felt the cold sweat beading on his forehead. His eyes darted about the room unable to focus. They labored to avoid dwelling on the stains of Arthur's atrocity coloring his formerly white shirt.

"What's the last thing she remembers?" Arthur asked.

Theo did not answer, looking away.

Arthur slammed his fist onto the table. "Answer me, Theo! How far does her memory go?"

Theo fixated on the bloody knife in Arthur's other hand and struggled to articulate, "She doesn't remember any time inside the sheath. I just erased her memory. She probably remembers back to the café . . . maybe just before."

"What café?"

"Where you called me."

"Good. If this works properly, my memory of taking care of Greg will have been placed in the girl's mind. She will believe she's done it."

"That's impossible."

"Impossible?" Arthur scoffed. "The inscription on the knife reads, 'memories of taking a life with this become truth for the trapped. Trapped in here is the murderer but not the truth.'"

Theo pulled his sweat-soaked shirt from his chest. His gut lurched as he recalled his handling of the entire sordid ordeal. A plan to escape that musty room dominated his rapidly working mind. Why he lacked the strength to endure pecked him incessantly.

Arthur pointed at the chair. "You're going to let her out. Get her into the chair and get her talking. Don't let her panic or move. Get her to admit she did it."

"What if she doesn't?"

"You have the power of amnesia. Just capture her and start over."

"And if that doesn't work?"

Arthur ignored him and set a chair directly across from Theo. He hid on the basement stairs and closed the door to but a sliver.

Theo shouted after him, "You promised nobody would get hurt! If she gets hurt any more, I'll never be able to explain it."

"Stop whining."

Resolved to end the ordeal, Theo knelt on the odorous carpet and again released Emma. As she took shape, he hid the sheath in his uncomfortable jacket. He swiftly took her hands and guided her onto the chair. A final shake of her shoulders brought her full attention to Theo.

"Um . . . hi," he said, sheepishly taking his seat across from her.

"What . . . where? What's going on?"

"You're in . . . my parents' vacation house. You passed out."

"Hey, what's the big idea here?" she asked, sitting up in her chair. She began surveying the room and fidgeting about.

"Emma, look at me," Theo said, spotting Arthur through the slightly ajar basement door. "You never went to a café. You have been here all day. You passed out."

"You're not making sense, Theo. God, I feel like a truck hit me," she said, rubbing her temples. She gasped, spotting the sore red contusions on her wrists. "What the hell happened?"

"You fell down some stairs."

She stared back incredulously.

"And hit your head."

Confusion twisted her face. Her smeared makeup unsettled Theo further.

"Hard . . . hard enough to knock you out," Theo said, fumbling for words. He pointed at the staircase on the far side of the room, "Those stairs, in fact."

"Well, this is a first, Emma," she quipped, inspecting the wooden staircase.

"I need you to focus. I need to check if you're okay. What is the last thing you remember?"

"Why didn't Chris . . . did I ride your motorcycle? Did Hanna see us? Where is she?" she asked, looking about.

"Focus, Emma," he snapped, "What is the last thing you remember?"

"Okay, okay. Why are you asking me? What's going on?"

"I need to figure out how much amnesia you have."

"From whacking my head?"

"Yes. Just answer the question."

"What's with the pushiness? Where's Hanna?" she asked, returning to looking about. Her attention veered from Theo and dangerously close to Arthur.

"What do you remember?" Theo nearly shouted.

"You keep asking what I remember?"

"Yes!" he exclaimed impatiently.

"I don't know, but I've got a splitting headache. And why are my clothes dirty?"

"What's the last thing you remember?"

"I was talking to Hanna . . . in the soccer fields . . . it was sunny."

"And then?"

"Then . . . then . . ." She shook her head, overcome by a bitter expression.

"*Then!*"

Her gaze fell to the table. Arthur silently pulled open the door just enough to flash his watch at Theo. "Oh Jesus," she mumbled, grabbing her head.

"What do you see?"

"You don't . . . I can't . . ." she murmured.

"Just say it, dammit!" he ordered, realizing his hands were in fists.

"There's no way," she said, standing up. "Let's go outside, huh? It smells in here."

"It's violent, isn't it?"

"Nope. Nah. What are you on about?" she said, dismissing him, taking in her surroundings. Theo scrambled for a question but merely mustered a doltish hum. Trying again, he said, "So you remember but you're just not saying?" but she merely waved her hand.

Emma turned only to be caught by Arthur rushing out from behind the closed door. She screamed while he forced her back into the chair. Struggling in his grasp, Arthur stood in front of her—a fist of her hair in one hand, the knife trained on her face in the other. Theo stood by helplessly. Over his shoulder, Arthur said, scathingly, "You don't have what it takes."

Emma's legs finally ceased thrashing about. He kept the knife pointed at her and with his other hand took out his cell phone. He turned the screen to her showing a picture of Greg. Staring down at her, Arthur asked, in a disturbing monotone, "Who killed this man?"

"*What?*"

"Who killed this man?"

"Hell if I know!"

"Who killed this man?" he shouted again, emphasizing each word. Theo moved to a spot just behind Arthur. Emma paused, staring up at the knife right in front of her. Tears welled in her eyes. Arthur repeated, "Who killed this man?"

Theo drew the sheath.

"Answer me!" Arthur demanded, pocketing his phone and grabbing her hair again.

Through terrible sobs, she shrieked, "I don't know! Please, God, don't kill me! I don't know!"

Theo shouted, "Just tell him already!"

Emma repeated, "I don't know! I can't remember!"

"Yes, you can," Arthur said, his eyes wild. "Who killed this man?"

Frenzied sobs overtook her. Theo shouted for her to answer but she only cried out for help. Arthur threw her head back and put the knife to her throat.

"I did!" she yelled.

"You killed this man?"

"Yes! Jesus Christ, yes, I did!" she yelled backing as far away from him as she could in her chair.

"How?"

"With a knife. Blood everywhere," she wailed.

"Where?" he asked leaning closer in.

"I don't know. A room? A dark room?"

"What were you wearing?"

"Wearing? A . . . uh . . . a white shirt. Hiking pants."

"Who was in that room?"

"Theo," she wept, her tear-stained cheeks red and body shaking.

"Why did you kill that man?"

"Because I wanted to kill him!" she cried. "I wanted to drive the knife into his chest! I wanted to feel what it's like to kill a man. Jesus Christ, please don't kill me!"

Arthur let her go. She sank in defeat, wracked by sobs.

It could have been Hanna.

The thought circled Theo's mind, refusing to recede into his subconscious.

It should have been me, he thought.

Arthur turned around to Theo, who asserted, "I'll take Emma back now."

"No. Change of plans."

"I have to bring her back! Her wrists are already too much to explain."

"You'll kill me anyway," Emma mumbled in a chillingly sober voice. Her head hung low and body, limp.

Over his shoulder, Arthur snapped, "Go down to the basement and put Greg in the sheath. We can finally test it on a body."

"And then?"

Arthur handed Theo the keys to Greg's car and a note. "Take him there and dump him. Take your time."

Theo took the keys, confused at the sudden change. He noticed Arthur's own address written just below the place to unload the corpse. He stood frozen in realization, but found himself evading a staggering Arthur. Emma had lunged for the knife in his hand. Arthur struck her down and wrestled her against the wall.

"Theo, do something!" she yelled between cries of pain.

Arthur used his left arm to pin her neck with unrelenting delight—his blood-soaked right hand, to snake the tip of the knife under her pink blouse's buttons, cutting them as it passed. Her arms struggled in vain against him crushing her neck.

Arthur snickered. "Don't fight it."

"You'll have to kill me first," she grunted through bloody, gritted teeth.

"Theo, bag her," he commanded.

It could have been Hanna.

The thought sliced through him again.

Resolve welled up. He lunged at a preoccupied Arthur and stabbed him in the neck. Unexplained pain raced up Theo's arm. A black aura flashed around the knife in Arthur's hand. Theo struck again, dropping Arthur to the floor. The same illogical pain shot up his arm.

Arthur staggered back, gasping. Theo recoiled and yelled, "How are you still here!"

Emma took her chance to escape but was soon caught by Theo, who trapped her back in the sheath. Enraged, Arthur returned to his feet, the knife still firmly in his grip.

Theo sprinted out of the house and threw himself at the driver's door of Greg's compact. He fumbled the keys out of his pocket, unlocked the door, and started the car. Backing up from the edge of the forested ravine next to the house, Arthur slammed into the driver's door to rip it open. Theo stomped on the accelerator pedal for all the car's little four-cylinder transverse engine could muster. Barreling up the winding driveway, he spilled onto the quiet road, raced along the verdant precipices, and dove back onto the main street. A red light gave him a reprieve, but the thought of Arthur's black SUV pursuing him brought him back to speeding through traffic. Unable to think, he set a course for his motorcycle— Emma's injuries becoming a festering ulcer in his mind. He drove along, his mind repeating: *what have I done?*

NINETEEN

LATE AFTERNOON SUN edged through the passing clouds. Theo sank back into the driver's seat. He set the bag of his favorite foods in the passenger footwell. Despite tempting himself to consume vital energy, he could not eat. He wiped the cold sweat from his face with the back of his sleeve. It was the fifth time he had done so. Thirty more minutes on the highway remained between him and the agony of bringing Emma back to Surgite. He pulled the center mirror to see himself. His appearance disgusted him. All color in his face had left and dark rings marked the skin under his eyes.

"Don't throw up in Greg's car," he grumbled, turning the key. He manipulated the dials to blow cold New Jersey air into the cabin. He rolled down the windows. The supermarket parking lot around him carried on making a heroic effort to ignore him.

"Think, idiot," he said aloud.

Arthur will kill me. I have the sheath. Greg knew where I lived, or at least parked. Does Arthur? If I go back to the city, will he find me? What do I do with Greg's car? Is Arthur following me right now? How do I bring Emma back? How will I hide this from Hanna? Should I? Would she understand? Is she okay? What happened to her on my motorcycle? Where is my motorcycle?

Theo's unsteady hands navigated the car back onto the highway. The cold air rushed in, comforting him. He imagined Hanna having crashed, or worse.

Find her. Find the bike.

Shivers overwhelmed him and he closed the windows, opting for the car's heater instead. He approached Surgite in a feverish panic. The police cars patrolling the main parking lot did not help. He passed by them, heading for the commuter parking lot. Its gate was closed. Met by suffocating frustration, he drove into town and parked by a meter, which he ignored entirely.

Maybe she turned around and made it back to campus, he thought, leaving the small car and drawing his phone. His jacket felt heavy—the sheath, dreadful. He marched up the sidewalk and called Hanna.

No response.

His pace quickened.

He called again.

No response.

The shadowy trees swayed in the dusk. Surgite's campus was in view. He called again. Finally, she picked up. "Hello? Who is this?"

Hanna sounded lost.

"It's me. Are you okay?" Theo asked hastily. "Am I not saved in your phone?"

Silence on the other end, followed by a confused Hanna, asking, "Are you Theo?"

"Hanna, come on, what are you doing? Did you hit your head in a crash? It's me, Theo."

"That's weird. Your phone number is already in my phone, but when did we meet?"

"Hanna, what are you doing?"

"Are . . . are you a student at Surgite?" she asked, her voice unsure.

"I go to Lincoln!" he nearly shouted, breaking into a run. "Where are you? Are you okay?"

"I'm . . . I don't know you. I shouldn't . . . how did I get your number?"

Theo rushed into Surgite's forest preserve, weaving between the black trees. "Hanna, talk to me. Did you fall? Did you crash the bike? Are you hurt? What do you remember?"

". . . I don't know."

"Where did you go to high school?"

"King's Prep in Wakefield, New Jersey."

"Who is your best friend?"

"Emma, since third grade."

"What's your sister's name?"

She hesitated.

Theo ducked under the branches of one last tree and stopped in the vacant commuter parking lot. Surgite's science building stood before him.

"I . . . I should go. I don't . . . know you," she said, speaking in staccato plucks of her melodic voice.

"Lily Popov! Your sister is Lily!"

"Why do you know that?"

Theo kept running, unsure of his destination. "We went to King's together! You play piano. You like sweet coffee. You love karaoke. I taught you how to ride my motorcycle. We've talked for hours into the night. What have I done!"

Apprehensive silence, then, "I remember King's. Your voice seems familiar."

"Yes! Yes of course!"

"Really? If we're going to keep talking, I should leave the library."

Theo changed course and dashed down the campus pathway. Under the orange lamplight between the rhododendrons, he spotted her. She stood alone in front of the campus library, passed by occasional groups of oblivious students. Inky night ensconced her. She intently pressed her phone against her ear. The lights of the warm campus library spilled out of its tempered glass facade. Theo hung up and ran toward her. At a few paces away, she saw him and gasped. He stopped and she lowered her cell phone. The earth marring her jeans and leather jacket brought Theo heart-wrenching guilt.

"Hanna, it's me," he called out. He had never seen such distant apprehension in her expression. "I thought I would find you here on campus. What happened to the bike? Did you fall? Are you okay?"

"What bike?"

"Hanna, please," he begged, stepping toward her.

She backed away from him, saying only, "I don't know you."

Theo stumbled to a stop, his boots scraping against the unforgiving concrete. Hanna kept vigilant watch of him. He stood powerless, in agony. Hanna turned. Theo grabbed her wrist. She tore it away, shouting, "Don't touch me!"

"You really don't remember me?"

Hanna glared back at him. A pair of passing students exchanged concerned looks.

"The amnesia made you forget everything?" he asked her, only to receive an empty stare.

Caution discarded, he yanked the sheath out of his jacket. *"What the hell did you do?"* Theo roared in Japanese. It merely sat inert in his hands.

"It really was you," Hanna whispered, her words drifting like smoke. "I knew you'd come back. They took you but you work with them, don't you?" Her voice, normally a flowing melody, bore only a single note.

"No! No, I don't."

"How did you get here? Do you have amnesia?"

"I . . . woke up in the city and took the train back here. I don't remember anything."

"How? What don't you remember?"

He could not answer.

"It's cruel, isn't it? When someone does it to you?" she asked. Ice ran through his spine. "Pretend they don't know you. Isn't that what you've been doing?"

Her lips quivered but her voice remained resolute. "Pretending you didn't know what I've said even though you remembered perfectly. Pretending to genuinely react to the things we've already said or done. How many times have you lied to me? Countless?"

Theo endured her vitriol in penanced silence. The will to form a word drained from his tongue.

"Did it mean anything to you?" she asked through hot tears. Theo looked away, resigned to his sentence.

"It was you. How were you doing it? How could you? Why do you talk to that thing? Is that what I translated?" she asked, striking painful sincerity in her voice. She grabbed his collar, "Answer me, dammit!"

"To learn the truth."

Dumbfounded, her eyes narrowed to a wince. "The truth? About what? You're not making sense. How were you erasing my memory? Who took you away? Why? This isn't who you are."

On the verge of collapse, Theo answered, "Power nefarious beyond your belief."

Hanna let him go and he stowed the sheath in his jacket.

"I can't show you here, but you're right. It was me. I was erasing your memory."

She shook her head. "No . . . don't say that," she whispered.

"I can show you how I did it—teach you how."

"That's not who you are."

"You could join me," he implored, "There's unfathomable power here and it's real."

She backed away from him.

"Hanna, I had to test it on someone I could trust—someone

close to me. I had to learn the truth about what it could do. If I were discovered, The Makers would kill me."

"Was it for those men that abducted you? Were they the ones abducting everyone?"

"No. I can explain everything, but not here," he answered, suddenly aware of the passing students' whispers.

"Did those men take Emma?"

Guilt choked him.

"Was she just disposable to you? Was I?"

The campus bell chimed the hour. They remained under its spell. A nascent sentence formed on his lips, but Hanna cut him off, saying, "Don't! You've already answered."

"What happened to you on the motorcycle? Are you okay?" he asked.

She wiped away her tears. "Your motorcycle is in the parking lot of the registrar's office," she began, in a seething whisper. "I ran off the road chasing you. Emma's brothers, Broc, and Chris came and rescued me. The four of them picked it up from the bushes I crashed in, put it in his minivan, and drove me back here." A sob rattled her. "It still works. Your helmet is still tied to it. Take it and go away."

Hanna threw the key at him. She tore through her pockets and threw her lilac earrings at him too. He picked them off the ground, accepting his fate.

"Theo, I wanted to love you," she said.

"Liar."

"Just go!" she yelled through fresh tears and disappeared into the warm lights of the library.

Shivering wind swept the refuse of autumn about the desolate campus. Huddled students trotted to inviting edifices promising warmth and comradery. A couple held hands following the comforting glow of the lamppost's vigil. Theo traversed the icy black lawns. The beauty of their nocturnal serenity struck him.

Like a tempest's clouds on approach, he marveled at the magnificence of the stout oaks towering into the night sky. One day, they would once again provide blissful shade on a warm summer day. The perspiration on his shirt chilled him to his soul. Traversing the main road, he spotted the police cars.

Take me. You'll find Emma, he thought. *You'll find the knife and they'll kill me.*

The blue motorcycle stood alone in the registrar's parking lot. Crisp winter moonlight poured through a break in the foreboding clouds, illuminating the solitary journey ahead. Theo rested his hand on its handlebar, garnished with clots of dirt. A turn signal was missing. The rear brake lever had snapped off. The exhaust bore conspicuous scratches. The memory of Hanna learning to ride pierced him—the warmth in her smile—her last words to him.

Look at yourself, he thought. *Just like your cello.*

Theo donned his helmet. It smelled like Emma. He pushed himself to fire up the motorcycle. Miraculously, it started. Hanna was not a complete liar. Greenberm's main road carried his lethargic merge and aimless turns. The machine was unsteady under his shattered confidence. He meandered back into town and parked behind Greg's car. To his surprise, there was no parking ticket. The compact's spartan key unlocked the manual door lock. The simple cloth seat supported him, close to collapsing—whether into tears or screams, he could not tell. He pressed on, emptying all the cash from his wallet into the bag of food from the supermarket that lay at his feet. A picture of Hanna in the purikura booth slipped out. Lost to its tender memory, he pocketed it carefully. He placed the bag and car's key in the driver's footwell.

Drawing the sheath, he said, "Take care of yourself, Emma. Take care of Hanna for me."

Theo surveyed the familiar worn-out streets around him. Not a soul stirred. He released Emma, tapped her again to erase the horror, and exited the small but valiant vehicle that had dependably carried them away from that wretched place. He closed the door and saw that Emma had been placed sitting upright in the driver's seat he had reclined all the way for her. Eyes peacefully shut and mouth open as if dozing after a long drive, the dried blood on her face and cut blouse ruined the illusion. He returned to his bike and set off into the heartless void.

TWENTY

VICTOR HUGO, Emma's older brother, stood and addressed the small gathering in his apartment. Hanna avoided his determined stare stopping at each person in attendance. "We will find whoever did this and make him pay. That's for sure."

Emma's younger brother, Luis, sat attentively on the couch. A pen flicked pensively in his hand. Chris and Broc stood flanking Hanna, who sat in a faded recliner. The modest one-bedroom Camagüey apartment just fit the five of them in its single combined living-dining-kitchen room. Hanna wondered if coming here had been a mistake. Fear had already swept through the campus, followed by wild speculation. Official university emails and dormitory meetings urging students to remain calm came next, then instructions from campus security and more emails to join together in fellowship in this unsettling time. Students were advised not to go out alone—especially at night.

Victor Hugo's piercing look returned to her. "Thank you for coming, Hanna. We appreciate your help."

She nodded, unable to express anything more. The black jeans and leather jacket on Victor Hugo suited his athletic frame, giving an imposing figure to a voice born for leadership. No blithe looks crossed the faces in attendance of his grim council.

"We don't have any leads, but we know Emma has amnesia. She woke up unable to remember anything except some kind of nightmare. She hasn't described it much. By the look on her face, we shouldn't ask her right now."

"Is she still not seeing anyone?" asked Broc earnestly.

"She said she doesn't wanna see anyone. She's staying with us here for the night—tomorrow too," Victor Hugo said definitively.

"She's not coming back to the girls' dorm with me? What about the campus safety orders?" Hanna asked, peering down the hallway at the closed bedroom door.

"The RAs don't need to know," said Luis. "She'll be back for class on Monday. Don't make a big deal of it, would ya?"

"You gotta be alone for tonight and Sunday, but the girls' dorms are perfectly safe," Victor Hugo said to Hanna, his voice softening. "Nobody's gonna mess with you. Monday morning, Emma will be back. If you don't feel safe going out, you can call one of us anytime. Broc can drive you back to the dorms—even home."

The thought of explaining it all to her family drew a limp, "That's okay. I'll stay," from Hanna. Fear gripped her as she remembered Theo telling of "power nefarious beyond your belief."

"Speaking of which, that brings us to why we're here," Victor Hugo said, steering the conversation back on course. "Nobody's gonna get abducted if we're smart about this. We gotta look at the facts and make a plan. It's been a crazy afternoon for everyone, but we need to review what we know before it all gets mixed up. The whole soccer team's already full of different accounts." He produced a notebook and handed it to Luis. "Take some notes, would ya?"

His brother nodded, clicking his pen.

Victor Hugo sat across from Hanna. Luis, Broc, and Chris took the couch. Hanna rested her elbows on her thighs, cupping her hot chocolate, the mud on her clothes a grim reminder of what had transpired earlier that day.

"Let's go slowly. Emma and Hanna were watching the practice. Then what?" Victor Hugo said, commanding the attention of everyone in the room.

Their expectant stares prompted Hanna to answer, "We were waiting for Theo and Chris. We were talking about the double date. Emma walked off to have a cigarette and—"

"We told her to cut that shit out," Luis interjected, shaking his head.

Victor Hugo gestured Hanna to continue. "Theo arrived on his motorcycle, Chris, shortly after. We went to the café."

"Nothing suspicious up to that point? The black SUV wasn't anywhere yet? Nobody follow you?" Victor Hugo asked.

"No. The whole date was . . . fine. We weren't there long. Then we came back to campus."

"I think you forgot to mention that Theo took a phone call in the café. He stepped outside," Chris pointed out.

Hanna nodded. "Oh, that was his history professor, the one with the translation Theo's been working on. Theo had to go back into the city right after the double date."

Luis kept pace in his notes at a furious rate.

"Did the black SUV have New York plates?" Victor Hugo asked.

"I . . . . can't remember. I didn't see," Hanna answered in a daze.

"It had a front license plate," Broc said.

"I remember Jersey plates," Chris tossed out.

"So Theo was in a rush," Victor Hugo observed. "And Theo was the last person Emma spoke to, right?"

All eyes returned to Hanna, who withdrew further from showing emotion. "Yes. I had asked Emma to talk to Theo alone. I . . . I suspected he may have been cheating on me."

"But you two seemed close in the café? Maybe that's just me but . . ." Chris remarked, his voice trailing off.

"It's complicated. Emma asked me to ride Theo's motorcycle

to buy her time. I had asked her to help me get to the bottom of things. She asked for time alone with him. She winked at me."

All men present exchanged confused looks. To clarify, Hanna said, "She winked at me like 'hey, trust me.'"

"So she knew what she was doing," Chris said. "Theo didn't force her to the far side of the parking lot. She told me to get the whole soccer team to watch you, Hanna. I guess she was trying to make a distraction."

"I think so too. She doesn't remember any of this?" asked Hanna.

Luis shook his head solemnly. His older brother stood and paced the miniscule space afforded to him. "And that was the last time any of you saw Emma?"

"Yes," they all answered.

"But moments later, Theo is in the registrar's lot and is grabbed?" he asked.

Nobody answered.

"You didn't see Emma in that SUV?" he asked Hanna.

She shook her head.

"It just doesn't add up," he said, shaking his head. Luis's furious notetaking subsided. All watched Victor Hugo as he recalled, "Steve disappeared in the commuter parking lot and was found in his car down by the train station two days later on the New York side of the tracks. He similarly had no memory of the events leading up to his abduction or what transpired during. He came back relatively unharmed, but suffered from exhaustion and a minor hit to the face. Emma disappeared in the main parking lot and was found in a car with New York plates down in town. The duration of the abduction was shorter than Steve's, but similarly, she came back suffering from exhaustion."

Anger flared across his charismatic face. "And like in Steve's case, somebody had hit her, but her clothes were dirty and the buttons on her shirt were cut. There was a struggle."

"What was different about this one? All the other abduction victims came back unharmed," Luis chimed in.

Broc joined the discussion with, "Emma fought. But that still doesn't explain what this guy's after."

"He's just growing more brazen in his attempts," Chris surmised.

"There's one connection," Victor Hugo announced. "Theo was present on both occasions. Hanna, what did Theo say about his escape? Did he remember anything?"

"He said he woke up in the city and took the train back here."

"Did he also have exhaustion or injuries?"

"He looked fine but shaken up."

"Again, the city," Victor Hugo said, taking a moment to think. "Did he say where exactly he woke up?"

Hanna shook her head.

"You spoke with him here?"

"Yes, earlier this evening. Emma called me a little while later."

"Why did Emma wake up in a car with New York plates and a bag full of food and cash? That's what I wanna know," Luis said.

"Was it Theo's car?" Chris asked.

Hanna muttered a soft, "No."

Luis continued, "She woke up in the driver's seat with the keys at her feet. Do you think she drove herself and passed out or something? Then forgot?"

"Maybe somebody rescued her," Chris said.

"Wait a minute," Broc said. "Theo said he took the train from the city. Emma woke up in a car with New York plates. On the other hand, she woke up only after he spoke to Hanna and had already left on his motorcycle. Maybe he woke her up. Or it's just a coincidence . . . I don't know."

Victor Hugo focused on Hanna. "You saw him ride his motorcycle away?"

"Yes. I waited in the library and followed him. I saw his headlight turn on and he rode off," she answered in monotone.

"You know that for sure?" Victor Hugo pressed.

"Yes."

"And you'd say only twenty or thirty minutes passed between the phone call in the café and the black SUV showing up?"

Hanna nodded meekly.

"And he met the black SUV in the registrar's lot?"

"You're not saying he's the *abductor*! He didn't touch Emma. He would never!" she cried back.

Broc said, "Hey, ease up, man. Hanna nearly died today on a motorcycle."

A silence swept over them. Victor Hugo took his seat, turning to Hanna. "We need answers from Theo," he concluded.

She stared at her inward-pointed toes and drank her hot chocolate.

Luis rubbed his chin. "Theo was abducted too, so even if he was somehow helping them, I doubt he planned it that way. Why did they yank Theo in the wide open? Doesn't make sense if you're trying not to get caught. Hanna, you rode over there. What was the last thing he said?"

"Run away."

"Did he fight when they grabbed him?"

"Yes."

"Was Emma in the SUV?"

"No. I didn't see her."

Luis adjusted his glasses and reviewed his notes. "There must have been a second car that grabbed Emma while we weren't looking. We don't know what Theo was doing, but we have no evidence he's working with these guys."

"True," Chris said. "He took his motorcycle, so he obviously wasn't thinking about carrying anyone against their will. How would he? Then he got stuffed in a car, presumably against his will, leaving behind his motorcycle. Hanna, how did he look when he came back?"

"Exhausted," she answered.

Chris continued, "I'm thinking maybe Theo was the main target and Emma was just a target of opportunity. Grabbing Steve might have been a mistake."

"Why would they grab Theo? How did he wake up in the city?" Luis asked.

"Ransom maybe?" Broc threw out.

Victor Hugo looked at Hanna. "What if we call Theo? Where is he now?"

"He probably hasn't made it back yet," Hanna answered, numb and shivering. Memories of his apartment swept through her, leaving a hollow soreness.

"Give it a try," Victor Hugo said gently. She flipped open her phone and called only to hear the automated voice mail message. "No answer," she announced.

After a pause, she added, "I never want to speak to him again."

Victor Hugo noticed Hanna's waning energy and said, "One last thing, Hanna. Emma mentioned you talked about having amnesia. Do you feel like there are any blank spots today?"

"How could I know?" she asked helplessly.

Luis set down his notebook and pen. "I think we should all get some rest."

Victor Hugo adjourned the session, and all but Hanna retreated to the nearby kitchen.

"Can I talk to Emma?" asked Chris.

Victor Hugo became defensive, but Luis slipped by him, merely saying, "Let's just ask her."

He came back up the short hallway a few somber moments later, shaking his head. "She doesn't want to see anyone."

Hanna gave him an imploring look. He merely shook his head and pursed his lips.

"She doing okay?" Broc asked.

"Tired, but alright. She's tough," Luis remarked. "But Mom's gonna freak out."

"She doesn't gotta know yet," Victor Hugo said. "We have

everything under control and Emma's safe. We'll figure out how to tell her in the morning."

To a wilting Hanna, he said, "You should probably get some rest too. Do you want to go home? Back to the dorms?"

"Dorms," she said, finishing her drink, its warmth gone.

Hanna followed Broc outside to his minivan, parked on the street. Not a word was shared between them. Lights of downtown Greenberm glistened through the minivan's rain-spattered windows. They ran down her window, tears of the earth.

The dented minivan carried them across town and up the hill back to Surgite, where Broc meekly greeted the security guard at the edge of campus. Access was granted by a trivial wave.

Broc walked her back to her dormitory. She stood under Broc's colorful umbrella at the door.

"So, um, what a day, huh?" he said needlessly. Hanna avoided his eyes.

"I guess I'll see you tomorrow morning?" he asked.

"No."

"Oh," he said in genuine surprise. "You're probably tired. You should sleep in. You can text me whenever and I'll come by."

"Sure."

Broc stood formulating a response. Hanna turned for the door, unlocked it in the rain, and thanked him over her shoulder. Clusters of gossiping girls huddled about in the common room. Some noticed her muddy clothes. Not a word escaped their shocked faces. She climbed the stairs and reached her dorm room. Safely inside, she showered and collapsed into her bed. Having eaten nothing, she cried herself to sleep.

Sunday witnessed her never once leaving the dormitory. Broc called around noon, inviting her to lunch. She lied about studying, wiping away tears as she spoke. She ate the last of her granola bars and sat rereading Theo's letter again and again. His handwriting was exquisite. She had kept it since last July when he had penned it —the letter declaring they should stay together despite attending different schools. Her heart pounded the day her mother discovered it in the family mailbox. Hanna presumed it was the end. But there he was committing, believing they could persevere. He would never forget her. His words carved deep wounds in her aching heart. She collapsed at her desk, sobbing.

You're not a criminal, Theo, abducting people with those scary men. This is the real you. What happened to you? she thought. She took a blank page from her notebook. By her unsteady hand, she drafted and redrafted, crossing out and eventually writing:

Dear Theo,

You always said you wanted to know the truth about this world. Some truths are best left unknown. I cannot be with you if you go down this path. You scare me. You're not the person I thought you were. I don't know why you talk to that thing in Japanese, what happened to Emma, or how you were erasing my memory. They must all be connected, and it frightens me to think how so. You had my heart and now you've crushed it. Was I not enough? You could have just said so. I'd have given you everything. I have nothing to give now. Get help. I pray for your soul that God may deliver you from the evil you are involved in.

Goodbye,

Hanna

She lay in her bed, where she remained for hours, wracked by tempests of sobs. The idea of calling him frightened her still. Dusk seeped through the windows. Returning students and lively conversations in the dormitory bled through the door. Hanna lay motionless and numb. She opened her eyes to Monday's bleak dawn. Outside the girls' dormitory, she saw Broc waiting on the patio.

"What are you doing here?" she asked.

"Oh, good morning. I knew you were going to get breakfast and thought, like, if you wanted me to walk with you?"

"You were waiting for me?"

"You and Emma always get breakfast at seven fifteen on Mondays, Wednesdays, and Fridays," he explained cordially.

". . . okay," she said, perturbed.

They dined under a blanket of silence. Broc's occasional attempts at conversation came like pecks of a needy bird. Hanna tolerated his presence.

After breakfast, he dutifully followed her to the classroom doors and parted when she took her seat. As the classroom filled, so did her heart with tender memories of Theo, followed by disgust and anger. Her hands were already sweating, and the week had barely started. Emma arrived. Hanna gave a friendly wave. Emma sat in the back row.

Bewildered shame tore Hanna away from calculus. The professor arrived, beaming and holding a box of new chalk. Equations unfolded before her, but Hanna struggled to focus. Integrals were solved, neatly employing defined theorems that left clear evidence on the blackboard. She wished the course of her future could be so tidily charted. Class dismissed, she gathered her books waiting for Emma to pass, but she did not stop.

"Hey," she called, running up beside her. "What's going on? Are you okay?"

"Leave me alone. I don't want to talk to you," Emma snapped.

"What the heck? What happened?"

Emma stopped and glared down at Hanna. "Whatever you're involved in, it's affecting me now. Not only did I get abducted on the day I decided to help you, but now I have vivid nightmares, courtesy of you."

She turned away but Hanna caught her arm. "What nightmares?"

"Oh, you mean you don't get those?" she seethed, wrenching her arm away.

"I'm serious. I'm trying to help. What's going on?"

Grave concern shaded Emma's unsteady movements. She pushed back her uncombed hair, her face flush with discomfort. "A violent nightmare I can't forget. I can't sleep, Hanna. I can't have a quiet moment without getting caught by these . . . horrible images in my mind. Every time I see you, I remember it." She shook her head as if to rid herself of those very images. "I'm probably gonna start freaking out again if I keep talking about it, honestly."

Without saying goodbye, Emma retreated down the crowded hallways and Hanna, into her own thoughts. She made for her next class accompanied by her newfound shadow. Broc's precise knowledge of her whereabouts disturbed her.

Hanna trudged back to the dormitory, exhausted after classes. She crawled under the blankets and hid her face. It was nighttime when she regained consciousness—still no Emma. Accumulating homework towered on her desk. Hanna lay motionless.

At eleven, Emma returned without a word. She entirely ignored Hanna, who quietly acknowledged their new terms. She heard their dormitory door open a couple times in the night, then caught Emma's silhouette slip out into the bright hallway. Emma was gone before Hanna awoke.

Tuesday succumbed to the new arrangement. Hanna's Asian history class witnessed Steve avoiding Hanna's presence, as he now opted for the front row. The professor asked for their homework and a student snickered when Hanna admitted she had forgotten hers.

For the rest of class, Hanna retreated to Theo's translation. Over and over, she read it for meaning. None seemed apparent. Later, she practiced it aloud in her empty dorm room. Memorizing it felt like revenge.

Wednesday, Emma walked alongside Hanna to the dining hall, testing how long she could converse. A brief exchange broached the limit of her endurance. Alone again, Hanna focused on Theo's translation.

She took the rubbing of the two illegible calligraphy characters to Sensei after class.

"*Kotodama,*" Sensei said, writing the kanji on the blackboard.

Hanna admired the ease of Sensei's confident handwriting.

"It means the soul of language."

"Like the true meaning?"

"You could also call it the miraculous power of language."

"How would you use it in a sentence?"

Sensei gave a dry laugh and admitted she could not produce one. Hanna thanked her and continued her day, absorbed by the translation. It was her only solace.

Night brought only more horrors. Emma woke up screaming at midnight. Hanna felt her insides churn and flighty adrenaline race to her extremities. Their suitemates rushed in. The RA came. A small therapeutic council took place in their room. Emma did not place any blame. All gave Hanna dirty looks.

Thursday morning, Victor Hugo met Hanna in the library. His leather jacket reminded her of the motorcycle in her life.

"I want to thank you for helping Emma through all of this. She may not say it, but she appreciates it."

Hanna offered an empty smile. "It's what friends do."

"Emma says she can't sleep. She walks around the dorm to clear her head several times a night . . . then the screaming last night. How are you holding up?"

"Me?" she asked incredulously. "Oh, hanging in there." She wanted to collapse and bawl.

He seemed to believe her facade. "Good. I was thinking maybe you could talk to Theo? Ya know, get some answers from him?"

Hanna felt her bitterness return.

"When you're feeling up to it. No pressure, but we need his side of the story. You're the only one who can contact him. Emma told me he ain't the receptive type. Chris said he couldn't get a read on him. Broc doesn't have any contact information."

"Yeah . . . that's Theo," she mumbled.

"Give him a call when you can. I'm sorry if I'm asking too much of you."

Victor Hugo placed a comforting hand on her shoulder. She

looked up into his understanding, avuncular expression and said, "I will."

He nodded approvingly.

Hanna headed for Japanese class. Sensei assigned a group project. Eddie and another film major were in her group.

An email from Sensei came later, rearranging the groups.

Eddie sent a message on Friend Link, apologizing and explaining that, "We already worked together, so I thought it'd be better we work with new classmates to foster creativity and test our abilities in new ways."

Hanna scoffed. "What does that even mean?" she asked aloud. Alone at her desk, she scrolled through Steven Chatsworth's long-winded posts about the abductions. His vows to bring justice garnered actionless support. She shut down her laptop and caught her reflection in the blackness of the screen: half-dead eyes, dark rings under them, and her face colorless save for an ugly pimple.

She took Theo's letter and her own out of her desk. Sorrow turned to wrath as she realized what could have been. The ceiling stared back at her as she lay flat on her bed, Theo's tear-stained letter clutched to her breast. Wasting away, she drifted out of consciousness until Emma opened the door. Hanna hastily hid the letters. Emma took no notice. She woke up fewer times that night.

Friday, a deluge drenched the campus. A lone crocus bloomed in vain along the pathway. Hanna observed its meaningless plight, the chilling rain soaking her hair and jacket. Katie's unending gossip irritated her to the point of rupture at any given moment. Why was that girl so preoccupied with others? Hanna dug her pen into her notebook, ripping the page. She casually flipped to the next amid whispers around her. Sensei shot her a concerned look.

That afternoon, Hanna stole away to an empty classroom in the science building, amid the rustling oaks. She sat by a window for some time unwilling to move, her cell phone on her desk. She recognized she had been wearing the same outfit all week. The thought to call her mother moved her to scoop up her phone and dial. No response. A text message came, saying she was about to enter a job interview. She asked why Hanna would call. Hanna felt the life drain further out of her stiff muscles. A thought to call her sister came, followed by a deep breath as if she had forgotten breathing's constant necessity.

She called her sister, who greeted her with, "What do you want?"

"Nice to hear from you too."

"*Tsh,*" Lily quipped.

"Are you home?"

"Yeah, but I'm going out later."

"Like on a date?"

"Look who's talking."

Hanna grimaced and murmured, "Would you just let it go already?"

"I know you were seeing that boy. You still are, aren't you?"

Hanna's silence answered her question.

"No boyfriends in high school. Here I am, following the rules, but I know I saw you and him together."

"We weren't even dating back then. We were just friends."

"You were all over each other. You talked about him all the time and even more after you 'officially' started going out. Ever since Mom said your grades suck on Christmas you haven't mentioned him once."

"Jeez, I wonder why?" Hanna shot back.

"I don't know why you haven't broken up yet. High school couples never last."

Hanna slumped in her seat. "Yeah . . . I don't know either."

Her sister asked how college was. Hanna lied that everything was fine. She asked Lily about King's. Her sister bored her with candid details. It was an adequate distraction. A confused batch of students stood at the classroom doorway, witnessing Hanna's conversation. Vexed, she pulled her backpack up and trudged out of the room. In the hallway, she continued the conversation.

"Is Dad home yet?"

"No, he's still at King's."

"He just works late to avoid us," Hanna muttered.

"How dare you!" Lily shouted, her voice shrill.

"It's not like it'll change anything."

"I'm telling Mom."

"Go on. Put her on the phone right now—oh wait, you can't. She's busy too," Hanna said listlessly.

"She's getting a new job. It's part time, but she can go full time. Mom says I can apply to more schools now—better schools."

Hanna had no reply. Lily continued, "You don't want to talk to her anyway. I showed her the video of you on the motorcycle. She says you're out of control."

After more stinging silence, Lily said, her voice dripping with venom, "I bet you didn't go back to Surgite early to study. I bet you saw him, didn't you?"

"Shut up, Lily. You don't know what you're talking about."

"God knows."

Hanna sighed. "I have to go."

Lily hung up without another word. Hanna passed through the campus a ghost to all. Everyone was so preoccupied with being social. The RAs and campus security made sure nobody went out alone—especially at night or near the parking lots. Rumors had spread rapidly. Nobody dared enter the forest preserve. Wildfires of speculation swept the campus about the mysterious Lincoln student who had been abducted but somehow escaped.

Hanna climbed the beige stairs of the library and took an empty armchair by the window. The glistening trees swayed in the misty breeze. She slumped down, put in her ear buds, and let the waves of rhythmic metal drench her soul.

A diffident finger poked her knee. She opened her eyes and yelped.

Standing before her, Broc said, "Sorry! Sorry. I didn't mean to scare you."

"Christ almighty, you did," she said, tearing out her ear buds.

"It's getting dark. You shouldn't be out alone."

"You shouldn't either," she griped, stowing her music player.

"You don't have to do this alone, you know," he said, sitting on the chair beside her.

"I want to be alone."

"I don't think that's true," he mumbled.

"Emma hates me. Theo's . . . I can't even. I still have missing memories. The whole campus is swirling with rumors about me. What do they call me?"

He remained silent.

"What do they call me, Broc?"

"Amnesia girl," he relented.

Her head fell back against the chair, her matted, greasy hair obscuring her eyes. Breathing felt like a chore.

"What do they say about me?"

"Everyone's just trying to figure out what happened. They know you were there and that you know the guy on the motorcycle."

To the beige ceiling, she whispered, "'Mr. Elusive.' Isn't that what Emma tagged him?"

"Yeah."

"Didn't she tag me 'Amnesia Girl?' Wasn't it her?"

Broc did not answer. Her voice fell to an emaciated whisper as she said, "I saw the posts. They sicken me. They think I did it somehow? That I helped?"

Broc shifted uncomfortably in his seat. "Hey, um," his childlike voice called out, "Maybe we should get something to eat. Warm food is good to clear your head. A solid meal always makes me feel better. You should eat something."

Hanna looked at him for the first time. His doughy face needed no more sustenance. She gave in and they walked to the dining hall.

Broc entertained her, sharing uncomplicated stories of the

soccer team and the benefits of regular exercise. She ate a paltry amount, picking at a misshapen muffin, and mostly focused on her black coffee. Just the two of them at their table, she could not escape the intimacy of the setting. They avoided the topics hanging over the campus.

After their meal, he walked her back to the girls' dormitory.

"So, good food, huh?" he remarked.

She gave no reply.

"How . . . were . . . do you like . . . when were you thinking of calling Theo . . . soon?"

"Not yet."

"Oh, okay," he said. Gathering what courage he was capable of, he continued, "But you will talk to him soon, right? I could help."

Hanna considered his proposal. She looked into his youthful green eyes, docile yet endearing in their earnest generosity, the dormitory's glow just barely illuminating them.

"I don't know," she said, tortured by the thought. He stepped closer, shielding her under his umbrella.

"You're the only one who can talk to him. You've got to get him to explain what happened to Emma. She's in danger—you're in danger—the whole campus is in danger until we know what really happened."

Hanna winced, wanting to be alone.

"I'm risking a lot being seen with you this much," said Broc. Realization of her surroundings crashed down on her. The whole dormitory was probably staring at the girl who had brought fear and death to campus.

"But I know you can do it."

"You really think so?" she asked, looking up through her wet bangs.

"You're amazing, Hanna. I know you can," he said, afire.

Under his umbrella, he leaned in to kiss her. She turned away, his warm lips gracelessly bumping her pale cheek.

"I'm sorry," he yelped.

She stood motionless, a husk unable to speak.

"I thought . . . I don't know. Emma said I should be more assertive."

The rain pattered on his umbrella above her, unable to wash over her and absolve her sins.

"You still have feelings for him, don't you?"

She let out a pained moan. Her heart felt up in her throat.

"Or maybe you haven't acknowledged that he could be the rapist."

"That's not him!" she yelled, shoving him away. Broc staggered back, bearing a stunned expression.

Hanna unlocked the dormitory door and wrenched it open. She looked back to give a perfunctory, "Goodnight," to Broc, who stood speechless. The clusters of students in the lounge were equally stunned.

Inside her room, a busily packing Emma unsettled her further.

"Where are you going?" asked Hanna.

"Home. My mom's coming to pick me up. I'll come back Monday."

"Don't go, please."

Emma sighed, her hands on her hips. "Don't do this."

Cold and weak, Hanna stood holding her own arms. Emma resumed stuffing her luggage.

"The nightmares won't stop, will they?"

"No," Emma replied curtly.

"What do you see?"

"I don't want to talk about it."

"Please, I want to help."

"Then don't talk about it."

Hanna watched helplessly as Emma avoided her.

"Why won't you tell me?" asked Hanna.

"Stop."

"But how can I help if I don't know?"

"You're on thin ice," Emma fumed.

"I'll be completely honest now, I swear."

Emma threw a textbook on her bed. It bounced violently. She stood with her back to Hanna.

"Okay, then, why did I wake up with a bloody nose and lip and a splitting headache? Why were the buttons on my shirt cut? Why were my clothes dirty? What happened to my wrists? Why'd I wake up in some random car from New York with a bag of chicken tenders at my feet? Why was there a wad of cash in the bag? Why couldn't I remember anything? Why did all of this happen the day we saw Theo? My brothers told me I was alone with him when I disappeared."

Emma turned to her, the vitriol in her eyes raging. "You wanna know what I see in my nightmares?"

There was no stopping Emma's vehement outburst as she cried out, "Murder! Bloody murder. A knife plunging into a guy's chest. Blood everywhere. Screams that haunt your soul. Gore. Parts of man never meant to be seen."

Hanna leaned back against the dresser. Emma closed in on her prey. "And you know the best part? I know his name. Yeah, I know who the victim is."

"Is it a memory or a dream?"

"I don't know, Hanna, and I don't care. When the cops drag me off, I'll plead insanity." She swore loudly and snatched the crumpled box of cigarettes from her desk. "I can't take it anymore."

Hanna backed away from the dresser. Emma resumed her scattered packing.

Suspicion brewed in Hanna. She called out, "You said chicken tenders?"

"Yeah. Why? I really don't wanna talk about it."

"And they were left in a bag for you? With money?"

"Yeah. I ate them and took the cash. Maybe they were

poisoned. I didn't care. I felt so shaky and horrible. Good chunk of change too. It'll go nicely toward my therapy. *That* wasn't a joke."

"Where were the keys?"

"At my feet."

Hanna sat on her bed, her mind rapidly reconstructing possible scenarios. She considered the time between Theo's appearance on campus and Emma's return. Emma's phone rang and she answered; it was her mother. A rare use of Emma's elementary Spanish hid the exchange from Hanna. Emma's expedient packing wrapped up shortly after.

"Look, I'll come back Sunday night," she said from the open doorway. "And Hanna . . . don't go see him. Don't even call him. You broke up, didn't you?"

"Yeah, but he's not who you think he is. He could have been the one that saved you."

Emma paused to spot the motorcycle helmet on Hanna's desk. "Stop lying to yourself."

The door slammed behind her.

Hanna sat under the dull buzz of the fluorescent lights. She flicked them off and removed her jacket and boots. Under the blankets, she clutched her phone, clicking through her saved pictures. The oldest one filled her screen. An ear-to-ear grin beamed across her face. Her high school uniform swayed in motion. She held Theo's arm to her body. Theo looked down at her in genuine surprise, oblivious of her advance. She loved the touch of joy just about to bloom in his expression. His own uniform framed him so fittingly. A lost friend had snapped the picture. Hanna had hugged her crush on a dare, the photo memorializing the occasion.

That Theo, she thought, *you're still in there. I know you are. Somehow, I'll find you.* But where was Theo on that Friday night?

Hanna knelt beside her bed. She clasped her hands, bowed her head, and spoke softly in the darkness. "God, Heavenly Father, protector of all creation, giver of life, who gave His only son for our sins, I beg you for strength. I know in my heart your justice is true and your path correct, and I ask only for the strength to stay on it. We are fallen. We are sick with apathy, wrath, and envy. Please grant me the strength to do the right thing. Please grant me the strength to find Theo. Please forgive him. He is lost and doesn't know the way. Please bring him back. In your hallowed name I pray. Amen."

TWENTY-ONE

THEO WOKE to the irritating buzz of his cell phone. Sluggishly, he pulled himself up off his bedroom floor. A mostly finished glass of gin sat next to a razor blade on his desk. He rubbed his bleary eyes and sat up. The bookshelves in front of him refused to stop spinning as he groped for his phone. Its ringing ceased before his unfocused eyes. He smacked himself impatiently and read the blinding screen again in the desk lamp's glow.

A missed call from Arthur sobered him. He sat leaning against his desk, his arms propped on his knees and head throbbing. He noted the time, seven fifty postmeridian, and calculated how many hours he had been out. The whole week had been a numb, muted blur as he tried to move on from his heart's gaping wound. Study without conviction preoccupied his aimless movements. He avoided his father entirely. Arthur called again.

Theo breathed deeply and said, "I'm not changing my answer."

"You took the sheath—my sheath."

"You finish dealing with Greg?"

"He's in a better place now."

"I'm not giving it back."

"I don't think you fully understand what you've done. Bring me the sheath with a girl in it like last time and I'll forget about your little episode—I'll even tell you where I got this kaiken. Return it without and I'll spare your life. Run or hide, and I'll hunt you down. Go public and the authorities will lock you up. You have forty-eight hours."

Subverted by the gin, Theo taunted him with, "You don't even know where I live."

Arthur told Theo his own address. The apartment number sobered Theo back to an alert panic.

"The Makers will find you. They'll take what's theirs," he said.

"I don't deal in myths," Arthur countered.

"You're finished if I go to the police about Greg. They'll lock you up."

"Then go," Arthur's callous voice said. "It's your fingerprints on his car. You don't have what it takes anyway."

Arthur hung up without another word.

Theo's hand fell to his side. He stood but stumbled against his desk. A final kiss of the gin's numbing fire, and he picked up the razor blade. Beside it rested a picture of Hanna and him in the purikura booth.

She'd never love me. Why would she? She enjoyed hurting me, he thought, cutting himself out of the picture. He pulled open his desk drawer and flicked the razor blade inside. It clinked against the sheath. "Don't judge me," he said to it and closed the drawer. Warm and distant from the pain, he collapsed into his bed, the dried blood on his sleeves an afterthought.

Saturday morning dawned on a hushed Jansen residence. Theo shuddered awake and quickly hid the glass. Outside, Mr. Jansen had already departed, setting about his busy weekend. A message from him asking about lunch glowed expectantly on his phone. Theo set about a shower and copious mouthwash to mask his transgression. The bleak void of Saturday stared back at him from the balcony windows. He sat remembering Hanna, the memories invariably leading back to her last words to him, until the lock on the front door clicked. No warm sweater to return this time.

Mr. Jansen came through the door, followed by a loquacious woman and her unending conversation. Her perfume invaded the apartment, and her coddling voice rang of desperation.

"Yes, yes, I know. Er, Theo?" his father said, gently interrupting this smiling woman. "I'd like you to meet Samantha. We met through work, and I thought it'd be a good idea to introduce her."

An effortless grin spread across her heavily made-up face. "Hello," she greeted.

"Samantha, this is my son, Theo. He's a freshman in college. A little older than yours?"

"Not by much, dear," she beamed needlessly.

"She has a son and daughter of her own," Mr. Jansen added, taking a seat on the couch. Samantha sat beside him. Theo merely observed the woman, who added meaningless giggles after his father's statements.

"We've been going out for . . . ah, what is it now?"

"Two or three weeks, I imagine," she answered, bubbly at his mere glance.

"Longer than most," Theo quipped, standing in the vast sunlight piercing the balcony's glass sliding doors.

Undaunted, Mr. Jansen said, "Samantha and I were thinking of going out to lunch and wanted to invite you."

Theo looked at this competitor for his father's attention. At once, he said, "I don't feel like it."

Samantha remained unfazed. Mr. Jansen urged, "It might be good for you—something new. You've been in your room a lot recently."

"Your father tells me you ride motorcycles just like he does," Samantha chimed in. "He says you're going to ride together this spring."

Mr. Jansen's eyes flitted between his two listeners. "Yes, Theo likes that little bike, but he's been taking it out a little too freely. I think sometimes he forgets he doesn't actually own it and needs to ask permission."

Theo silently accepted the censure.

"Theo's been feeling a little down lately," Mr. Jansen announced, standing up. "Just had his first break up. They had been going out since school started."

Samantha followed him like a puppy, hanging on his words and giving acknowledging "*mmms*" throughout.

"Since prom," Theo corrected.

"It's alright, sweetie, I'm sure you'll find somebody new. Love takes time, but you'll find the right one someday," was her attempt at consolation. He gave no comment.

"Why don't we make some coffee like I showed you?" Mr. Jansen said, leading her by the hand. Their fiasco of chatter and her constant sycophantic "*mmms*" and "*ahhhs*" continued into the kitchen.

Samantha was enamored by the coffee machine she convincingly feigned was positively magical. After his father saved her from her believable ineptitude to start the machine, he stole away from the preoccupied Samantha and stood beside Theo.

"Don't tell me you're still down about the mousy Jersey girl?"

Silence sufficed as an answer.

"Stop it," he ordered. "You're all bent out of shape over a first girlfriend. It's not a big deal. Girls come and go. You can't drag yourself through the mud like this." His father shook his head. "And shave that damn scrap you call a beard."

"Hanna was different."

"You'll always think that because she was your first. Those memories never go away."

"She cared about life," he said to his reflection in the sliding glass door.

"Move on. Find another girl. You need to focus on you."

"What's the point?"

"You probably drove her off. What happened?"

"I lied to her about some stuff. She found out."

Mr. Jansen winced, his eyes narrowing. "Did you lie about other girls? I know you've been going out to those concerts and nightclubs. Dating multiple girls at the same time is irresponsible, Theo. I wouldn't recommend it." He compulsively checked his cell phone and then turned to Theo. "What I would recommend, though, is dating more casually. Don't get so overinvested. If you go into every date with a wedding ring in your pocket, you'll just get hurt."

Theo took in the scattered clouds above, broken, like her trust.

"Enjoy women for what they are, Theo," his father said. "Don't get involved in the toils of their lives. They will rip out your heart. You've been moping around for a week, wasting away. You stopped working out. You even lost the two fifty off an exit ramp. I'm still not thrilled about that. You've been treating that bike like shit. Man up. Move on."

Mr. Jansen walked off, beckoned by the calls of Samantha's coffee concerns. They both returned a short time later, bearing beverages nothing like when Hanna had made them. Samantha offered a steaming mug to Theo—an olive branch to his cold hands. He examined it and simply said, "Cat tongue."

Two confounded expressions met him. He shook his head and added, "You two look happy together. I'm glad for you."

Samantha beamed at his sudden approval. His father expressed an interrogative edge but refreshed it into an imbecilic grin when Samantha leaned on his arm, suggesting, "Why don't we all go out for lunch? It'll be lovely. Theo can tell us all about his first year at Lincoln."

"Sure. Why not?" Theo answered.

Samantha swooned. Mr. Jansen remained dubious. Samantha all but pulled him toward the door. They departed into the vexingly sunny day. Mr. Jansen led the party to the Fair and Debonair. Theo could not conceal his disdain of the choice.

Sure. Take me to where I took her. Rub it in my face more, he thought, following the steps to the dark, dizzy lounge in the sky.

In the booth, Samantha cautiously peppered him with questions, growing bolder as Theo surrendered answers. His life was profoundly uninteresting, but Samantha found it riveting. His father ordered a second round of drinks. Theo lazily sipped his soft drink, considering a potential plan.

There's no way he actually cares about this woman. She disappears. Arthur gets what he wants. Would Dad move on this time? He's way too knowledgeable about her family. I erase this Samantha from his memory. If I fail, I'm dead anyway.

An impulse to throw his glass against the wall infiltrated his mind.

Look at yourself. You're actually thinking to hand this innocent woman over to that killer? he asked himself. *You disgust me. You're just an animal like him after all*, his mind's voice said to himself. His chest tensed up and hands balled to fists momentarily. Samantha and his father were oblivious, absorbed in their meaningless saccharine conversation.

A chilling calm came over Theo. Thoughts carried his already spinning mind away from the conversations that drifted like passing ships in the Sound.

But there would be none of this if Arthur were gone, he thought.

The blissful couple dragged him to a department store after lunch. Theo chose nothing. His father pointed out his gloom in line for the register, only for Theo to rebuff him with, "I'm just tired."

Mr. Jansen's parental instinct flaring, he pulled Theo aside. Samantha suddenly found her recent purchases fascinating.

"What's wrong? Why are you so lifeless? You're embarrassing me."

"You going to ask me to leave the apartment for a while? Or do you make her send her kids away? All the hotels must be getting expensive. She picks nice ones, doesn't she?"

His father sighed. "Theo, I've been divorced for six years. I got you through high school and into an elite college. I kept my job through multiple layoffs in this global financial crisis. I bought us a great place in the city. Don't I deserve a little something for myself?"

"She's not my mom."

"But she's my date. Don't be so selfish."

"Forget it. I don't care what you do," Theo said, walking back to Samantha. He struck up a conversation about her work. Samantha enthusiastically obliged, telling him all about her thrilling career selling software to banks—anything to avoid speaking to his father more.

The afternoon waned and Theo was at last released from their insufferable party. He returned to his desk and began planning confronting Arthur. Night encroached without his notice. His notes spread like wildfire. He paced about his room unable to contain his energy. He took the sheath from his drawer. The prospect of its use sickened and excited him.

Arthur wouldn't believe me if I just told him someone is trapped in this, he thought, scanning the engraved characters on the sheath. *The only way to convince him would be bait. I'd need to reveal someone is in here, get him close, then capture him. But how?* he thought. He stowed his notes and retired to the kitchen for a solitary meal. His father's return pushed him back to his room, where he found himself online in Demon World. He ignored his guild's messages and invitations, as he had all week. The fires of resolution smoldered while his mind chewed the cud of revising his attack.

Theo continued his character's quest for total game completion. His phone buzzed. He picked it up, nearly dropping it.

"It's you," he said in disbelief.

"Hello, Theo," replied Hanna, stiff and reserved.

". . . what do you want?"

"I . . . I want to know how you were erasing my memories."

"You don't."

"I do," Hanna insisted. "You owe me an explanation at least."

"You got your revenge. I owe you nothing."

"I want you to teach me. I need to erase Emma's memory."

"You said we'd never talk again. You forget?"

"She told me about her nightmare."

"Oh," was his only response.

"She's suffering," Hanna said in an unsteady pitch. "Please, I… need your help."

Emma could be bait for trapping Arthur, he thought. The Hanna in his mind distracted Emma and he made Emma disappear. Hanna's approving smirk afterward stirred him. Imagining Hanna getting taken by the sheath stole his mind's eye. *Hanna could be the bait too,* he thought, revenge's satisfaction snaking its way through his mind.

Hanna broke the silence with, "Can we meet tomorrow? I want you to show me."

"Alone. My place."

"No. Not until I know what happened to Emma. Not until I know the truth."

"You're one to talk."

"I'm not backing down."

Theo scrutinized the conviction in her voice. He heard her expel a breath.

"Central Park. Today," Hanna declared.

"It's already dark," he said, readying a blank page in his notebook. A new plan was taking shape, but he needed time.

"Tomorrow morning at ten. Central Park. Alone. You'll find me on the bench by the lake, just like on Christmas."

"Alright," she said. Both sides were unwilling to speak or end the call. Questions swarmed him but Hanna gave a curt, "Goodnight," and hung up. Theo penned, "Final," at the top of the blank page in his notebook. He logged out of Demon World and set about his work, starting with shaving off his scraggly beard.

———

HANNA SIGHED and carelessly set her cell phone on the table. She sat back in her uncomfortable wooden chair in the common room of the girls' dormitory. At least the university permitted the first-floor common room to be coed. Maybe they hoped it would engender collaboration and further studies. Saturday night saw little of that. Other groups seemed so happy in their obnoxious conversations. Hanna despised them. She messaged Broc, "Meeting Theo in city tomorrow."

Seconds later, her phone rang. She gave a perfunctory, "Hi."

"I'll come with you," he offered.

"I have to go alone."

"Don't! Don't even go! Why can't you just talk to him over the phone?"

"Look, I'm just telling you so that I told someone. Theo and I are just going to talk."

"What time are you meeting him? Where?"

"Central Park at ten a.m. It'll be outside. I'll be back well before dark."

"Are you going to ask him what happened to Emma?"

"Yes."

"I'll come too. I want to know."

Oh, Jesus, he'll tell Emma for sure. How am I going to erase Emma's nightmare if Broc tells her I'm going to? It'll just make more memories to erase, wouldn't it? she thought. Hanna employed more subterfuge for Broc, saying, "I'll tell you right after. He's not going to explain anything if someone else is there. He's skittish."

"You really shouldn't go alone, but it's your choice," Broc said, unconvinced.

Hanna ended the call and retreated to her room, which she had grown to loath. So much of her recent existence she had spent there, unable to escape the reality of her situation. Sleep eluded her exhausted body.

Sunday dawned overcast. Hanna rose well before her alarm. She packed her backpack, carefully going down a list. She triple-checked for her pepper spray and her green journal. Both letters lay neatly tucked in an envelope with their purikura pictures. Walking to the station, the recent habit of wearing her leather jacket and boots found her appearing as if going for a motorcycle ride. Theo's spare helmet swung toylike from her gloved hand by the fastened chinstrap. Climbing the steps to the station platform, a voice behind her called, "Wait!"

Not surprised, she grumbled, "I said I was going alone."

"You're cute when you're mad," replied Broc.

She turned away from him.

"No! Hey, come on. I was just making a joke. Emma said I need to get better at making jokes."

Hanna cradled Theo's spare helmet in her arms. It, too, stared expectantly for the train. "You're not riding today, are you?"

"No. I'm giving it back."

"So you're actually going through with it?"

Chilling wind shook her resolve. ". . . yes. I better not see you on the train. You're already being creepy."

"I . . . sorry," he said beside her.

"Don't worry about me. I'll be fine."

The train's headlight pierced the distant corner and signaled its imminent arrival. They remained silent as it pulled up slightly early. A few passengers rushed the doors, though many seats remained open.

"I have to know the truth, Broc. I have to do this alone," she said and climbed the steep steps of the train car.

"Good luck!" he shouted behind her.

She paused in the empty aisle to spy him descending the steps of the platform. Hanna took her seat. The plan was underway.

Several moments later, the train lurched to motion. She purchased her ticket on board using what little cash she had.

It's not like I'll need it for karaoke, she thought.

Hanna avoided thoughts of him. Still, her imagination produced a zoetrope of pictures of Theo embracing her, explaining, exploding in anger, pulling out a syringe, taking her out to lunch, apologizing, grabbing her wrists, drawing a knife, kissing her. She watched the passing bare trees thinning into blurry tired buildings. Penn Station's copious stairs passed under her apprehensive feet as they rushed her upward. Midtown's popular streets witnessed her brisk march. Central Park's southern sidewalk caught her stopping to catch her breath. Only a few minutes stood between her and the hour of meeting. Hanna set off, the black motorcycle helmet swaying in her arms, running right into Theo's trap.

TWENTY-TWO

INCESSANT GUSTS WHIPPED across the frozen lake. A lifeless Central Park bristled under the suffocating fog. The city that dared to raise its brow against the yoke of humility funneled cruel wind through its endless buildings. Neither dead nor alive, Theo sat waiting on a rocky crag jutting into the ice. It felt impossible that this place had once welcomed him and Hanna in balmy warmth under autumn's ephemeral crimsons. Litter was now trapped under the ice, a tomb for the city's morality. Looking up at last, Theo spotted six towering buildings. The wind was relentless. It pierced his coat to his breast. He imagined a great windmill on the far side of the lake generating the gales in monumental swings. Striving upward—struggling against the fall—pretending to have never wanted more: the city with three faces, once so beautiful, was now the prison of his abandoned soul.

Face her, coward, he thought.

All night, competing thoughts had fought for dominance. None succeeded. Doubt rotted him. He checked his watch: only a minute until the chosen hour. Inability to decide always evoked self-loathing. Hanna would be late anyway. He still had more time.

Man up. She's no greater soul. Once you show her, she'll hate you.

The memory of Emma's screams sickened him—then numb disconnection. The irreverent minute hand struck twelve on his watch. Footsteps marched up behind him and pattered to an unsure stop.

On time, he observed, surprised.

———

THERE HE WAS. The frozen lake spread out before them. Not a soul stirred in the inhospitable wind rustling the unverdant greenery. Finally, the moment had arrived, and Hanna could not produce a word. She stood watching him, motionless on the solemn precipice.

"It's beautiful, isn't it?" he said, his voice traveling across the bitter wind. "The terror of the ice."

Hanna did not answer.

"It fascinates me, like a hurricane razing ships in the sea, or a chemical fire licking the night sky."

Hanna inched closer in determined steps. Theo's hands remained unseen in his coat pockets. "How were you erasing my memories?" she asked, her sole question lingering between them.

He hopped down from the granite ledge. His ossified expression eschewed sympathy. "You don't have the right to know, liar."

Aghast, her parted lips were unable to form a word.

"Impulsive, passionate social liar Hanna," he hammered out. "Truth is yours to disfigure into neat, palatable bites. All for what? Easy conversation? Maintaining so-called friendships? Fun? You shape the truth at your whim, uncaring of the consequences, you little liar. Your family must love you. Where's God's thunderbolt for *your* sins?"

Hanna set the helmet down on the ground.

"What happened to Emma?"

"What happened to you?" he snapped. "You aren't the sweet

Hanna everyone takes you for. You saw me get abducted before your very eyes and what did you do? Lie in wait to stab me in the heart, you snake. Where is she anyway?"

Shocked by his vitriol, she stood in dizzy disbelief. Theo repeated his question, anger mounting in his voice, to which she answered, "She went home. She blames me."

Theo merely checked his watch and clicked his tongue.

"You can't take me to her right now?"

Rage's embers flared up in her.

"Useless," he remarked at her silence.

Hanna exclaimed, "I won't fight you, Theo! I just want to know what really happened. God knows, Emma is in pain."

"Does he? Omniscient and omnipotent, why didn't he stop me from destroying myself in your mind? Why did he create Arthur? Why did he create such terrible power to cut the memories clean out of someone, and abduct another for implanting those horrible deeds? Who would allow such a thing to be made?"

"I don't know what you're talking about, but I want to know how you were doing it," she reiterated, realizing her hands had curled to fists.

He gestured to the sky. "Ask him. I'll wait."

Hanna thrust her shaking hand onto the pepper spray in her jacket pocket. Theo's expression grew wild, his movements unpredictable.

"Could you actually fall in love with me? Admit it. You pity me. That's what made it so easy to hurt me—your pity ran out. You saw me for the wretch I am."

Hanna turned away. He called her name and she yelled back, "What is wrong with you!"—she fought to restrain her frenzied voice—"Theo, why are you like this! Why are you saying these things?"

He stepped closer, sensing her fear. "To justify hating you."

Theo stood but a couple of inches from her.

"I'm not afraid of you," Hanna said looking up at him, but her voice betrayed her.

He grabbed her forearm. As she winced under his merciless grip, a passing stranger caught their terse engagement.

"I'll scream," she whispered. Theo's eyes darted for an escape. The moments passed like posing for unwanted pictures.

Hanna twisted her arm out of Theo's grip and hissed, "Stop. Touch me again and I'll have you locked up."

He retreated back to the crag.

A welcome moment of respite spread out between them. Temptation to flee reasoned with her. Resolution to help Emma waned. She gulped a deep breath and approached him.

"Like I said, I won't fight you, Theo. I know a better you is still in there."

"You don't even know what I've done."

"I want to know. I won't judge."

He wiped his hand across his brow, then his mouth, then his brow again. Thoughts raced behind his calculating eyes scrambled by an unseen melee.

"You should hate me, yet here you are. And for what?" he asked. "To save Emma? How can you be so stupid? She'll never forgive you."

Hanna replied, "Maybe so, but I have to try. Emma is my friend. I know of something that could help her. I can't unknow it. To walk away when I know I could have done something is the greatest sin. She's not the only one in pain."

Theo snarled. "You going to bitch about how much I've hurt you?"

Hanna's gritted teeth barely held back profane shouts. She resisted. An image of her screaming at him flooded her imagination. Seconds fell like bleeding droplets between them.

"Go on. Go on, I said!" he shouted, prodding her.

"Emma is not the only one in pain. You are too. Look at yourself! You're lashing out. And for what? I won't fight you. I know there's still a future for you."

"Name one I care about."

"Then at least care about the present you've made for yourself. You have a chance to explain yourself. I will listen. We can help Emma. Tell me what really happened. Tell me what's going on. You can still come back."

Theo turned in aimless circles, avoiding her stare. He stopped and scoffed. "I'd come back a saint if it meant anything. I've been holding this secret—harboring this knowledge of power beyond belief . . . running these errands in a madman's nightmare for a chance to uncover the origin of mankind's revolution—only to be unsurprised what humanity would actually do with it. There has to be more than just carnal primitivism and the tranquil quiet of death."

"It's destroying you! Tell me what happened to Emma," she shouted. Theo retreated further toward the ice. Hanna pursued him with, "Maybe pretending to forget you was spiteful. I didn't want to do it."

"Liar. You lie so much." He was seething.

She nodded gravely. "Maybe so. I am only all the decisions that brought me to this point—bad ones and all. I may have been reckless with my lying. I made mistakes."

Her temples throbbed and throat felt choked by invasive doubt. The stone beneath her feet felt like the thin ice spread out before them.

"But I will not lie anymore."

"Just like that? And for what?"

"For you."

He charged up to her as if ready to strike. He sensed weakness and began a retort, yet stopped.

There she was, bare and vulnerable to his attack. She held out her arms and gestured to her body. "Go on. Do your worst. Say how stupid I am. I'm, at least, an idiot."

They remained locked in a gaze lasting winter's coldest night. She refused to retreat, her entire being urging her to strike her adversary. Theo's lips twitched to snap out a word. Then his expression softened and a calm came over him. He looked away.

Hanna exhaled and shook her head. "I know you were erasing my memories—as much as that hurts me to know. I understand something bad happened to Emma. Part of me is terrified to find out what happened, but I will face the truth."

"You said you won't lie anymore. You're serious?" Theo said to the overcast sky.

"Yes."

"For how long?"

"I . . . I don't know. Forever?"

"I propose a deal: I will tell you the whole truth and you will never lie to me again."

"Deal," she promptly shot back.

Theo blinked in disbelief. "You . . . did you even think about it?"

"I guess not, but I don't have to hesitate about the truth."

"Did you mean it when you said we'd never talk again?" he asked, sincerity shining through in his voice.

"I don't know," she admitted. "I was just . . . I wasn't really thinking that far ahead. There was too much to digest that day."

He turned and faced her. "What does Emma remember?"

"She has terrible nightmares," Hanna all but whispered. "She remembers killing a man. She wakes up screaming in the night. She hasn't slept in days. She avoids me because I remind her of it."

"She's convinced she did it?"

"I didn't really ask her that. Can we erase her memory . . . like you did mine?" The addition awakened a deep pain in her.

"Possibly," he said.

"Talk to me straight, Theo. No lies," she demanded.

His eyes narrowed. "You can't even fathom what kind of power is at work here."

"Show me," she said. A chill ran down her spine as he came closer. This time, she slowly backed away, unable to read his expressionless face.

"I suppose the sheath would be reasonable to show you," he answered, producing a small wooden object from his coat pocket. It was the same one he had berated in Japanese on the night he came back.

"Those engravings. That's what I translated for you," she said, drawn to it.

"Half of it. The other half is on the knife, which Arthur has. This is the sheath."

Hanna's eyes strained examining it, her brow working.

"Okay . . . but . . . why are you showing me this?" she asked.

"This is how I was doing it—just this ordinary object."

"Does this have something to do with erasing memories?"

"The spirit inside it abducts people. She can erase memories. Sometimes she thanks me."

Hanna's eyes widened in disbelief. "Theo, are you okay? You weren't slipping me something? Poisoning my food? Injecting me behind my back? Signaling a nanochip in my brain?"

Theo stood, unphased. "You'd never believe how. I can show you, but not here. We have to go back to my place. I'll show you the notes in my desk."

"Alone?"

"I've kept it a secret this whole time. You can't tell anyone."

Hanna bristled with curiosity and fear. "You've been erasing my memory somehow for weeks, or God knows how long, and you show me this . . . thing and want me to go alone with you to your apartment?"

"Yes."

She stared, perplexed.

Theo's face changed back to one she recognized, if only momentarily. "It will make sense," he said. "I know I have no right to ask you this, but trust me."

Theo scooped up her black helmet, which had been observing them from the safety of the ground, and gestured her to follow.

She chased after him, calling out, "Wait!"

Through the maze of subways and sidewalks she followed him in silence. Hanna's unsure knees felt ready to buckle. The dread that this had been a horrible mistake continued. She vigilantly monitored Theo. His thoughts remained masked by contemplative gloom.

He paused at the door to his apartment. "Why did you pretend not to remember that night? Why did you do that to me?"

Caught off guard, her stomach sank and pulse rose further still. "To figure out if you were really erasing my memory."

"That's all?"

She sighed. "And partly out of spite."

"Do you hate me?"

"No, Theo. I don't know what to think right now," she replied, exasperated.

"You probably will."

He unlocked the door and gestured her inside. The familiar warmth greeted her. He slipped off his shoes by the door. She kept her boots on.

"My dad should be out all day. It doesn't matter if he comes back. I guess he would be surprised to see you."

"I'd be too," she said, following him. She prompted him for a thorough explanation of her amnesia. He agreed, seemingly mollified by the safety of his bedroom. Hanna remained apprehensive.

"I don't really know where to start," he stated, "but Emma's abduction is the most reasonable place, from your perspective. That day, she separated us. You were on my motorcycle. I walked her along the edge of the parking lot out of your sight. I had been given instructions to abduct someone I could talk to after running a test. We wanted to discover the full extent of the knife and sheath's capabilities. I was foolish not to realize what that entailed. I am disgusted to admit it, but you were the intended target that day. I was running out of time and spotted Arthur's SUV in the parking lot. Out of options, I put Emma in the sheath."

Hanna's face twisted in repulsed confusion. "Put her in the sheath? What are you talking about?"

Theo removed his coat and hung it on the back of his desk chair. He drew the small wooden sheath and his cell phone out of its pockets and set them on the desk. Hanna peered at the sheath. It appeared as if nothing more than a museum piece.

"Don't be insane, Theo."

"No, I'm telling you, this is how I did it."

"Theo, don't be like this."

"The abductions in the news, Steve, Emma—that was me. Your amnesia only of our memories together—all me. That was me using the sheath's amnesia on you. Abducting someone charges it up. When touched to someone's bare skin, it erases their memory for however long it was charged. I've catalogued everything in my notes. I have them all here."

Flustered, she paced about his room. "My uncle was mentally ill. He never got better. Here I was, expecting some kind of confession and you're telling me this . . . this nonsense? If you are telling the truth, how am I supposed to believe you?"

"Think. It all makes sense. Central Park, ice skating, the café, the clinic—your memories of all of them are missing. All of those events centered around our relationship. You think you started the green journal because you were worried about being abducted. That's not true. You started it because you suspected you had amnesia. I erased not just your memories of me, but also your memories about your amnesia itself and your journal."

Theo pointed to the top of his bookshelf. "It's all there in my notes. I can get the keys in my desk and show you."

"Shut up," said Hanna. She began to shake.

"You have to believe—"

"*Shut up*!" she shrieked. Pallid with rage, she snatched the sheath off his desk. He grabbed his cell phone and rapidly tapped through its screens. He turned his phone to her, displaying the picture of her in the café. Her tepid smile greeted her again.

"You didn't go alone that day!" said Theo.

He flicked the screen to the next photograph. There they were. His forgotten kiss, her surprised expression, the exact same background in both, their clothes the same, the same customers and lighting—doubt was torn away by tumultuous waves of ire.

"What have you done to me?" she whispered through quickened breaths.

"I figured you would not take this well."

"How did you do this? How did I not notice?"

"It happened several times. Most recently while you slept with me."

Hanna shook, barely containing herself. She grabbed a fistful of his shirt. "In my *sleep*! You were giving me amnesia while I *slept*? What have you done to me! You touched me!"

He remained limp and avoided her livid glare. "Nothing you don't remember. We never went all the way. The spirit in the knife comments about the memories I erase. She can see them somehow. I didn't want to embarrass you."

"Embarrass? You've been toying with the fabric of my being, and you're worried about that? How dare you! I'll never touch you again!"

Hanna shoved him away and turned to his bed. The sight of it repulsed her.

"You make up this supernatural garbage and expect me to believe you? You disgust me!"

"I understand if you never forgive me. I suppose I will always remember our time together with regret for my reprehensible behavior."

"*Let's see you remember now*!" she screamed and lunged at him.

"Hanna, no!" he shouted, but it was too late. She thrust the sheath blindly at him. It contacted his raised hand and violet light burst from it. Black lines shot out, surrounding and pulling him into the darkness radiating from her hand. In a single breath, he was gone. She fell through the vaporous light and crashed into the hallway.

TWENTY-THREE

"THEO?" she called to an empty apartment. Silence enveloped her like a disease. She called his name again only to receive haunting stillness in reply. She crawled back into his room and waved her hands through the space he formerly occupied. She called his name one last time like a lost child. Again, no reply. She clambered to her feet and searched for the weapon of his destruction. It surprised her how far the sheath had flown from her hand. She picked it up and inspected it. Plain and ordinary, nothing stood out. Humoring a ridiculous thought, she peered inside it for a shrunk Theo. She slumped into his chair and dropped the sheath onto his desk. "No way," she said, astounded.

Hanna flicked open her phone and called him. His smartphone buzzed on his desk. She hung up, disappointed in herself. She investigated his room, then the entire apartment. She combed through it as if it were a game of hide-and-seek turned sour. Ripping open the door to his father's room, she realized the extent of her trespassing, but pressed onward. By the time she pulled back the shower curtain in the master bathroom, she conceded that her search was pointless. He was gone. She paced about his living room bathed in the overcast sunlight, unable to fathom what she had done. *He really was telling the truth*, she thought.

The lock on the front door clicked. Flighty adrenaline burst through her as she raced for Theo's room. She closed the door behind her and, without thinking, picked up the sheath. She stood holding the last trace of Mr. Jansen's only son, poised to strike his father. Several successive knocks on the door rattled her further.

"Theo? I know you're in there," his father called through the door.

Hanna's heart drummed in her ears. Her body pulsed, ready for an action her brain had not yet decided. Running off the road on his motorcycle felt trivial in comparison.

"Theo, open the door," he ordered. "Let's talk. Samantha's coming over later and I thought we could all have dinner together."

Could she impersonate his voice at all? No, it was much deeper than hers. Could she mimic his footsteps? No, his gait was much too different from hers. Should she reveal herself? Should she reveal what she had done to this man's son? Should she reveal what he had been doing? *Does he even know?* she thought. Petrified, she stood gripped by indecision.

The interrogative footsteps receded to the kitchen. Hanna's lungs strained for air. She hardly breathed, attempting to conceal her presence. Her sweltering jacket was unbearable. Her ears remained trained on Mr. Jansen's movements. Some errant kitchen noises later, he departed. Theo's phone lit up with a message from his father: "Let's talk tonight." Hanna collapsed to her knees and pulled off her backpack and jacket.

How much time she had until Mr. Jansen's inevitable return pressured her scrambled mind. She inspected the plain wooden sheath in her hands and carefully set it on Theo's desk. Recalling his mention of his explanatory notes, her sweaty hands rummaged through his bookshelf. She looked up and saw the book he had pointed to earlier. Her memory replayed their conversation, and she reenacted each part to reveal the next memory. She clung to them, desperate for a way out. The book on the top shelf easily escaped her reach. She rolled his desk chair closer and carefully stood on it. The chair wobbled on its pivoting stand under her nervous boots.

"Sorry," she whispered.

Hasty hands snatched the books on the top shelf and tossed the irrelevant ones aside. None bore any secrets, until finally, one merely posing as a book revealed itself to be a locked box.

"This must be i-i—" she said, falling to the floor, betrayed by the pivoting chair. Hurt, she staggered back to his desk. Tempered breaths had no ameliorating effect on her palpitating heart. The locked box demanded a key. *But where would he hide it?* she thought, inspecting his room. Frantic, she ransacked his desk, pouring out notebooks, pens, staples, memos, and anything else caught in her abject quest. So many memos—they fell like snowflakes as she spread out the contents of each drawer. A model airplane was toppled in the chaos. Her hopes burst free of despair when she located a locked drawer, but were quickly dashed when the key had not presented itself in the contents strewn about his floor.

She pulled on the locked drawer again. Predictably, it did not open. She pulled several more times in mounting frustration. "Dammit, Theo," she said, crumpling to the floor, tears imminent. His phone rang on his desk. Terrified, she craned her neck to spot the phone above. Lo—there was a key taped to the underside of his desk.

Thanking the Lord, she sprung up and grabbed the key. The name on his ringing phone caught her.

"Arthur," she read aloud and thought, *Jesus Christ, he wasn't lying.*

The key opened the locked drawer, and the contents of the drawer found their way onto the pile of his belongings, hastily strewn about as if a tornado or burglar had been through. Feverishly, she pillaged his motorcycle magazines for another key, until the dissected drawer itself revealed a second key taped to it. Nearly slamming the box onto his desk, she unlocked it and poured out its prolific notes and a journal protected by a combination lock.

The handwritten pages were beautiful. Spreading them across his desk, she paused to admire his magnificent cursive. "I never knew you could draw like this," she found herself remarking at his illustrations. Between the handmade maps and neatly penned tables, a hand-drawn diagram of the sheath itself came out of the pile. Her heart leaped and she held it to her nose, then at arm's length. Without her glasses, she squinted the graceful letters into focus. His phone chimed, bearing a message from Arthur. She yelped as if struck.

Hanna grabbed the sheath. Determined, she followed the diagram and spotted the inconspicuous leather belt loop near the top. Per Theo's instructions, she pulled it.

Violet light burst from her hands. She dropped the sheath, falling back onto the pile of his notebooks. Watching the black lines rapidly reveal a body, she scurried backward, afraid and mesmerized. The lines carefully set Theo down on the floor between the scattered drawers. The last black line laid his head down like a child to sleep. Theo's face was peaceful before beleaguered confusion contorted it. Pupils dilated, his eyes darted about. Pained observation met Hanna in the silence, interrupted only by her rapid breathing. His eyes rested on her. Realization came and a calm washed over him. He sat up and said, "Hey."

"Hi."

"How long was I out?"

"I don't know. It hasn't been that long."

"I see you found the two keys," he said, noticing the mess that formerly comprised his desk.

"I panicked."

Theo pulled himself to his feet but struggled against apparent exhaustion. "So this is what it feels like," he mumbled, slumping back down. Clammy and shivering, he wiped the perspiration from his brow and leaned back against his desk.

Hanna leaned against his bookshelf across from him, imitating the way he sat.

"Are you okay?" she asked.

"Cold. I feel so tired."

"It's real—the sheath."

"It is," he said gravely.

"What happened to you? Where did you go? Do you remember anything?"

"I don't know. I remember you coming toward me. Next, I woke up here. Had I not known what really happened, I could have assumed I hit my head and was knocked out. It's disorienting. What happened?"

"I looked for you. I couldn't believe what happened. I still can't fully comprehend it. Your dad came back. I hid in your room. He knocked, thinking you were here. He had no idea. He left and texted you something. I remember you pointing to your notes, explaining how it all works. I found the fake book box and, well, you see what happened."

His eyes struggled to focus on his combination journal, which lay between them.

"Arthur called," she added.

Despair played across his face.

"I'm sorry about the mess," she said in a placating tone.

"It's alright," he said, pulling himself up to his phone as if his legs were useless. Taking it, he slumped back to sit against his desk and sighed at the updates. The screen's glow illuminated his saturnine expression.

"Is that the same Arthur you mentioned earlier?" she asked.

His hand fell to the floor, still gripping his cell phone. He strained to fill his lungs and began, "I should start at the beginning."

Hanna hugged her knees and nodded.

"It was September. I was online in Demon World and my guildmates were joking about some post they'd seen hyping a mystical shop in Tarrytown. They sold healing crystals, bracelets that improve circulation, magic trinkets for aching joints—things of that nature. They were all having a laugh about it, but I looked up the shop. I read somewhere that it was a good idea to periodically give gifts in a relationship, particularly when unexpected. A day later, I went to the self-proclaimed new-age health and wellness store. It was quiet and small. Their shelves were full of items boasting impossible cures for every malady. They sold candy too. Nobody was in the shop. I browsed the incense, and the cashier appeared, asking if I needed any help. I recognize now that was Greg. I dismissed him and left, not finding a gift for you."

"But when I got home, there was something pulling me to go back. Maybe it was the way the shelves were so crowded or the way all the tables had boxes as if full of secrets. I wanted another look. The same cashier was there. Greg was genial and left me alone. This time, I perused the mind-clearing herbal remedies. A few claimed they could erase nightmares. The healing crystals said they could absorb traumatic memories. They were all, of course, unclear on their exact efficacy, and many bore labels indicating they were not FDA approved. The whole section was titled 'Memory Therapy.' I remember thinking what a racket it all was. I assumed some people must believe in it because the store existed. Maybe they made their keep on the weight loss foods they featured prominently. The misleading 'eternal youth' skin care section also took up a good part of the store. Somewhat bored and questioning why I had come again, I found bottles of elixirs and enchanted stones with Chinese characters on them. There was a little sign declaring them 'Secrets of the Orient.' I found one with Japanese. It had the names of stars and constellations written on it. I tried to read it aloud. A few moments later, Arthur appeared."

"You were being watched?"

"I suppose so. The whole store is a maze. He introduced himself as the store manager and complimented me on my pronunciation. I was immediately suspicious, and he seemed to pick up on that. He started a conversation about Japanese and made me read more. I didn't realize he was testing me. He asked if I was a student and if I was interested in a part-time job. I said I'd think about it since I lived in the city. He asked me what I was looking for. I said a gift. He asked me what I'm really looking for. He played a psychic pretty well when he was trying to be pleasant, but those piercing eyes always stared a moment too long. I didn't know how to answer, so I said I didn't know yet. He gave me a business card and told me I could apply to work at his store. I thought that was odd, but he hurried off to another customer. On the back of the card he had written instructions for me to return at midnight."

"I rode back that night and he let me into the locked store. He showed me the knife and explained its power. He asked me to read it. I pretended I could, and he seemed convinced. He explained this Japanese item had untested and unbelievable abilities. I didn't believe him, of course, but felt intrigued. He offered me employment to test it for him on the condition I would not tell a soul. In exchange, I would be allowed to join the venture he was planning. I agreed and thus began our arrangement."

"What was he going to do with it?"

"Start a cult. He wanted to make the Memory Therapy section into his own religion. Apparently, it was his idea. The store owner didn't like it much since it didn't make money, but Arthur kept selling and believing in it anyway. Once we discovered the true workings of the knife, Arthur would make his secret society for those seeking his mystical therapy for their traumatic or unwanted memories. He would show them the path of enlightenment, and if they followed his way well enough, they would be granted the amnesia they sought. I was to assist as a right hand. So I began testing the sheath's amnesia-inducing capabilities."

"Just like that? He let you take it? He had just met you."

"*Borrow*. He explained that if discovered or arrested, I was to deny everything and hide the knife, or just pretend it was nothing special. Who would believe what it could do without seeing it first-hand? His only concern was making sure it couldn't be traced back to him. I wasn't being paid for any of this except the vague promise of a future partnership in Arthur's cult. I suppose he trusted I'd keep my mouth shut. Maybe he even wanted me to get caught with it, but I didn't. The thought crossed my mind to run away with it, but I just . . . couldn't. Even if I went on the run, I felt like he'd find me—or The Makers would. Having been instructed that the kaiken, as we later discovered it was called, could poten-tially erase someone's entire memory, I vowed to never use it on myself. Arthur said it was full of evil mind-destroying power. My first test was on a classmate at school. I was shocked. It worked."

"Under the guise of 'Memory Therapy,' I would help Arthur bring customers to a secluded room in the store to 'test' different crystal and incense therapies. He would hold their attention with some snake oil, and I discreetly touched the sheath to the customer. He or she would be trapped and, simultaneously, the amnesia would charge. We'd let them out and erase their memory trying to grasp what effect it had, but it was chaotic. These amnesia events were not useful, since we were just erasing a few minutes of their recent memory. How do you ask someone what they don't remem-ber? One woke up panicked and yelling, so we had to find a new way to test. Arthur charged me with testing it on someone I knew and could interview while not revealing the kaiken and its power. I had few choices. Charging the amnesia, too, was entirely up to me. Again, I think he sent me out almost wanting me to get caught."

Theo tipped his head back against the desk.

"When did it start? I can't even remember," asked Hanna.

"November. I did not yet know I could direct it to erase specific memories. I erased an hour of an afternoon together here, some time in my apartment there. I tried not to interfere with your schoolwork, friends, things like that—just memories of me."

"Why did you do it to me?"

"I thought . . . convinced myself you would break up with me.

Everything I read online said we wouldn't last. You'd meet someone new at your school . . . tell me the inevitable. Every day was a fog. Nothing interested me or bothered me. Life happened and I watched it from afar. I didn't play a part in it. I began thinking nothing would change if I died. I couldn't see you as much. You said you were busy with school. I thought you had found someone else. If I kept telling myself you were already gone, it wouldn't hurt as much when it really happened. Arthur's errands occupied my time. I stopped caring if I got arrested or hurt . . . or what happened to the people I trapped."

"I would ride the bike late into the night traversing the city aimlessly. My father didn't notice. I didn't care if a car hit me or if I crashed. I'd just point the bike at a turn, twist the throttle, and see what happened. I'm surprised nothing happened. Maybe that disappointed me too."

"Was I not good enough? To tell?"

"What do you mean?" he asked innocently.

"You could have told me," she said in a broken voice. "How could you not see I cared about you? We could have talked about it."

"That was my fault too. You were far away, slower and slower to respond. I was more and more involved in Arthur's errands. I was . . . I don't know . . ." he said, groping for the words, "I was waiting for it all to come crashing down, like I deserved it. Surely, I'd be arrested at some point. I didn't want you to see that. But you came to the apartment. We spent more time alone. You talked about a future for us. I was still going out to charge the kaiken's amnesia mechanism. The guilt piled up."

"The abductions . . . they were you all along?"

Theo gave a sullen nod.

"This is insane," she said gently, rubbing her bruised shoulder.

"One small contact and someone is completely gone. You saw it yourself. The longer they remain in the sheath, the more it charges the amnesia power. The more charge, the farther back the amnesia goes. Pull the belt loop, and the victim is released. It's unbelievable, really, but you get used to it. Charging it took up most of my time. Nightclubs and concerts were frequent choices. I wasn't much good at small talk, so usually I played a drug dealer."

"The Long Island incident . . ." Hanna said, straining to articulate his crime.

"A mess. I wanted to charge the sheath and put the victim back without them noticing. If they suspected me, I'd have to erase their memory and start over. Sometimes there were complications. Long Island was an unfortunate case where I was followed by her friend."

"Theo, they were real people. How could you do that to them?"

"Part of it was my focus on the kaiken's origin, part of it was I just didn't care for them. Ideally, they didn't even notice their own absence. Discretion was important, but Arthur still let me run around making people vanish."

"And Steve?"

"He had it coming."

She forced a chuckle, saying, "He's such a jerk," but refocused her attention on an enervated Theo. "You never . . . you just captured the girls and let them go, right?"

"Ask the spirit."

"Who?"

"There's a voice."

"Theo, you're scaring me."

"I'm telling the truth. It comes from the kaiken. She only speaks Japanese. I would try to understand her. I'm certain she's the one actually erasing people's memories. They must go to wherever she is. I would talk to her. She commented on the people I abducted and the memories I erased. She likes you."

Perturbed, Hanna asked, "How do you talk to her?"

"As long as the kaiken is close, she can hear us. You can only hear her if the knife breaks your skin. It doesn't take much—just enough to draw blood."

"How often did you . . . talk?"

Theo pulled back his sleeve. Witnessing so many scars made Hanna's stomach churn. He pulled back his other sleeve and she averted her eyes. She rested her cheek on her knees, pulling them close. Eventually, she gave in to the only words that felt appropriate: "I'm sorry."

"Don't be. It's my fault."

Theo's listless blinks hinted at a confession held back. The cavernous depths of his suffering brought out an ache in Hanna to console, but a selfish fear of the unknown came too. Yet his heart seemed bare and within reach.

"I feel that way too sometimes. I feel worthless and fake, like I don't deserve happiness." Hanna explained softly. "My sister is a much better daughter than me. My parents are so happy with her. I said I'd go into teaching to make my dad not regret having me. It was just another lie. Look at me now. All of Surgite hates me. Maybe it's right to feel this way." She paused, noting his receptive silence. "I'd punish myself for being such a mistake. I'd put my finger down my throat . . . make myself . . ." She gestured the outcome.

"It stopped when we saw each other more—when the amnesia started," she added.

Her eyes met his again. They were apologetic.

"Was it only to talk to her?" she asked.

"It's been a habit for a while."

He took in his own scars. Having dammed up years of unspoken words, they were finding their way out. He took a shaky breath. "She was an excuse. I was afraid. I didn't know how to tell you . . . never mind the supernatural criminal activities and voice I was hearing. I didn't know how you'd take it . . . any of it."

"Have we had this conversation before? Did you erase it from my memory?"

"No, this is the first time."

"So I haven't told you . . . about my problem before?"

"No, I put it together from some comments you left on Friend Link. A friend of yours was struggling with an eating disorder. You offered to be someone she could talk to. You sent her a message saying you had gone through something similar, she answered you, and so on."

"Do you think less of me?"

"No, not at all. More that you told me."

"You weren't supposed to know, but I guess now you do," she said, her voice quiet. Then her cheeks grew hot as she connected the dots. "How could you see those messages? You don't have an account."

"I saw you type your password once."

"Creep."

"I used your Friend Link to manipulate your amnesia. I'm not proud of what I did."

"So I didn't post the picture in the café?"

"Mea culpa."

Silence blanketed them again. The central heat whirred to life, bringing balmy warmth to Theo's room. Hanna remained unsettled by tremulous nerves. Her limbs felt unsteady and icy. His words felt unreal. Reality kept drawing closed her imagined escapes from the magnitude of the little wooden Japanese object still abandoned between them on the floor.

He cleared his throat. "I've been manipulating you. Little stuff, but keeping track of it all. I wrote everything in the notes. You're welcome to read them. I don't know if you want to."

At a loss, she remarked, "In a way, you know me better than I do. You have entire parts of me—what would have made me the me I was supposed to be—not who I am now. What are we but our consciousness up to the present?"

"I know," he said, battered by remorse. "If you want to kill me, that's fine."

She left him in his torpid lull.

"Were you really going to join Arthur's cult?" Hanna asked at last.

"I didn't care for it. I wanted to know where the kaiken came from. The Makers are real. I know it's true. Arthur was a means to an end."

"Who are they?"

"A real secret society that crafts these powerful items. There isn't much you can find online that's true. The campus libraries had nothing. Texts on the occult aren't taken seriously. Arthur was always dismissive, convinced that the kaiken was somehow made by the US government during the Second World War. It didn't make sense to me. We have no idea how old it is."

"Do you still work for Arthur? He called earlier."

"No. I saw his call. That's another problem."

"When did you stop working for him?"

"When he murdered Greg and tried to rape Emma."

Hanna's horrified expression prompted him to explain, "It was the day of our double date. Arthur had asked me to capture someone I could interview. He said we were going to test the knife. We knew what the sheath could do by then, but your translation of the inscriptions gave us clarity on its ability to transplant memories. I admit truthfully that you were the target."

Hanna gasped, pulling her legs closer for some semblance of comfort. The raw pain in her eyes was almost too much for Theo to bear, for he had been the one to put it there.

He continued, "I understand if you hate me. I was going to abduct you and erase your memory after. Nothing was supposed to happen to you, because I thought I'd just cut myself with you trapped in the sheath. I was so clueless. Emma cornered me in the parking lot when you were on the bike. Arthur and Greg showed up shortly after. You must have been suspicious by that point."

Hanna's eyes were wet with unshed tears. Her pent-up breath escaped her in the beginning of a sob. "I was. Somehow, I thought it could be you all along, but convincing myself hurt too much."

His lip quivered for a moment, and he mournfully recalled, "I abducted her. Now you understand how quickly she disappeared. When I saw you on the motorcycle, the guilt was like a heart attack. They took me away and I saw you chasing after us. And for me? The one treating you like a lab rat? Idiot Theo." He shook his head as if to dispel the thought. "They took me to his house up in Tarrytown. He murdered Greg using the knife while Emma was in the sheath. It was horrific. Gruesome. I already don't remember parts of it. How I wanted to disappear from that basement."

He forced himself to keep going. "He made me interrogate her after. I couldn't do it, so he assaulted her. She confessed to killing Greg, remembering it as if she'd done it herself. I still can't block out her screams. She attacked him. He pinned her against the wall and told me to leave. His intentions were obvious. I fought him off, captured Emma, and ran for my life. I drove Greg's car back to Surgite to find you. You had your justified revenge. I rode back to Greg's car, released Emma, and left."

"You rode back alone that night?" she asked, belying her previously accusatory tone.

"I didn't care if I died."

Struck, guilt ensnared her this time.

"If you never forgive me, I understand," he said, his voice barely above a whisper. "Just know I never meant to hurt you. When I came back that night and you pretended to have forgotten me, I couldn't . . . I just couldn't. I thought I was going to erase myself from your memory one day, but seeing you that night . . . I felt a pain I could not have foreseen."

Hanna remained very still. Her tender heart pumped by her unsteady breaths. Theo looked back at her, regret heavy in his apologetic expression. She met his eyes, eager to comfort him. The short distance across his room felt too far.

Memories of that pain stole the breath from Theo's lungs. Taking a moment to compose himself, he added, "I always thought it would be better for everyone if I slipped away. I planned to disappear into The Makers. After everyone forgot me and years passed, I would come back a different person. Maybe I'd even visit my mom."

Hanna took in his unguarded words. She strangely found herself at ease.

"What was she like?" she asked.

Theo hesitated, the memories long since buried. "Not kind, but not mean. She was quiet. My dad talked over her a lot. She didn't like that. She bought me a cello when I was in middle school. She wanted me to learn and said I should have no problem. I was good in school, so she had high hopes. But I was unfocused and prone to fits of anger. I was acting out for no reason, yelling at her and fighting about stupid, random things. It was a nice cello. I remember its finish had a pleasant reddish tone. It felt nice to hold, like you should take care of it. One day, I took it out alone. I smashed it to pieces in the living room."

Hanna covered her mouth with her hand, her eyes wide.

"When my parents came home, they couldn't understand. They kept asking me why, and I couldn't answer. I told them it was their fault and that they did it. They became very quiet. My mom took it hard, blaming herself and dad. She drank more. My dad took me to my first psychiatrist. Mom hated me . . . called me 'demonic' . . . 'unfixable.' Dad didn't like that. She disappeared for hours at a time—then days. She talked to Dad less and less. She'd say her life was a waste and out of control."

Theo gazed at the model airplane crashed on the floor before bringing himself to say, "The divorce started not long after."

"When was the last time you saw her?"

"I can't remember. Just before Lincoln?"

"When will you see her again?"

"My dad handles that. We haven't been talking about it."

"What do you want to say to her?"

Theo drew a deep breath. "I don't know. I've thought so much about forgetting everything that it never crossed my mind."

"Did you think about erasing the cello from your memory?"

"Something always reminds me of it."

They both sat in the silence of the broken cello. Remorse drew anguished lines in his pale face seemingly aged a decade by the ordeal. Hanna blinked in a despondent torpor.

"Theo, we don't want to forget you," she said. "You know I was here for you this whole time."

"I thought about inviting you into all of this, but I doubted your strength."

She shook her head. "If I'm not enough, just say so. I wanted to fall in love with you, Theo. I'd have given you everything. You are smart and passionate, and now look what you've uncovered. I mean, this is incredible. I still can't fully grasp that all of this is happening, and here you are, acting so matter-of-fact about it. If someone offered me supernatural power, I don't know how I'd respond. Maybe other people would have joined his cult or taken the power for themselves. You didn't mean to hurt me, but you did. Maybe you thought you were only affecting yourself, but it hurts, Theo. Part of me is gone."

Hanna met his sincere eyes. "God only knows for sure, but I think your heart is still in there. You did bad things. You hurt people. You fell down the wrong path, but you can still turn back."

"You don't think it's too late for me?"

Hanna's frown melted away.

"Never," she answered as her nose tingled, warning of imminent tears.

"What would you have me do?" he asked, sitting up at last.

"We have to make it right," she said, standing up. She collected her jacket and backpack. With newfound reverence, she stowed the sheath in her backpack.

"It's charged, isn't it?"

"Yeah. However long I was out," he affirmed.

"We need to help Emma. She's suffering. Then we need to stop Arthur . . . somehow. Will you help me?" she asked, extending her hand to him. Underestimating his strength, she tottered helping him pull himself up.

"Promise me you'll atone for what you did. You'll help Emma and apologize to her, to everyone . . . to me," she said, still holding his cold hand.

Theo took her hands in his. "I won't apologize until you know I mean it."

Back to his full height, he stood full of newfound purpose. "But first," he said, gesturing at the mess of his desk scattered on the floor. He picked up the model airplane and carefully set it back on his desk. She handed him the stand, which had snapped off.

They reassembled his desk drawer by drawer, but were interrupted by her phone ringing. She answered, seeing Broc's name on the tiny screen.

"Hey, I told you not to follow me. I'm at Theo's."

"Is that so?" a callous voice asked.

She gasped and froze.

"Who is this?" she asked. Theo came to her side.

"Broc here tells me you're the translator girl Theo's been hiding. He's told me a lot of things."

Theo held up a scrawled "Arthur" on a notebook page.

"I'd like to meet you. Your work is most appreciated."

"Where's Broc?" asked Hanna, breathless, her heart threatening to burst.

"He's right here."

Broc's distressed cries filled the speaker. "Hanna, I'm so sorry! I was following you! I know I shouldn't have. I saw you go to Theo's apartment, but out of nowhere—" he was cut off by a blunt strike.

"Tell Theo to bring you and the sheath to my house within one hour. If I see one cop, Broc joins Greg."

"Leave them out of this," Theo demanded. Arthur hung up.

Hanna closed her phone in disbelief.

"You were being followed?" Theo asked, his question ending her disturbed trance.

"I told him not to!" Hanna explained, exasperated. "He was worried about me seeing you. How did Arthur know where we were?"

"He knows where I live. He must have been watching me. He saw me go out and come back with you. Broc must have been following you."

"We've got to save him."

"How?" he shot back.

"Maybe we can convince him to stop using the kaiken?"

Theo threw her a skeptical look.

"Okay, um . . . maybe we can take it from him?"

"He stabbed Greg to death. He pinned Emma with one arm."

"Oh . . . no," she said, deflated. "But you beat him once, didn't you? You fought him off and got Emma out of his house? There are two of us this time. We have the sheath. What's our plan? We can surely think of something."

Theo scrubbed a hand across his face. "I ran away. He has the knife. As long as he's holding it, he can't be captured," he said.

"We can't just give up!" she cried.

Thought absorbed him momentarily before he raced for his smartphone. He entered an address from a folded note and announced, "Thirty miles. We'd barely make it to his house in time."

"We're not giving him the sheath?"

"No. He's keeping Broc there. It's in the woods, out of the way."

"How would we get there? What would we do?"

"My dad took my keys to his car and the two fifty. The trains would never get us there in time. All we have to do is get Broc in the sheath. We can outrun him."

"On your bike?"

"No—my dad's."

Tingling fear darted through her as he explained, "I don't know exactly what will happen when we get there, but it'll be a fight. We have to find Broc and get him out. He knows we have the sheath, so he's probably hidden him away somewhere in the house. He wants us to give it back. My guess is he'll want to make a deal. You have the sheath in your backpack?"

"Yeah."

"You stay with the bike. I'll get Arthur talking. He'll bring out Broc, and that's when we'll grab him."

The weight of a life laid its gravitas on her unprepared shoulders.

"What if we don't find him?"

"We don't have time to ask what if."

"Do you think he's going to kill him?"

"Yes."

"And he knows your address?"

Theo gave a single taciturn nod. Hanna let out a pent-up breath and shook her hands.

"Okay, okay," she said to convince herself as much as convince Theo. "We need to do this. We're actually doing this. We can do this together."

Theo disappeared and returned in his motorcycle attire. In the lull, she stole a prayer. He handed her the black helmet, saying, "I'll make things right."

She took it from him. "I trust you."

A streak of confidence emerged in his countenance. He grabbed the single key left on the hook by the door.

"We need to stay outside of his house," he explained, leading her to the parking garage across the street. "He'll probably have Broc tied up somewhere. Don't take out the sheath until you see Broc. Just have it ready. I'll negotiate a trade. Whatever happens, we absolutely can't go to the basement."

"What if it's not just him?"

"He works alone. He can't risk exposing the kaiken."

Theo pulled the cover off the red motorcycle, celestial even under the parking garage lights. She trembled yet more while Theo handed her his smartphone.

"You'll have to navigate me when we get to Tarrytown. Just hit my shoulder and point before the turn."

His eyes became sharp, his jaw clenched. He said, "We won't be able to talk once we go. It could get violent. Are you sure you want to do this?"

"There's no reverse, right? We'll just have to pull ourselves out," she said, gripping his phone tightly. He put in the key and fired the ignition. It roared proudly to life, announcing its awakening. He put on his helmet, and she did so too.

Theo mounted the bike and lifted it off its stand. Hanna climbed onto the pillion seat, even more slender than the two fifty's. It angled her body aggressively down into Theo's. Frightening power rumbled through the whole machine as it breathed a crackling growl. Hanna held his smartphone, showing the way, in one hand, Theo's body tightly with the other. Theo lurched the bike forward, attempting to maneuver the parking garage. At the entrance, he gave one last look over his shoulder at Hanna. She nodded and they took off. Hanna prayed to God for their safe return.

TWENTY-FOUR

STRIKING afternoon sunlight poured down the city's corridors. Hanna clung to Theo as though he were a buoy in a hurricane. The machine's brutish power insisted on her untimely departure off the back. Theo wrestled it into focused bursts. The roar was deafening. That morning's mist had cleared, revealing indolent Sunday traffic enjoying the relative warmth. He pulled them to an impatient stop and smacked the tank in frustration. A second later, he ran the red light. Unprepared, Hanna screamed, groping him to stay aboard. She pocketed his phone and frantically wrapped both arms around him. He briefly released the handlebars to reset her arms solidly around his torso and twisted for more power. Manhattan morphed into a blur on their unsanctified passage through red lights, around traffic and irate pedestrians, and up sidewalks.

A sudden dip, and Theo swept them onto FDR drive. The serenely sunlit East River left her breathless as the expanse of road before them morphed into a runway. The red motorcycle indulged its gluttony for hideous speed. Traffic flittered past them like autumn leaves. She gripped Theo tighter.

Would I even feel anything? Would we just die on impact at this speed? she thought.

A slowdown came, and she exhaled at last. Theo's insuperable concentration navigated the traffic and brought them charging northbound. He plunged them forward in clifflike decelerations, then tore open the throttle, charging explosive accelerations. He kept their velocity ever changing. The seesaw of being crushed into him then torn away exhausted and embarrassed her. Theo reached back and gestured her for the smartphone. In the din of the engine and wind, she had completely forgotten. Keeping one arm firmly around him, she recognized the route the map plotted. They were still on target, precious little time remaining.

Hanna tapped his shoulder and was awarded his shrewd attention. She pointed at the coming intersection and the direction to turn. The red motorcycle was promptly aimed at the correct course. Success. They bore down a wooded lane. Chills buzzed across her skin as she recognized they were mere moments away. Another successfully navigated turn brought them closer yet. She felt her heart pounding. Theo executed the winding turns flawlessly at her direction; she almost wished they could ride on.

The engine reverberated the forest, its baritone screech following Theo's aggressive downshift. Arthur's serpentine driveway swallowed them up. She followed his body and the motorcycle into his determined leans. The awesome power of the bike inspired confidence in her—Theo's astute control over it even more. Hanna reached to pocket Theo's phone but missed in her sudden weightlessness.

Earth, blue sky, trees, dried leaves—how they swirled about surprised her. She found it strange her feet were up in the sky. *They look so out of place up there*, she thought, watching her flight like catching a shooting star through a telescope.

———

BROC!

The thought sliced through Theo as the motorcycle violently bucked, slamming him into the ground. He narrowly avoided hitting Hanna's friend, bound to a pile of cinderblocks spanning the road. His father's toppled motorcycle vehemently pulled him off the road in a burst of sparks, his leg trapped under it. Down a slope, he flailed in the leaves, struggling against the inevitable laws of physics. Gracelessly, the motorcycle collided into a tree, whipping the beam of its headlight across Theo, tumbling and disoriented. Following an icy splash, he found himself thrown to the bottom of a ravine. Temporarily immune to inevitable pain, he pushed himself up from the submerged mud and stones, freeing himself from the shallow creek's lifeless waters. He clambered to dry land, calling Hanna's name. She was nowhere to be found.

Theo glanced about for his bearings and saw the motorcycle's half-submerged corpse. Spotting the trail of mangled bodywork, strewn like confetti, he made his way to the wreckage and pulled off his helmet. Deep lacerations were carved into its formerly round and smooth fiberglass. The consequences of his grave error came into focus. He turned the motorcycle's key, shutting off its cracked headlights.

"I'm so sorry," he said to the magnificent machine that had breathed its last. He set his scarred helmet on top of it. "I will come back for you."

Theo raced up the muddy slope. Pain ignited in beleaguering surges in his leg. He pulled himself up by hand in a determined effort to reach the road above. Only Broc lay bound to the pile of cinderblocks maliciously placed across the road. Broc squirmed against the plastic cable ties, yelling through the tape that silenced him. Theo shoved off the cinderblocks, easing the immobilizing weight tied to Broc. At last, Broc could frantically slide himself and his blocks out from the pile. Theo pulled off the copious tape covering his mouth.

"Forget about me!" he burst. "He took Hanna!"

"You're still tied up."

"I can move enough. I'll get free and go get help."

Indecision paralyzed Theo.

Broc yelled, "Just go! They went to his house!"

Theo bolted down the driveway, passing her nearby discarded helmet. Debilitating pain seared through his leg, but spotting Arthur's black SUV ahead surged encouraging energy through him. He focused his attention on the front door, left ajar, bounding up the stairs of the dilapidated front porch. Across the threshold, he froze at the sight before him.

With one hand, Arthur pulled a struggling and crying Hanna by her hair. In his other, the knife coerced her movement, evidence of its punishing bites staining her shirt. Arthur effortlessly knocked Hanna to her knees and faced her to Theo. A faint vile odor seeped up from the house. Arthur raised the Japanese blade to her neck and said, "You've really outdone yourself bringing me one this sweet."

Hanna ceased her teary struggle as the black steel paused at her throat. Theo scanned the room for solutions: nothing but the front door behind him and the kitchen doorway, which led to the basement.

"Where's the sheath? Give it up!" Arthur ordered.

"Lower the knife."

"The sheath, Theo."

Theo stepped forward.

"I'll gut the bitch!" Arthur bellowed, pressing the knife against the side of Hanna's neck. She cried out, hyperventilating at the steel's insidious touch.

"It's more fun when they scream," he said, pushing the blade harder against her neck. Crimson life spilled onto her white shirt. Theo's burning ankle involuntarily buckled and he fought to regain his balance. Hanna wrestled her screams into a stifled grunt and yelled, "Wait! Just wait!"

"Where is it, Theo?" Arthur demanded. Hanna's jacket, sweater, and backpack lay strewn about, having been ripped off her. Theo's eyes darted to the backpack at Arthur's question, belying their subterfuge. Another second slipped by, and the situation spun further out of his control. Hanna's death materialized into harrowing possibility. Hopelessly, he struggled to know what to do.

The blood pooling around her collar nauseated Theo, but shock overwhelmed him as he spotted Hanna's determined hands taking the blade and keeping it pressed to her neck. Stunned, Arthur stared in fascination at the girl accelerating her own demise. Words formed in her suffering voice. Theo recognized them as Japanese. She spoke in perilous spurts. The strength of her voice surged. Before Arthur realized it, Hanna yelled the end of the inscription on the kaiken and shouted, "*Kotodama!*"

Blinding violet light shot out of the blade. Arthur staggered back. Theo spotted the sheath shining through Hanna's backpack. Hanna flailed and struck Arthur, stunning him. Burning with determination, Theo charged Arthur and drove his fist into him. Theo fought the knife out of his hand. It tumbled across the floor. Hanna crawled away and snatched it during Arthur's vehement retaliation. Arthur's enraged blows battered Theo, who wavered, retreating on his crippled leg.

Just keep him off Hanna, he thought, tackling Arthur. Their bodies crashed into a bookcase. Theo protected himself relying on his jacket's armor, but Arthur's infuriated blows kept overwhelming his guard. Theo fell back, losing focus on his opponent. Arthur wrestled him to the floor and pinned him under his weight. Theo gasped for air. His arms became sluggish. His evaporating strength failed to throw Arthur off. Arthur's blurry fists wetted his numb face in his own blood. Insidious ringing in his ears enveloped the growing silence. He fought back, but darkness consumed him.

HANNA STUMBLED to her glowing backpack. The abominable sounds of Theo and Arthur's combat had filled the room. "Please be right!" she pleaded breathlessly, tearing open her backpack, the knife beside her. Revolting pain flared in her neck. She dared not think of the wound still pouring blood. She felt herself becoming stiff and weak, desperate to cover the gash in her neck. Her trembling, blood-soaked hands located the sheath. The sounds of the melee had ceased, leaving only Arthur's labored breaths. Mortified, Hanna turned back to see Theo defeated and unconscious on his back. Arthur rose, approaching her. Those remorseless eyes stared back at her.

"God, please!" she cried, jamming the glowing knife into the sheath.

The light exploded. She dropped the kaiken, scurrying away from the blinding nova. Arthur shielded his eyes and retreated from the echoey bang. Hanna glimpsed a woman amid the light. Black clothes cloaked a lithe form. Her black hair obscured a face set on the man rushing away from her. Her deft hand readied the kaiken—her kaiken—and she sprang after him. Hanna shrieked at Arthur's escape, ended by a single adroit strike. The woman dug the blade deeper into his back and forced him to his knees. Her voice boomed an emphatic command in Japanese. Hanna frantically crawled to Theo's motionless body, clutching the dripping wound in her neck. The woman repeated herself. Hanna recognized the Japanese.

"I won't allow it!" she said, smothering Arthur's terrified shouts with her hand. He sank lower. She ripped the knife out of him and tore it across his neck. Hanna shielded her eyes from the chaotic splatter. Arthur spilled onto her feet. Once so full of movement, he breathed his last, becoming very still as if calmly entering sleep. The woman kicked him off and sneered. *"Annoying."*

Flicking the blood off her blade, she inspected it, tossing it from hand to hand curiously. Maniacal laughter engrossed her, and she roared in her native tongue. Hanna comprehended only the final word of her verbose outburst.

"Finally!" the woman repeated with clenched fists.

Invigorated, energy pulsated through her. The woman ran her

hand along the walls, feeling the mundane wallpaper and panes of the windows. She came back to Arthur's corpse, grabbed it by his shirt, and threw it into a corner as if tossing a pillow. Another fit of laughter took her. Hanna cowered at her incongruous strength. The woman raised her disturbing glare to Hanna's petrified face. She approached Hanna and a defenseless Theo.

"*Get away from him,*" the woman ordered, flicking her blade. Hanna rose. Gasping for breath and clutching her dripping neck, she stood blocking the woman's way.

"*Stop,*" Hanna shouted back.

"*Move, I said,*" the woman commanded with evident irritation.

"*Stop!*" Hanna found herself yelling back in her own language.

The woman recoiled, then glanced at the weapon she held pointed at Hanna. Her head tipped, catlike, and she dexterously returned it to the sheath affixed to the back of her waist. The kaiken was clearly at home with her.

"*I see. You are the translator, aren't you?*"

"*I am.*"

"*You helped Theo release me. He could not understand me,*" she said, her tone dismissive and biting.

"*Thank you,*" she added, though Hanna doubted her sincerity. She wavered and fell to her knees. The woman approached her and knelt beside Hanna, who winced at her proximity.

"*Calm down. I will help you,*" she said flatly. Her clothes were difficult to make out being all black. They resembled a judo *gi*, but much tighter. Body armor was concealed beneath the folds of elegant fabric. She was not particularly tall and rather slender. She unwrapped a scarf about her waist unseen to Hanna a moment prior and wrapped it about Hanna's dire wound.

"*Let go,*" the woman ordered. Impatiently, she repeated her command two more times, but Hanna merely shook her head. The woman disappeared to the kitchen and returned shortly with hand towels that she indicated would serve as gauze. She ordered Hanna to remove her hand and used her black scarf to secure the makeshift bandages.

"I pity you. You better see a doctor," the woman said, tightening the scarf. The adrenaline was wearing off and Hanna felt herself slipping away. She wrestled herself back to ask the woman, *"What is your name?"*

"Mougo."

Hanna recognized the word from the inscription. Mougo knelt beside Theo and turned his face to the ceiling. Blood ran down his swollen cheeks and eyes. Bruises were already discoloring his face in putrid purple and yellow blotches. She stroked his hair. Hanna's vision started to dim. She shook her head, the relentless throbbing pain igniting an anemic second wind in her.

"You saw the things Theo did?"

"Yes."

"What did you see?"

"The memories he took from you. The people he brought me."

"Really?"

"You love him, no?"

Unprepared for the question, Hanna coughed, pain flaring up in her neck.

"Did he . . . what happened to Emma?" she asked, regaining her composure.

Mougo hesitated before answering, *"That loud one? He saved her from the disgusting man."*

"Did he . . . did Theo . . . the girls he captured . . . did he touch them?"

She smirked. *"I get it. You are his lover after all."*

Hanna clutched Mougo's arm for support.

Gently rubbing Theo's chest, Mougo said, *"He talked to me so many times despite the pain. It was never for long, but he tried. I yearned for his voice—any voice after all this time, even if he couldn't understand me. He had such doubts about that disgusting man. He promised he would discover how to release me. How he despised the girls. Touch them? He disregarded them. He gave them to me for power—nothing more. His heart was set. I enjoyed the variety he sent me. It was fun seeing Americans and their strange clothes. Watching your dates was fun too."*

"You have them? My memories?"

"Yes, what he gave me."

"Could you give them to me?"

She faced Hanna. *"That disgusting man's death grants me power to use my abilities to their limit. I need that power back here in the moving world. I can, however, use some of it to grant you a favor. I suppose I could give them back to you. I could also erase memories. I could erase this entire ordeal. I could erase this evening. I don't know what you want, but I could erase you from his memory too. Whatever you choose, you will graciously allow me to thank you by this favor."*

Hanna clutched Mougo's arm and took in a deep breath. Theo's unconscious breaths continued weakly.

She fought to ask, *"You really could give me back my memories?"*

"Yes."

There, again, was that pang of sympathy. His face looked like raw meat—his suffering immense. She could only imagine how he would feel waking up. He would blame himself for the crash.

"Just one?"

Vexed, Mougo said, *"Look, I will share some of this charge. I need the rest."*

"Could you . . . erase a memory from his childhood?"

"Childhood? How long ago?"

"Six or seven years."

Mougo frowned. *"That is difficult. It's buried deep, but I suppose I could. To reach that far back I could not erase much —certainly nothing else."*

"Just one memory. I ask you to erase the time he destroyed the cello from his mother."

Mougo blinked. *"Cello, you say?"* she asked, placing her hand on his forehead. A moment passed and she blinked again. She shook her head, lost in recollection.

Coughs soon roiled through him, and he regained consciousness. His eyes peered through his swollen face as they took in the room. Struggling to sit up, he coughed out blood, wheezing. He blinked several times between the two faces watching him intently. He fought back another cough and managed to say, "Hey."

"Hi."

"How's your neck?"

"Not good. Mougo gave me this scarf."

He gazed upon the black-clad Japanese woman peering at him.

"You look different than I imagined," he said.

She turned to Hanna. *"What did he say?"* she asked in her tongue.

"He said . . ." Hanna began but collapsed onto her hands. Mougo and Theo both helped her up to her unsteady feet.

"We have to go," Mougo said, pulling them to the door. Hanna and Theo both froze at the horrific sight of Arthur's half-decapitated body splayed in the corner. Mougo forced them out the front door into the chilly late afternoon. Theo's limp worsened. Blackness encroached on Hanna's vision.

"Stay with us. It's not much farther," Theo reassured her as they approached Arthur's SUV.

"Ask her to get the keys," he told Hanna.

Addressing Mougo, her voice, rapidly deteriorating, only produced, *"Arthur's key."* Hanna weakly pointed at the SUV, then sank to the ground, clinging to Theo. Mougo darted back into the house.

"We'll be right back," he said to Hanna, propping her up against the wheel.

Hanna hovered on the edge of total blackness.

Seeing her slipping away, Theo said, "You have to stay awake. We'll get Broc and all drive to the hospital. I'll be gone for just a minute," he added, removing his jacket and placing it on her. She took it, comforted by its weight and warmth, and avoided dwelling on the turgid, blotchy flesh constituting his beaten face. He limped back into the house, struggling against his injuries. Her breaths became short. Her blinks frequent and prolonged. The pain was incessant. Sweat beaded on her forehead. She looked at her formerly white shirt, now stained scarlet by Arthur's cruel strikes, the blood obscuring the kittens and hearts that patterned it. The trees swayed in the frosty breeze. She shivered in her torn jeans. Winter still held spring away in its clutches.

"Where's Broc?" she called out in vain.

"Mougo? Theo?" she cried, but only relentless pain cried back.

———

THEO HURRIED to gather Hanna's sweater, jacket, and backpack, the tattered straps of which dangled about him, lurching in unsteady heaves. He took care to collect its scattered contents and locate her cell phone, his having been lost in the crash. A solemn wave moved him as he spotted her bloody fingerprints on two letters. He returned them to her backpack.

"Do you have the keys yet?" he called over, but Mougo ignored his English. The Japanese woman approached him bearing the promising jangle of keys. She handed them to him and took Hanna's jacket out of his hand.

"*Mine,*" she said, swiping the dirt off it. Her exotic clothes were now somewhat concealed. She did not mind the scratches down the jacket's back, courtesy of the crash.

Theo led Mougo back outside, only to discover Hanna slumped on the ground. He tried to run, but his ankle finally gave out and he collapsed. Mougo raced past him and picked up Hanna, deathly pale. Holding her, she shouted, *"Hurry!"* Theo unlocked Arthur's SUV, having to crawl to it. He pulled open the back seat door and Mougo lifted Hanna up, placing her onto the row of seats. Theo took the driver's seat and started the vehicle. The SUV jerked down the winding driveway. He hung on the steering wheel for vital support. They turned the driveway's corner and came upon the cinderblock trap. Broc had wriggled himself off the road, still bound by two blocks. Theo parked the vehicle and opened the door.

"Broc! You okay?" he yelled, hobbling to him. Broc began a prolonged answer, but Mougo swiftly moved past Theo, unbeknownst to him. She cut the plastic ties and pulled Broc to his feet. A shivering Broc looked astounded as he beheld Mougo. Shifting his focus to Theo, he yelped.

"Dude! What happened to *you*! Who's she? Where's Hanna? What happened to Arthur?"

Theo's injured leg dragged him lower as he said, "There's no time. You have to drive us to the hospital right now."

Broc sputtered more questions, but Mougo impatiently grabbed him and pulled him to Arthur's SUV. She ripped open the door to reveal Hanna lying on the back seats stained by the blood oozing from her neck. Broc shrieked, backing away. Mougo grabbed him by his collar and pinned him against the vehicle. She yelled at him in Japanese, evidently impatient. Theo heard Hanna's faint voice from the back seat say, "She said drive the car."

"It's really more of a truck," Broc said demurely. Mougo shook him violently and roared another command.

Through labored breaths, Hanna struggled to say, "She called you useless."

Broc nodded. "Okay, okay!" he said and scurried to the driver's seat.

A faint, "Sorry, Broc," could be heard from Hanna as Mougo assumed the passenger seat. Theo made for the third-row seats, but Hanna called him to her. He set himself in the footwell beside her. Broc's nervous reassurances to himself filled the cabin as if he had never operated a motor vehicle in his life.

They moved at last. He kept reminding Mougo it would only

be a few more minutes, fiddling the navigation on his cell phone at every stoplight.

"I'm sorry, Hanna. I don't know what to do, but I'm so sorry," Theo told her. "For everything. It's all my fault."

Hanna opened her eyes. Unable to turn her head, Theo leaned nearer to hear her in the car's darkness cut by bars of passing streetlights.

"Don't go," she said.

Her battered voice was just audible above the road noise as she continued, "I believed in you, and He answered my prayer. Pray for me, Theo."

Powerless, he held her icy hands keeping pressure on her wound for the rest of their brief journey. *If you're real, God, please help her,* he thought.

Time passed in a fog. Broc and Mougo were both speaking. Hanna tried to move. The vehicle stopped under the lamps of an awning. The door opened and Broc beckoned Theo out. In a daze, he found himself driving the vehicle to a parking spot, Mougo seated beside him. His leg and ankle burned, the pain agonizing. How he longed to lie down and drift away. Broc carried Hanna in his arms into the hospital's emergency room reception. Theo abruptly stopped the black SUV in a quiet spot, out of the parking lot's vigilant lights. Mougo did not stir. Hanna's life was in capable hands now, yet Theo's heart remained restless.

Logic could not assuage him. Time was unbearable. Only a few minutes had passed since their arrival at the hospital. He reached for his jacket behind him and gingerly put it on. Next to it was Hanna's backpack. Digging through it for her phone, he came upon the two letters. He discovered his own handwriting on one. Theo read his own words. The memories came back.

That Theo, so hopeful and energized when a new friend—his only friend—had grabbed his arm. Eyes and smile so bright, she hung on him, excited just by his presence. He could only fathom who put her up to it or what trick it was—but it was no trick.

That Theo, not much younger than the bloodstained one reading the letter, wrote to her, able to overcome plaguing cynicism. How she fought against the Theo he was becoming. Why could he not?

He opened the next letter. A silence gripped him. There were her stark words. Her mind was set. Theo folded the letter carefully and returned her final decision to her backpack. She was safe with Broc now. He sighed heavily, aware of comforting unconsciousness seemingly just moments away.

"I'm sorry," Mougo said, breaking the silence. Theo shook his head, unable to speak. She leaned across the center console and peered into his swollen eyes. He could hardly tell her age in the shadows of the vehicle, but she was older than him. Her voice was deep and dismissive. A mature confidence accompanied her curt words and actions.

"Thanks," she said, holding up the kaiken.

"It was mostly Hanna," he said, shaking his head.

She softly touched her cold fingertips to Theo's face. Motionless, he accepted the contact. She withdrew her hand and inspected his blood on her fingertips, then licked one. She licked another and said, *"Hanna will be okay."* She added another sentence, which was lost to Theo's poor Japanese. He sat passively, unsure how much longer he could stay conscious or let the inexplicable actions pass unquestioned.

"Torakku kiizu?" she asked in her heavy accent. Oblivious, he searched the front seat, but was interrupted by Broc knocking on the window. Theo opened the door and Broc asked, "What happened?"

"Is Hanna okay?"

"Yeah," said Broc. "They took her in, but what happened? Where'd she come from? And what happened to Hanna's neck? And—"

"Arthur's dead. Hanna set her free," he said, gesturing to the Japanese woman. Mougo exited the vehicle and pulled Theo out of the driver's seat. She set his arm around Broc's shoulder, handed Hanna's backpack to Broc, and pointed at the hospital.

Theo shook his head. "Just drive me home. I'll sleep it off."

"Dude, you look like hell. You can't even stand. She's right. You should go to the ER," Broc countered, propping him up.

Mougo repeated, "Torakku kiizu?" to which Theo produced them from his pocket, having finally remembered. She took them, pointed to herself and the kaiken, and raised her index finger to her lips.

"Take care. See you," she said and climbed into the driver's seat.

Broc shouted, "Hey, wait!" as she pulled the door closed. She started the engine and drove off. They looked on at the red tail-lights receding into the blackness.

"What did she say? She can drive? Did she really just steal Arthur's truck?"

"Yeah," Theo answered.

"But that's a crime."

"He won't be using it anymore."

Broc sighed. "Guess I'll call Emma to bring my minivan. Oh God, what's she gonna think about all of this? What am I going to say to her?"

Theo sank to his knees. Broc hoisted Theo's arm around his shoulders and started walking him across the parking lot. They shuffled together in an unsteady gait to the emergency room entrance.

"Who was that woman anyway? She Japanese?" Broc asked.

"You can never tell anyone about her."

"Dude?"

"She was a prisoner. We set her free, but people will look for her. She's a fugitive. She killed Arthur."

"Oh my God. Now she stole his truck too," Broc said, his already frayed voice growing higher and yet more frenetic. "Where—when—exactly is she from? Was she wearing some kind of, like, armor? How can she drive? Can she even drive in this country? Don't they drive on the other side of the road in Japan?"

"Broc, focus. You can never tell anyone about this woman. Your life could be in danger."

"Can I tell Emma?"

"No—especially not her."

"She's gonna yell at me. Maybe that's for the best. She's still having nightmares and all. Oh yeah, Hanna was supposed to ask you about that. Did you guys talk? I followed her through Central Park. I saw you two talking and then I kept following you to a really nice-looking apartment building, and that's when Arthur grabbed me—right off the sidewalk too."

"You were abducted by Arthur alone?"

"He came up behind me and said he had a gun. What was I supposed to do?"

"He didn't," Theo told Broc, shaking his head.

"So what are we going to tell the police?" Broc asked, clearly frightened. "There's going to be a police report and everything. The hospital's gonna ask us questions."

Theo stopped before the awning's lights, causing Broc to stop beside him. He struggled for breath and wondered if Hanna was already in surgery. He asked Broc to put him down on a bench beneath the awning. A man talking on a cell phone moved away from them.

Using the last of his strength, Theo fought to grab Hanna's backpack, tucked under Broc's arm. "Her cell phone is in here. Take it and call her parents. Tell them you rescued us after I crashed the bike. You brought us to the hospital. Give her backpack to her parents when they arrive. Make sure they find her."

"What about Arthur?"

"Say you saved us from the abductor."

"No way," Broc said in disbelief. His petrified voice and frivolous worries belied his fit but round physique.

"It's believable," Theo assured him. "Tell them it was you that saved us. You were never abducted. I crashed the bike with Hanna. The abductor got us. You fought him off. There was no Japanese woman."

Broc went pale and whispered, "What about the body?"

"I'll say I killed Arthur. If the cops come down on you, I'll step forward, turn myself in . . . plead self-defense."

Broc leaned back. "This is some heavy stuff. What if they throw you in jail? What if there's a trial?"

"She saved Hanna's life. I will keep her secret."

A somber moment passed between them. Broc took back Hanna's backpack from Theo's failing grip. He slung Theo's arm around his shoulder and lifted him up. With generous care, he walked Theo to the light pouring out of the hospital entrance.

"Hey, Broc?"

"Yeah?"

"Did the hospital take in Hanna right away? Will she be okay?"

Broc gave a knowing smile and answered, "Yeah. She's gonna be all better in no time. Now let's get you inside, buddy."

TWENTY-FIVE

"FRACTURED EYE SOCKET, broken nose, chipped tooth, multiple torn ligaments in your ankle, contusions in your knee, two cracked ribs, a sprained thumb," Mr. Jansen read aloud, flicking the pages of the medical report, "totaled my motorcycle, lost your cell phone, wrecked your gear and her helmet, weren't even wearing a helmet yourself, you idiot, put that poor girl in the ER, hours in the ER yourself . . . am I missing anything?"

Theo remained still, lying on the couch. Monday's afternoon clouds formed an uncomely haze over the city outside the living room windows. Mr. Jansen flipped through the report another time. Theo strained to add, "You'll get all the tickets from the red light cameras too."

"What is wrong with you?" His father sighed and began pacing the room. Theo closed his sore eyes. Any movement was a chore. His father carried on his censure, saying, "And no police report? How am I going to make an insurance claim? Where did you say you crashed it?"

"It's in a creek by some house in Tarrytown."

"You're such an idiot—joyriding my motorcycle with her on the back. What were you thinking? What were you doing down some private road?"

"I didn't realize it was a driveway. It just looked like a twisty road," Theo said, burying the truth further.

"I thought I raised you smarter than this." Mr. Jansen scoffed, then asked, "How did you crash again?"

"I was in a turn. I was going too fast. Panicked—stabbed the front brake. It slid out from under me—pulled me by my leg into the ravine. Hanna fell off. Her friend took us to the hospital," he said with rehearsed precision.

"You low-sided the bike onto your leg? You weren't going that fast."

"I overreacted."

"But you were going fast enough to do that kind of damage in a driveway?" his father hammered, giving an incredulous look. "And on cold tires even! They were new. I never even got to properly scrub off the edges. What were you thinking?"

Theo opened his eyes to escape replaying the crash he had seen every time he shut them. His father continued his tirade with, "To think you not only got on a motorcycle after I took your key, but you took Rosetta! Without my permission, and crashed her on your first ride? More importantly, you endangered the life of a passenger! And you weren't even wearing a helmet! How could you! I should have seen the signs. My lovely dinner with Samantha was interrupted by your call. Thank God she came along to deal with my depressed bike-crashing son in the ER."

A vein on Mr. Jansen's forehead looked as if it might burst. "You've even been through my liquor," he blurted out, shaking his head. Theo avoided his piercing glare. "What a surprise when I poured myself a glass of spiked apple juice. You really are your mother's son."

Theo sat up through stinging soreness. He took his crutches and prepared to stand up. "Anything else?" he asked.

Mr. Jansen grimaced. "What do you have to say for yourself?"

Theo heaved himself onto his good foot, his left bound by a

cumbersome brace. Crutches and bandages slowed his silent retreat to his room. He closed the door and collapsed into his chair. Demon World soon opened on his screen.

They'll find the body. They'll find the bike. The police will knock on the door. Why not say it was Mougo? She must be far away by now, he thought. Remembering her in the hospital parking lot, he reconsidered. *But she saved Hanna's life and yours.*

The consequences of that fateful night swirled outside his room. He felt the urge to yell for help, followed by the desire for unending sleep moments later. His fault—all his fault. *But here I am, alive,* he thought. He focused on the game before him. His character stood in an azure pasture. Down its winding paths, he sought solace. No enemies, no other players, no quests—a veritable retreat, blank and inviting. An hour or so passed. His cloaked ranger came to a stop. A message in the game appeared from Ray.

"You available?"

Theo ignored it. His strength for human interaction ceased to exist. He retreated farther into the fields and found himself under a tree. Another message from Ray came and went. A missed day of school—he criticized himself for his truancy. Hanna would inevitably miss days too—maybe weeks. The blame he felt surrounded him like numbing cold water. The scattered contents of his desk still lay about his feet. He sat under the tree until the afternoon faded into a blazing sunset. The idea to call Hanna's cell phone from the apartment's landline came and went too. Was she even out of the hospital? Not even twenty-four hours had elapsed.

An unread email from Ray sat atop his inbox. He clicked it.

"Are you okay? We're worried about you," it read. Still numb, he reread the words. The aches in his bones dragged on. He clicked back to the game but accepted Ray's invitation. Ray came walking up the grassy knoll clad with his bow and ridiculous hat. He sat his character beside Theo's.

"Hey, you can hear me?" Ray asked.

"Yeah."

"Grapefruit sunset, huh?"

The strength to speak failed Theo.

"Come on," Ray prodded.

"All I feel is pain."

"Oh. What's got you down?" Ray asked, his voice losing its usual pep. "Why haven't you been on any raids or anything?"

"It's a pointless guild in a stupid game."

Ray was silent for a time, then said, "But it's our pointless guild."

"I can't even stay in a guild."

"Why are you so hard on yourself? What happened? Do you want to talk about it?"

Theo offered only silence.

Ray's courage failed him before he finally asked, "I know . . . I'm going out on a limb here . . . it's that girl, isn't it?"

"I miss her so much."

"It's okay, bro. What happened? Did you break up? How bad is it?"

The headset was painful on Theo's bandages. "I crashed my dad's motorcycle throwing her off the back. We were trying to save her friend from the cultist I was working for. I got in a fistfight. She almost died."

". . . dude."

Ray's silence invited Theo to explain, "We went to the hospital together. I lost my phone in the crash. It's been a day. I haven't heard from her. She was in surgery. I don't know what's going on or what to do. She wrote me a letter saying we're done and good-bye. I found it last night in her backpack. I can't stop thinking about her. He had a knife to her neck and . . ." but the recollection choked his voice.

"You don't have to say, man," Ray said gently. "I'm sure she'll be alright. The doctors will take care of her."

Breathing strained Theo, who let the words fall out: "I hate myself for how much I miss her. I feel sick thinking about her, but I can't stop. I'm such an idiot. We were fighting just yesterday, at each other's throats. I can remember so clearly the anger in her eyes. Yet then my stupid brain remembers how warm she feels in my arms. I remember the night she ripped my heart out, and the very next moment, I remember the little bows and lace on her clothing. Why is their clothing so much softer than ours? The way she sneezed too. She actually says 'achoo' in this little squeak she does. Her socks were always mismatched and colorful. And her laugh . . . what cheer. I'm such a loser for saying all of this. It's pathetic, isn't it?"

Ray replied, "Yeah, girls are soft and they smell nice. It's a gift you had that time in your life."

"I'll never hear her voice again," Theo said, forlorn.

"You never know. You might hear her beautiful voice again," Ray said, ever the optimist.

Theo scoffed. "Like you know what she sounds like."

"Actually, I do. We talked to her when Emma played with us. She was all worried about you, asking if we'd seen you. She probably wants to talk to you about everything that happened."

Her jovial singing danced in his vibrant memories, but Theo could only say, "She'll never talk to me again."

"You never know. Why don't you try calling her?"

"She wouldn't recognize the number," Theo mumbled, recalling the landline in his apartment. Would she not recognize the number, though? Would she even be awake? Ray urged him further, but Theo snapped, "Even if she did pick up, she'd just blame me for the crash and everything."

Ray receded into his own thoughts. Theo overheard him clattering away on his keyboard. Sleep's reprieve beckoned Theo away from the slog of consciousness.

"What about Emma?" Ray asked suddenly. "Can't you talk to her?"

"She wouldn't talk to me either. I ruined her life too."

"You don't know that," Ray retorted. "You gotta have a little faith."

Ray's words smacked his unreceptive face. Ray pressed on, "I'm going to need some help on this." Several moments later, a familiar sorcerer appeared on his screen and Necro's flat voice filled his headset with, "You're alive. You've been blowing us off for a while now."

"Don't you have somewhere else to be?" Theo asked.

"There's no place for me," Necro replied, approaching them.

Ray chimed in, "Theo's going through some stuff. Tell him he should talk to his girl."

Necro asked, "Did she break up with you?"

"Yeah."

"And?"

"And what?"

"How'd she do it?"

"What a stupid question," Theo uttered in confusion.

Necro pushed on, saying, "Ray said I have to be serious. I'm asking you seriously."

Theo sighed. "She wrote me a letter. I found it in her backpack. We already broke up last week, but she came to see me and we had a fight. Then . . . how do I even explain . . . we agreed to work together, and all of this happened."

"Did she give you the letter?"

"Not . . . directly . . . no, she did not."

"What was the last thing she said to you?"

Theo peered into his memory of that moment. Her agony was painful to recall. His own pain flared in his wounds, but there, in his recollection, were her whispers. Hanna's last words to him echoed in the void of his heart.

"She said she believed in me and to pray for her."

"You're still in it."

"What?"

"Did she give you the letter?"

"No, but I found—"

"Grow a pair and talk to her," Necro said.

Theo closed his eyes. "I don't deserve her. I've caused her so much pain."

Continuing his nasally encouragement, Necro said, "You deserve to give yourself a chance. Take it from me, I know a hard no. She still wants to talk. You broke up, what, a week ago? But she came back. Stop ignoring that. She thought she could work things out with you. I don't know what went down last night, but you sound horrible. Imagine how she feels? Alone in some hospital maybe—who knows? Maybe she's worried about you and you're making it worse by not calling. From the sounds of it, you can't make it much worse, but here you go, finding a way. You gotta get out of your own head. Don't overthink it. She never gave a hard no."

"What's a hard no?"

"She say she'd call the police if you kept talking to her? Had that happen once," Necro answered.

Ray added, "When I asked a girl to prom, she said she'd rather be expelled."

"Oh," was all Theo could say.

"I always knew you were different from us," Ray said, his avuncular tone comforting. "Necro had doubts, but we always figured you'd be the one to have a real chance—to not end up so alone. You still have a chance to make up with Hanna."

"She wouldn't want to talk to me."

"Have you tried?" Necro asked.

"Then you don't know," Necro said confidently, Theo's silence telling him all he needed to know.

"What does she look like?" Ray asked.

"Why?"

"She sounds like she has a kind heart and will hear you out.

She probably wants to know how you're doing as much as she'd appreciate you caring how she's doing."

Theo navigated to Hanna's Friend Link account asking, "If you two are such experts, why are you still single?"

Necro chuckled. "I'm twenty-three, living off disability in my grandparents' basement."

Ray tossed out, "Oh, I try, man, but after enough rejections, you come to terms with it."

Not having an account himself, Theo saw that Hanna's account was hidden from the public. She must have put her security settings to their highest. He began typing her username and password to log in as her.

Have you learned nothing? his mind's voice asked himself. He stopped. Theo grimaced at his only option. There was no time to edit the photographs with his friends urging him to share. Theo chose a picture saved on his computer. Hanna's radiant smile stung his heart. She stood beside him in the photograph. He sent it to Ray and Necro.

"Aw, dude, she's adorable. How could you put her through this?" said Ray.

"Flat and plain," commented Necro.

"Come on, Necro. She looks like a nice girl, albeit one with a fangy smile," Ray remarked.

"Her teeth are really sharp," Theo added.

Ray and Necro both chuckled, then laughed. Their infectious laughter pulled a ripple of laughter out of Theo, bringing sharp pain too.

"You look exactly how I imagined. Man, you're like a foot taller than her," said Ray.

"She's rather short," replied Theo.

"You look older than I thought. You're a freshman? Both of you need to eat more," Necro said, his usual judgmental tone coming out.

"Do you really think she would talk to me?" Theo asked.

They both exclaimed affirming answers. Theo's extinguished embers of resolve caught a spark.

Ray asked, "So, um, do you have a picture of Emma? Just curious."

A few clicks later, his guildmates were presented a picture of Hanna next to her best friend.

"Good Lord, we were talking to *her*!" Ray shouted.

"That ass," Necro remarked. "Could you have picked a photo that showed it off more?"

"They're all like that," dismissed Theo.

"Clap and Two-D have got to see this!" Ray exclaimed. Seconds later, the boisterous monk and the nervous healer logged on, asking, "What's the code red? Where is the girl?"

Necro said, "No, dude, just pictures of the girl Theo put up to playing with us."

"Oh yeah, Emma. I can't—" but his verbose answer was cut short by his gasp at seeing the picture forwarded to him.

"Wowzers! As long as I have a face, she'll always have a place to sit," said the nervous healer, who clearly had gained tremendous confidence that day.

The guild decried his comment. In the ensuing commotion, Theo quietly messaged Ray, "I'm going to try calling her."

Ray sent back a smiling face next to, "See! You're literally hardwired to find hope!"

Theo sent back, "It might be a couple days before I log in again. I have promises to keep."

Ray's message saying, "Good luck," sprung onto his screen.

Theo logged off, heaved himself onto his crutches, and gimped his way to the kitchen. There sat the seldom-touched landline. Memories of her anger, then cries of pain, her cold bloody hands— Theo leaned on his crutch. The phone felt heavy in his hand. The dial tone was uninviting. He put it back, lost to a wave of guilt.

"Have a seat. You're in pain," his father said from the doorway.

Theo turned. "No, I'm fine."

Mr. Jansen took a seat at the table. Memories of Hanna's benevolent touch pervaded the space too. The silence grew between them. His father appeared at a loss for words.

"Do you want me to go away?" Theo asked.

His father sighed and cursed under his breath.

Theo asked, "Do you hate me?"

"No. How many times do I have to tell you?"

"You don't mean it."

He smacked his fist against the table. "Dammit, Theo!" he said and took deep breaths to steady himself. Mr. Jansen began, "I understand I may have come down too hard on you. What was I supposed to do? You, my only son, almost died. How do you think I felt seeing you at the hospital like that? I hope you never have to feel that in your life. All this to get you here. Do you know how hard I fought for you? That custody battle became the longest years of my life. Your mother and I were not good for each other. It's better this way, for your sake. I know I don't do a good enough job keeping her in your life." His father lost his usual confidence. "But I don't know what to do. Do you want to talk to her? Would that help?"

The familiar feelings from the cello surfaced, but he failed to envision it. He struggled to recall and sat at the table, shocked at his inability to summon the memory. Concentration strained his bandaged face. He could not remember. What did he do? Helpless, he asked his father, "Why did Mom leave?"

"I was too stubborn," Mr. Jansen admitted. "In marriage, the only things you'll fight about are money and kids. We fought about both. She fought me on every purchase—every little thing I wanted. She never thought I was doing a good enough job raising you either. Maybe she was right."

"Wasn't there my cello?"

"That? Your mother got upset you broke it. You were eleven. I don't know what she expected."

"I can't remember. What did I do?"

"Nothing," his father told him. "Kids break things all the time. She overreacted. She said you were a psychopath and I had ruined you. We had a fight. She called an attorney."

Mr. Jansen reached for his phone but stopped himself. He fidgeted a pen in his hands. "It was my fault she left."

Theo connected the gap in his memory to the only person who could erase them. *While I was out?* he thought.

He returned to the present conversation and asked his father, "Was I the reason?"

"No. I didn't believe she could forgive. She couldn't forgive a child for being childish. She had such hopes for you and that cello."

"I still break things."

"Yes, but you've learned, hopefully."

"One day, I won't be a child anymore. I will have to learn on my own."

"But I will always be your parent."

"I'm sorry."

Mr. Jansen looked into his son's broken face. "I chose to be a parent. You don't have to be sorry." With that, years of unspoken words were laid bare between them.

He placed a reassuring hand on his shoulder. Theo felt welcome in his presence for the first time.

"But I should be sorry I didn't add you onto Rosetta's insurance policy. How am I going to figure this one out?"

His hand returned to his cell phone. Whisking through the screens, he asked, "How was she anyway, Rosetta? Great bike, huh?"

"The power is unreal. I thought it would be much harder to turn, but it leaned right in."

"She'll take off on you coming out of a turn hot."

"She launches like a jet. It's incredible."

"That was nothing." His father smirked, looking into his eyes.

"You get her on a track and when that front tire comes up, you'd think wings'll come out of her."

A grin broke through on Theo's face. He indulged in remembering Rosetta with his father, the memories still fresh and vivid.

After their candid talk, Theo made his way to the phone and dialed Hanna's number.

TWENTY-SIX

SWEAT TRICKLED on Theo's brow. Saint Augustine's pages drew Theo's attention for mere moments, just for him to close the book again. His ankle throbbed in its brace. The classroom desk was ill-equipped to accommodate his awkwardly outstretched leg. His crutch slid and clattered onto the floor. The clamorous echo flashed memories of the hospital to him. His pen wrangled the date and lesson into his view. He perused the syllabus for clues. The classroom door flew open. Flush with adrenaline, he clutched his desk. Two students shuffled in banally. Theo exhaled. Visions of the police arresting him remained, menacing him. He imagined their inevitable interrogation. The two students desperately ignored him. Another flock of students clattered in, prattling about their weekends. Two of them noticed Theo and inquired if he was okay. He told them so, but their incredulous looks persisted. The door swung open again. He flinched.

The professor entered and tripped at the sight of him.

"Are you okay? What on earth happened?" she asked, righting herself. The unavoidable attention of the class was suffocating.

"Someone tried to steal my motorcycle," he murmured back.

A wave of avaricious questions roiled through the classroom. Theo refrained from twisting the story further and fortified his silence. He wondered if gods bemoaned that only the needy prayed.

The professor silenced the class with a flick of her wrist. "You can go home if you'd like," she told Theo.

"I'd rather be here," he answered. It was the truth; his classes distracted him from the pain. The professor nodded and adjusted her smart vest. "Case in point about the reading today: Saint Augustine . . ." she began and took to the blackboard.

Theo concentrated on the lesson, but his impatience limited him to a lost stupor. The peppy lecture whisked past his ears, which were trained on the door.

His history class saw a similar scene unfold, his classmates again sinking their fangs for details. He hated playing the part. By lunch, he abandoned his remaining class and headed home, nauseous and trembling. He collapsed into his bed, imploring his body to sleep. Consciousness did not relinquish its grip. Exasperated, he stared at the dim ceiling. His fidgeting eyes focused and the contours of the crown molding materialized. He closed his eyes and whispered, "If you can hear me . . . help her."

Enhanced by the effects of his painkillers, the morbid memories kept spinning behind his eyelids. Stale evening greeted his unrested eyes. The kitchen felt just a couple of his sluggish footsteps before he found himself in front of his computer again, back among the demons.

His father's absence brought visions of the police banging on the door. Eventually, his father returned and checked on him. Theo feigned cordiality. Theo called Hanna again—straight to voice mail. Another anxious hour was tossed onto the heap of them since the hospital. Her last words were his only solace. He held his head in his hands as if the memories would fall out.

A message appeared on his screen. He blinked, not believing the name.

Emma.

"Hey, I'm okay. Thanks for checking," she wrote. "Meet tomorrow at Surgite?"

"What time?" he wrote back at once. Seconds turned to minutes, betraying her facade of enthusiasm. Theo sank in his chair, decrying the plan as asinine. At last Emma answered.

"Two?"

"Okay. Can you talk now? Is Hanna out of the hospital?"

No reply.

"Why can't you just answer?" he snapped under his breath.

Emma finally sent back, "She's at home recovering. Let's talk tomorrow. Meet me at the benches in front of the library."

Theo shut down the game and hobbled to the kitchen. Being near the phone comforted him. His father ordered a lavish meal for them. Mr. Jansen set the table for him and said, "I'm going to find my bike tomorrow. It's in a ditch on a private road to a residence, right? Where were you? Do you remember the name of the road?"

"Don't."

"Why not? I have to go get her."

"It's not even there anymore. The homeowner probably found it by now and had it towed," Theo lied, its ripples slipping through his mind's grasp. He had given up on tracking the lies.

"Look, I'm getting my motorcycle back. I'm filing a police report."

"Don't call the police. Nothing happened," Theo stressed, but in vain. His father coaxed Arthur's address out of him. Defeated, Theo retreated to his bed, the silence of the phone weighing on him.

A sleepless night later, Theo embarked on a restless day of travel. Each arduous footstep laid bare his foolish plan. He braced himself with the station's frozen handrail as he descended another step. His bookbag jostled against his back, exacerbating his poor balance, one crutch painfully jammed into his armpit. Another step. A passerby brushed against his shoulder rushing down the frostbitten stairs of

Greenberm's train station. Another step. He exhaled a foggy cloud. The daylight was painful. Flurries dusted his coat. His watch held hope he could still arrive on time—his ankle did not. Another step.

Through the town, up the hill, the barren branches of the birches swayed above. Frozen wind swept past his ears, painfully cold and bare. Greg's car was gone. A moment's rest held him. He leaned on the great stone walls by the campus entrance. A specter of Hanna in the parking lot not far off played in his mind. Theo finished the march to the library's brick patio. Passing students averted their curious looks. Biting breezes jostled the rhododendron he stood by, where he was spotted. Emma made a chirp, like a singer entering the wrong part of a song.

"It's you," she said in awe.

"You said to meet here, didn't you?" Theo answered, propped up by his crutches.

"Holy moly. Broc didn't say you looked this bad."

Snowflakes graced her eyelashes, melting onto her astonished look. She beckoned him to a bench away from the passing groups of onlookers. "Come on, don't just stand there, dummy."

He clumsily placed himself on the bench beside her.

Emma stared straight ahead, stealing occasional glances at him. "Did you catch the bike with your face *and* every punch? You should have told me you were all mummified. I wouldn't have made you come here."

Her sight left the refuge of her well-worn sneakers for a glance at his fresh gauze pads, still dotted red by his healing wounds. Theo drew a sore breath.

"Do you still have the nightmares?" he asked.

"What are you talking about?"

"Hanna told me."

Disappointment drew a grimace on her expressive face. "There she goes again."

"Are you okay?"

She held back a chuckle. "Nobody's asked me that before. What gives?"

"I want to make sure you're okay."

A passing student greeted Emma; she gave a little wave in reply. She resumed the conversation, saying, "Me? What are you talking about? I'm not the one you should be worried about."

"I am."

"Come on, seriously? You limp all the way here just to check on me? Get outta here," she said, shaking her head.

Theo picked up his crutches to stand. He heaved himself up but spotted the familiar benches nearby. A pack of students gathered there. He wondered if the benches remembered their jovial conversations, their embraces, their accomplishments, their fates.

Just forgotten and meaningless? he thought.

Theo drew a determined breath and set himself back down. He leaned back and stared into the ashen sky. "I believe . . . you are in pain. I'm here to listen . . . to make things right. It is my fault. I know I can't change that . . . but I want to help."

She murmured an inaudible reply and fumbled her long pink coat closed, then open again. The barbican of a faint smile she always wore faded. She sat as if lost in a daze. "The nightmares never went away," she said in a near whisper.

"Still every night?"

"Every night," she said, pursing her red lips. "Maybe I shouldn't tell you this . . . but . . . no. It's just . . . I can't sleep anymore."

"What do you see in your nightmare?" he asked, knowing what Arthur had seen. She folded her arms just to unfold them and impatiently push back her hair. "Nothing."

"It never happened. What you're seeing is just a dream—like a bad hypnosis. None of it's real."

"You're not good at this."

"I know."

"You act like you were there."

"I was."

Emma cast a disturbed look at Theo, wincing at his bandages but furtively sneaking more looks. "You were, huh? So what really happened to me, then? What did you see? Why did I wake up with a bloody nose and lip? My shirt was cut. I was in a stranger's car—food and cash at my feet."

"You and I were abducted and—"

"By the guy?" she cut in. "The one abducting everyone?"

"Yes."

Theo drew aching breath to explain, but Emma cut in with, "Ya know what? I don't want to know just yet. I got enough from Broc at the hospital. When you and I were nabbed . . . well, it was you, wasn't it? It was you that got me away from him. How else did I get back? I can't remember a thing. Maybe he really did hypnotize me."

Hysterical laughter lightened her words. "Maybe he actually had spooky nightmare powers. I don't know," she said, then paused. Her pupils grew wide. "You drove me back in that little car, didn't you? You left the cash and food for me?"

Theo solemnly stared back into her imploring gaze. His silent affirmation sent her looking everywhere but him. "You fought him off," he said, remembering her screams. "I helped you escape."

Emma pulled back her sleeves, revealing the still-healing wounds dug into her wrists.

"How did we escape?"

"I woke up somehow. Maybe the sedative wasn't strong enough. I saw what he was going to do. You were already awake... fighting back. I stopped him, but you hit your head . . . knocked out."

Emma rested her elbows on her thighs. "Broc says he saved you and Hanna from that abduction guy—fought him off. He told the whole soccer team—anyone that would listen, really. Everyone on campus thinks he's a hero. Hell—everyone believed him. The soccer team practically threw a parade in his honor. My brothers were over the moon that Broc avenged their little sister. The wrongdoer was brought to justice. They all ate it up. The story grows by the day."

"He said he beat up the guy, but Broc's hands are pristine," she said quietly.

She delicately took Theo's right hand and turned it over. Her touch was warm and gentle, her sharp nails careful not to scratch him. Her index finger softly traced the bruises and cuts on his swollen knuckles.

"Broc was so scared that night," she continued. "He didn't even call Hanna's parents. He called me first. I called them and broke the news. They showed up at the hospital not long after I did. Broc was shaking and mumbling to himself. They asked him what happened, and he almost fainted just telling them. Broc and I kept them company during Hanna's surgery. Twelve stiches in her neck. It was practically dawn when they let us in, and her mom and dad just bawled. They took her home and she could barely speak. Broc cried too when I drove him back to campus."

They watched the passing students recede into their buildings, time dictating their self-absorbed schedules. The view hung like a pall between them.

Emma faced Theo. "It really was you, wasn't it? Both times?" He left her unanswered, save for an understanding look.

She asked, "You and Hanna didn't get abducted—Broc did, didn't he?"

Theo stared at the snow-kissed rhododendrons and gave a single nod.

"I knew it. Oh, I knew it," she said. "You can't hide the man you are. I should've talked to you. I can't believe Broc was stupid enough to tail her and still get his ass abducted. He even texted me, saying he'd call if anything happened. I shouldn't have told him to go."

Emma smirked, taking in Theo's bandaged face. "Mr. Elusive,

eh? I can't believe you—fucking philosophy major. So what really happened when Hanna went to see you Sunday?"

Theo pulled his crutches closer, the painkillers no longer suppressing the burning in his wounds. "We had a fight. We talked about . . . a lot of things. The abductor called Hanna's cell phone from Broc's. He said he'd kill him. We took my dad's bike to save him. I crashed where he was keeping him. We got out of there . . . Broc drove us to the hospital."

"You don't wanna talk about it?"

"I will if you want me to."

"No, it's okay," she was quick to reply. "You don't have to. But, I guess, can you tell me where'd you and Hanna . . . uh, leave things?"

"I don't know," said Theo to her and the world. "She wrote me a goodbye letter. It was in her backpack. I read it. But I promised her I'd check on you." His mind worked on withholding the account of Mougo. Deflecting further questions, he asked, "You've had these nightmares since we were abducted. What happens in your nightmare?"

"Listen," she said, turning toward him, "it's not like . . ." but drifted off. She considered her words momentarily, then said softly, for his ears only, "I see . . . something terrible. Someone is dying. I can't remember his face anymore, but I know him and hear such terrible pain in his voice. My heart is racing. Blood covers my hands. God, that screaming . . . I feel like I'm the one dying. And it's my hand that's doing it. I'm using this black knife. I can remember how it feels and how heavy it was. It felt so satisfying. It took way longer than I thought it would. It caught on his bones. I remember how sticky the blood felt on my fingers. It's horrible and just goes on and on, and I can't stop it."

Emma held her own arms. "But I'm the one doing it. I know the victim's name: Greg. Sometimes it's just parts, sometimes it's from the beginning, but I always turn around . . . and then I wake up."

Emma's red lips twitched in unsteady starts, unspoken words fighting their way out, but she remained silent. She stared at her feet again and blinked as if at a loss.

At last, Theo said, "I want you to know it was just a dream."

"Really?"

"The abductor was using heavy tranquilizers. They had hallucinogenic side effects. I don't know how I woke up from it that day. He must have made a mistake. Your mind put together the scraps it could, reformed what it saw into a cohesive memory, even if it was far from the truth. And then it turned dark, becoming your nightmare. I'm sorry you must bear it."

Emma gave a sullen nod.

"If you ever need anything . . . someone to talk to . . ."

"Don't worry about me, Ted," she answered. "One way or another, I'll find my way past these nightmares."

"Great," he said and asked earnestly, "So you are okay now?"

"I don't know how she did it," said Emma, exasperated.

"Neither do I," Theo replied, and Emma shared a chuckle with him.

"Just promise me one thing."

"What is it?"

"I just . . . I need to know that one day I can talk to you more about my nightmare. Not tomorrow—not anytime soon. Can you promise me that?"

"Yes," he answered in their newfound kinship.

"How is Hanna? Have you heard from her?" he caught himself asking.

"At home, recovering. She missed class Monday and yesterday. I talked to her a little bit this morning."

"Does she sound okay?"

Emma paused but feigned a worriless expression. "Yeah, champ, she's getting better. She said her parents are going to drive her to school. It may be for the rest of the semester. You want me to tell her I saw you today?"

Unprepared, Theo fumbled for words. "Tell her . . . yeah." He dropped his crutches, then picked them up, asking, "Could you call her?"

Emma pulled out her cracked smartphone without hesitation. "Sure. Let me see . . ." and held it, ringing, to her ear. She listened, but checked its spiderweb screen.

"Voice mail. She's probably resting."

Theo retreated to his morose thoughts. Emma let out a great sigh.

"It was spring yesterday," she said, brushing the snowflakes off her shoulders, some falling onto him. "Look what you did. You made it snow. It's because you didn't wear any green."

Theo stared, confused. Emma opened her jacket, revealing a green sweatshirt.

"Saint Patrick's Day, hello?"

Theo found himself distracted by the words "Kiss me, I'm Irish" boldly splashed across her chest. He turned his captivated stare to his crutches instead. Emma stood up and stretched.

"Come on, Teddy, let's get inside. Why are we freezing our asses off out here anyway?"

Theo pulled himself up as she asked, "Where are you heading next?"

"Home."

"Helluva walk to the train station."

"Miles to go before I sleep anyway."

Emma deftly twirled her cell phone. "Come on, I'll get Chris to drive us," she said, and messaged him. They waited by the sandwich shop in the library's tunnel. Emma praised its pretzels between frustrated, hushed remarks about her text conversation. Sitting beside her, waiting, he watched the students ensnared by the delectable sandwiches again and again. Emma punched his sore arm.

"What?" he asked, vexed.

"Tell ya what, Teddy," she proclaimed boisterously, "if you won the lottery, what would you do with it all?"

"I wouldn't care."

"Oh, come on. Have some fun. What would you buy? What do you really want?"

"I'd go away. Somewhere far away from everyone . . . a house by a lake."

"What would you put in that house?"

"A piano," he answered, closing his eyes, imagining her lovely playing.

"Nerd," she said, sneering. "You know what I'd do? I'd host a radio channel. It'd go like this." She cleared her throat. "Broadcasting from the Great Swamp," she said, assuming a sultry voice. "Playing the raunchiest hits of all time and the craziest shit we can find. The FCC can only fine us if they can find us. Keeping the Garden wild. We're all horned up and have lost our minds. Ninety-nine point nine WSUK: The Nut. Jersey's dirtiest."

Theo stared vacantly at the sandwiches diminishing from the glass case, his chin in his hand. Emma's nose wrinkled.

"What? You don't find that even a little funny?"

"No."

"We're all gonna have to chip in for the surgery. Even you couldn't afford it."

"For what? I'm fine."

"To buy you a sense of humor," she quipped.

The sandwiches had all disappeared. Chris eventually appeared, absorbing Emma's saccades of attention. Chris paused at the sight of Theo.

"Wow, you got your shit kicked in," he remarked.

"I know," Theo answered flatly.

Emma said, "Yeah, yeah, he looks like he got run over by a truck. Are you parked in left field or what?"

"Yeah, in fact, I am," Chris answered, his annoyance flaring.

"Lighten up. It'll only take five minutes," she replied, but he shot back, "There you go again. You just—" but he stopped himself. Theo trailed behind their brisk pace and hushed conversation, an intentional distance growing between them along the salty paths. They reached the low burgundy sedan, which Chris started hastily. Emma opened the back door for Theo. The couple's spat subsided and they turned their conversation to the tenacious winter weather.

At the station, Emma pulled Theo's crutches out for him and helped him out of the car.

"Hey, thanks for coming here and checking on me. What's your number anyway?"

"I lost my phone in the crash," he answered.

"Oh wait, I can see you in Demon World," she remarked, closing the car door behind him. "Don't be a stranger," she said through the window and was whisked away into the flurries.

Theo placed himself on a bench, the next train a distant thought. His ankle throbbed. His heart pumped warmth to his frozen fingertips. The train was late. Time crawled by in noticed lurches. He ignored his watch telling him he was unlikely to arrive before his father came back. His unannounced absence and lack of cell phone was sure to cause an issue. "Miles to go . . ." he whispered to the crows above, perching on the awning's filthy beams.

A woman sat beside him. It struck him as peculiar that she did not sit inside with the other passengers. He continued to observe the crows descending to the platform and hopping about.

The woman asked, "Do you think they're self-aware?"

Theo looked over at her watching the birds too.

"The crows?" he returned.

She nodded.

"We'll never know for sure, just inferring from their actions."

"I think they are. Man is not alone in this capacity. Your philosophy classes cover this?"

Theo craned his neck for a closer look at this woman. Her dark pantsuit gave a hint of some refined profession—her combat boots did not. Her wool coat added size to her already grand muscular frame. A short-cropped haircut completed a rugged appearance. She wore a disinterested look, seeking reprieve in the hopping birds. Unsettled, Theo pulled his crutches to stand.

"Calm down. You can't run anyway."

"Who are you?" Theo asked, leaping to his unhealed feet.

"Davenport," she said, picking up one of his dropped crutches. She handed it to him, but he did not take it. "Theodore Sakamoto Jansen," she said, her tone unenthused. "You bear your mother's maiden name. You came here to find Hanna, did you not?"

Theo backed away in tremulous lurches. "That's not my name. What are you talking about?"

Davenport pursued him at an unhurried pace. "You're an undergraduate at Lincoln University. You live with your divorced father, Earl Jansen, who is right now at Arthur's house looking for the remains of his cherished motorcycle you crashed. My colleague, Juliet, is advising him that Arthur is away on a family emergency, the house is being listed for sale, and the wreckage of his totaled motorcycle has already been cleared."

Theo's heart pounded. The drab station platform melted into the gray sky.

"There's no point in resisting. We've wiped the area clean—Greg and Arthur included. We didn't find what we were looking for."

"Who are you?" Theo asked in a breathless whisper.

"You know the whereabouts of the woman in the knife," Davenport said, emotionless, her words as cold as the wind. Theo stopped against the stone railing, bumping his back. Cars sped past on the street below.

"Or if you don't, we can get it out of Hanna."

"Where are you keeping her!"

"Come with me and you'll see."

Rage shook Theo. Davenport extended his dropped crutch to

him again. "Go down the stairs to the black car. Get in the back seat. It's unlocked."

He carefully took the crutch from her, not taking his eyes off her stocky physique. She stood a touch short of his height.

"And Theo," she added, "don't do anything stupid. We want to talk."

Theo descended the frosty stairs to an idling black limousine.

TWENTY-SEVEN

DAVENPORT SAT motionless on the right side of the limousine's pit of a back seat. Theo remained vigilant, though all was quiet. The car impressively subdued the road noise. He noticed that her right hand rested inside her coat. Theo had the impression he was not to leave her sight. The driver remained mute and made no notice of the hostage in his back seat. Though seemingly preoccupied, Theo detected his occasional checks in the mirror.

The drive took little time. A concrete building of spartan styling loomed at the edge of an office park, which they entered via a keycard and gate. Its full parking lot and lit windows were unconcerned with their swift approach. The car pulled them up to another gate, this one with a security guard. A flash of a badge and they were through, swinging around to a garage door on the building's backside. A fingerprint scan and the large metal door retracted, revealing a dim concrete cell of a garage full of mysterious equipment lining its edges. Theo was ordered to exit. Davenport escorted him to a creaky metal door that screeched in the echoey garage. The driver remained with the limousine. A voice from the intercom asked, "Are your shoes dirty?"

Theo found the question bizarre and discovered himself looking down at his own mismatched shoes.

"No, perfectly clean," he heard Davenport answer. A loud click sounded.

Theo followed her blunt orders to open the unlocked door and awkwardly pushed himself through on his crutches. An empty corridor met him. The lights were off. Only Theo's anxious breaths broke the silence. Adrenaline from his fright erased the pain in his ankle, which he was cognizant he should be feeling. He was ordered into an elevator.

"Who is the woman in the knife?" he asked on the ride upward.

"Don't play dumb," she said behind him.

"Who are you?"

Silence.

"What have you done to Hanna?"

Yet more aggravating silence.

The door opened and he entered a dim hallway. "Just tell me what's going on!" he shouted. He was answered by a shove in his back. Davenport ordered him brusquely past several doors. A locked one made them pause. Davenport brandished a metal key, unlocked the door, and pushed it open. His eyes strained, adjusting to the flood of sunlight from the windows. He made out a conference table's silhouette. He felt himself shoved into the room and losing balance. A gasp and scream pierced his ears. The door slammed behind him. Theo stumbled on his crutches, then crashed onto the beige carpet.

<hr>

CARS MARCHED along the distant highway like ants. The overcast heavens relinquished the last of their precipitation. Daylight waned in the sun's post-noon descent. A hawk hastened to rise through the chaotic crosswinds of winter's parting gift. A squirrel scurried up a tree. A pair of hunched suits left dotted trails across the lot. Vehicles patiently awaited their impatient operators to rush them into the distant stream of ants. Hanna sat taunted by the normal day unfolding outside the conference room's windows. How carefree they were in their banal routines. But those outside had struggles of their own. She wondered if hers could ever return to such normalcy.

The memory of those reflective moments stayed even when she ran away from the commotion at the door. The clatter of crutches had scared her. Her unintentional exclamation, his loss of balance, the door slamming closed, and Hanna was kneeling beside him.

"Theo!" she cried.

"Hanna?"

"Theo, it's me! Are you okay?"

Theo raised himself up to Hanna, who was terrified and breathless taking in his bandaged face. She clumsily helped him up with one arm, her left bound in a sling. Stitches and tape kept her neck rigid, causing her upper body to turn as a single mass.

"Oh my God! Are you okay?" Her flush face contorted in anguish.

"Don't cry. I'm fine," he answered, on his four feet again. His solemn eyes took in her injuries, the sight leaving remorse etched into his expression.

"How'd you get here? Where were you?" she asked.

"I was coming back from Surgite. They got me at the station."

"Surgite?"

"I went to see Emma."

"Is she okay? Why'd you go so far?"

"I made you a promise. I was checking on her nightmares."

Hanna wiped hot tears from her cheeks, at a loss for words.

"What happened?" he asked.

"They just left me here," she answered, rubbing her nose on her sleeve. "I tried calling you, but I forgot your phone was gone, and I was in the hospital and I had to recover. They said I had a torn rotator cuff, and they took X-rays and they didn't want me to leave and then my parents took me home." She rambled shamelessly, "Then I couldn't find my phone and then they brought me to school this morning because I've been missing so much. And then a black car showed up and a lady with an English accent said she was with the FBI and it's about Arthur's murder and they said I had to get in the car, and they left me here."

"I'm so sorry I put you through all this," Theo said, regret filling his voice.

"Theo, who are they? What do they want?"

"The knife," he whispered.

"But we don't have it! Do *you*? They aren't really the police, are they?" she whispered back hoarsely.

"The Makers . . . they must be The Makers. They know what happened to Arthur. They're after Mougo. She's on the run."

"Oh God."

The door opened. They both turned, frightened at the sudden sound. A man entered carrying a manila folder.

"Good afternoon," he said, his dark suit and tie complementing his professional tone. His bald head and stout musculature stood out. Theo remained standing firm. Hanna realized her good hand gripped the lapel of Theo's coat in a tight fist, her left helpless in its sling.

"You must be Hanna and Theo," the man said, walking to the lengthy table's other side. "Have a seat," he told them, taking his. Neither moved.

"I insist," he added in the same professional tone, and both sat in the hard plastic conference chairs. Theo kept his crutches in hand. Hanna trembled. The man placed his folder on the table and clasped his hands together, his formidable shoulders evident in his crisp jacket.

"We weren't looking for two people," he began. "We should have been prepared for that. You weren't hard to find after what happened to Arthur."

The man paused long enough to let their memories bring up the sordid affair. Already, traumatic parts were becoming distant and blocked out.

"What happened that night?" he asked, moving convicting eye contact from Theo to Hanna.

"He abducted our friend, Broc. We went to save him," answered Hanna.

"And?"

"There was an altercation. We escaped and went to the hospital," answered Theo.

"Where did the Japanese woman come from? Where did she go?"

Theo fell silent, unsure if to speak. The man remained firm, "You will tell us everything you know. We need to find her. We know you don't have the knife, but you were there when that woman escaped. Where did she go?"

"Her name is Mougo," Hanna stated. "You won't hurt her if you find her?"

"No, but let's start with what happened," he answered plainly.

"Are you really FBI?" Theo asked.

The man watched him, unamused.

"Are you really with The Makers?" Theo pressed.

The man considered the questions for a moment, but answered, "Consider me on your side. I am not here to arrest you. Nobody is going to jail. I'm here on behalf of the man that can help the woman in the knife and you. There will be people after you. They may find you if you don't cooperate. It's in your best interest to tell me everything you know. We are already aware of that woman's capabilities to make people disappear, erase memories, transplant memories, and take people into the Static Realm. She may be capable of even more. Don't hide anything. There's no point. We've brought you here to talk—just a straightforward explanation of what happened."

He leaned back in his chair. "Let's rewind a bit. Why did you go to Arthur's house that night?"

"He called us saying he had abducted Broc," answered Hanna.

"He'd kill him if we didn't go. So we did," answered Theo.

"And this Mougo was not out yet?"

"No, not yet," Hanna said. "We had the sheath and Arthur had the knife. There was an inscription on it. Theo had me translate it earlier."

The man opened his folder and slid a photocopy across the table. "This one?"

She read it, careful not to move her neck. "No, I don't recognize that."

He took it back and slid several copies of handwritten Japanese notes across the table. She inspected them, then patted one with her good hand. "This one."

"Can you speak Japanese?" he asked Theo.

". . . no."

"Would you call yourself fluent in Japanese?" he asked Hanna.

"Not fluent, but I've been studying it for three years and I've been to Japan."

"Does Mougo speak English?"

"None," Theo and Hanna both answered.

The man took back the photocopies. His tone was ruthlessly professional. "You arrived at Arthur's house on the motorcycle. Your friend was being held hostage. There was a struggle? What was the altercation?"

"I crashed the bike," Theo said. "Broc was tied up to cinderblocks laid across the driveway. I was going too fast and lost control. We both flew off. Arthur took Hanna into his house before I could get to her. Broc told me which way they went, and I ran after them."

"Is that what happened?" the man asked narrowing his dark eyes on Hanna.

"Yes, as best I can tell," she replied. "I remember sliding a lot in the crash. I didn't know what was going on yet. Everything was spinning and happening so fast. Arthur cut my chinstrap and pulled off my helmet. Every moment of it was horrible."

"Did you have a headache? Was your vision blurry?" Theo asked her in a softer tone.

She began to answer, but the man cut in, "He had Hanna. Broc was still tied up. You went into the house. Then what?"

"Arthur put the knife to my neck," Hanna recalled morosely. "I could hear Mougo's voice. It was cutting me, and her voice was super clear. She told me to say the inscription out loud. When I said it, I thought to also say, 'kotodama,' and the knife and sheath started glowing. She told me to put them together. Theo fought Arthur. I put the kaiken back in its sheath and there was like a lightning bolt. It was this brilliant flash of light. She appeared in the middle of it."

"And?" the man asked Theo.

"I was knocked out for this part," Theo answered, ashamed.

A sickly feeling overcame her. Hanna felt uncomfortably warm in her puffy jacket. She focused on the folder between them. "Mougo ended his life. Put the knife to his neck . . . blood everywhere . . ."

"Did she have any trouble?"

"No," Hanna said, shaking her head, but searing pain soon reprimanded her carelessness.

"Elaborate."

A fog already blocked the particulars of Arthur's gargled shouts and the thud of his corpse. Hanna struggled to say, "I mean ... he was running away. She caught him, no problem ... stopped him, just like that. She started laughing after. She was saying all kinds of stuff and running her hands along the walls. I thought she was going to kill us. She easily picked up and threw Arthur's body."

The man focused on Hanna. "And she still has the kaiken?"

"Yes, both parts," Theo answered.

"Did you speak with her? How did she escape?" the man asked Hanna.

"We talked a little. She did her best to bandage my neck. I was really lightheaded, so I don't really remember it all, but she thanked me for setting her free and offered me a reward. We talked about Theo. She told me her name, Mougo, and she told me everything Theo had been doing."

"*Everything*?" Theo asked, alert.

"The months of my memories you were erasing, the abductions, how you talked to her."

The man asked, "Did she say where she was going? What she wanted to do? What reward did she offer you?"

"I can't remember. I know she was telling me I needed to see a doctor. That's when I started fading out, but she let me erase a traumatic memory as her way of thanking me."

The man's expression was unchanged, immovable like stone. He asked, "How did she escape?"

"I don't really know. Theo and Mougo took Arthur's big car. We got Broc and all went to the hospital," answered Hanna.

Theo chimed in, "After Broc carried Hanna into the ER, I talked to Mougo a little. She thanked us for getting her out. She touched my face and licked the blood off her fingers. It was odd. She said we'd talk again."

"Licked the blood, you say?" the man asked, intrigued.

"Yes. When Broc came back she told me to go to the ER, took the keys, and just drove off."

"Did she say where she was going?" he asked.

"No. It all happened quickly. I told Broc not to say a word about her. He didn't see what took place anyway. He was trapped outside. I told him to say he saved us from the abductor. I'd take the blame for Arthur's death."

"We've taken care of that," the man stated before asking, "What did you tell your father when you got home?"

"Nothing."

"Nothing?"

"I said I crashed his bike and wasn't wearing a helmet. I

explained that our friend took us to the hospital. There was no Japanese woman or abductor."

"And to your folks?" the man asked Hanna.

"Same."

A pause elapsed, long enough for him to weigh her taciturn answer. He carried on, not revealing if he was convinced. "And this Broc friend, where did he go?"

"Back to Surgite," Hanna answered.

"He's a classmate of yours?"

"Yes," she answered, jittery.

"I told him not to say anything about Mougo," Theo was quick to reiterate. "I told him to just explain he saved us and omit her entirely."

A careful weighing took place behind the man's heartless expression. He carried on, "I understand you've been in possession of this kaiken for some months. You ever run into the police or any authorities during your use of it?"

"No."

The man raised his eyebrows but relaxed in his seat. "You were foolish to grab Steven Chatsworth. That tipped us off."

"I planned it poorly," Theo admitted.

"But you evaded detection?"

"Not entirely. She found out I was erasing her memories," he said, indicating Hanna.

"When?"

"Just less than two weeks ago," Hanna answered.

"You knew for that long?" Theo asked, turning to her.

"Since spring break. I had to keep it a secret from you. Sorry."

"No, I understand," he said, but asked, "So you knew when you followed me on the bike?"

"I did. That's why I couldn't let you go. I had to know why."

"You ride too?" the man asked.

"Not really. He taught me and I just started."

"What were you planning to do with the kaiken? Why did you carry this out for so long?" the man asked.

"I suppose because I had to know where it came from," Theo said, his tone taking on wonder. "I never wanted to join Arthur's cult. At times, I considered running away. But I couldn't escape the drive to answer why Mougo exists."

"Why did you confront Arthur? It led to his murder," the man pushed, zeroing in on Hanna.

"We had to!" she exclaimed. "He was going to kill Broc! He was going to brainwash innocent people in his cult. He dragged me to his basement and nearly beat Theo to death!"

The man was unmoved by her outburst. "Your thoughts?" he asked Theo in the same merciless monotone.

"He didn't care where the kaiken came from or what it was for. He was going to abuse its power. We did not plan his untimely death . . . but ultimately, we could not stop it either. He had Hanna. Mougo attacked him and she knew what was going on. Had he lived I don't know if he would have changed."

The man nodded, deciding that nothing more was to be discussed. He collected his folder and stood. "Wait here," he ordered and disappeared out the door behind him. Hanna was unprepared for the palpitating fear coursing through her.

THEO TOOK stock of Hanna's deteriorating state. She sat slumped in her chair, cradling her arm in its sling, her head drooping and expression blank. Dried tears stained her ruddy cheeks. So full of life before, she sat a husk of her former mirthful self.

"I'm sorry, Hanna," he said, turning to her. Consequence cast its fateful pall over him. She drew an unsteady breath, on the verge of collapse like a trampled flower.

"They'll kill us, won't they?" she asked.

"Don't say that," he implored. "They're looking for Mougo. They'd have no reason."

"We know too much," she whispered.

The man's inevitable return weighed on them both. Frustration thrashed in Theo. A sole resolution was born of it. He sought to express it to her, but the words did not come. His mouth was agape, obtuse, and incapable of the simplest articulation. He gnashed his teeth for a moment at his ineptitude, just to spot silent tears rolling down her cheeks.

Struck by a wave of helplessness but a desire to do something —anything—for her, his heart felt as if it were falling through him. Theo searched his pockets and produced several napkins. He handed them to her. She took them and thanked him sincerely. She wiped her tears and sighed, on the cusp of copious sobs. "Ow," she mumbled, tensing up after blowing her nose.

"Hanna?"

"Yes, Theo?"

"I promise I will get you out of this—no matter what happens."

———

THE DOOR'S opening chased Theo's hand away from hers. The cold left by the absence of his reassuring touch left her hurt. The man took his seat again and set the same folder down. New contents thickened it. His expression appeared the same as before, revealing nothing. Hanna wiped her puffy eyes and met his, determined to hear their fate. The man let slip a sliver of surprise. He placed his rough hand on his folder, saying, "I would like to thank you two for your candor."

"My name is Gus and I work for The Makers. I don't know what Arthur had told you or what you've heard, but it is likely untrue. Mistruths are part of our work. What is true, though, is what you've seen firsthand. That Japanese woman is real and so is her weapon. We will track her down and bring her back. She is armed, deadly, and possesses supernatural power. Her whereabouts and motivations are unknown. The potential responses from the public and the authorities are unpredictable and dangerous if she is discovered. That kaiken, though, belongs to us—and so does she. Nobody can know about her, but you set her free."

He opened his folder. "Which is why you're going to help us find her."

"What?" they both asked.

"You're going to fix this. She knows you both. She will seek you out. Hanna, we need your language ability. You would join our organization to translate and interpret. Your efforts would be solely focused on bringing Mougo in. Tracking her down will be a task, but once we've got that done, we'll need to make contact. You'll need to facilitate, as well as assist in the research and preparation leading up to that encounter."

Aghast, Hanna blinked, uncomprehending. Gus looked at Theo. "And you. Your skills are needed as well. You have tested the kaiken for months, evading detection and developing a relationship with Mougo. You will tell us everything you know, as it will be paramount to the success of our tracking her. You would join our organization to facilitate the planning and execution of tracking down Mougo. You will be needed to bring her in, as she has a personal connection with you."

"You're offering us jobs?" Theo asked, astounded.

"You could call it a summer job. The Makers have assumed different covers over the years. We currently exist as Mallory and Agitur, a private equity and consulting firm. You would work directly under me in our Manhattan office under the guise of an internship, though our search would likely take us far and wide. The true nature of your work must remain absolutely confidential. You are to use the stories we provide when you tell your family and friends about your internship. The best number of people to keep a secret is zero, of course, but here we are."

Gus produced two documents from his folder. He set one

before Hanna and one before Theo. "We may find use for your motorcycle skills too," he tossed out.

Hanna inspected the document. A contract, titled in raised lettering, spelled out a rigorous arrangement with the prestigious firm. Dozens of lines stipulated a complex internship covering vast responsibilities. Intrigued, her eyes pounced on the header about confidentiality, the lines below a blur without her glasses.

"When would we start?" she asked.

"Immediately," Gus answered nonchalantly.

"But we have school!" she protested.

"It's of less concern. The prompt capture of Mougo is now your primary concern. You'll need to heal up first anyway. You won't come into the office for a few days."

"A few days," Hanna said to the table. "Our lives . . . my parents . . . Theo can't even walk yet."

"And when we find her?" Theo asked.

"We don't know how she'll react, but force may be involved. This search could take us out of the country, depending on her abilities. She could still be here in this area. We have no idea."

Hanna's disbelief did not recede. "When you say, 'force,' what do you mean?"

"Your personal safety may be affected," Gus replied, guiltless.

"And what about our families? Are we supposed to keep this a complete secret from them?"

"Yes."

"But—"

"You will keep it strictly confidential," Gus interjected. "We will give you a cover story and furnish all the details. Your work may involve trips or absences. We will cover all expenses. If you break this confidentiality, though, there is nothing I can do to protect you from the consequences."

"You'd kill us," Theo said.

Gus nodded, as if Theo's statement were a perfectly normal

thing to say in an interview. "Your lives are forfeit, should you not cooperate," he added in his merciless, professional tone.

"Will you let us go once we get Mougo back?" Theo asked.

Gus wore a grim frown. "I can't promise that. It depends on her and how it resolves. Our normal protocol is for nobody outside of our organization to know of our true existence or the items we have made. This Japanese kaiken emerging in the civilian realm has admittedly taken us by surprise. You two know about it. I am offering you a chance to make things right. Take it," he said sternly.

Hanna cradled her injured arm. "We have no choice. We'll sign and keep your secret."

"You'll just erase our memories as soon as we get her back," Theo shot. The man made no response.

Theo hammered, "How much would you erase? All of it? The last year?"

The prospect of more amnesia sickened Hanna. Theo crossed his arms. The man offered nothing, though his silence did not refute Theo's accusation.

Hanna shook her head just slightly. "There has to be a way. There has to be some way we can go home and be okay."

"What do you propose?" the man asked.

She paused to consider, then said, "We will sign and help you find Mougo while keeping your secret. We understand the consequences of failure. But if we win your trust by the time we find her, if we do a good job and you know for sure we won't do anything bad to you ever, you will let us go with our memories intact?"

"Hanna, how will he trust us enough to just let us go like that?" Theo asked in a low voice.

"Deal," said Gus.

Hanna and Theo shared surprised looks. Gus gave a joyless smirk. "You can't comprehend the full extent of what you just agreed to, and there may be things you will want to forget, but I accept the terms of your bargain. Win our trust by the time we bring her back, and we will not erase your memory. Should you fail, of course, you'd never know since you'd have no memory of anything you did. Should you defect, you die."

Those last words weighed heavily on a lightheaded Hanna. The world felt far out of her control. Theo remained rigid, deep in thought, and reluctant to move. Hanna took the weighty pen and signed her contract.

"Wait. Shouldn't we think about this more?" Theo asked her in a murmur.

"We just have to do our best," she told him, and he followed her lead with his own elegant signature. Gus stood, unphased by their plight, and collected their signed contracts.

"We will be in touch from now on," Gus said, producing two sleek smartphones from his jacket pocket. He gave one to each and they both noticed the phones were already powered on.

"My number is already in your contacts, including the Manhattan office. We'll reach out to you about coming into the office soon. There's more paperwork to be done."

Gus turned to the door opening behind him. A tall, stocky woman entered in a dark suit like Gus's, and he addressed her, saying, "Dav, take Hanna back to her university."

Dav gave a silent nod, and Gus handed them each a glossy folder bearing the firm's name. Hanna opened it and scanned the blurry orientation papers in disbelief, her glasses forgotten in her backpack. Her internship was already dated to start that day. Hanna stood, prompted by Dav's gruff order. Theo was instructed to stay.

"Wait! What are you doing with Theo?" Hanna asked, alarmed.

"I will take him back to the city," Gus replied, buttoning his jacket.

Dav escorted Hanna out of the conference room despite Hanna's wistful and painful glances over her shoulder. "Let's talk!" she called back to an attentive Theo, already up on his crutches.

"I'll call you!" he shouted back as Dav pushed her through the doorway.

A quiet elevator, a dark garage, the echoey chime of the black car as it started, and not a word came from the scowling Dav. Her plain short fingernails made no sound as her hands operated the car's controls. Small lacerations speckled her knuckles.

"Do you work with Gus? Are you, like, in the same group?" Hanna asked. Dav backed the car out of the garage in silence.

Putting the car in drive, she, at last, responded, "Yeah." The conversation ended there, and Dav drove them the unmemorable distance back to Surgite. The newly acquired cell phone pinged in her pocket. She gasped, seeing a new message from "Theodore Jansen."

"Hey, it's Theo," it said.

"Hi! I'm almost at Surgite," she wrote back.

"Gus is driving me back to the city."

"Are you talking about anything? Dav isn't much for conversation."

"He asked me about my hobbies and where I grew up. I don't know why."

Hanna cradled the new phone in her hands, enjoying the cool touch of the glass screen. She messaged him more, thrilled at the expediency of the touch screen. An elated smile sneaked out of her in the dreary car at his immediate replies. Pulling into the parking lot, Dav finally broke her silence with, "Tell your parents you had an interview today and you got a summer internship. Your backpack and phone are in the trunk."

"Okay."

"Gus's taking a huge chance bringing you on. Don't let us down."

"I . . . I'll do my best."

"You'd better," she said, pulling the car into a spot. Caught off her guard, Hanna opened her mouth, not knowing what to say. Dav ordered her out of the car and the trunk lid popped up. Hanna opened it to find her backpack neatly laid beside hard black cases enclosing mysterious contents. Hanna slung her pack around her good shoulder, closed the trunk, and the car sped off. Hanna stood alone and perplexed in the gusty parking lot.

What just happened? she thought, flipping open her own cell phone. Messages and missed calls from her mother about the snow filled it. She called her back and arranged her pickup. An hour slipped away in the student center on the quiet campus, blanketed in winter's parting gift. The reality of the perilous bargain they had made was still planting itself in her mind. Hanna pushed herself to check her classes' syllabi for the contents of yet another missed day. She surmised Emma was out at the dining hall. A groan of pining came from her empty stomach while she walked to the parking lot where her mother was waiting to take her home.

TWENTY-EIGHT

"ABSOLUTELY NOT," Mrs. Popov answered in heated frustration. Hanna avoided her rebuking glare. "Talk some sense into her, Alex! She's been all corked up about this for months, just inviting more and more of the devil's havoc into her life. You let her get this way. She's completely out of control, getting tangled up with that boy and his motorcycle!"

Mr. Popov gestured his wife to calm down and said, "You can lower your voice, dear. We can all hear you."

"Clearly, she cannot!" her mother shot back, growing shrill. "The first day we bring her back to school and she's already back in trouble. She's not doing an internship in the city and certainly not with that Theo boy. Why, are we just going to ignore that it was him that did this? The nerve of him taking our daughter out against his father's permission on a speeding joyride! Irredeemable! The Goddamn fool! A dozen stitches in your neck! Lord only knows the medical bills coming our way. Our insurance won't cover it all. Hours in the ER, overnight stay, pain killers, follow-up visits— they won't cover even half of it, I say! She has to stay home." Mrs. Popov turned to Hanna. "Tell your father what you did today," she said, her voice hoarse.

Hanna cradled her arm, feeling the pulses of pain from her shoulder, desperate to heal. The interrogation room of the kitchen table was drafty and lit by sickly fluorescent lights. Her eyes, heavy with lack of sleep, slid away from her parents' stern expressions.

"I saw him again today at the interview . . . Theo."

"The one that's caused all of this!" her mother shrieked.

Mr. Popov coaxed his wife back to her seat and asked, "And he got you this internship?"

"Yes."

"You would work together?"

"Yes."

"Mallory and Agitur is a prestigious firm, dear," he said, turning to an irate Mrs. Popov. "Private equity in Manhattan was not at all what I would have guessed, but she'd be . . . well, er, what would you do?"

"Translate Japanese," she said, feeling the lies bury her alive.

"Is it a paid internship?"

"I think so. I don't know how much. It didn't come up."

Mr. and Mrs. Popov exchanged puzzled looks. "And when would you start?" he asked, picking up the pristine glossy folder.

"Today was already my first day."

Mr. Popov reserved himself to a hopeless expression; Mrs. Popov was livid. *It'd be easier to tell them I eloped,* Hanna thought. Her father rubbed his unusually ragged scruff of a beard and ordered Hanna to rest in her room. Hanna considered studying. God knew, she was behind in her classes.

"May I please have my phone back?" she asked, wincing as she stood.

"Absolutely not," her mother answered definitively.

Hanna trudged to her room in the wake of her parents' heated whispers. She flicked the door closed and carefully laid herself on her bed. From behind the stuffed animals, she pulled out the clandestine company cell phone. A message already awaited her behind the cool glass screen. Under the orange glow of her bedroom lamp, she read Theo's message: "How did your parents take it?"

She typed back, "Not well. My mom was super upset. My dad doesn't like seeing my mom mad. They're fighting about it right now."

"I'm sorry to hear that."

"It's not like I have a choice."

"What did you tell them?"

Hanna's thumbs raced to type, "What Gus sent me. They kept questioning me, though, because the story changed."

"What do you mean?"

"When I first woke up, I told them everything."

"Everything?!" he wrote.

"I told them we had to save our friend. I told them God sent an angel to save us. They didn't believe me and said it was all the drugs the doctors had me on. We were talking about it again today after they brought me back from school. They kept asking what happened to my neck."

His reply, instant up to that point, stalled. Hanna asked, "What did you tell your dad?" The touchscreen keyboard was amazing to her unfamiliar fingers. Typing another message remained a constant temptation.

"He was understandably mad about me putting you in danger and wrecking his bike, but I told him about the internship, and he thought it was great. He was almost proud. He has no idea."

A knock came at her door. Hanna shoved the sleek smartphone under the covers. Her mother entered, weary from battle.

"That neck still looks mighty painful. Let's have a look," she said and set about inspecting the wound. She concluded once again it was a terrible thing that had happened to her. She pursed her lips, the creases in her face deepened yet more by Hanna's recent transgression.

"I raised you right, my little Jessamine. First year of college almost done and not one broken bone, ER visit, drug use, pregnancy scare, failed class—not so much as a single cigarette. Nothing. The Lord kept you safe—got you all the way here. We kept you proper, taught you the straight and narrow—why, you get to go to college! Not everyone does. Your father and I saving up every penny for you and your sister. And now look what you've done—thrown it away, that's what."

Her mother looked away, visibly hurt. "You put us through this and for what?"

"Mom, I'm sorry."

"Are you? First day back at school and you're right back in the thick of it. I can't understand."

Hanna's good arm twitched to action but came to a defeated rest. The Makers' contract forbade her speech. There was her mother and her dutiful attention, the safety of her childhood room, the security of knowing meals were ready, schedules were set, the frightening terrors of life outside shut out. Her mother left to bring the medical kit. Hanna watched from her bed as if she were a ship drifting from dock. The phone beneath the covers stayed out of her mother's sight. The current of the inescapable arrangement pulled her out to sea, the candor of childhood lost.

"Mom—"

"Get some rest, dear. You have school tomorrow."

Following a careful shower and considerable time for new bandages, Hanna lay down in the darkness. She closed her eyes, which refused her sleep.

God, what am I doing? she thought. There seemed nothing left but to return to the secret beneath her covers. Several of his messages filled the screen. He offered a phone call to listen. He concluded he had taken a misstep. He conceded her silence as a rebuke for his misstep. She called him in the darkness under her blankets. He answered on the first ring.

"Hey."

"Hi," she whispered. "I didn't mean to ignore you."

"Oh."

"I don't want to lie anymore. It's rotting me from the inside. Doesn't it get to you?"

"Not really. I've been lying and obscuring the truth since I got the kaiken, but I don't have to lie to you anymore."

"That's true."

"It'll all be over soon enough. We'll find her. I'm sure of it."

"I hope so."

A meaningful pause preceded his, "I hope so too."

The newfound care previously absent in his flat affect comforted her.

"Thanks," she whispered. "I just . . . needed to hear your voice. Let's talk more tomorrow?"

"Anytime."

"Goodnight, Theo."

"Goodnight."

The memory of their conversation looped in her mind, mercifully transporting her from the haunting recollections of the death of Arthur, Mougo's maniacal laugh, and the agreement she had made with The Makers.

Midnight arrived to a Hanna sick by lack of sleep. Remembering Theo's voice brought along the memories of his transgressions. Her pillows and blankets watched her drag herself out of bed, careful to not use her left arm. She stood in the kitchen, eating ravenously in the refrigerator's glow, despising herself.

Back in her bed, she drifted out of consciousness around three.

Her father met her for breakfast at seven and urged her to eat more. She lied about her previous meal, avoiding the conflict. Few words were exchanged. Shame silently brewed in her.

Time in her father's car was a rare gift. Not since he had moved her belongings to Surgite had she been in his car. He was quiet, driving her the hour or so back to Surgite in the early morning light. The highway passed in a murmur of wind and road noise. He remained in austere silence. The debate with her mother must have been vicious.

Hanna finally asked, "Is Mom still mad?"

"No, dear, she isn't. She was just upset seeing you in the hospital."

"It's my fault you were fighting."

"That's true."

Hanna slumped farther in her seat. Mr. Popov noticed her lack of reply and asked, "How is your neck?"

"I just want the stitches out."

"Soon. We'll take you to the doctor on Monday. I've already made the appointment."

"Can you pick me up later tomorrow? More like six, or even seven?"

"Why so late?"

"To study and catch up."

"On a Friday night? Is it really just for your classes? Are your friends worried about you?"

"Yeah," she answered vaguely.

"Are you planning on seeing him again?"

"... no."

"Don't lie," her father said, his tone sharp. "It will destroy your relationships and eventually you."

"I guess I'm not very good at it."

"No, I think you've been hiding Theo from us for quite some time. What really happened that night? Was there actually a motorcycle? Did he hurt you?"

"No! He would never."

She filled her father's consequent silence with, "I'm sorry I lied to you about it. God, I'm such a mess."

"You'll be working with him this summer?"

"Yes."

"Did he help you get the internship?"

". . . yeah." She slumped in her seat.

"Do you feel ready?"

". . . no."

"How do you feel about it?"

"I'm scared." She crossed her legs and held her injured arm. The car's heater could not fend off the shivers rattling through her.

"You don't have to do this."

"You said it was a good idea."

"Only if it's good for you. I still think you should be a teacher. You'd be so good at it, your guidance counselor recommended it, Surgite has a great education program, and I could help you avoid all the mistakes I made. There are still so many reasons to switch back. It's not too late."

Hanna stared at the blur of passing trees, an old wound open again. They gently swept through the exit ramp. "I know you want to make your own choices, but just remember one thing," Mr. Popov said, adopting his trademark comforting tone. "The truth always comes out. If you ever want to keep those precious to you, honesty is the only way. Lies will destroy you and erode the trust of everyone around you."

His words stayed in her thoughts for the remainder of the quiet drive and her walk to class. She entered the empty classroom and tackled the reading she was woefully behind on. Each student silently shuffled to their seats in front of her. Steven Chatsworth sat beside her, snickering. "You remembered class today."

"Nice to see you too."

"Didn't Broc save you? That's what everyone is saying."

"Yeah," she answered and buried her nose in the reading. The professor made no notice of her injuries and kept a chipper attitude. Spring was coming. Nobody seemed on edge anymore about the abductions, despite there never having been a police report or news story about the abductor's apprehension. The class sailed by Hanna—the quiz not as much. Violent flashes of that fateful night kept battering her already strained concentration.

Japanese demanded more courage to enter the classroom. Passing students observed her curiously. The campus was awash in fresh rumors. Theo's appearance the day prior may not have helped. What were they saying about him? How was he faring in his own classes? A voice behind her asked, "Are you going to open the door?"

"Oh, I'm sorry," she said, noticing she was blocking the entrance. Katie opened the classroom door and politely gestured her inside. Hanna obliged and put on a cheery face, but Katie's seemed even less sincere. Katie avoided a conversation with Hanna and the unavoidable acknowledgment of Hanna's sling and gauze. Maybe a scarf would hide her ugly neck. The ugly lies, though, had come out.

"Hey, I'm sorry for lying to you about Theo's major," Hanna called after Katie.

"It's no big deal," she replied through a hollow grin. "I'm sure we'll both forget about it."

Katie's tepid smile persisted, then vanished the moment she turned back to her already whispering friends. Hanna returned to her notebook, shaken, and blinking to bring the kanji into focus. Today's lesson was reporting on past events. An example they gave was reporting on a recent conversation. Hanna remembered the dripping kaiken pointing at her and its owner's pernicious glare. She shook her head to escape, but the memories chased her, followed by burning pain in her neck. Eddie's exuberant call broke the spell.

"Hanna! *Daijobu*?"

"I'm alright, Eddie. Thanks."

"I heard all the stories! Everybody's talking about it," he said, sitting beside her.

"I'm sure they are."

"Broc was crazy, but I'm so glad he went and saved you. Did

he beat up the guy? Did the police arrest him? What really happened?"

Hanna shuffled her notes. "I don't know, Eddie . . . whatever Broc said."

"Well, um, that's the thing," one of the film majors said, coming over alone, boldly separating herself from the flock. "What really happened? Was that guy on the motorcycle there? The one from Lincoln?" she asked in a whisper.

". . . yes," Hanna answered. What fresh hell would this bring, she wondered.

"Did he know the guy doing the abductions?" the brave film major asked.

"No way!" Eddie countered. "Know him? He was abducted! Broc said so himself, and he was there. Ain't that right, Hanna?"

"Yeah," Hanna replied, playing along.

"Absolutely," Eddie said, nodding. "See?"

"I'd rather not talk about it," Hanna responded.

Eddie recoiled. "Ah, oh, *gomennasai*," he said in his usual overexaggerated manner.

The brave film major retreated, bearing news from the front for her hungry comrades. Sensei entered and Eddie started a great commotion just to say, "Hey, the Haru Matsuri is next week. We're all going to get together with Sensei to plan it. Want to come along?"

Hanna smiled, her itchy neck burning from any movement. "Yeah, that sounds like fun."

Eddie gave a welcoming thumbs up. Sensei set her notes at the lectern, but discreetly diverted to visit Hanna's desk. She squatted beside her.

"Are you okay? We heard you got hurt in a motorcycle accident," she asked.

I just want to lie down, Hanna thought, but instead politely replied, "I'm fine. Really, I'm okay. I'm sorry I missed Monday's midterm. Can I make it up somehow?"

"Of course," Sensei answered, ever the optimistic educator. "Come to my office after class and we'll figure out a time."

Sensei stood and began the class precisely on time. Austere but understanding, she conducted them into their lesson on reporting conversations. Hanna avoided her immediate memories for examples.

Afternoon relinquished her from her troubled classes. She hid in the library, frantically catching up on her studies. Absorbed in her ear buds' lush music, a finger gently tapped her shoulder.

"Who's there?" she asked, twisting back rigidly.

Broc smiled. "It's good to see you."

Notice of his approach had escaped her. She pulled out her ear buds and whispered, "How'd you find me here?"

"You usually study here. I'm glad you're back. Emma's brother wanted to talk to you. I'll get him now."

"Wait! What does he want to talk about? Why me?"

Broc leaned closer to whisper, "Everybody thinks I'm a hero, but you're the real hero," and took off down the labyrinth of book-shelves, out from under the mezzanine. He returned with Emma's oldest brother. Consternation etched itself into his charismatic face.

"Hey, um . . . I just wanted to say thanks. You really came through for us—for everyone," he said. Mawkishly, he added, "And I wanted to apologize."

Hanna shook her head, resulting in another flare of pain. She let out a weak moan and Victor Hugo was quick to say, "No, really. I shouldn't have pushed you to face Theo. I don't even know why I was so convinced he would do anything to hurt my little sister. She saw him the other day and she said he was there to check on her and personally apologized for everything. And I wanted to apologize to you. You got to the bottom of things. Thank God Broc was there. I can't imagine what would have happened otherwise."

Broc stared at his feet. "I'm sure you would have done the same."

Victor Hugo placed his hand on her good shoulder. "I'm glad my sister has someone like you as a friend. Thank you."

Hanna drew strength from his validating touch. He withdrew his hand, but its ameliorating effect stayed with her. He looked at Broc. "That's all I wanted to say. We shouldn't bug her anymore."

He parted, giving a friendly wave. Broc followed, but ran back to Hanna and whispered, "Thank you. Tell Theo I am forever indebted to you both. Really. Get well soon."

She replied, "Thank you, Broc. You were really brave."

He smiled knowingly and left.

A warmth filled her, and she tackled her studies with newfound fervor. She reported the encounter to a receptive Theo, who messaged her back. A sinking feeling of unresolved matters between them, though, stirred in her.

Evening saw her flip phone buzzing with her mother's messages. A swift pick up, and Hanna was headed home, pecked by her mother's questions.

In the house, Lily's upcoming piano recital dominated the family dinner's conversation. Hanna enjoyed not being the focus.

After dinner, Mr. and Mrs. Popov took an evening trip to the supermarket. Hanna slipped away to the vacant piano in their absence. Koushka brushed against her leg invitingly. Hanna eased into an improvised melody. She closed her eyes and melted into it, her useless left arm dangling in its sling.

"Still sounds the same."

Lily stood by the lowest keys. Hanna stopped under her sister's judgmental stare.

"I can't help who I am," Hanna said.

"Mom and Dad are still fighting because of you. Mom said she missed an interview on Monday because you were in the hospital. They're scared of the bills. She keeps telling Dad to get control of you. Dad thinks you'll make money on your internship—maybe enough to make up for some of this—and you should do it."

"Anything else they don't want to tell me?"

"Anything else you want to tell us?"

Despondence crushed her.

Lily added, "For there is nothing hidden that will not become visible, and nothing secret that will not be known and come to light."

When that day comes, forgive me, Father, Hanna thought.

"Don't forget it's Mom's birthday next week," Lily said, disappearing into the warm glow of her bedroom, Koushka trotting behind her. Hanna returned to her room, stung by the shame of having forgotten. The evening ambled by, Hanna carefully bathing and changing her bandages, studying, and stealing another clandestine phone call with her new internship partner. She slept better than the previous night.

Friday dawned, overcast and bleak. Mr. Popov made conversation to guide his misguided daughter. Hanna's hidden organization and secret rendezvous remained perilously so. She waved him goodbye. *It's only until we find Mougo,* she thought.

Twenty minutes until eight in the morning had never been such an ordeal, but she fought to focus on the daunting lesson in her calculus textbook. Exasperated, she traversed the empty classroom to draw out some life from her exhausted body. It sufficed merely to remind herself of her predicament. But she was alive—had survived. *He* was alive. He had lost his way but found it again. There remained only the matter of finding a safe home for the runaway Mougo. Perhaps the quest would take her to Japan.

She stopped at the sill under the blackboard. New chalk graced it. She took one and drew a tiny smiling sun shining in the corner of the board. A student entered and Hanna returned to her seat.

The ever-lively professor came in, flanked by more sleepless students, and perused the chalk. He savored the untouched chalk, reveling in its crisp perfection, then selected the one Hanna had started, pleased with his discovery. He basked in the cleanliness of the board and triumphantly wrote the day's lesson. Just as the hand struck eight, he greeted them all. Emma rushed through the door.

Without hesitation, she sat beside Hanna, smirking. "Not actually late," she said in a low, jovial tone.

Emma hurried to take out her notes and pick up the lesson. Hanna read her own notebook pages, hopelessly missing swaths of multiple classes. New intimidating symbols inhabited the blackboard. Emma nudged her good shoulder and slid over her notebook bearing an explanation of the mysterious hieroglyphs.

After class, Emma helped Hanna pack up her backpack and asked, "How are you holding up?"

"It's been a long week."

"No kidding. You home this weekend?"

"Yeah, my dad is coming to pick me up. I have a doctor's appointment Monday. They are going to look at the stitches. I just want them out." Emma carefully slung Hanna's backpack over her good shoulder.

"Any plans?" Emma asked.

The second cell phone in her backpack had not suggested any yet. Hanna innocently answered, "Just rest."

Emma raised her expressive eyebrows, prompting Hanna to reveal, "And I'm seeing Theo today after class."

"He's coming here again on that busted ankle?"

"I offered to see him in the city, but he insisted on the café here. We're starting a new internship together. It's supposed to be this summer, but it kind of started already."

"A new internship, eh? How'd you swing that? You were just in a motorcycle crash."

Grim fear shut her mouth. She backpedaled, saying, "It's a long story. I'll tell you some other time."

Emma gave a shrug and a nod, before saying, "It sure is a hike for him, but if he wants to come all the way here, that's his prerogative. Give yourself a day off, though. It's just an internship. Haven't you put yourself through enough already?"

"He's in pain. He needs somebody to talk to."

Walking beside her, Emma shook her head. "You got some

will, kiddo." She waved Hanna off to her next class, but not before saying, "Just keep off the bikes, would ya?"

Hanna's Japanese and western literature classes felt like a return to normalcy. Hanna wore a cheery face, participating beside her classmates oblivious to the origins of her injuries and the true reason the abductions had stopped. Everyone enjoyed the peace, though, and spirits were high. The university continued urging students to be vigilant, but already, she overheard bold weekend plans shared in both classes. Hanna quietly left and walked down the campus to the great stone gates.

Alone, she passed through them, her itchy stiches ablaze. She pulled out her flip phone and messaged Theo she was on her way, but remembered the conversation had been on her new company smartphone. He responded, confirming his punctual arrival.

Hanna continued to the station. The salt crunched under her flats, her leather boots having been discarded from the bloodstains. Off in the distance, she spotted him carefully working his way down the platform's concrete steps. She rushed up to him, unsure what to say.

"Anything new from Gus?" he asked, his stern expression mollified at seeing her.

"No, you?"

He shook his head and drew closer. Reservation stayed his voice. She said, "You look better. Much less swelling in your face."

"How's your neck? Your shoulder?"

"Getting better. I still can't move my arm much."

Theo resumed his usual frown. "Let's go," he said and led her to the café, swinging his cumbersome braced ankle along by his crutches. She followed and rushed to open the café door for him. He was quick to pay for her. Seated and served, the activity of the café receded from her thoughts.

Pale afternoon light brightened their table by the windows, tranquil and tucked away from the other customers. Theo carefully rested his crutches on the windowsill and cupped his black coffee. Hanna sipped her creamy coffee and asked, "How are you doing? What did you want to tell me?"

"Neko jita," he said.

"Where'd you learn that?" she asked innocently.

Theo had trouble summoning the breath needed to speak. His eyes downcast, he said, "We have been here before, spoken these words—made these memories already. I took them from you. I didn't know how to tell you—still don't. I was scared of how you'd react. I understand if you hate me. I won't deny what I did. I'll just tell you now. It's a staining guilt, making me feel like the world will crash down any moment. I deserve it. I've come to think I deserved what Arthur put me through. But you didn't deserve what happened to you. Your neck will bear that scar for the rest of your life." He cleared his throat unable to speak further.

She swallowed audibly. "How do you feel?" she asked.

"The guilt is incessant. This whole week I've felt nauseous. I can't sleep. I can't focus on anything. I felt like the door was going to burst open and the police would drag me away. There's no way to repent, but the desire to won't go away. I've pulled you into this. We're both inside of this lie. We've already had to twist and warp what happened for the doctors, your friends, and our families. There's no way out of what we've caused. Nobody will ever have the whole truth. You'll forever be separated from them. For that, I came here to apologize."

Theo reached into his peacoat and produced a letter. "I'm sorry for everything." Delicately, he placed it between them. Hanna recognized her handwriting on the folded page bearing bloody fingerprints.

Theo pressed on, "I understand your decision. I accept it. This internship will make us work together. Knowing what they can do, I'm sure we will find her. She has your memories. We can get them back. I owe you that at least. Once The Makers have Mougo back and your memories are restored, we can ask her to erase whatever you'd like."

He avoided her heartfelt gaze. "If you want to forget me that's fine," he said, the quaver in his voice unmistakable. "Maybe you want me to forget you. I can understand that too."

Hanna stared at the letter between them. Theo produced his original letter to her and placed it beside hers. She blinked, staring at her letter juxtaposed with his letter's graceful handwriting. She leaned closer, now able to peer into his unswollen, unbandaged eyes.

At last, she said, "You owe me nothing but to be yourself."

His perplexed expression prompted her to continue, "We'll find her . . . together. I know she has my memories. She already offered them to me. I said no."

"Really? When?" he whispered.

"We talked while you were unconscious. She wanted to repay me—to say thank you for releasing her. She offered to restore my memories."

"But you didn't want them? Why?"

Hanna cupped her coffee. "Of course, I want them back," she began solemnly. "They are a part of me. Without our memories, how can we grow and mature? But that self-reflection can be poisoned. It can turn dark, returning over and over to a single terrible memory. We will both bear the truth of what you did forever. But I don't have to remember *that* you—not when I know that's not the real you. My heart could not take it. Believe me, I want to find her. She can still help Emma. And those memories are mine, so in a way she has a part of my soul, having seen and felt what I have. She saw the Theo that could not feel. But when I saw you suffering in so much pain . . . I just"—she took in a deep breath— "I couldn't bear to see a Theo that was lost and hurtful. I know that Theo led to the one who fought to admit the truth to me, save Broc, set Mougo free . . . stand up to that man. I will never forget that Theo. You will never forget who you were to become who you are now. That's what's important."

Theo sat up, deep in thought. He came back quickly to say softly, "But you had already written the letter."

"I wrote that, yes." Hanna looked up at his face, braced for her stinging rejection. "But I never gave it to you."

He struggled to comprehend her words.

"Theo, our lives are a mess. We're trapped under so many lies. If my parents ever found out . . . I don't even know. They'd probably question why God would create such power—if they could even wrap their heads around it. And The Makers? This is no way to live. I was stupid to have been lying to my parents. And now there's all this between us. I just want to be honest again. But now, at least, I can be honest with you. And your honesty is . . . well"— she wiped her eyes—"what I wanted all along."

A contrite Theo sat with his thoughts for a moment. From his pocket, he produced a small notebook clasped by a combination lock. "This has everything I did. The abductions, the sheath, the knife—everything. You can see the truth."

"Destroy it. Leave behind the evil that consumed you."

He entered the numbers and unlocked the notebook, flipping through its pages one last time. He closed it and clasped the lock. Hanna breathed again at its return to his pocket.

"Promise me you'll destroy it and never look back."

"I will."

Hanna breathed deeply in the interlude, enjoying their drinks' aromas and realizing her breaths had become short and strained.

Theo said, "We may carry the weight of hiding Mougo and The Makers for the rest of our lives. Maybe they will erase our memories of her at the end."

"What will they do to Mougo? She's out there, lost and confused in a world she doesn't understand. I want to help her. Maybe we can convince them to let her go and find her way home," Hanna proposed in a low tone, realizing they had not broken from leaning in close to each other.

"Do you want to talk about the night we set her free?"

She grew tense beginning to recall any part of that dark house. Her heart drummed in her ears and mouth ran dry. Hanna gazed out the window for reprieve. The sky began to drizzle on the tranquil afternoon. She whispered, "We will never speak of that evening again."

"Okay. Never," he affirmed, and she added, "But let's both take a vow. We vow to never lie to each other again. We must live under the lie of The Makers, but if we're ever going to get Mougo and our lives back, there can be nothing between us."

"A vow?" he asked.

"Yes."

He took her hand in both of his, their warmth stirring her racing heart to new heights. "A vow," he confirmed.

"Of honesty."

"Between us."

"Forever."

"No matter what."

"No matter what," she affirmed, and he let her hand go, the deed done, but her heart begging to reach out.

Theo took his first sip of his black coffee. He leaned close to her, as if anything more than a whisper was not safe around the passing customers. "Per our new vow, I have to break your rule about that evening just once. After you set Mougo free, she killed Arthur and offered you a reward. You said she erased a traumatic memory. What did she erase?"

"One of your memories."

"Of what?"

"Breaking the cello."

"But how?" he asked, gripped by wonder. "That was years ago."

"She said that death charges her abilities. I suppose she has that memory now—your memory."

He shook his head, lost in recollection and resting his hands on the table. "I remember feeling a terrible guilt. There are so many interconnected memories, she must have not been able to clear them all. But I was talking to my father the other day. We started talking about Mom. It's been a long time since we last did." He ran his fingers through his wheat-like hair. "I remember taking cello lessons. My mom would take me after school. What did I do? Why did I break it? How?"

Hanna pinned Theo's eyes with her own. "It doesn't matter now, does it? I could tell you the story that the previous Theo gave me. But I think you should ask Mougo. She has your memory, and we'll tell you together—my recollection and your actual memory from her, side by side."

"I'd . . . like that," he managed to say. "We'll have to ask her when we find her. We can't let The Makers take her away."

"I'm sure she'll want to talk to us. We are the only people she trusts. I wonder where she went?"

"I don't know," he replied and let his gaze fall to the letters between them. The café quieted down as the last few customers exited and braced themselves against the chilling rain outside. For the first time since the incident, Hanna forgot about the stiches in her neck. Theo met her eyes.

"And . . . since we're being completely honest . . . about us?"

Hanna took her letter penned to Theo and tore it in half. She answered, "I was thinking about it, and maybe we could start over? We can go slowly and take our time. We're going to be working together. Who knows what the future holds?"

"Start over?"

"We'll take it slow, get to know each other, start from the beginning," she said, putting the torn letter on the table. She took his letter and placed it in her backpack dangling at her feet. Theo smiled at her radiance. Tenderly, he produced the lilac earrings from his pocket and placed them on the table between them.

She gasped, covering her mouth. "You still have them."

"I'd never forget."

The earrings rested between them. Before her sat an earnest Theo, awaiting her reply.

"One day, I will get my memories back from Mougo. But before that day, and since we're starting over, I'd like to know from you," she said, leaning forward, "if you've given me these earrings before? I want to know what really happened, but I want to remember through your eyes."